Also by Vince Passaro

Violence, Nudity, Adult Content: A Novel

CRAZY SORROW

VINCE PASSARO

Simon & Schuster
New York London Toronto Sydney New Delhi

Simon & Schuster
1230 Avenue of the Americas
New York, NY 10020

Disclaimer: It is an incurable habit of the imagination to sculpt the past, or an incurable habit of mine, anyway. The novel that follows is set in a small collection of known places and known periods of time, populated by known personalities. Yet it remains a work of imagination and no factual reality should be imputed to whatever actual persons, places, organizations, or events appear here; they should be understood as part of an entirely fictional narrative, created for artistic purposes. History can be an energizing element in literature, as can alien creatures from other worlds, should one choose to include them. Of the two, aliens might be the more comprehensible.

First Simon & Schuster hardcover edition September 2021

Interior design by Lexy Alemao

Manufactured in the United States of America

10 9 8 7 6 5 4 3 2 1

Library of Congress Control Number: 2021943099

ISBN 978-0-7432-4510-4
ISBN 978-1-5011-3488-3 (ebook)

With love to John, James, Paul, and Jonah,
who have endured much.

As I looked to the east · right into the sun,
I saw a tower on a toft · worthily built;
A deep dale to the west · and a dungeon therein,
With deep ditches and dark · and dreadful of sight.
A fair field full of folk · found I in between,
Of all manner of men · the rich and the poor,
Working and wandering · as the world asketh.

—Piers Plowman

Are not two sparrows sold for a copper coin? Yet not one of them falls to the ground without your Father knowing it. Even the hairs of your head are counted. So do not be afraid; you are worth more than many sparrows.

—Matthew 10:29–31

|| PART ONE ||

if tonight were not a crooked trail

1

July 4, 1976: the night they met: mere children but they didn't feel so. A night of celebration, a million or more marched from subways to the river, George among them, Anna too, his first real vision of her on the train, amid that throng. When they got to the street the crowds expanded, the people like pilgrims, like pictures you saw of pilgrims, moving in a stupor of faith down Cortlandt and Rector, up Water and Wall, a multitude of believers in the moral force behind the founding of the republic. The nation's tarnished history lay light on their shoulders—they were partygoers, after all, it was the bicentennial and a redemptive-seeming election was on. The country hadn't yet slow-squeezed the hope out of all but its richest citizens and this grand show was their official fun in the silvered darkness, requiring only a fifty-cent token for the trains. They were here for the fireworks, which came in culmination of a long, decent day, absent so far as they knew the customary lies and assassinations—a day full of tall ships on the river and barbecues and beer on its banks. Now they walked and walked until the water stopped them, with the mammoth towers behind them to the east and the blackening Hudson to the west—a crowd ready to see these fireworks, fireworks such, allegedly, as there had never been, to be set ablaze in the smudged twilight sky above the harbor, with its gathering of sailing ships from around the world. The ships were at anchor, sails furled, creating a seascape of spindly masts like crosses, each awaiting its thief, its zealot or its redeemer.

George had a special interest in the boats; he was an adequate sailor and had worked for three years in a shipyard in Connecticut. He had never seen the likes of the largest of these vessels, which he'd viewed passing that afternoon up the Hudson, two dozen enormous eighteenth-century ships. You'd have to go to Newport to set foot on anything even remotely close. Of the smaller ships, which were small only relatively, there must have been more than a hundred.

The piece of property on which the crowd gathered was a landfill, a moonscape of gritty dunes plunked into the river behind the Trade Towers, beyond the gothic remains of the old West Side Highway, which they passed beneath to reach this place, an unexpected gray beach; it was covered with many manner of Americans, mostly youthful—the walk required it—but of every kind, locals and tourists, rich and poor, the colors and the races, giving each other room but still, together. George Langland would come to know that there were moments like this in the life of a city when everyone joined—everyone was fused—in a semi-unified emotional experience. This was his first such moment; he would be twenty come November, an eastern Connecticut boy, and he found himself (usually detached, notoriously a cynic) stunned, unbelieving, at how many people there were, chaotically grouped and thoughtless as bison crossing this sandy nothing. And how genial. The city functioned every day as a dotted map of safe zones amid swathes of jagged hostility and potential violence: but there seemed to be none of that. Here was a new colony, half-stoned, a cheerful drove in milky light, settling the moon—the moon, which had been conquered seven years before, it seemed two or three lifetimes back, George twelve, his mother still alive. She woke him at two a.m. to sit on the couch with her while she smoked Raleighs with her bare legs curled beneath her, to watch the men—dressed as Diver Dan and moving as slowly—stiff-walking and bouncing, looking absurd, across gray desert, planting the flutterless aluminum USA flags to claim the place for their kingdom. He remembered his mother remarking, well, this flag-planting thing was *always* a good idea, historically, it never caused a problem, it went over well with all concerned. And next day came the golfing, spraying the lunar landscape with Titleist, those boys from NASA—static crack static *roger Houston* static *that was ahh* static static *about ahh* static *fifteen hundred yard* static crack—electric wash and white noise and whistle and hum of two hundred thousand soul-breaching miles. *Sure wish we* static static static *drive them like* static *back on the big blue, over* static static static. *That's . . . roger Eagle.* NASA hadn't trained ground control in jovial banter. Cronkite translated for them, adopted a cheerful tone and twinkly half smile—since the day John Kennedy died, the man's eyebrows had spoken the mood of the nation—to explain how, gravitationally liberated, the astronauts could jump ten feet straight up from the surface, even in their stony costumes, and their golf balls took off like missiles (*one-sixth the gravity*, he intoned, *that holds us to the planet Earth*). And who—who?—would have thought they'd have stashed their clubs and balls and tees and whatnot in the tight little cabin of that spider-legged, foil-wrapped pod they'd arrived in? Whatever you do, boys, don't forget your golf clubs when you're heading up to the fucking moon.

≡

SEVEN YEARS LATER almost to the day, the small dunes of New York City rose and fell and the gravity was pure sea-level American East Coast. The landfill sand was dense and firm and seemed darkish in color, unpleasantly crunchy beneath their sandals and sneakers, inexplicably moist in an unhealthy, oily sort of way. Some serious hippies were humping it barefoot, which George felt was a little . . . what? Unwise. Over-ideological. He tried to imagine where the powers in charge of New York City infrastructure could have gotten all this dingy moist sand, tried to imagine what befoulments might be in it—and how they could have deposited it all right here. Much of the denser stuff—the schist and rock and paltry earth—would have come from the foundations of the towers behind them, dug up there and distributed here to the riverbed. *But whence the sand, brother?* And now, tonight, standing upon it, so many people—the subway had been as crowded as it was possible to make it, completely jammed full, including George, going into his second year at Columbia that September, staying on campus for the summer, and his friends, most of whom had left town in May but returned for this, a national display. They'd all been in Riverside Park that afternoon smoking weed, watching the ships cruise by, stunning and romantic, full sail, with the uptown Puerto Rican and Dominican families picnicking all around them in the thick heat on the closed West Side Highway, folding chairs and hibachis, blankets and shoes and kids' toys all planted right out on the radiator asphalt, a kind of miraculous dispensation.

At this moment George, no longer stoned, but in that pre-headache state which followed, everything in sharp outline, a hollow acutance, was interested only in the girl; he had not yet learned her name. She was small, dark, and gracefully curved, with green eyes that offered a view into what seemed a calm and melancholy set of rooms. Rough bangs and brown hair hanging at her shoulders. A red cotton plaid shirt, old and soft, opened and pulled backward by its own weight revealing neck and upper back more than chest. She was not wearing a bra; her breasts were lovely. He felt himself drawn to certain women based on hints of liveliness and danger in their intelligence; alert, quick to laugh, vivid-eyed. Again, his mother flashed through his mind. She never let up, even dead. Especially dead. The girl, to accompany the shirt, wore cutoff Levi's. Keds with open laces. A patriotic outfit, purely American. She was a friend of Geist's: translation, she had slept with Geist, a prosperous Lothario from Princeton, but, according to Michael, who had run into her and invited her, she was not sleeping with him now.

George carried a mini-cooler with the neck of an actually decent bottle of Chablis, already corked, sticking out of the unclosed top, plus, buried in a withered-looking baggie in his shorts' pocket like a codpiece, a quarter ounce of good Colombian: tawny weed with big sticky buds, three joints already rolled. He and she and everyone else slogged up dune and down and up again, they were like a million dumb explorers who'd all decided to go to the south pole at the same time, the grayish brown grit dusting up beneath their sandals and All Stars and forest-green Pumas: the crowd knowledge homing in on the not yet visible southwestern tip of the landfill.

Her name was Anna. Anna Goff.

Some of their friends were ahead, some left, some right, and, in their own small group, besides George and Anna, was Robbie, a year ahead of George and his mentor at *Spectator*, the campus daily where George was an assignment reporter and Robbie was news manager; dragging a few feet behind, the elaborate genius-math-major-stoner, Logan, who came from Hawaii and spent all his non-toking time, especially midnight to five a.m., in the mainframe computer bunker located under the physics building. This was one of the rare occasions when he could be seen without his rubber-banded stack of beige punch cards.

They sat finally, in that grubby dirt-sand. The fireworks started to gasps and a cheer. A joint was passed and soon they were stoned again. George was lying back, seeing directly above him not so much the fireworks display, which went on and on and on, but the flashes of color higher up, ghostly paint spills come and gone across the charcoal fabric of things.

He sat up, took a drink of the wine, handed it to her. The wine was good. He flopped back down again.

This wine is good, he said.

It is, she said. It is good.

Too bad we're not in Spain, he said, and this isn't a Hemingway story with a somehow miserable but inconclusive ending. In which some things are good and other things are not good and what we have is that we know what's good and what's not good and the others don't know, they confuse what's good and what's not good. Which is not good. But we know. This is what makes us good.

She was watching the fireworks, like blossoms of colored light. Logan and Robbie were a few feet away sharing one of the fat joints and discussing the election.

But we're doomed of course, she said. We can never be together. You were injured during the war, you know, down *there*. And I'm a nymphomaniac.

What? said Logan. What was that?

It's from Hemingway, George said. Don't get yourself excited.

I never get excited, Logan said.

Unless you can get Fortran to spell *fuck* on a screen, Robbie said.

I've done that, Logan said.

Why am I not surprised, Robbie said.

George took advantage of Anna looking at the glittering color to look not at it but at her. Her face, impossibly sensual. It was the mouth, the cheekbones and chin. Her eyes threw out enough intelligence to knock you backward if you didn't love intelligence, weren't drawn to it as George was—a taste his mother had induced in him. He pulled his eyes away from her, looked at the mini-cooler and the neck of the bottle. The wine would soon be finished. He would leave his stupid little cooler here. Make it part of the fundament.

Andrew and Robbie had relighted the joint. Robbie took a pull at it and a seed popped, essentially blowing it up as if it were a trick cigar.

Fuuuck, Robbie said.

Somebody didn't justly clean this leaf, Andrew said.

I've been busy, George called out. I was memorizing the Declaration of Independence.

Well, you've fucked up my pursuit of happiness, Robbie said. Piece almost went in my eye. Plus you're named George, not a good sign during the revolution.

George Washington, George said.

Robbie said, George the Third, fucker, is who you are if the joint blows up.

He repaired and relit the bone and handed it across the informal space that marked George and Anna apart from the other two. Time stretched itself out like a tablecloth spread on the grass. Behind them, the two towers, like huge magic boxes: they reflected the harbor lights and the fireworks, in long panels, geometric slices running in impossible rows down the side of the building, thinly divided. Like a mural—narrow strips, cut up. An abstract. George touched her shoulder to show her and they turned to face opposite, watching the flat fragments of incoherent colors on the two looming immensities. A million other people were staring in the wrong direction. Within a few minutes they were lying closer together but only the upper portions of their bodies. Shoulder to shoulder, heads tilted in and touching.

Would it be a cliché to refer here to the black monolith in Kubrick's *2001*? George said.

Yes, that would be a cliché, she said.

Then I won't do that, he said. Did you see when that French guy crossed between the towers on a high wire? Petit?

I never saw it, she said. You don't pronounce the *t*.

What? George said.

Petit. You don't pronounce the final *t*. It's like *putty* but the accent's reversed.

Thank you, George said. Putt-EE. I was looking at it on television and I couldn't accept that it was true. And he stayed out there for a long time too. Dancing around, taunting the cops. Forty-mile-an-hour winds, a hundred stories high. Helicopters zooming around up above him. There were shots from the ground, he looked tiny as an insect with the pole sticking out, you couldn't believe it.

She stared for a time, as if trying to imagine it.

How enclosed he must have felt, she said. Or been able to feel. That's what I can't imagine. The state of mind.

I never got that far, George said. I'm all about the insane height.

You wouldn't maybe notice the height, she said, if you were all wrapped up in yourself, in this magical space you're occupying.

Again quiet. And then she said: I can't decide what I think about these buildings. I like them right now, but sometimes I can't bear them.

I always like them, he said. I have an uncle who worked on them.

Tonight, she said, when we're lying right underneath them—

She paused. He made an approving, go-on sound: Hmm?

They're beautiful, she said. It was weed profundity. George could hear that she felt it—they're beautiful. They *were* beautiful. The size was part of it, the widths were massive too: you didn't notice this from greater distances. So was the twinness. So was the coloration of the glass and steel, in the changing light of all the days and nights, the dawns and dusks, the skies gray or pink or occasionally that divine, transparent blue.

≡

THE JOINT HAD gone out and, with the boom of the fireworks behind them, he relit it. Then they lay back and answered questions about their lives. She was at Barnard, same year as he, studying comp-lit Spanish and politics, the closest she could get to Latin American studies, which Barnard did not have; she was trying to take most of her courses in the department at

Columbia but there were no end of hassles and, as she bluntly put the matter, they hated women. The English department too, he told her, was known for hating women. Yes, she'd heard that. He wanted to touch her, pull her close to him and smell the back of her neck and down between her shoulder blades, where, he'd seen in the inches-away proximity of the train, a hint of dark fuzzy hair ran down; that rearward scoop neck, the skin of her upper back, but they'd only been together what? Ninety minutes? She was from Pennsylvania. Where. She didn't want to say. Why not? Just didn't. Central, she said finally. Not far from Harrisburg. Okay, he said. Eventually the show was over, the deep booms and the quick pops, the crowd's somehow insignificant pleasure, given its vastness, what seemed like thin applause in the humid night; he preferred the sky imbued with its own light—he had not realized it before but fireworks didn't merely bore him, they actually irritated him. There it was, another adult fact to file: he still savored it, his daily autonomous creation of himself, the grown-up version of himself, a peeling away of childhood propaganda and family myth and incorrect hometown articles of faith. He had spent his childhood and adolescence burning for freedom. And here it was, as sweet as he'd imagined it would be. He was, he now knew, a disdainer of fireworks. They'd be fine if one were a primitive—shit, you'd worship them—but now, cinema and books and premarital sex had been invented, so why was everyone standing there slack-jawed staring at the sky? Ooh. Ahh. All across the harbor and up into the mouth of the Hudson were dozens of the anchored works of art and engineering, the elaborate masts, sails lowered, tied to booms, needle-sharp silhouettes, a fabulous clustering of aquatic woodwork. Everyone rose, collected, brushed, tramped in ragtag retreat out of the landfill and back toward West Street.

Robbie called after him: Your cooler!

I'm leaving it for the future, George said. Then he and Anna angled northward and Robbie and Andrew were lost behind. The crowd, with everyone departing at once, soon became enormous, frightening, like some night exodus from a war-torn land, the bottom of Manhattan. He kept himself adjusted to the angles of the towers—really you couldn't imagine the mass of them until you were near, and once departed you couldn't reimagine that mass again until next time you stood beneath them. They were almost completely dark, now that the light show was over, like two rising tunnels into the black attic of the universe.

They moved ahead along the northern edges of the crowd, went out via Chambers Street, and managed to get an express train there, heading uptown. No one spoke on the hard-packed train. All the pop and boom and daylong celebrations had drained the crowd of sound. It was perhaps 110 degrees in the car. Everyone's face was moist, shirts darkened. From 14th to Penn Station, Anna and George were forced into the middle of the car with nothing to hold on to: he was tall enough to place his fist against the low ceiling for balance: she held on to his belt. This made him a little crazy. A few times they caught each other's eye, or both eyes, stared a moment, but they were too close, it was too much, they looked away. At 96th they were disgorged. Here was the transfer point between the express trains and the local, which they would need to take in order to continue up Broadway to the campus. Several other expresses had already been through and the station, holding so many transfers waiting, became so dense with people that the most recent arrivals seemed in actual danger of being shoved off the platform and down onto the tracks, where if a train didn't get them, rats the size of eggplants might. They were like rodent alligators down there. George took Anna's hand and pulled her along with the bulk of the assembled, who were exiting the station. They would walk the last twenty blocks.

I never walk down here, she said.

By *down here* she meant anywhere from 110th down to 79th Street, a stretch of pimps, whores, junkies and drunks, mad Vietnam vets, and other traditionally crazy-ass people just out of the state institutions and living in the single-room hotels that populated most of the side streets.

George offered his arm, which she took.

But I like seeing it all, she said.

Along Broadway the bars, the bodegas, everything had a mean fluorescent glare. It was loud. The music was entirely salsa and it was everywhere tonight, down the streets both east and west in impromptu festivals and schoolyard dance parties. When they got to Morningside Heights, the quiet set in, the usual few drunks on the benches in the Broadway median, the students heading home in small groups or alone, the nurses from the hospital going in early for the night shift. They entered the campus at 114th. He had a room in the big freshman dorm, a double normally, rented during summers as a large single for cash-paying visiting students. He paid for it with his social security money.

What are you doing now? he said.

Sleep had occurred to me, she said.

It was past midnight. She was living in a Barnard building on 116th and Claremont.

We could listen to some music. Get high.

Right, she said. We already are high. And then?

And then what? he said. Who knows. Talk about Nietzsche. Read *Zarathustra* lately?

She had a pleasant laugh, musical. Yes, I have, actually. What music?

He recognized this immediately as a question that stood in for about a dozen larger ones.

Whatever you like, he said.

Whatever?

Sure. I have, you know, a bunch of different stuff. What do you like?

I'm looking at you, she said. You have Dylan, I know that. You have Joni Mitchell, you definitely have the Doors. You have some bad suburban shit. Lots and lots of the Who, I bet.

Okay, that's all true. I mean I have three albums by the Who, that's not excessive.

Yes, it is, she said.

She said: You have *Kind of Blue* by Miles. That was like a big deal when you got that.

Whoa, he said.

I'm sorry, she said.

It's all right, I can take it. Keep going.

Do you have Janis Joplin?

I have the Holding Company record.

Good, she said. Glenn Gould?

Who's Glenn Gould? he said.

Oh, my, she said. How about, let's see. Do you have Procol Harum?

Procol Harum? he said. Really? Procol Harum? It so happens I do have Procol Harum. Do you actually listen to Procol Harum?

No, she said. I mean, occasionally but never mind. Do you have Tito Puente?

No. Just Santana. You know, with the Puente song.

Ooh, she said. That's bad. How about Eddie Palmieri?

Wait a minute, that's bad? That I don't have Tito Puente and . . . what? Eddie Palmieri? Are you kidding? Yeah, sure, I have Eddie Palmieri *and* Tito Puente, I got both of them. Right. Look at me, yes, absolutely. I was the only guy from coastal Connecticut with my Topsiders who was into Tito Puente and Eddie Palmieri. With a whole salsa collection. I had to hide the tapes from all my burly white friends, in *their* Topsiders, Jesus. You're lucky I'm not making you listen to Renaissance.

No, *you're* lucky you're not *trying* to make me listen to Renaissance.

You're testing me with all this? I'm just a suburban white boy strung up halfway between the haute bourgeoisie and working class.

Which side was which, she said.

My mother was toney but mostly cut off from the money. My father was a high school teacher. Civics and health. One step above gym. Where he was asked to fill in from time to time. He was a good-looking guy. Loved boats.

Was?

Both dead, he said.

Oh, she said. Oh.

He said nothing.

She said, That's hard. I'm sorry.

He never knew quite how to react to this. Honesty would have been a grating howl.

He said, Yeah. But don't let it bring you down. As Neil Young would say.

No Neil Young, she said.

Not a moment of Neil Young, he said.

You give up so easily, she said.

I take the long view, he said. Skirmishes are never the war. I'll have you stoned and listening to *4 Way Street* and you'll be singing along and suddenly look up and go, what?

She screamed: *No no no.*

Two guys on the way into Carman Hall looked at them.

George sang in falsetto: *Old man sitting by the side of the road . . . with the lorries rolling by . . .*

No! No no no no! No! She was laughing.

This will happen, he said.

They walked. She said, How about Charles Aznavour? Do you have any Charles Aznavour?

He stopped. She had to turn around and wait, staring at him. What? she said.

That's so fucked up, he said.

What's so fucked up?

I shouldn't even know who that is.

But you do, she said.

I actually have Charles Aznavour. I have a cassette I bought in high school and I *did* keep it hidden from my friends. I like him.

The eternal recurrence, she said.

He looked at her.

Things happen over and over, she said. I thought you'd read *Zarathustra*.

I never said I'd read *Zarathustra*, you said *you'd* read *Zarathustra*. I'm still working on *The Birth of Tragedy*, which I was supposed to read last year. My analysis so far is, Nietzsche probably would have dug the Stones. They have the whole Dionysian-Apollonian thing down.

I'm not seeing the Apollo part, she said.

You must be hard to please, he said.

You have no idea, she said.

They were standing now, and had been, near the entrance to Carman Hall, against a cinderblock wall painted a cold white that glowed in the lamplight. They were quite close and inching ever closer.

The silence fell between them, the locking of eyes that they hadn't had nerve for on the subway, and then she kissed him. He kissed her back, slowly, easily. Her lips were soft, like the soft, unimaginable lips he'd felt in certain eerie dreams. He didn't want to remember those dreams, not now. He wanted to hold this woman. They went upstairs, to his room. They kissed and smoked some more and he put on *Sketches of Spain*, turned medium low, music like a watery poem with glints of reflected starlight leaping up from its small waves. The sound of night air. A little sad. Whatever happened he wanted it to be slow. They lay on his bed and kissed and kissed and he moved his hands across her body, barely touching her, just grazing her skin, like the wind. She arched toward it.

2

Ferris Booth Hall, a dollop of modernity dropped amid the neoclassical effusions of Columbia's McKim, Mead & White–designed campus. He was fond of this misplaced little imitation Philip Johnson building, with its terrace of slate and walls of polished granite and glass. That wall against which he had stood and cooled himself last night, where the granite of the façade met the white cinderblock rear wall of FBH, as it was called. Through the doors the triangular café to the left and ahead, farther on, more granite, a white staircase with chrome banisters curving to the second floor. The other buildings around FBH dwarfed it: Carman looming behind, a federal housing project type nightmare; the library looming to the left, colonnaded, stone, Caucasian monumental; old Furnald Hall, another dorm, brick and stone, looming to the right. Ferris Booth was completely incorrect but lovely, like an elegant child in a white dress waiting in the fallen-on-hard-times gloom of her grandparents' parlor.

Second floor, the offices, a more utilitarian ambience, black and gray tile floors, cinderblock walls, fluorescent lighting behind grids of tin. *Spectator* was, in summer, a minimal operation. The paper, an eight-page or sixteen-page daily during the school year, was reduced from June to September to a single broadsheet once a week. George found only Louis there, typing a feature on the tall ships and fireworks—one of his first-person things. He was summer editor for now, would return for his second term of being features editor in fall. He was the only out-of-the-closet homosexual George knew. He often turned his chair back-to-desk, knelt on it and rested his ass on his heels as if he were offering a fuck in a tent near the campfire. Louis had given George the horrors for most of freshman year but three facts, which would prove decisive in so many of George's relationships with men, overcame all other considerations: Louis was smart, funny, and observant, which meant he was usually correct.

Who puts the *bi* in *bicentennial*, baby? Louis called, without looking up from the typewriter.

You're not bi, George said. So far as you let on.

A, that's not true, B, how would you know, and C, everyone's at *least* a little bi, Louis said. Including you.

What the fuck is going on with your feet?

What feet?

The ones down there at the end of your legs, in the centurion-style sandals, George said. They were nice sandals actually, leather with brass rings: the biblical look. It was the Chiclets variety pack display of unshapely toenails at the front end that was disorienting.

You mean my gorgeous nails?

I have to hide my eyes.

I gave myself a pedicure and I bought five different colors of polish because I just couldn't decide and it was the bicentennial. But the red and white and blue thing is a cliché.

And look! What joy! And . . . (finger tapping George's chest) they . . . are . . . beautiful . . . to . . . me. So, in short, my broad-shouldered friend, fuck off.

He went back to his copy.

Then: Are you here for a reason?

Just seeing what's going on, George said.

Nothing's going on. You're going on. The herald cries of your coital activities.

Jesus, already?

I saw Joe at Chocks, he was drinking with Robbie and Logan last night at the West End. Where Joe learned you'd gone off with the lady, not to be seen again. He gave you up in about, oh gosh, I don't know, six or seven seconds.

We discussed Nietzsche. There was hardly coitus, George said.

Give me a break, Louis said.

Okay, there was—until this morning, okay. But before that were hours of near-coitus.

Ohhh, Louis said, as if being shown photos of a baby or a kitten. That's so nice.

Discussion of coitus, George said. How we feel. What it means. Why not to. Lathery kisses. Application of hands. More talk of how we feel. Family histories, in brief. Watching trails made by our cigarettes. More kisses, more talk. We were naked in a cold comforting sand, powdery and dry. Except it was my bed and we had underpants on. First Miles Davis then Blind Faith playing, on repeat. Which I have to say, but for Presence of the Lord, much of it doesn't bear repeating. So then Billy Cobham on repeat, though with Cobham you can't tell you're hearing something a second or eighth time. Trippy shit, all the sensations. Then finally we went to sleep. A sweet awakening.

A hard-on like from the petrified forest. She was amused, she was interested, she was a little excited. She was for a time truly enthralled, or so it appeared. And then she settled herself upon it like a tablecloth settling over a table in one of those commercials where tablecloths fall in slow motion and settle over a table. I'm sure you know the ones.

Like they've been washed in Woolite? Louis said.

Exactly. Or Breck.

Breck's for hair, Louis said.

It falls, George said.

Yeah, it falls. Anyway, you're making me *all hot and bothered.*

Down boy, George said.

It started with petrified forest, Louis said.

Keep it to yourself, George said.

I'd like to take it as my own, Louis said. Then I'd keep it to myself.

Note that I'm ignoring you, George said. Anyway, afterward we hung out and we'll see each other again tonight. We went for breakfast. I'm in love. There. You happy now?

Happy? Happy? I'm never happy, Louis said. Where did you go for breakfast?

Jesus, George said.

Details, details! Louis said. Details are the story.

Mac's. We split the eggs-pancakes-bacon special.

You took her to Hungry Mac's? That's disgusting.

We sat at the counter.

They're going to have to incinerate that place after the next inspection.

Great breakfasts. Pancakes eggs bacon juice coffee, one sixty-five.

You're just tipping the executioner.

Is that why the counterman has a hood?

I don't understand straight people, Louis said.

What are you writing?

My personal impressions of the—his voice shifted almost professionally into song—*bi-bi-bi . . . centennial celeBRAAAA—shun.*

I hope you're putting something patriotic in there for the alums, George said.

You don't hope that at all, Louis said.

Arthur came in. Arthur was a photographer.

Mr. Pennybaker, Mr. Langland, he said. Pictures. He half-bowed with his usual ersatz formality. He would have been the summer photo editor, but this was a problem since he wasn't enrolled and hadn't been for a year or, more likely, two. His full name, Arthur Augustine Townes. Pronounced, he would be quick to tell you, Ah-GUS-tuhn, like the theologian, not AWE-gus-teen like the city in Florida. A light-skinned black man, round of shoulder and belly and voice, he was the adopted child of a white minister and the minister's wife, an otherwise childless couple, in the Midwest. Methodists. With all that ramrod certainty of grace. How he had convinced them to let him go to school with Communists in Harlem was a wonder. He dressed out of the Eddie Bauer and L.L.Bean catalogues with an occasional Brooks Brothers shirt received, George assumed, at Christmas from his mother; in his oxford cloth and khakis, he was a study in racial mixed messages, late in graduating, hairline just beginning to recede, language hectic and repetitive yet precise, black beard with a gray hair or two already coiled within, vivid-eyed, excited to tell you a story, focused mostly (as were the majority of people George knew) on the comic absurdity of the world. He was a Photographer, with the capital *P*. He'd been *Spectator*'s full-time photo editor for two years, the yearbook's for one, now superannuated. He remained a frequent ghost in the halls and because he was *there* and because he had regular meetings with the dean about readmission—working putatively on some prodigious number of incompletes—he qualified as an actual student of sorts. He possessed many keys to various offices and supply cabinets. Darkroom. Photo equipment. Film. Beside photography—directly beside it—he had made himself expert in photocopy technologies; he knew the capacities, the time requirements, what the machines could take, he knew their dark, black-dusted innards and, like a farmer with his cows at dawn, he could be heard speaking to them in low singsong or cursing them lyrically when they were overheated and jammed. He had taken a work-study job in the printing center and had quickly risen so that now he assistant-managed the core of the university's enormous paper-production facilities—through which passed, for printing or copying and binding, the reports, the committee reviews and projections, the presidential speeches, the staff directories, the schedules of classes and bulletins of offerings, the faculty tenure documents (eyes-only stuff that was), the assessments and refinements, the curriculum reviews and accreditation preparations. The director of printing went to meetings and left operations largely to Arthur, who was becoming the Robert Moses of the university's paper flow.

As for the racial ambiguities, George had heard him address it once, near the end of the spring semester, with a tale of how on an early-darkness winter day back in Milwaukee, in ninth grade, at home, late in the afternoon, he realized he'd forgotten a book—Four thirty or something, he said in that way of his, yes, close to lock-up time, it was, yes, the building where he attended a medium respectable private high school closed at five so what could he do—he dashed out the door into the Wisconsin gloom and ice and ran to the school and then returned with the book, successful. His mother was waiting for him in the kitchen, where mothers, George thought, oft waited in their anger.

Arthur said, Oh yes. She was pissed. She was *pissed.* She said you do not run out of this house after dark, you do not run, oh no. No no. You're a young black man running through the streets after dark in Wisconsin. You will be *shot.* It was a simple fact, okay, jump off the chimney you will die, right? Run these streets, black kid, you will be shot, okay? Like, what are you thinking, right? Like, the point is not debatable, uh uh. No no no no. This is Wisconsin. This is one of the biggest KKK states in the country. Men in sheets. More than Mississippi, right? Yes. And so what did I say? I said, Okay. Right. Right you are, Mother. Yes. I won't do that again, no. No, no, you don't. You don't run down the street in Wisconsin. Ha ha ha. No.

For the bicentennial, Arthur had taken many rolls of film, this known because he always took many rolls of film. Crowds by the river, tall ships. But the paper, at one page, had room for a single picture, which would be badly reproduced. Arthur developed his rolls in the FBH lab, he went over the strips briefly with the loupe—they were dull pictures, he said later, dull dull dull: but he picked out six of the least dull and made five-by-seven contact prints. For the kind of horrifying repro used for the summer paper—cheap offset, one step ahead of mimeograph—you wanted to lower the contrast. The one he liked: strange faces in the foreground, in focus, a man and a woman, the man in profile and his face and neck and upper chest and shoulders painted blue with white stars; on the parts of his body more distant from the lens, stripes, even in black and white a recognizable pattern. The woman held a sparkler and laughed. And behind them, out of focus, like a dream they were having together, a four-masted ship on the river, that whole Horatio Hornblower scene. So he'd brought the prints when dry to the office. The one he liked was third in the pile.

Pictures, Arthur said again.

Yes, yes, Louis said. Pictures. He looked through them quickly, picked the third.

Bless you, Arthur said.

You always put the good one third, Louis said.

No no. Not true. No. Sometimes fourth. Occasionally on the bottom, as a test.

But never on top, Louis said.

Well, if you put it on top, then they *know.* And they'll reject it.

Who's *they*? Louis said.

They is you, Arthur said. In this case.

But I *always* pick the good one.

Well, you're good, yes, you're good. With an eye. Still, give nothing away. My father told me this, many times, from when I was young. Reveal nothing. This is America. Whatever it is, shut up about it. Just keep quiet.

Wisdom from the heartland, Louis sang.

I'm glad you're happy, Arthur said.

I'm not happy, Louis said. I'm semi-hysterical. But I'm glad *you're* happy.

Let's not exaggerate, Arthur said.

Well. You remain cheerful.

Yes, that's right, yes. I remain cheerful. I'll remember that. Remain cheerful.

And he left. Remain cheerful, he called from the hall. Louis thought he was gone but then there he was again, Arthur at the door: Continue to be driven by your overbrimming self-confidence, he said.

Fu-u-uck you-u, Louis sang.

≡

THE NARRATIVE THAT George had sketched out for Louis of his evening and morning had been a fading approximation—such things were never as one told them. Indeed the telling could easily ruin what nuance memory managed to hold. Twice that night he had almost come when she was rubbing him through his underwear and kissing him and the second time, when he pulled away from her, she said it's okay, I'd like it if you came and he'd said no, he didn't want to, the idea of coming in his underwear was too depressing and junior high and she said what about in my hand and he said no, real thing only, lady, and started to crawl up between her legs causing her to back up laughing and he had tasted it, the power struggle, an iron tang like the taste of blood. It was going to be that way between them; and his simple principle, principle being the fancied-up word for one's immutable inclinations of personality, hidden beneath his kindness and his attempts at humor, was never, ever, ever to give in. This inclination—this attribute—he recognized as the endowment of his mother—here she was, the trope of the dead mother and the fact of her, he hated confessing to it, so he rarely did—she had been absolutely relentless. Hide if you must, disappear if you must (his father had, after all, or after what was not nearly all), lie if you must, pretend if you must, but *never surrender*. Pretend to surrender, if you must; even after you've seemingly surrendered, keep fighting. Like the Viet Cong. His mother had grown fond in her later years of the Viet Cong, in their tunnels, enduring and vanquishing. The North Vietnamese Army. She was the only mother in Saybrook, he'd venture, who knew the name of General Giáp.

And so the morning had arrived, they'd slept, on and off, only a few hours in the single bed, she in her underpants pressed against him, the light pale blue on the west side of the building, the room cool with the fan. He'd taken off his underpants and she kept touching him—checking if he was still there, checking if *it* was still there, the hard-on, holding it and dozing. Finally they slept and then it was as George had told Louis, he'd woken very hard, needing to piss of course but holding that off, her hand had gone to it again and not been able to pull away and he drew down her panties and she'd climbed on top of him. There was something miraculous about her compact body, about her dark and intelligent beauty—she knew herself, she knew her own beauty. Or no, not that: she knew her own body, was at ease in it, did not live in it as if it were something he was looking at, some alien tool to be used for seduction and sex, but as if it were her own domain. He'd not encountered that before, the lack of an impulse to pose; he would have called it *confidence*, and thought of telling her later that's what he saw, but for his suspicion that it was something other than confidence, his sense that almost certainly she'd deny any feelings of confidence—at times, in fact, as they'd moved together and apart, before he began to drive into her very quickly, he'd seen moments of uncertainty and alarm in her eyes. It wasn't confidence but integrity. She was herself in an immutable way. And it wasn't that she had no fear. It was that she liked it, she liked being aroused, she liked what her body was feeling, she even liked being a little afraid, and it was not fear of her body or of his body or of some forbidden thing, not fear of sex, but fear of what was real, the emotional vulnerability that stands behind sex, between it and the sunlight, casting its shadow. He stared into her as an explorer would and she had not looked away, not until she came; he'd whispered to her, he'd whispered as he moved very deep into her, "I want to open you up," by which he meant both things, looking into her and fucking her, and this moment had set them off, brought on the speed, the hips, the climax. He believed she'd climaxed. She appeared to have done so at least the once. After, she'd been flushed in face and neck and chest. For a few minutes she'd been shy, her face buried away. He had spooned against her, his arms around her, ready to go back to sleep, but after three or four minutes—certainly not five—she squirmed out of his pupal embrace and said, I'm hungry. Are you hungry? I'm really hungry.

Women—how they look at change and adapt to it and move on. He was flattened, by exhaustion, by the sex, by the power of his feelings. She meanwhile was readying herself to go out for breakfast.

3

Anna's lasting memory would be him wearing that T-shirt, which had been washed many times, the subdued red shade of raspberry sherbet, faded, filled with shoulders she wanted to have her hands on, wanted to have her teeth on, her mouth. Big rounded solid-looking hunks of meat. She'd said to him at one point that he looked as if he lifted weights or something, and he looked down at himself, right and left, and said no, he had crewed and repaired boats, sailboats, out of Old Saybrook for most of his adolescence and this was the fading remains of that work, the first summer in five years he had not been in a boatyard. He had the mashed-up Topsiders for it, the ones he'd gone on about. No one who wore them ever, ever had new ones. Ever. She would remind herself to inquire into this strange New England Protestant phenomenon—no clothes are ever new—at some future point of easier familiarity. He spoke slowly. He took care with his words, which was appropriate, it turned out, as he wrote for the paper and wanted to be a writer or journalist of some kind. As such it took a long time to find out if he was interesting; she felt as if she were still finding out. Somehow his physical presence made it difficult to determine what if anything was going on there.

Here was what had finally, thoroughly, taken her: the way he stopped and stared at her after she'd said Charles Aznavour. He'd been funny about Eddie Palmieri and his deck shoes but the Aznavour, that was real. Sometimes you make contact with another human being and it's like an electric current. Zzzzzp. That frightening buzz as when your finger touches the prong while the plug's still largely in the socket. The little story of his cassette tape. Purchased after his mother died. Aznavour on *The Mike Douglas Show*. She'd gotten it out of him, this little tale. So many records have a story. Your story, with them. Carole King's *Tapestry*. Shit. Not even worth thinking about. It was like the march of thirty million women to buy *Tapestry*. But *Sgt. Pepper*? She couldn't even look at the cover anymore: her brother when it came out, his air of thrilled absorption. His records were hers now, among all else he'd left behind. She had a Japanese edition of Wilhelm Kempff playing his transcriptions of the Bach chorales. Mark, her older brother, had played piano. He'd been very good, and then at fourteen or fifteen he stopped. No longer interested. But he still played the records, the piano music, once in a while. The Kempff album was a Japanese release, the cover indecipherable. A warped cover and the record within it warped too: the arm of the turntable rose and fell like a conductor keeping time to the wrong piece of music. But it played. Or Ohio Players. The honey dripping on the body. She wanted warm honey dripped on her body. Ever since she'd seen that album cover she'd wanted *that*. She'd never told anyone. Maybe she'd tell this one. Maybe he'd get it.

He was sturdy and he was clearly wounded, and this was how she liked to think of herself but she didn't express it physically the way he did; she wondered whether this was what turned her on. He was red, a little more golden red than his T-shirt, a white boy used to the sun. He wasn't working this summer, just reading and writing stuff; he had social security survivor benefits from his mother and his father both, he'd told her, the orphan's ransom. It would last until he was twenty-one. She didn't realize children got social security. In his room after they'd finally picked a record, she'd held him around his neck while he kissed her and put one leg on him and then the other and essentially climbed up him, rubbing and rocking. There was a marvelous bulk and solidity. Like warm lumber. She so so so had *not* wanted to fuck him on the first night. She so so so believed this was a dooming habit of hers. Thus she held him off and held him off while she knew she was driving him crazy and driving herself crazy too, and pointlessly really, some rule she'd decided to adopt, and in the morning, that strong cock in her hand, leaking onto her fingers, she couldn't hold off anymore and wouldn't and didn't and after all it was not the first night anymore, was it? In the pink and powder-blue light of dawn. Her panties on the floor. God, sliding onto him. He was thick across the hips she had to stretch herself out she felt opened up and then later that's what he said, he wanted to open her, and that sent her over the edge and she came and came a second time and she loved the feel of his body, which never happened, she never loved their bodies until later, if at all. She liked the smell of him. Always important. They went for pancakes. They kissed at the counter with syrup on their lips. They were a little gross but she didn't care. The guy behind the counter looked like a sleaze and kept leering at her.

4

Soon they were together, a couple. When do you say, I love you? It catches in the throat but won't hold there for long. Autumn came, but first August, she went home for two weeks—it was Hershey PA she was from, that was what she hadn't wanted to say—and George found a place to crash for the week when the dorms were closed, having no home to go to. It was long distance so they only spoke twice; he wrote to her, she wrote to him, interminable separation. Then exciting September, russet October. Of course he loved her. And she loved him. Why wouldn't they love each other? They dropped acid on a windy clear autumn night that followed upon a crystalline day of crisp miraculous blue—and how he loved her. The day was limpid! pellucid! George was reading Conrad and the language was infecting him like some ancient virus that survived by spreading Latinates through the victim's cerebral cortex and out into the world. The night sky glowed with starlight, more stars than one generally saw in New York. A wind was coming up, it blew dramatically at times, it had blown every trace of cloud and moisture from above the land—after heavy rains the night before—and it threw their hair back and brought a cool fire to their faces. It seemed at times a supernatural wind, a biblical wind, there was death in it, a complicated death, it carried a portent of wonders, of God's wrath and his arbitrary, gorgeous salvation. George and Anna had dropped the acid at about eight thirty, everyone but them on the floor gathering in the lounge to watch game four of the World Series, which the Yankees were about to lose; George couldn't believe they would subject themselves to it, unless they were all from Cincinnati. Most of the College, half at least, was from the tristate region. Games one through three had demonstrated with efficiency that these were two clubs playing presumably the same sport but with different orders of skill. Munson of course the exception. He was phenomenal. The rest of the team looked like scared cats. George wanted to be as far away from it as possible and the acid would take him very far from it indeed. Anna was pleased after losing him to the first three games to have him back. Those games had put him in foul humor. Now he was liberated, almost joyful; she felt it was for her.

George went down to the pub to have a beer. Anna, having gone back to her room, was planning to meet him in the lobby. The place was nearly empty, because of the game and because it was still relatively early, and while he was standing with his mug, ready to finish it off, the dean walked in. The fucking dean. He was about six six, and stooped, a scholar of Russian language and literature who spoke in an inaudible murmuring stutter. He was slightly hunched and all angles and he looked like a pterodactyl. He had a dactylic name: Harrington.

The dean needed someone to be talking to, not standing there looking freakishly tall, tweedy and out of place, and George was it, the only soul positioned near the entrance. The dean smiled. He was a courtly yet awkward man.

How are you, Dean? George said. He reached out his hand to shake, which he instantly perceived was a little weird with a school authority, but too late: Harrington took it, pressing his own hand around George's; it was a large, soft pillow of a hand, almost baby-smooth, that George could hardly get his fingers to the far side of.

Fine, Harrington said, with his many teeth. It's g-g-g-g-good to s-s-s-s-see you. The Ya-Ya-Ya-Yankees are losing. I th-th-th-thought I'd t-t-t-t-take a walk.

George, being five eleven, or just enough above five ten for him to believe for a few seconds at a time that he was five eleven, gazed up at Harrington, who stooped even beyond his default stoop in order to converse over the sound of funk guitar, a Hammond, and Donna Summer groaning. A smattering of white kids, dancing. There were black students in the College, constituting some five or six percent of the class, but where the white kids hung out, one rarely saw them—the social segregation was a dual-sided commitment.

The Series is a foregone conclusion, George said. It's over.

S-s-s-s-so it s-s-s-s-s-seems. S-s-s-s-sad. And s-s-s-s-so th-th-th-th-this is where the ac-ac-action is, Harrington said. Again the teeth, lips pulled back, horse's teeth, large and yellow. George was already stoned and the acid was beginning to outline the edges of things, and what took over his full brain at that moment—because of the teeth—was *Equus*. He'd sat on the stage, in student seating, and watched through the stage lights, the audience invisible behind the blinding wall of white, observing with horrified fascination the backlit Marian Seldes spray Anthony Perkins with spit for three acts; the red-haired girl lay down nude five feet in front of him, his first real redhead, with her ginger pubic hair and all-pink genitals—while the boy ran around blinding the horses, George just stared at that girl, the pale white of her body there before him, almost translucent. She was breathing hard, her stomach rising and falling, it mesmerized him. This acting was work. What, Dean? Can't hear? Oh, this was the dean smiling. He was a nice man, it was plain, shy and kind; yet his severe face gave the smile a look of grimacing in pain. He was genial and he didn't want trouble and, all in all, George thought, he must wonder how the fuck he ended up in the squall of running things—he was that worst of all appointments, an interim dean—his tongue and mouth betraying him so many times a day, holding him back, which was fine as he wasn't supposed to say much of substance anyway.

A moment of awkward silence—how long?—and then the dean's face began to shift and move. His head elongated and shimmered. The wall behind him undulated pleasantly. And then, oh god, what? He started talking again. What?

A g-g-g-g-great place to unwind after classes and stu-stu-stu-stu-studying . . . ? Something. George envisioned Harrington suddenly morphing into the very pterodactyl he already resembled—the shattering caw, the brown paper explosion of his unfolding wings, his taking off with George hanging from his beak, gripped by his upper leg, with thrown back arms behind him and face of terror. The eyes wild and out of control—what was that face he had in his mind now? One of the Greek deities devouring his son. Fuck Western civilization, man, too much carnage.

Have you ever noticed, George said, then stopped.

Wh-what? Harrington said.

Have you ever noticed, um, how much carnage there is in Western civilization?

Oh indeed, said Harrington. He looked delighted. Nothing could have pleased him more than this comment from a student in the pub on a Friday night. Western Civ—the very identity of the place.

I've been thinking about that, George said. Like this Goya painting . . .

He drifted off.

Oh indeed yes, ma-ma-many of them. Quite b-b-b-b-bloody. Harrington almost had to spit the last word out. He shook his head to throw the words forward: again the horse.

One of the gods eating his children, George said, vaguely.

I b-b-b-b-believe it's the T-T-T-Titan Cronus, Harrington said. I-I-I'm not an art s-s-s-scholar b-b-by any means. B-b-b-b-but I I thi-i-i-ink s-s-s-s-so, yes. In L-L-Latin S-s-s-s-s-s-s-s-s . . . He took a breath. S-S-S-S-Saturn. I think.

Such a gracious false humility. That Saturn was the giveaway—he could barely spit it out of himself—because he *knew* that he was showing off.

Yeah, Cronus, yeah that's right, George said. He couldn't shut it off, the chatter, though inanimate objects were moving quite explicitly now, the eyes and faces, the slatted paneling on the walls, oh my god—

Funny, he actually liked this man.

Okay, George said, for instance, right, Goya, Cronus. Saturn. And then there's this diner over in the 90s on Madison, I think—maybe Lex? No, Madison. They have this huge painted mural covering the whole wall, the entire length of the dining area, of Achilleus dragging the body of Hector around the walls of Troy. It's huge. It looms over everybody's lunch.

You know, I-I-I-I'd like to s-s-s-s see that, Harrington said. I-I assume they're G-G-G-Greek?

Yeah, said George. Greek diner. No Coke, Pepsi. Yeah. It's on the east side of the avenue. Madison.

Well then, it m-makes pe-pe-perfect s-s-s-sense.

George got it, with the acid it seemed revelatory in some special way: Harrington used phrases like *oh indeed* and *well then* to launch his mouth into the sentences he needed to say.

Dean, I have to go, man. I mean, not man, sorry. I have to go. Have a good time! I was actually on my way out, actually.

He was frantic and inarticulate. Harrington gazed at him with large friendly eyes. I'm meeting a girl, George said. He said it with an absurd theatrical air of manly conspiracy. To explain his departure, which didn't need explaining. Society and its fucking psychic demands, Jesus. The universe picked up speed. Everything his eye landed on began to pulsate.

Oh e-e-e-excellent, the dean said. That large hand again. Something unbearably tender in it, slightly clumsy and gentle. Other humans. George turned and waved vaguely and ran up the stairs, toward night, freedom, Anna. She was waiting five feet from the stairwell, on the edge of the multi-doored lobby.

We have got to get out of here, George said to her.

This is so wild, she said. I just saw Ichabod Crane, I swear.

That was the dean, George said.

Right, but he looked like Ichabod Crane and now I'm watching for the headless horseman. Which would be a bad thing for this trip, right? A kind of Art Linkletter moment there? It is *such* a bummer to see anything headless when you're tripping.

I was *talking* to him, George said. Downstairs. Ichabod the dean. His face started like *decomposing* while I was talking to him. The walls were moving and his face was melting and I thought it was going to fall off in front of me—

Right, Anna said. He would have *become* the headless horseman.

Then, in a segue that George mysteriously understood, she stepped back and twirled in a ballet kind of pose and made a sound like wheee.

George covered his eyes. Oh my god don't do that, I can't take it, he said.

Anna twirled and seemed to laugh. We are soooo fucked up . . . Two girls heading down to the pub looked at them and laughed. They didn't laugh nicely. Anna continued twirling—George's eyes were seeing four of her at once, or five, trails of her, an endless sequence.

Don't, George said. I'm going to lose it, I swear.

She stopped. Poor baby, she said. Let's go. Oops, I'm a little dizzy. Here, hold my arm.

She had changed, into a flowered skirt, a cotton knit shirt, and the arm that took his occupied one side of a time-soft denim jacket. Nothing pleased him more than to hold it. Twenty-eight twenty-seven—that was her phone extension. It was burned so deeply into his skull that if he saw a campus phone, such as the one that had just come into his sight on the lobby wall of this old World War I officers' dorm, some inner spiritual muscle in him leaped, wanting to dial her, no matter at all that she was already with him, which proved the Pavlovian power of the image of the phone.

They left the building, out into the quad, into a gust of the changeable wind rubbing up against them, a hundred brief caresses.

5

It would be their companion through the night, that wind, it spoke to them—an animated being with thoughts and will that they came to know and that they felt able, with the acid, to interpret. They went on the subway and the other faces were almost too much for them and the graffiti and the smells and the shifting patterns and smears and stains of the linoleum tiles on the floors of the train. The enormity and thousand-voiced scraping-steel noise of it. A million cigarette butts and gum stains, which were black or else lumpen gray not yet dinged to black. Anna suddenly could see *every* figure who'd dropped his gum, her gum, his cigarette butt on that floor, men in suits and drifters and workmen and Puerto Rican girls from the Bronx, and nervous old women and nervous old men, they multiplied like a rapidly replicating society in her mind, nurses, secretaries, cops: it was like a weird Ad Council public service spot about *community*. She closed her eyes, tried to shut it down but she barely subdued it, the image grew and grew like some kind of virus-infused kaleidoscope until it was all crowds in her eyes, a massive swirl of faces.

She murmured in George's ear, Petals on a wet black bough.

He looked at her.

Oh man, he said. Not the Pound shit. Then he started laughing.

She laughed too.

Apparitions! she said.

No, he said. No no don't. Still laughing. Bending over.

Obviously they were insane.

Faces! she said. Crowds!

Then she looked away and let her eyes and consciousness drift until she found herself focused on the flashing by of the soot-dark I-beams holding up the tunnel, think of that shit why don't you, the whole fucking street is up there, held up on poles. Then he said, *One year floods rose, One year they fought in the snows . . .*

Oh no, she said. No Pound shit for me, so no Pound shit for you.

You *had* your Pound shit!

Oh, the sounds: steel on steel, rattle and bang, millions a day, millions a day, the rails seemed to sing it hoarsely: and George was singing it to her now, singing it low, to her hair, where he imagined her ear was. She pictured this mental process, determining the ear beneath the hair. He sang: *millions a day*. She and he almost huddled together but she wanted them to keep the appearance of normality—doesn't every woman want this, why does it matter so little to so many men, and indeed worst of all it matters least to the most desirable ones—she wanted them to *sit up straight* and not stare glazed and frightening at some pulsating dot on the wall next to someone's head. With every new onslaught she just kept muttering oh my god and closing her eyes, except then the dizziness would get her and she'd have to open them again and for a minute somewhere in there she thought she'd have to get off the train, pull the brakes and get herself off the train or she'd throw up and then, worse, die . . . but it passed. She tried to find some Zen inner tranquility thing, some strength-spirit entering through her open palms. Noise: clanks and squeals of stressed metal, the doors banging open and closed, bells and hollers and *completely . . . indecipherable . . . messages . . .* through the ancient loudspeaker system, like the voice of a ridiculous god who'd given up even trying to be understood, the sound of bad wiring and ominous truths just missed. Mixed in with a few slurred electric words—electric words, ecstatic words—that they *thought* they could understand.

He's saying, *My god, my god, why have you forsaken me*, Anna said, after a conductor's announcement.

George said, Actually, it was, *Franklin Street next, watch the closing doors.*

Ohhh, don't be a total shit, she said, and hit his denim thigh, not too hard, but hard enough to make a point, and then they both stared at the spot on his leg that she'd hit, as if they could see the concussion of fist on quadriceps, occurring and occurring again, in super slow motion. They stared and stared.

Wow, George said finally and they started laughing again. They were together, that was what held it in place for them, made the heightened world bearable: they would look at each other in amazement or amusement or both and each would know to the depths of reality and to the depths of spirit what the other was thinking, feeling, wondering, hoping. Acid clarity, acid truth.

George said, If I said what you're thinking right now—

Long pause. Anna said, You'd be right. Of course.

Long pause. Yeah, George said.

Longer pause. I know, Anna said. You remember it and tell me later and I'll remember it and tell you later.

Holy shit, that would be totally impossible, George said. I mean, think about it.

Pause.

I can't think about it, she said.

Pause.

George said, I don't even remember now.

Pause.

Anna said, Remember what?

George said, Exactly, man. That's the thing. I mean, *that's* the *thing*. Remember *what*? Remembering is living. But it's the opposite of living too, because when you're having the experience to remember you're not remembering other things, right? And then there's too much to remember.

And too much of it painful, Anna said. She knew what she meant by this. He had his own version, she could see it, some dark shape like an inner shadow.

They clattered and clanked with stretches of time—eons—lost on each other and to the world, until they were down to South Ferry, where the train turned impossibly to make the curved station, screaming during the turn as if the elements of iron and steel and aluminum themselves were being rent. And then moving ridged steel panels like rows of teeth slid out mechanically from the platform to meet the train doors, monster teeth covering the wide gap caused by the severe curve of platform unfitting the ruler-straight form of each subway car. Steel teeth. Black and silver and glinting reflections. She and he went up the stairs and out into the air. At the top she wondered had they gone up slowly or fast? She already couldn't remember. The smell of harbor and sea, the molecules palpable in an infinite assault against their faces and down into their bronchi and lungs; the erotic air penetrated them, wrapped itself around them, touched them—right there, right there at the center of their sex it brazenly rubbed against them, with intent, lifted them off the ground—and he said, Do you *feel* that? and she made a sound, that unmistakable sound, low and quiet: she felt it—this air, this night, these air-feathered fingers, all things living and sentient and so intense they were hardly bearable: exquisite. And the light: they could walk on the beams of it, skip on the million stones of it that glittered on the water. He stopped her.

We cannot walk on water and we cannot walk on air, he said.

She said, I know that.

We have to remember that, he said.

Got it, she said. I mean, I was already there.

Good, he said. He looked reassured, she was happy to reassure him.

Don't worry, she said. None of that aforementioned Linkletter shit tonight, baby.

≡

THEY WANDERED ONTO the ferry stiff-legged, dumb, beamed from another planet, unaccustomed to the particular gravity—PEOPLE OF EARTH—they stared this way and that, George almost frozen in place by the unimaginable fist-size lugs and bolts in the thick brackets that held deck to bulwark, all ridged with soot and grime; by the long-cracked linoleum floor; by the voices, the faces. They went upstairs and then outside onto the upper starboard deck, and sat, and felt the wind and the impossible rumble of the ferry's enormous engines departing. It ran to starboard for a quarter mile then made its sharp tack to port to gain the harbor channel, the famous immense strange statue, verdigris patina'd, illuminated and shimmering over the waters, casting fragments of luminous green that looked like neon eels on the choppy surface.

Who would build such a thing? George said.

The French! Anna said, and he laughed. She approved of the project. Behind them the insane immensities that had grown right up to the edge of land and water: an impossible palisade of corporate stone and steel and glass. One after another after another and then at the very end, far to the west side of the base of the isle, the two black ones, dwarfing all.

Who would build *that*? he said.

Us, Anna said, more flatly.

I didn't have nothin' to do with it.

Not true, your uncle, you told me, she said.

My uncle was just tacking up the drywall, he said. I mean, who decided and who enacted? They really are huge.

This led to kissing, touching, on the bench. It got serious.

Oh my god stop, she said. I can't take it. Too much.

He sat back.

Are you sorry you missed the last game of the Series? she said.

He said, You know, I lived and breathed and died and ceased breathing over this team since I was seven. Now. Hmm. Not really. That was all before I'd been exposed to quality—to dazzling women such as you.

You were going to say *pussy*. You were about to say *quality pussy*.

No, I would never. That would be vulgar and demeaning.

Right, and you were about to say it.

Never. I would never.

She kissed him. Suddenly she could kiss again. That merest hint of swagger in him had moved her somehow. He'd told her she was the softest kisser imaginable. There wasn't much of anything else in sex she liked in the oh-so-gentle mode but in kissing she wanted slow, pliable, hungry, wet. It haunted him, what it reminded him of. Sometimes she rubbed her cheeks lightly on the bristle of his unshaved face. She took a strange, stupid little bit of pride in pulling his attention to her and away from his baseball team. What was that?

Your kisses, he said.

Yes? A topic of interest.

My mother used to come to my room and kiss me at night.

Like when you were a kid, to kiss you good night?

No, he said. Not like that.

Oh, she said. Oh.

I'll tell you sometime. I can't now. My brain would explode.

Oh, babe, she said.

Later, George said: It's very important to remember your lies.

What? Anna said.

You know, remember your lies so you don't fuck up and contradict yourself.

Were you lying before about your mother?

No, he said. But you know what I mean. Like I told a guy on my floor that I played high school baseball. Just ninth grade. In fact I thought about trying out but I didn't. Now I have to remember he thinks I played ball.

Oh my god, Anna said. I can't stand when people fuck up that way. It makes me lose faith in the workings of the universe.

But you've never done that, right?

Oh, the wind, Anna said. God the wind. George laughed.

The wind. Time elongated in it, rose and fell and lapped with the corrugated water, grew new dimensions inside itself—Anna whispered in his ear at some point because she knew it too, and knew what he was thinking, she whispered: *days sift down it constantly, years*, he knew exactly what she meant, *exactly*, the lifelongness of it, of life! And beyond, lifelong after lifelong after lifelong, bay, light, wind, the meaning of it went deep through the water and into the earth, oh the intensity of meanings, of meaning itself! You can't even think of it. Meaning! Standing out in the wind—what does the wind mean?—her nipples hardened beneath the cotton of her shirt and he whispered in her ear, what he was going to do, he was going to just barely touch her, and she nodded and his flat-handed palm grazed the tip of one and the other and back again while her eyes closed and he understood that he had to put his other arm around her waist and hold her. This was only a few seconds, but it stood out, as everything else had, like a bas-relief in time. The *present* was eternal, sure, the problem was learning how to experience it that way, so it was after an eternity holding each other and leaning on the rail in the starry wind, a rare night of such clarity even the New York sky was flooded with light—we gotta call Carl Sagan, he told her at one point, this is too much—the ferry docking at Staten Island, engines enormously and loudly in reverse, pulling against the momentum of the boat and the boat crashing hard into the pilings BOOM and BOOM again, throwing George and Anna nearly onto the deck, the cracking creaking yielding of the wood along the retaining wall, the noise like a giant outpouring of coherent and distinct noises, the pilings each cracking and moaning, wood stretch, wood groans, a harem of them as boat slid into slip, a machine-made modern symphony of steel on wood—the mind lost itself distinguishing all the sounds; all the anguished faces.

Wet black bough, he said to her.

Yeah, yeah, yeah, she said.

How about wet black bow of the ship, he said.

Was prow, now bow, she said.

Very good, he said. That's very good.

I knew you'd like that, boat boy.

Eventually the boat relaunched, they came back across the harbor, and the wind grew steadier and more forceful; he thought he was flying home on it, home, he realized with explosive clarity, being *the here and now.* They were both so cold they thought they would freeze in place. They staggered inside to the electric dry heat of the long gray metal basilica where the commuters sat on the interminable boat pews every morning.

Home is the here and now, he said to her. That's where home is.

On the ferry? she said.

On the anything, he said. He wrapped his arms around himself. Now. Here. Wherever.

Oh, she said. She pried open his arms and stepped inside them to his chest, and his arms closed around her again as if designed for the task.

I wish that were true, she said. But home is a little more . . . ontological than that. As it exists in our psyches anyway. It's an ongoing category of moral life. Far-reaching.

She was mumbling into his chest by this point.

It's like original fucking sin.

God, your life is hard, he said.

She laughed.

They got back uptown a little after one a.m., having first gotten off the subway and wandered around an empty Lincoln Center, the reflecting pools behind the opera house black with lights sparkling on the surface, tempting to wade into it but they didn't, galvanized and even a little frightened by (or *he* was a little frightened by) the massive abstract sculptures standing ominously mid-pool on stone platforms. Bronzes, dark as the water. He took out a joint from his jacket pocket, lit it, held his puff, stared at the statues.

George said, What are those?

Henry Moore, Anna said. English sculptor. Reclining figures. You gonna share that? We sure there's no one around?

He handed her the joint.

You see anyone around? he said. Except these giant nudes, who look mellow. Once you get used to them.

She took a hit, held it, and after releasing she said, I love Henry Moore. He understands bodies.

Their own two bodies leaning into each other, looking. Anna gave him back the joint. She could feel his solidity, like the solidity of Moore's statues, which every time she saw them she wished to slosh out to and lean against in much this way. She expected them to be warm as if in perennial sunlight. She wanted to attack them face-first, arms outspread. The famished lover. Now she had *him* to lean against and she could transfer the desire to this, to now. She tried to do that. She leaned harder. His legs almost gave way and they both staggered leftward. Anna laughed and laughed and tried to explain it—you were supposed to be solid, she kept saying—and he laughed too, but he didn't understand precisely what had happened and she knew it. Which, then, they both knew: that *she* knew what was funny and he *didn't* know and she knew he didn't know and he knew she knew that: which made them both laugh over again, and him saying, What? What? but there was no answer to it and every time he said it—What?—they laughed more. They wandered from there farther back into the complex and found an open area with a bandshell and behind that a fence from which they could look down on the barren scape of Tenth Avenue, the residential towers and housing projects beyond. They smoked more of the joint but didn't finish it. He went to save it in his pocket and she stopped his hand. Don't save it, she said. He looked at her, then flicked it out between the wires of the fence and it sailed onto the sidewalk beneath their high post. They walked back then and climbed up onto the stage of the bandshell and they sang songs and declaimed from the stage in an intoxicated mockery of actual performance which they fully understood and deeply enjoyed and neither of them, recollecting the bandshell, would be able, ever, to remember what they said and what they sang there on that cool-winded night. George remembered best that he could, in fact, charm her; more than that, he never lost this new sense of stunned liberation.

Afterward they got themselves back to Broadway and walked for perhaps two blocks before it became exhausting and overwhelming with the noise of traffic and the moving lights and so, though barely competent, George bounded into the traffic and hailed a cab and magically, with full knowledge, avoided a splattering death—she watched him, knowing somehow he would not die. He might never die. For his part he could see it play out in the acid cinema of his mind, but his mind made it into a dance, a beautiful promenade, honkings and veerings of no import and the cab pulling up beside him with the door spotted exactly to his hand, for his opening,

Anna just watching him, calm as could be, and he and she then in the cab. They sat close in the back and closer still until their lips touched, and tongue tips touched and George entered a staggering tunnel of desire. They kissed slowly and precisely as if each new movement of the mouth and tongue was a dissertation in response to the previous movement by the other. His arm across her lap and hand on her far hip, tilting her toward him, the feel of that extraordinary folded spot where so much flesh meets. Speaking in this wordless, mouthy way. Until she pulled away—

Dry mouth time-out, she said.

He had it too.

We have to get something to drink, she said.

I have a can of Coke in my room.

Oh my god, Coke, she said, and began sliding down in her seat and laughing again. He hoisted her up.

They arrived at 114th Street. Sorting out the money was comical. George found a five and paid. They got off at Broadway and walking down 114th they came upon a tree behind Carman—a young, small tree, recently planted, it was uprooted and brutal and spilled on the sidewalk, torn from its stingy rectangle of dirt, yanked down by that wind, which had been with them all night, the gorgeous, unthinking wind, and after staring at that, the roots and tendrils of roots hanging like nerve endings or guts or miniature bones, so wrong when you see the living insides of something pulled out, then finally walking on, imbued with a tragic sense, they looked far down the block and saw the rest of it, near Amsterdam, the police cars and the dark silhouettes of the half dozen cops, with their distinctive hats, gathered there, the red and white light passing so quick and bright, a momentary return to the hallucinogenic.

For years after, through separate lives, they would associate that night, that wind, the sadness of that yanked-out tree, young and destroyed, and their own first sense of irretrievable loss, with Jeffrey Goldstein's death out a window on a high floor of John Jay Hall, a living thing, tender and new, ripped like that tree from his place in the world and dying that night on a New York City sidewalk.

6

They walked down the long block toward Amsterdam through a thickness of knowing and dread. They got as far as the east gate on 114th, between Butler and Jay, stairs up to the walkway past the tennis court—Anna stopped, held his hand, kept him from going on. Something deep told her not to see this, something beyond how it might be awful or bloody or very sad—something having to do with herself, her essence, her own suddenly threatened animal survival: as if it were her death they were walking toward, as if she were the toppled tree, a fallen body.

Let's go up, she said.

George: I can't. I have to see what it is.

The paper?

Yes.

A moment's silence then George said, why don't you go up and I'll come later? She stood, head down, shaking it no. She pulled on him, but he resisted. He was so thick. Physically and right now in other ways too. He gave a small tug. So she went. They came around the corner to the body on the sidewalk: not even taped off yet, a uniform standing there to keep them from going on. Move along, he said. His colleagues were backing a few people away on the other side, north of the body, so they could tie a cordon around the signposts. George took in that Arthur was already there, shooting, flash going off and whirring in re-charge, trying to get as close as the cops would let him. He had some kind of bogus-looking credential hanging on a chain around his neck. Farther on, George saw a detective looking at him. George told the guy he was with *Spectator* and asked him, was he shot?

He jumped. Or fell.

From John Jay?

That this building?

Yes, this is Jay.

Then from John Jay. The cop was smoking a cigarette and when he inhaled he looked as if it was ripping his lungs out.

He said, I thought for a minute you meant the college on 57th Street.

George just looked at him.

I didn't know there *is* a college on 57th Street.

You from out of town or what? the detective said.

Eastern Connecticut, George said.

Right, said the detective. John Jay College. It's City. Criminology is their main thing. Therefore well known by the likes of me.

Did anyone see what floor? You willing to give your name? You from the two-seven?

Everyone said the two precinct numbers separately.

Actually I'm from the two-five but I was on 110th when the call went out. I'm Detective John Snetts. No jokes. S-N-E-T-T-S.

The two-seven is coming or you guys have it?

Homicide Division is coming, Snetts said. Manhattan North. I'll be assisting with preliminaries.

Homicide? George said.

It always starts with them, Snetts said.

George thanked him. Anna was facing away from him, staring at the boy on the sidewalk, at his misangled limbs. George touched her back. They watched Arthur with his camera, working around the body, the cops basically ignoring him now, something avid and surgical in his interest, his absorption in the specificity of the thing. He kept looking around, searching out sources of light. A pudgy man—something about him led Anna to wonder if he was a virgin—but intense and quick-motioned. He looked at them for a solid two count, nodded in his Arthur way, went back to work. George pointed toward the other side of Amsterdam, a change of focus. Across there—but 150 feet away—was, almost bizarrely, the hospital, St. Luke's, and closest of all, the glare and buzz and the two parked orange-sided ambulances of the ER, black-silhouette figures of cops and medical techs moving into and out of the double doors at the head of the bay. The boy had jumped and died right in front of the emergency room. The cop car lights, the ambulance lights: a moment of spinning nausea; surreal, but everything was surreal tonight. George had the feeling he was momentarily tuned into a foreign television channel: something in German or Polish or Russian, with weird lighting and production values. The language didn't convey.

Three medics from St. Luke's were kneeling beside the boy but soon they stood: there was no need for urgent measures.

He'll have to be pronounced at the hospital, one of them said to Snetts, who nodded.

I'm noting the time, oh-one-thirty-nine, he said.

Two of them were pulling the stretcher out of the truck. Snetts said, We gotta wait for the homicide division and the

ME so don't take him yet. Anna's face was still, deep, without horror—as George too was without horror, he realized then. It was some form of acid detachment, or no, they should call it acceptance—there it was, the seemingly real, unsolvable, unchangeable, implacably mysterious, the *facts*, the present, you can't plan for it or play with it in memory and alter it, because there it is and in this head you accepted it. He tried to imagine the pain. Perhaps from now forward this is how he would be in the face of death: can acid change your relationship to death? There would have been only a second of pain: he counted it off: one one thousand. Then you settle into darkness that looks like sleep. God how brutal that impact. Anna's face beside him so solid, so silent, silver-pink with the flash of red and white passing over it, a poh-lice disco strobe.

I can feel this, she said. I can feel myself falling falling falling like nothing that's ever fallen. The look on her face was distant, her voice as calm as pond water and as unrevealing of what lay beneath.

But it wasn't you, George said.

She looked at him then. Oh? she said. I can *feel* it. I can see it, a whirling darkness and then a brilliant light, falling falling falling. Falling. I've never imagined falling. It takes the stomach and shoots it skyward. You fall and what's in you wants to stay up where you were. Your lungs up in your throat. Your skin mashing upward on your body, wrinkling like water. It's insane. It's hideous. It's also comfortable in some bizarre way, alluring. Flight. Such as it is.

He wanted to put his arm around her, hold her close to him, but felt it wasn't wanted; he rested it carefully on her shoulders and back. Comradely.

We can't fly and we can't walk on water, he whispered.

People keep saying.

Four cops standing near one of the patrol cars: Snetts said to one, Jimmy, gimme your radio, who's upstairs on this?

Karelsen and Dumbo.

Apparently they have a guy they call Dumbo, George said quietly to Anna. She looked at him without amusement, just taking it in. Facts. Guy called Dumbo.

Couple of mopes, said Snetts. What's Karelsen's number? Cop mumbled, Snetts pressed the side button and said, one-fourteen come in one-fourteen—he let the button up and what felt to George like a long delay—two seconds probably—before the static and *Yeah this is one-fourteen, over.*

Detective John Snetts of the two-five. Confirming you're in John Jay Hall, gimme your floor, over.

Confirm John Jay, thirteenth floor, over.

Snetts says: How many witnesses, over.

Could be twenty to thirty. Nobody saw it but almost everybody heard it, over.

All right, I'm coming up with Jimmy and what's his name—Snetts snapped his fingers at the cop named Jimmy, pointed to his partner.

Tommy Tonelli, Jimmy said.

Double T, said Snetts. Over.

Affirmative, over, said the radio.

George said to Anna: I have to go upstairs too. She turned to him; her movements seemed a little slowed, cased in gel. Her eyes were far off.

Can you feel the hardness of the concrete? she said, low-voiced. Its coldness?

For reasons he didn't understand, and would wonder about later, he said: End of time.

Hey, *Spectator*, said Snetts, behind him. Show me the quickest way into this place.

Let's go, George said quietly to Anna.

They walked in silence. Snetts followed but in the lead, asking if this was the way. The two uniforms followed behind. After the stairs up from 114th to the campus, George gestured to Snetts, indicating the pathway around the old tennis court. Snetts went fast, then, ahead of them, ahead of the uniforms, but all four caught up with him at the elevators as George knew they would; the things were practically medieval. One finally rattled down and Anna rode with them as far as the fifth floor. What about my Coke? she said to George.

You know where the key is, he said. Wait for me or find me later at *Spec*.

≡

THE ELEVATOR DOORS closed behind her, that beautiful woman, and George looked at Snetts. All of reality seemed to be moving slowly, the elevator doors clanking and banging shut, and he could hear all the individual sounds, and see all the details of Snetts's face, the detective's eyes rising to meet his own. He heard Anna's voice, and the word *Coke*, in his head. Coke. But wait.

Coca-Cola, he said to Snetts. You know, soda.

It felt as if half an hour had passed since she'd said *Coke* and now he was a fool and Snetts wouldn't even know what he was talking about but of course they'd barely moved a floor upward so it was only a few seconds.

Snetts gave him a half nod and quarter-mouth smile.

I'm guessing you might have had something a little stronger than that earlier, he said. He held up his hands: I'm not asking. Not my department.

We enjoyed a period of enlightenment, George said. We, uh, rode the ferry.

Oh, enlightenment, said Snetts. Not that many people find satori on the way to Staten Island.

George thought about this.

With her I could probably find it anywhere, he said.

Well, yeah, Snetts said. There's that.

≡

FLOOR THIRTEEN. McKIM, Mead & the long-dead White had shown no compunction nor did the university about the unlucky number, unluckier tonight than ever. The endless corridor—of narrow single doors opening into narrow single rooms—was in a state of disturbance that George felt the moment he was off the elevator, as if there'd been a fire drill or a bomb scare, doors open, people standing talking in the hall, women with tangled hair and long cotton shirts, some with teary eyes, hugging each other or hugging men in shorts and T-shirts. It was cool out but hot here: always hot on these upper floors of Jay. The building was stolid and oversized and brutal and inside it was cheap; these upper floors were the last stop for the rising heat of the other floors plus the building baked beneath the copper-clad roof and the inevitable sun. In summers it could kill you.

Down near the window, one bone-thin young man, in khaki pants, safari-type jacket despite the heat, cowboy boots, and a western hat. He was squatting with his back against the wall, smoking a cigarette and tapping the ashes behind the radiator beside him.

Snetts homed on him like a falcon on a field mouse. What's your name, son? he said.

Tex.

Of course it is, Snetts said but not unkindly. He too squatted. George stayed upright, looking around. Snetts said, So Tex, have you seen some police officers up here?

They're down by the windows onto Amsterdam, said Tex. He gestured with his cigarette.

Do you know the boy who fell?

He didn't fall, and yeah, I know him.

What's his name?

Jeffrey Goldstein.

Snetts went to his notebook. Jeffrey with a *J*?

Yeah, I think so, yes.

You said he didn't fall?

He was pushed, Tex said. Or else he jumped. Gon' be hard for y'all to find out which.

What makes you say he was pushed? Snetts said.

I said he didn't *fall*, Tex said. He was pushed *or* he jumped. He was with some guy. There was an argument.

You saw this?

I heard it. Everybody heard it. Jeff was screaming and crying.

What about? Snetts said. He lit his own cigarette. He smoked Parliament. With the plastic filters so he could hold it with his teeth, it turned out. Tex was smoking Lucky Strikes, with no filters at all. White pack, red-and-black-circled target on the floor beside him. And that thin band of green.

You couldn't tell, really, he said. It was like the usual shit: you said you loved me. Et cetera et cetera.

He pronounced *et cetera* like Yul Brynner meets Jimmy Rogers.

Snetts was looking at him.

Tex looked back.

He was gay, Tex said.

You mean he was a homosexual?

Tex looked at him with large eyes, unhostile, brown, mildly curious. Fundamentally unreadable. He held the look a beat longer than he might have. That's what it means, yessir. Common moniker. I heard them. I was in the lounge. Then I went to the outhouse and took a shit. Had a bowel movement, I guess I should say, if you're writing it down. *Shit*'s the common moniker.

That one I get, said Snetts.

Then I come out and the fellow was gone and Jeff was out the window.

What were you doing in the lounge?

I was watching the TV.

He pronounced it TEE-vee.

What were you watching? Snett said. A cop's automatic question with verifiable answer.

Harry O, Tex said. Love my *Harry O*.

Snett nodded, as if he knew the late-night schedule and *Harry O* checked out—maybe he did know the schedule. George slipped for an instant inside Snett's life, home alone watching David Janssen reruns at 1:30 in the morning. Eating beans and franks out of a can.

Did you hear or see them struggle?

No sir. I heard them *argue*.

Tex's voice was mid-range and resonant—it was large—and made all the more dissociative from his small body by the fact it issued forth without him looking at you or making any but the smallest facial expressions.

They were being very loud, he said. Other folks heard it. You can ask 'em. Tex gestured with his chin down the hallway and carefully dropped a long ash behind the radiator. Snetts, as if cued, flicked his Parliament in the radiator's general direction. He missed widely; but the carpet was a hideous green plaid that no amount of abuse could make worse.

Snetts stood, thanked Tex, and went off. George stayed.

I'm with *Spectator*, he said. My name is George Langland.

I've seen your name in there, Tex said.

Did you know the guy? George said.

Yeah. I mean, we didn't *socialize* but I'd talked to him in the lounge and shit.

Tex pulled a furtive hand to his mouth and inhaled the last draw on his cigarette. The words came out of his mouth like a line of small boats in a river of smoke.

I think the guy he was with didn't want to be ID'd as a fag. I think that's what it was about.

Is there a gay community on the floor? Or in Jay? Like a tight group?

This drew a hard look.

I'm Tex, he said. I live in Jay but there is no Tex community, far as I know.

I'm just trying to get a handle on the scene here, George said.

Tex waved his hand around in a circle like a helicopter blade. Go on, wander around and check it out, my brother. This is the scene. And it ain't no scene. It's John *Jay*, son. Man was burned in effigy but hey, he was one of ours, Kings College, the year seventeen-whatever.

George had a pen, he always had a pen, but nothing to write on. Do you have some paper? he asked. Tex rose slowly from his crouch and went into his room across the corridor, came out with three sheets of loose-leaf paper. George folded them lengthwise into a tall booklet shape, folded that again to half height, and carefully ripped the bottom fold creating pages.

What's your full name, Tex?

You're putting me in the story?

George looked at him. I don't know yet what the story is or what will go in it but I do know that I don't want to notice in two hours that I have no name for you. Then it's like *said one floor resident who didn't provide his name.* Because the reporter didn't ask for it, that means.

Robert Wallace, he said. But use Tex. If you put Robert Wallace no one's going to know who the fuck you're talking about.

Scottish? George said.

My father's people, in the 1700s. Since 1831, pure Texan.

George said. What year you in?

Sophomore.

George moved down the hall to where Snetts was with the other cops; he was looking at the open window, around the frame of it, leaning out of it. In the lounge, which was an end-of-the-hall area with some furniture and Tex's TEE-vee, George saw a kid he knew named Kenneth; every time George saw Kenneth's face he thought of Montgomery Clift. He was in George's Keats class. He was crying.

George said, Hey.

Kenneth said, Oh, hi. He wiped his face on a sleeve of a

black turtleneck, with the usual silvering effect of mucus on black cotton.

I'm here for the paper, George said.

Oh yeah, you write for it, Kenneth said.

You knew this guy? Jeff?

Jeffrey, Kenneth said. Yeah. He preferred Jeffrey.

I'm really sorry, George said. Were you guys friends?

George was undergoing his usual set of anxiety and misgivings asking these questions. The conflict: he wanted the story and he wanted not to be an asshole. But mainly he was supposed to want the story. More excitement than sorrow once you were after the story.

I mean we were friends, yeah. Not close but yeah.

What happened? George said.

Jeffrey *al*ways wanted these *jocks*, Kenneth said. Always always always.

Kenneth too had a shockingly deep voice, plus a huge Adam's apple for such a small guy; he really did look just like Clift. Heavy beard shadow almost always. The voice had a strong tinge of mid-Atlantic Brahmin.

Big butch guys, you know. Maybe it had to do with his father, I mean I don't know. I mean, that's just a guess.

Kenneth's cheeks were still wet with tears and he wiped his nose on the back of his hand. George's eye was caught by the sheen now on the hand, a hairy hand, like dew drops in morning grass, only—not. Snot.

Jeffrey was *desperate*! Kenneth said. He told the guy—I think his name was Thomas, maybe it was John Thomas, ha—he said, *You think I won't tell your parents? I'll tell them.* Threatening the guy, you know? Which was stupid. And the guy Thomas was like, *You're going to blackmail me into something?*

Like you think you can blackmail someone into being your friend? But Jeffrey was going full Joan Crawford. He said something like, can you imagine, *Your father will want to kill you.*

George almost said, but didn't, I need a line I can quote here, Kenneth baby, and *Jeffrey was going full Joan Crawford* probably won't fly.

7

Anna was in George's room and there was the can of Coke on his bookshelf, as promised. She found a cloudy glass and washed it with hand soap in his room's little sink. She didn't like soda from the can, she liked it poured out. You had to let it *breathe*. This made her laugh: as if it were good wine. She peeled off the tab and decanted.

Oh my god, it was so good. Even warm. It was so so good.

She poured some more. Oh my god.

Then more: she tried to go slowly. But then—it was gone!

And with that, a flickering sense of trivial sadness and she saw again the broken body of the boy on the pavement. And up it came: she barely got to the sink: Coca-Cola and bile and oh fuck, the drain was a little clogged. So many hours since she'd eaten. Fortunate.

She washed out her mouth, got the sink clean, opened his window for the smell—she could hear the wind but it was passing along the building side and didn't come in. She lay down on his bed, her hands landed between her legs, and thoughtless of it she pushed down onto herself, massaging, then fingertips on her clit. Oh. She realized when she touched herself that she'd been wet forever, all night? No, couldn't have been. On the subway and in the cab and the moment on the ferry she remembered now the moment when he'd whispered in her ear that he was going to touch her breasts and then he touched her breasts, how hard her nipples were and how sensitive in the cold wind. She thought of this and kept her right hand on herself outside her skirt and underpants and her left came up to her breasts. Nipple tightening in her fingers. Oh. And she arched to it, to the feeling, but then it was over, blink—she was breathing and nothing of it left in her anymore, just the hint of bile and the boy the boy the boy, Lord, he was dead. He looked like her brother. So many of the skinny ones like that, with the stringy hair, looked like her brother. Lying like that. Where? In the yard. Just sleeping. Probably stoned or drunk or both. Sleeping it off. In the middle of her small lawn. He was sixteen probably so she was nine? He left for good right after his seventeenth birthday, which he was not home for, and they heard from him twice, each time for money. The second time her father said no—the first round of money her father had wired him, Mark had been supposed to use to come home, that was the point of it—so this time no, and Mark said, That's it then, and her father had said, No, there's lots more than *that* to talk about, and Mark had hung up. Just hung up. This was a story in the family as sharp and hurtful as the tale of an accidental death, the pipe coming off the truck on the highway to pierce the windshield, the stumbling fall off the mountain, the new husband pulled out to sea in a sudden wicked current. Bad stories. Mark had called collect from Santa Fe, New Mexico, then he'd hung up, and they'd never heard from him again. Nine years. He'd be twenty-six now. Her father had called the police down there and telexed them a photograph and other life details but no one had ever called or reported anything about him. It made her cry to think of him—more so now, tonight, with the dead boy on the pavement, because that was the problem, of course, she was seeing *him* dead and had long suspected him dead, and every time she cried over him she grew angry that *she* was crying, angry at herself: *she* wasn't someone *he* had ever cried about, that was for sure, she would have been easy to find if he'd missed her.

She used to think: maybe he's in New York.

But no one was in New York now. Not the faux hippies anyway. There were people Mark's age in white wigs and black eyeliner downtown playing in ironically crude rock bands and painting ironically crude imitations of masterpiece paintings and writing barely ironic imitations of Wordsworth but very few staggering fucked-up Neil Young imitators who'd started out with the greatest sincerity wanting to burn down the system. They were gone. There was worse, but not that many in New York either, the Todd Rundgren imitators. Like the ones in the suburbs, like the guys with carefully managed metal-band hair and rock-tour T-shirts still wandering the towns outside Philly and Harrisburg. Like the Loud brother who wasn't gay and wasn't interesting—not Lance, in other words, but the next oldest one—just stoned and pissed off in Santa Barbara. *That*. That guy. Those guys were not in New York anymore. She kicked her legs up and down like a kid having a tantrum. It felt good. She did it some more. It made her laugh, face still wet from crying. She had a moment—here it was—she loved herself. She wanted to hug herself. She wished George were here to hug her for her, to kiss her for her, to touch her for her, to put his mouth against her cunt for her. Oh that. And her hand again. But again it didn't go. She decided to walk over to the paper. See him. That would mean fixing her face: cleaning it anyway. Eyeliner running to clown's tears. That picture of Anna Karina weeping. *Vivre sa vie.* The mirror. The face. Living her life.

She washed her face in the tiny sink; she splashed and splashed then rubbed it with his towel, smudging it with black. Oh dear, the school-issue white towel. She'd wash it for him later if he cared. Outside his door before letting it lock she pushed his key into the torn bit between the carpet and the wall.

And then she was out. Out in that wind again. Like hands in silk. She stopped in front of the library on the long terrace and leaned up against the stone wall and let the wind have her, closed her eyes and felt it run across her body and felt it slow and stop and rise again and gust so that she shivered.

Well—she heard a voice but didn't open her eyes—if you aren't the sexiest goddamn thing I've ever seen.

Her friend Susan. Voluptuous Susan. The voice.

You're Susan, Anna said. Her eyes were still closed.

Yup, Susan said.

Anna opened one eye. As she'd expected, there was Keith, her gangly boyfriend.

That does look good, Keith said.

That. He referred to her as *that.* He had a look on his face . . . How to describe it? Stupid? She closed the eye again.

You should try it, she said. She said it very low.

She ended up with Keith on her left and Susan on her right—You feel it, right? she said, and they said yes, the warm stone, the cool wind—and then somehow she ended up—in a deeper sense of ending up—in Susan's room at Barnard smoking another joint and in no time at all—she couldn't even remember the concept of time passing and, of course, how could it have been otherwise—she was on the bed and legs open as wet as she could be with Keith on her left and Susan on her right and they were kissing her and touching her and Susan was saying, Just close your eyes. Close your eyes like on the terrace.

Just close your eyes. The blue and orange of low flame and high flame. She slept after, they all slept, but she was still aroused and kept half waking with her mouth wet—drooling essentially, but in a controlled way, her face next to Susan's rib cage and Keith on the other side. She slept again and then, when she rose again slowly out of sleep, she felt a mouth kissing her body, in a slightly greedy unpleasant way, she felt hands exploring her, and she was dreaming of her brother, it was Mark, somehow they'd been reunited, oh my god it was Mark, grabbing at her with his mouth like that, but she was still so happy they were together and it was natural they would do this, she wanted it, it wasn't pleasant but it was good . . . but then she was waking more and it felt too real—was it real? Yes, it was real, how real it was—but oh my god was it Mark? She screamed. Not a little scream, but a big scream. A clarifying moment.

This put a damper on skinny Keith, though she told him it wasn't his fault.

I was having a really bad dream, she said. Really bad.

What was it? Susan said. She was sitting with her breasts loose and hair a mess and sheets covering her to the waist. Anna just gave a little shake of her head, waved her hand. Susan flopped back down on the bed, reached for her boyfriend. Anna rose and dressed.

≡

George at the paper, writing the story, Richard, the editor in chief, hanging over his shoulder—three thirty in the morning, they were holding up production, they'd halted a printing and trashed it, it would cost them a mint—Richard finally said, We're gonna do *personal problems* and *rife with speculation*. Nothing specific.

George said, Why is it always *rife with speculation*? Why can't it be *rich with speculation*? *Dense* with speculation. *Dappled and strewn with feverish speculation?*

Fuck, I don't give a shit, Richard said. He was working his ice cream cone, licking around the sides to hold back the inevitable gravitational flow of melting green drips. Mint chocolate chip. New York: twenty-four-hour ice cream.

Hurry up and write it if you're writing it, he said. We're holding the presses here, mucho dinero. Write that part how you like. Then I'll just change it to *rife with speculation* and then, like the man said, all things shall be well and all manner of things shall be well.

It wasn't a maa-aan, Louis sang from his desk, not looking up. *It was Julian of Norrr-wich, who was a wo-maaan . . .*

No one acknowledged him.

≡

When Anna got back George's door was open against the latch—it was maybe eight thirty in the morning. She had to work later and felt as if she were falling off a cliff. George was sitting at his desk, chair turned at an angle, away from the desk and toward the room and the door. He had the black-streaked white towel in his lap. He looked stricken.

Where were you? he said.

I was going to *Spec* but I ran into Susan, Anna said.

She could feel how slippery this was already; the cliff was going muddy underfoot. Which image reminded her, as it always had, muddy terrain, of the story she'd heard growing up from her father, about the retreat in Korea, in winter, troop trucks sliding off the mountain roads and falling two thousand or three thousand feet, no one knew how far, in those mountains. Nobody's family was ever told your boy died sliding off the side of the mountain in a truck during a massive panic-stricken retreat. That's how this felt now, like that: she could see herself sliding over the side.

George looked at her, waiting for more.

We went to her room and smoked a bunch and I ended up falling asleep for a while.

Pause.

He was staring at the wall, his hands fidgeting with the towel.

I'm sorry about your towel, she said.

Yeah, what is that, he said. Now he was looking at the towel.

She readied her lips to speak. Eyeliner, she wanted to say. Due to weeping. She looked at him. She would tell him about her brother—she wanted to. But his face looked so needy—fuck fuck fuck. She couldn't then. Normally she respected his face. What was this? He was wounded. Resentful. This irritated her. It was a form of entanglement she wasn't ready for. She hadn't realized she wasn't ready for it until she saw it there. She didn't want this, these syrupy strings.

Oh, just trippy shit.

Yeah, he said. He held up the towel as if it had cooties, which, in fact, it did.

Listen, she said. It wasn't just Susan, baby, it was Susan and Keith. And we had sex. The three of us.

His face. Oh god, he looked as if he'd been shot in the groin. If the soul had a groin, that's where she'd shot him.

He turned away from her. Like, gave her his back. She wanted to say this was effeminate but then what would she be standing for? She was surprised how furious his reactions made her. She had gone unexpectedly all testosterone to his femme—she wanted to hit him. Of course this was stupid stupid stupid. How did she *think* he'd react? She'd said it to hurt him because he was pouting and pissing her off and now look: she'd hurt him.

Please, she said. Please please please. Don't do this. To me *or* to you. I was high out of my mind. It was sex. It wasn't, you know, planting a nuclear weapon or poisoning babies. It's not a *relationship*. It was just sex.

He stood up. Jesus Christ, he said.

Well, I *was* high but I'm pretty sure he wasn't there.

This did not get a laugh—as she could have predicted, it made him angrier. He started to leave—he walked brusquely past her, nearly shouldering her to get by in the small space, but it was his room, which he must have realized, because he stopped. He finally looked at her.

How did it happen? he said.

He was still holding the towel, so she decided to talk about that. It's eyeliner, she said. I was crying.

Wait, why were you crying?

Okay, here it was. She hotly—for a moment—wanted to say it: I was crying about my brother. She'd not told anyone of her brother. No one here, that is. Not George, no one. A few friends at home knew. Probably more than a few but only a few she would acknowledge. In any case, home was over.

I was sad, she said.

What I meant was, how did the sex happen?

Look how he moved right past the sad, couldn't give a shit.

I told you, she said. I was high.

Yeah but how did it *ac*tually happen? How did it go down?

How does sex ever *ac*tually happen, George? We're all together in Susan's room, we're getting high, we end up prone, someone kisses someone, someone touches someone, Bob's your uncle.

No, George said. No. Bob's not your fucking uncle. Someone kisses someone and you say, Oh, hey, what? Look at the time. I have to go.

C'mon, George. Really. Can't you see this from the perspective of living, breathing, stoned human beings?

You wanted to have sex with another woman?

The fact is, George, I had been wanting to have sex with *you* but *you* weren't *there*. Which is fine, I know, you were doing something important. But I was very turned on. I was on my way over to the paper to see how it was going, hang out and whatever, and ended up pinned by the wind to the stone wall of the library and like having semi-orgasms there with my eyes closed when they found me. So I was ripe for the plucking. Jesus, George. I'm sorry but I'm having trouble seeing this as a big deal. Haven't you ever been horny?

Yes, I've been horny.

There it was, that face again. Oh, the fury. She wanted to smack him. But not really. She wanted to scream. But she wouldn't. So what the fuck would she do? Here, she would say this, which was true:

I can't *stand* the feeling of being owned. And I can't *stand* the Mommy-you-abandoned-me face you're giving me.

He was silent, looking at her.

Oh my god, I'm sorry.

He said nothing.

I'm so sorry I said that. It was completely thoughtless.

He sat on the bed. He said, Fuck it. I'm going to lie down. It's been a long night. Strange and beautiful and then terrible. An eternity of changes, this night.

He lay back, half on the bed, feet still on the floor. Anyway I'm tired. Let's talk about it tomorrow. Which is today. I'd like to fuck Susan. Can she come over and fuck *us*?

There was something childish in whatever salaciousness he was mustering here. Like the sex humor among the fourth-grade boys.

George, I'm sorry. For what I said.

I know. You should go. He pulled his legs up onto the bed. Desert boots and all, on the bedspread. He wouldn't look at her. She wanted to take his boots off: it looked so uncomfortable and wrong. And he would never have lain down with her that way, if she'd been staying.

Go, he said again, voice muffled by his arm over his face.

So she went.

8

It was close to noon, George had slept for two and a half hours. There was a hole in his middle when he thought of Anna and he could hardly manage to think of anything else. And there was this story that needed more writing, continued writing.

Richard said, You've never called the grieving family member before, have you?

No.

You scared?

George kept his eyes on his typewriter. I'm . . . horrified, he said. Harrowed. Don't want to see and hear what I'm going to see and hear.

They could just tell you to fuck off, Richard said. That's what I'd do.

For some reason this stirred him to dial. The heavy resistance of the steel wheel on the old phone: GRamercy7-5128. The phone chicka-chicka-chicka in his ear clicking out the numbers onto the wires. George waved the receiver at Richard, indicating he should go away. Privacy, he said.

It rang. And rang. And rang. Finally the sound of it being picked up, fumbled, a woman's voice, distant and frail. Hello?

Hello, said George. I'm sorry to disturb you, My name is George Langland and I'm calling from the Columbia University *Daily Spectator*, the campus newspaper. Is this Mrs. Goldstein?

You should speak with my husband, the woman said. She put the phone down, loudly. It sounded as if she essentially dropped it onto a table. George envisioned the Gramercy Park apartment: the mahogany phone table in the hall, a fresh pad and nice pen. A lamp perhaps. A dark wood chair with upholstered seat in maroon and silver stripes. Everything frozen in 1948 finery. Really he's thinking of his grandparents' generation. These people could be Danish modern.

The phone swept up from the table. A man's voice, deepish, unyielding: This is Bernard Goldstein, to whom am I speaking please?

Hello Mr. Goldstein, this is George Langland, I'm a student at Columbia and a reporter for the Columbia University *Daily Spectator*. I'm calling about Jeffrey.

This is, to say the least, a difficult time, Mr. Langland.

I know that, sir. I'm really sorry for your loss and Mrs. Goldstein's loss. Did Jeffrey have siblings?

No, Goldstein said. He was an only child.

That's so hard, sir. I really am sorry.

George felt . . . what did he feel? A shocking calm. Maturity. What could they do to him after all? Either Goldstein or Richard? He was just a messenger really, on either end.

His mother was recently dead. His father was long gone. He too had no siblings. Nothing mattered.

He said, Sir, as you might know the paper had a story about Jeffrey's death in today's edition with no identification. Now that the ID is official we need to print it, and we want to be as accurate as possible, and not make mistakes. Particularly important on a story like this. So I'm hoping to confirm some things with you, facts about Jeffrey.

I tell you what, Goldstein said. We'll talk to you people. We're not talking to anyone else. Jeffrey liked the paper very much. He admired the features man.

Louis Pennybaker? George said.

Yes, that's it.

Well, that's good to hear, George said.

You'll come downtown to see us, Mr. Langland. Bring Pennybaker. I'd like to show you both a little bit about Jeffrey. My wife might be upset but I will be able to talk with you.

What time, sir?

As soon as you can get here, Goldstein said.

It was not yet noon. George had missed one class already and was on the verge of missing another. Keats was the first. The other was American Society After 1945. This latter a giant lecture with no attendance taken and virtually nothing of substance one couldn't get from a Time-Life series on the decades. He was sorry he'd missed the Keats, he wasn't keeping up with the readings either. He could feel that class slipping away from him, like a fish at the last moment coming off the hook, sinking away into the dark water.

That's fine, sir. Just for now, though, in case anything happens, allow me to verify the main facts: you've identified your son, as the police have stated?

Yes.

What is Jeffrey's full name, sir?

Jeffrey Benjamin Goldstein.

George verified age, residence, high school. Then he asked: And you've not been informed of any note Jeffrey might have left?

Silence.

Sir?

Why don't we talk about that when you get here, Goldstein said. Do you have the address?

Yes, George said.

Fine then, Goldstein said, and he hung up.

Richard had slipped back into the chair across from George's desk—the news desk, technically, which was an arrangement of two aluminum desks and an old wood table—and he sat slumped comically low, ass out by the edge of the seat, feet spread out in Converse All Stars. The chair squeaked brutally as he rode it left to right, left to right. Some kind of nubby hiking socks under the sneakers. George, a basketball snob, did not approve of such socks with sneakers.

George, eyeing the socks, said: I think there's a note.

Really? Richard sat up, looked around. Dave, he called out, there's a note.

I *think* there's a note.

A small crowd filled in the space around the desk, four editors, another reporter.

Richard: What did he say?

George said, It was at the end of the conversation. I said something like, And you've not been informed of any note? And there was this long silence. So I said, Sir? Hello? Note? I mean, I didn't, I just said, Sir. Then he said we'd talk about that when we get there.

Richard said, Call Snetts. Or the homicide division, they must have taken it by now. Who's the detective in charge again, what was that guy's name? Baker? Get them on record. Say you know there's a note. Find out.

This, George would come to understand, was where the

tire-treaded sandal sole hit the road, among the disciples of journalism. Either you were totally dedicated and excited to find out about the possible note, or else some voice in the back of your mind said, the kid's dead, what does it matter really, leave him the fuck alone. Breslin said every story is five flights up. You want the story, you climb the stairs. George kind of wanted the story, THIS story, he would climb the stairs, but he felt the first inkling that his interest would not carry on, that as days turned into weeks and story after story after story came and went he wouldn't continue to care, wouldn't be able to bear avid discussions urging him forward to pursue story after story after story: which is what you had to have to be a decent reporter. Louis of course didn't have it either and didn't pretend to. He cared about what he cared about. They were all going to be *his* stories or there would be no story.

You guys are going to have to do that. Goldstein wants me to come downtown to see him. Or them. He says he wants to, quote, *show me a little about Jeffrey*, unquote.

Richard scratched his beard. Really? Wow. Scratch scratch. That's great. How'd you do that?

I was polite. Kept using the words *Columbia* and *campus.* Other than that, nothing.

You have the touch.

It's not a touch.

Personality.

Presentation.

You're a sophomore reporter I'm a senior editor in chief so shut the fuck up.

Right.

Just kidding.

No you're not.

You're right.

He mentioned Louis, George said.

Who? The father?

Yeah. Said Jeffrey admired *the features man.* He recognized Louis's name when I gave it. Wants me to bring him.

Richard called out, LOUIS! Where's Louis? Is Louis here?

Everyone looked at the features office doorway, from which Louis, with a hint of pause for effect, emerged.

I love when you talk that way, he said.

≡

GOLDSTEIN HAD LARGE eyes behind John Dean–style round tortoiseshell glasses. The ne plus ultra in lawyerly eyewear. Thick lenses. The earpiece a flexible steel curl. Louis and George were dressed neatly in slacks and loafers, junior lower quality of Goldstein himself. Mrs. Goldstein was a fashionable woman, a kind of Kennedy-era remnant, a taupe dress with white piping along hems and collar and exaggerated hip pockets. Pumps a shade lighter than the dress, cream, with square toes and blocky heels. Ferragamo, Louis said later. George didn't know quite why the shoes had struck him so. Then he did: his own mother would have worn them. Mr. Goldstein introduced his wife, who shook his hand faintly, and immediately announced in a flat tone that she would be retiring, that she wouldn't be taking part in the interview.

I'll leave you to it, she said, barely above a whisper. Please have some coffee and something to eat. Everything's out.

George thanked her and she receded down the carpeted corridor and went into what George presumed to be, by its location, the bedroom. She closed the door with a faint click.

Now *there* was a thing: how rich did you have to be in New York before you got an apartment in which the doors properly closed and clicked, not clogged by thirty years of landlord paint? Goldstein brought them from the foyer down two steps into the large living room. A coffee service on a silver tray. Sugar cookies and quartered oranges. Could people really live this way?

≡

It ran after the op-ed with a double byline, George Langland and Louis Pennybaker. A feature. Photograph by A. A. Townes.

INTERVIEW WITH A GRIEF-STRICKEN FATHER

NEW YORK, NY Oct 23, 1976—He is unusual, this 48-year-old man. His son was a homosexual and he knew it and he loved his son and he supported his son. And now his son is dead.

The son is dead because, in part at least, he loved a man and that man for whatever reasons did not love him back. So you could say that Jeffrey Goldstein died of a broken heart.

But that probably wouldn't be true and, besides, it's a cliché. "Jeffrey's life was an ongoing struggle because of his sexuality," said Bernard Goldstein, father of Jeffrey, age 20, who died early last Friday morning, having plunged, it is not yet known *how* or, fully, *why*, from the window in the lounge on the thirteenth floor of John Jay Hall.

"He'd had a very nice year the year before he entered

Columbia—he took a year off before starting—actually living with a young man, they started Columbia together, and they seemed to love each other. But they broke up. They were young. That's not unusual."

Goldstein, tall, well-dressed, an attorney, sat on a damask armchair in the sunlit living room of the spacious Gramercy Park apartment he shares with his wife, Sheila Goldstein. Mrs. Goldstein did not wish to be interviewed for this article.

In truth, about the suicide, we have *some* idea why. Jeffrey wrote in a notebook:

I really DO love him.

Cross my heart and hope to die.

Then he'd left the notebook open on his desk—as easily a note to himself for his journal, which is what the book turned out to be, as it was a note for anyone else's eyes. It needn't have been some kind of explanation or goodbye. But now it is, inevitably, and the irony—*cross my heart and hope to die*—cuts like a blade. It is the living, never the dead, who are cut by the blade, and the elder Goldsteins, quiet, polite, seemingly prosperous people who until two days ago had many reasons to be at a satisfying place in their lives—they are the ones bleeding.

There was more, about Jeffrey's childhood, his teen years, the Goldsteins' feelings when they learned about their son's sexuality—*It wasn't easy, for him or for us*, was what the father said. George had asked, were there fights? And Goldstein had said, of course. Of course there were fights. But we worked it out.

This article, which he and Louis had worked out almost

line by line, was the most matter of fact and open the paper had ever been about homosexuality, an entirely new treatment—a way of life, not a disorder or a freak show. Louis's presence, his advocacy and his humor were largely responsible for this: utterly unapologetic, assertive, often funny. The other reason was Jeffrey Goldstein's father. It was as if the alumni—of which he was one—had called in and officially approved a new approach. George, Richard, et al. would discover in coming days that the alumni very much had *not* called in to approve a new approach, nor had the administration that dealt with them, when they were phoning every office from alumni affairs right up to the president.

The other young man, Jeffrey's presumed lover, was not found; the death was ruled a suicide at the inquest that took place the following week and the body was released to the parents, who buried it in Jewish custom albeit delayed. Not long after, they held a memorial service which George, with Louis and Richard, attended. It was at a small reform synagogue on 17th Street, a modest place of worship fitted into an old town house. Just down the street was the Quaker Meeting House—proximity to the Quakers was always reassuring. Afterward Louis had shaken the Goldsteins' hands, *père et mère*; the *mère* was cool, the *père* was not, gripping his hand for an extra beat, thanking him. Ah—a look George caught when she was shaking Louis's hand: there it was. She had never accommodated her son being gay. It grieved her and angered her and it grieved and angered her still.

That story, the Goldstein story, marked the height of George's journalism career. His heart was never really in it after that. The job required an ongoing passion for what constituted *news*, what made *a story*. Or as journalists were fond of saying, *a great story*. Each story fed into the next story—or was erased by it. The narrative mind became a palimpsest with everything earlier rubbed away and only the current visible. A month after Jeffrey Goldstein's death no one spoke of him or very much thought of him—but every time George walked by the blank square of dirt where the little tree had fallen, he saw that boy's body on the hard concrete and the red and white lights flashing against a curtain of autumn darkness, in a night of wind and loss. Something you couldn't put in the paper.

9

A surprising day in March. Warm, but still with that pale angular light of late winter. George and Anna had been apart for almost five months. Awkwardness, all over the neighborhood, avoiding each other, veering off at a long-distance sighting, looking the other way at Momma Joy's delicatessen. She'd stopped at his table one night at the library and said to him, We can say hello, you know. It won't kill us.

Hello, he'd said.

He'd said it again the next time he'd seen her, and thereafter, until it was a joke: Hello. The hellos got bigger: Hello! HELLO! So this day of late-winter spring, they abided on the opposing edges of the same large group, first time since late October, gathered on the steps that ran along the north side of College Walk. Anna was watching him, he was watching her. They were separated by four others, all friends more or less; he and she both were wearing jeans, they each noticed the other's, but hers were rolled up a bit and there were those Keds again. Interesting how she made them look sexy. Those ankles of hers, he wanted to have one in each hand with his arms outspread and her open beneath him . . . He looked away. Took a hit of a joint that was making the rounds. She was amused he had on his desert boots. Desert boots or, on the colder, wetter days, the duck boots; soon the beat-up brown deck shoes would come out again, for summer. Men were infuriating in that way, each got his look and just stuck with it for fifty fucking years. Or more. Until they died. She could see him at seventy in the same many-times-washed oxford cloth shirt. Beneath the same dark red crewneck sweater. Grizzled and gray. Not bald, no. Hair a bit shorter, uncombed. As if knowing her thoughts he pulled the sweater off and dropped it in a mean little pile beside him. There it was: that chest. Those shoulders.

Along these hundred and fifty feet of granite steps that rose up to Low Library—which was neither low nor, any longer, a library—were bodies, some stretched across three ridged lines of step, with shoulders and elbows propping from the top, butt down on the second, calves across the third, luxurious and suggestive in the pale sunlight of uncertain spring; others were sitting hunched like Times Square addicts and petty grifters because you tended to curl up when smoking weed here, folded inward against the wind and possible hostile observation. You could shoot up every day on the steps and find no *institutional* disapproval; campus security was nonexistent, an inheritance of the riots, the philosophy since then to leave the kids alone and keep them drunk, stoned, strung out, just as long as they were not *engaged* and taking the dean of students prisoner in his office again. But certain uptight individuals still complained. High above them: Low. Built in 1898 it had begun to sink under the weight of books by the 1920s and been turned into an administration building: leaden minds, apparently, did not endanger it. It was the geometric and gravitational center of the monumental neoclassicism of the original campus, rising behind them, laid out before them, stone and columns wherever you looked. The newer library, broad and squat, perhaps a hundred and fifty feet long, looked like a prison for criminal Greek statuary and stood across campus, militantly facing them, slightly downhill and nearly two city blocks away, separated from them by brick paths and three swards of patchy dirt and grass. Both these so-called libraries were massive architectural advertisements for the Western canon, not that the Western canon needed promotion or defense to these students; they had been exposed to no other and believed in it almost automatically, like the youngest children in a religious family, who are the last to question their faith. The Columbia students, which is to say, the males, far more than the Barnard women, were armed by virtue of their core curriculum with a newsmagazine writer's familiarity with that classical canon's major figures and its broadest points; they shared, too, the newsmagazine writer's accompanying lack of skepticism. Some of them were magazine writers of a slightly higher standing than the others; some of them even knew a little Latin or Greek and one or two had continued with its study. None of them was thinking of Herodotus at that moment in the midafternoon of that first spring day, except perhaps in terms of his actual name, facing them from where it was carved on Butler's frieze in meter-high glyphs, the seraphed, all-uppercase letters at eye level across campus from them: HOMER HERODOTUS SOPHOCLES PLATO ARISTOTLE DEMOSTHENES CICERO VERGIL. No one George knew had ever read Demosthenes or referred to him or quite likely knew a thing about him. For the perhaps fiftieth time George made a mental note to look Demosthenes up. The rest were like teams in the National League East (PHILADELPHIA CHICAGO ST. LOUIS PITTSBURGH MONTREAL

NEW YORK . . .), crusted with particular characteristics in one's mind, a set of colors, a vague sense of permanent qualities; and each author, like each team, admired by some, disdained by others, weathered by moments of intellectual victory that generally had been snatched from the jaws of the far more common defeat. Perennial .500 teams or worse. The foundational texts were, in literature, *The Iliad* (which George had to admit, even in the overworked and rather dry Lattimore translation, had its moments), and, in politics, Plato's *Republic* (in George's view there was no salvaging this book, it didn't matter which translation). Only a certain percentage of students, a plurality or at best half, could be expected at this late date to force themselves all the way through these texts and take intellectual nourishment from them; there were drugs and whiskey and beer to be consumed, cigarettes and joints to be smoked, women (though not enough of them) to be longed for and pursued, talk to be talked, flippant remarks to be made, visions of one's identity to be formed and smudged over and redrawn—and nights, so many nights, to be spent in the College Library Reading Room intermittently reading but mostly flirting with Barnard women. It was important though to know of these authors and these works in a general and accurate way, to know portions, to know the general thrust; it was part of the culture of the place to know that, just as it was to know that you should never go into Morningside Park, or to know the price and constituents of the Ta-Kome special hero sandwich, the meats and cheeses, the onions and shredded lettuce and oil and vinegar.

George went and sat with her.

Hey, he said.

She looked at him.

You want me to leave? he said.

No, she said. I just wonder what you want.

I saw you and I was stirred, he said. I don't like it—that we avoid each other. Feel we can't talk.

Well then, she said. Let's certainly end that. What else? I sense there's more.

Okay, he said. I saw you and I wanted to kiss you. I want to touch you. We can entertain each other in this way.

He handed her the joint he'd brought over, fingertip over fingertip.

There are other kinds of entertainment, she said.

None as cheap or nearly as good, he said. Or none with that kind of cheap-to-good ratio, would be more accurate.

Not a pre-spring walk in the park? she said.

Surely you're kidding.

Not in the least.

It's certainly as cheap. I'd say only half as good. But yes. Fine.

He had the joint again, took a pull, offered it to her and she shook her head. He put it out and stored it with the weed and papers in his pocket. Let's walk then, he said. He offered his hand, she took it, he pulled her up.

The temperature was in between.

They descended the steps and turned west toward Broadway, whence they descended farther, to Riverside and its long narrow park. He felt loose. This was the thing he'd become so familiar with about weed: that sense of mental and physical unbinding.

You're going to be successful, he said to her. They were walking along. She looked at him. He stopped, they stared at each other until he began to laugh.

What? he said.

She had never looked so deep in him, penetrated so far. She was searching to see if it was true. Neither he nor she had realized, until that frozen moment, that the question was so important to her; that this prediction could change her. It changed her and then, seeing how important it really was—how the insistent, timid lack of success of her mother and father had maddened her as a child and teenager—feeling all *that* changed her again. While they stood there. He kissed her then, couldn't not kiss her, and he felt her body yielding toward him, and his, hardening, pressing—and then she pulled away. She shook her head and they walked on.

≡

Late winter-spring, uncertain weather, fast-changing sky. The stuff of five hundred bad poems and three good ones. George had been with her, she had grappled with him, enjoyed him a little too, and now he was gone. What he had been proposing—what she had let him nearly enact—was some kind of open relationship. He liked the sex, he'd said. He'd wanted points for putting it plainly. Fact was, she'd liked the sex too—goddamn him.

He'd said to her, What does it mean, you don't want to *share* me? I'm not a dish of ice cream. When I'm with you, you have all of me, and when I'm not with you, you don't. You have memory, expectation, you have your own life. It doesn't matter if I'm in the library or playing ball or fucking someone. I'm not here then, and you're doing what you're doing.

The question regarding George was, and she had asked him this: When did you become such a dick?

He turned his head like a bird to look at her, face crooked, conveying something like, *Really? That's how it is?* But he didn't say those things. He was going to say something and didn't. Then he was going to again, opened his mouth to speak, and again didn't. Then he said, in a low voice, I don't know.

But Anna had realized when she asked the question that his answer might well be, When you broke my heart. She didn't accept that she had broken his heart, she believed he had looked at it on its shelf and fingered it off the edge to the floor, that he'd made a choice about his heart, in relation to her—but she was susceptible to the guilt arising from his belief that she had broken it. Or perhaps he didn't believe that at all. Someday perhaps she would ask him.

Now, she was sitting in her room on her bed, legs crossed and head bowed low, *Hejira* on the turntable with its mournful overdubbed guitar and straight roads dividing the desert. Her hair hung down. She could see herself: she was watching as if from above, transom-level, in the doorway; she was a sleeping monk. Unwashed hair and unwashed feet and a faint smell of musky body—she needed a shower but to take a shower you had to love yourself, or at least like yourself a little. A man could walk through that door now. What would he look like? Tall and lean or short and thick? God, she needed to get laid. Maybe George was right. Why not? Had she not been aroused? To feel a body against hers, pushing, pounding, insistent wanting, avid for her, needing to have her, to be in her and fucking her, and at this thought she stirred. *Amelia, it was just a false alarm.*

It would be wrong to think she wanted love. She wanted flames. To be consumed. One of her friends, Tracy, was busy converting to Catholicism, enraptured (Anna suspected) as much by the forceful young campus priest as by notions of Trinity and sacrament and Incarnation, though Anna would not say this to her. She'd asked her, nonconfrontationally, Do you have a crush on him? and Tracy had said, No, I really admire him. Tracy was smart not to go on from there, to object too much, to overdefine. That would give it the lie. What was to be envied in Tracy's conversion was the unifying engagement she was experiencing, of mind and spirit—the soul's swoon and lift with the beauty of an idea, an idea you believe entirely is potent and true. Not half man, half god, Tracy had said to her in one discussion. *All* man and *all* god. Anna could sense the electricity coming off her friend's skin. What a beautiful thing, faith and grace. But really, who could believe that shit? *Just how close to the bone and the skin and the eyes and the lips you can get—and still feel so alone.*

There was Recent-Alex. That's what she called him to her friends: Recent-Alex. Recent-Alex was beautiful, he was a drummer in a jazz fusion band playing on campus and a few gigs downtown and as with all drummers it would require a dozen drumsticks and some surgical tools if you ever wanted to drive an idea into his head. He smoked weed and sat around with no shirt on, long arms topographed and sinewy as the village smithy's and his skin tasted of salt and sweat and she could just fuck him all day, especially if she was on top. However, always a however: his mouth on her was one of the worst sexual experiences she'd ever known, slack, distracted, a wet thing without the least want in it, like a small unintelligent animal between her legs—a horror. Yet he kept doing it. The less he did, the better: with his pot and the music flowing in his head he was too calm a presence when above and fucking her—but lying there with his reliable and sizable cock pointing skyward and that beautiful chest to grab on to . . . just do nothing, she'd whispered to him, let me do it . . . Once he consented to having his hands and feet tied to the bed frame with three scarves and a pillowcase, and that was the pinnacle of her pleasure with him, he was a living cock doll. Of course it turned out that—life being so difficult and all—she couldn't fuck him all day, the days proved too long and so did the nights and without a kit around him he was a creature of little interest. Nice enough, but not so he'd notice what you said or needed. He was Recent-Alex.

What happened to men like that? The passion when he was soloing on the drums: the sweat and the hair flying and the choreography of his arms, that lightning-fast, coordinated wildness. There he seemed to have a vision of himself against the backdrop of the world. Outside that context, even using cattle prods, you could not have elicited this wildness or purpose from him. It was clear that he wasn't going to make it through life as a drummer, he wasn't quite at that level of good and he didn't seem to have the ambition to become so. Big beautiful stupid men. Like cattle in a field. They stand close together under a tree when it rains. She knew the female versions: like that but they had to be smarter, just to survive the assaults. From age ten, attracting the wrong attention, and some learned to trade it because they needed to, because they needed the affection or the protection or the affirmation or the salvation or the material reward, which is to say, finally, the money. Once they were grown, the more fortunate ones, the economics of their looks was turned to the capturing of the earner-husbands; many found this exciting, a fulfillment of white-lace expectations. Some knew better. Either way it turned into a job. And then the efforts as they aged to remain socially and sexually viable, the civic clubs and diet pills, the spas and seasonal wardrobe overhauls. The good-looking children. Except when they didn't and the children weren't and it all went to hell—that was an ugly scene. In her world growing up in Central Pennsylvania the money was disappearing not from their own accounts necessarily but from the ground beneath them, opening up social sinkholes where the underlying sense of community had been slow-burned away. The uncertainty undid some of them. And, always, alcohol took a place somewhere on the stage. Gin and vodka: these gals hardly ever went for the brown stuff. The diet pills took them up and the alcohol evened it out and the sleeping pills brought them down and after forty you could see it in their faces. She had seen them all in Hershey and later in Harrisburg, serving them at the hotel restaurant where she waitressed and hostessed for two summers and Friday and Saturday nights in the school year. These aging vixens were up against the high-energy WASPy wives who kept it together—never even close to being as erotically compelling, these women were competent, certain, and strong—frequently they were a little . . . boyish would be the polite term, with short haircuts and square Bermuda shorts, with pastel loafers and nicknames like *Andie* and *Tommi* and *Bobbi*. The kids were athletes and the husbands, not showing it much, drank a fifth a day. Andie and Tommi and Bobbi *hated* the former queens of lovely tits and good sex who, loosed from first marriages but still about, were a lure to their husbands. Perhaps their older sons as well. It was tennis-club Altamont.

What was she to be? (*The pills and powders. The passion play*. She could hardly wait for the fucking passion play.) Was she to be a poet? Fucking laugh. Suicide poet-girls with their long brown hair and big eyes and sweaters with breasts aching beneath, sexual hunger you could use to fuel a convoy of eighteen-wheelers, the real thing, nothing fake in it but always—always—misunderstood. Tide in, surf rising. Parched ribs of sand. A man and a woman sitting on a rock. She sat up on the rock. She wanted to run into the sea. The cold, cold sea. Across your upper thighs and crotch and your arms and belly the probing salt tongue of the sea. Like a stranger's touch, full of intention. She was trembling.

Travel the breadth of those extremities, baby.

There's comfort in melancholy. An opposite of hope that becomes hope, hope in the lack of hope, the hope that says there is no chance—no chance—so just make the best of it and carry on and maybe somehow you won't feel so humiliated and repulsive and as if you barely existed. That would be nice, right?

I'll walk green pastures by and by.

10

What George noticed first in the devil-owned summer of 1977, before the true depths of the heat wave, before Son of Sam, were guys on the subway platform, one or two dancing while another guy played wild beats on upturned joint-compound buckets, the dancing guys taking running starts and landing on one hand or shoulder, sometimes getting up onto their heads, using flattened cardboard boxes as matting, spinning, flipping, bending, all to the beat. The kids did breathtaking moves: you could imagine it as a perilous Olympic event. And a few times he encountered similar beats on the subway, a group of guys, with standard 'fro and one pant leg rolled, sitting across from each other maybe three on one side, four on the other, doing a kind of scat singing, made up rhythms and rhymes. Somebody keeping that new beat on the edge of the bench. He saw this three times that spring and early summer. The lyrics were always amusing but the only line that stuck with him, he would repeat it for years after, was *We from the streets of Brooklyn and you know we good-lookin'.*

As summer went on, the nights became darker somehow. Perhaps the financial crisis—fewer streetlights, or dimmer ones, maybe they were living in a constant brown-out no one had been informed of. Because of the heat that had come in and seemed determined to stay with them, the heat, the heat, the heat. He came out of the consciousness-obliterating helicopter-loud air-conditioning of Tom's Restaurant early one afternoon—breakfast at one o'clock, life of leisure—and the heat hit him, or he it, as if it were a solid mass that he walked into like a garage wall. Blinding glare; no actual direct sunlight, just TV-screen white. Two bedraggled older men were arguing on Broadway's median, moving around each other, loud and angry. What made the scene particularly galvanizing was that one of the men held a primitive-looking handgun. Four other men—colleagues in bedragglement—waited on the benches, watching, a little too close for comfort it seemed to George, but none of them was getting up to run away. The man with the gun was yelling, the other man yelling back, you couldn't tell what—after a minute or less the angrier man, who stood farther away and was facing George, shot the other man, whose back was to George, in the leg, just shot him, pop pop: two shots. The wounded man went down yelling and screaming. And within twenty additional seconds, it couldn't have been more, three Checker cabs pulled up, two from the uptown side of the median, one over in the downtown lanes, each with two plainclothes cops riding in front (he'd seen these cars many times before, a police strategy that seemed reasonable on its face except that no Checker cab had two white guys riding in the front seat, off-duty lights on, except the cops, so how undercover were they exactly, but here they were and a good thing. Somebody must have seen the gun and called it in. Out the cops leaped, guns aimed at the shooter. George was amazed, so many, so fast. He filed the observation that should any of the cops shoot and miss, the bullets would be sailing across the sidewalks on either side. But they didn't have to shoot; the man gave up, they cuffed him, two of the cops working over the guy with the bullets in his leg. It amazed George to consider it, how little journalistic desire he had left—nothing seemed less appealing than the prospect of talking to these strangers about another in the city's endless supply of moments of psychic breakdown and violence and possible death. He walked the two blocks down to 110th—he was staying in a sublet there, working fifteen hours a week as a shipping clerk, the only one, for a small European book import company run by an old German and his wife near Lincoln Center, most of their business in the Langenscheidt language dictionaries with their bright yellow covers. The rest of his time he spent reading Carlos Castaneda alternated with some Hammett and Chandler. There—that was a mix to reflect his state of semi-depression and spiritual flux. For weeks women had been avoiding him. Perhaps they could bio-sense the sluggish sperm such a man as he would put out, ambivalent and self-hating. Nights at the West End bar, at least for an hour or two, nothing; and watching old movies at the New Yorker and the Thalia. He walked downtown, slowly. The hot evening streets smelled of rotting garbage and piss. At the Thalia they had a punch card; if he went ten times, the eleventh was free.

≡

If your bus departed from the basement level at Port Authority, as the buses to western New Jersey did, the diesel fumes filled the hallways, stung eyes and lungs while waiting. Snacks available at the newsstand in the middle, just before the restrooms. Stay away from these. George had broken through his lethargy and begun a short-lived relationship with a soon-to-be sophomore girl, named Susan, she went by Suzy, with high ambitions, high energy, a vivid face. She had almost no bust but this was compensated as is so often the case by gorgeous legs and ass and, not often the case, a wild jungle of red hair. He was at Port Authority to put Suzy of the stunning legs and ass on her bus home, after an afternoon and early evening of what Henry James called *intimacy*. She had a libido, that girl, she just wanted to come and come and come, and they were sexually suited in a way that allowed him with relative ease to oblige her. How she presented from behind . . . Her hair—it almost defined her—that luscious golden red. She was working that summer of 1977 at a big PR firm and living with her parents in Clinton, and these once-a-week trysts usually started with George picking her up outside her office in Midtown. They would go somewhere, a quick bite, definitely drinks, then to his summer sublet apartment on 110th to fuck and sweat in the heat. If it was a Friday, as it usually was—she had Friday afternoons off in summer, the place closed shop after one p.m., but she hadn't told her parents so—it meant they had all afternoon and into the evening. They walked uptown commenting on people's looks, clothes, movements—women's mostly, she was an eagle for the social signifiers women took charge of displaying—and if he commented approvingly on a woman's looks, she was cheerful in discussing it, only growing dark, he soon learned, if the compliment went to the other lady's hair.

═

SOON HE DROPPED her—dropped her entirely before the end of July, rudely, crudely, in a cowardly way he would forever regret—simply stopped calling, wouldn't answer his phone. The problem was, she really liked him. That night, though, he was still in it, and he left her boarding her bus for Clinton, an hour west. He went up to the street.

And—suddenly the lights went out. Times Square. It was insane to see the lights go out here, of all places. For a moment everyone stopped. Looked around. In this state of charcoal darkness, after the minute or two it took for him to become accustomed, the scene struck him as a horror movie. Silhouettes without detail against a murky background. Instant traffic jam. He had intended to walk across 42nd Street to Seventh for the IRT uptown but that was pointless now—he'd need to stay on Eighth for a bus. After the passing of another minute, no more, the streets became a carnival, impassable with humans mingled unnaturally out in the street with the autos. The people, the cars, bright headlights burning through the exposure. The cars moved inch by inch; sometimes the kids outside banging on the hoods and roofs, the car drivers' faces behind the glass showing a kind of staved-in panic. George, face dripping, shirt soaked with sweat—it was even hotter out on the macadam with the two hundred idling engines on 42nd and Eighth—he wished he had a camera for the faces of the drivers, their windows clear, the zombie-movie effect with the drivers underlit by dashboard glow, the terrified wives, grim-jawed husbands, with kids gazing out as if into a circus they were not allowed to go to, no reflections on the glass but for the taillights of the cars ahead of them. Some of the drivers cursed him out and gave him the finger and gestured at him to go away but none of them dared get out of their cars. And the faces on the street—none of *them* looked panicked, oh no, on the street there was nothing to lose, it was a kind of arsonist freedom, with everything, the entire social order, gone in minutes. The powers of darkness claiming us for their own . . . There were, suddenly, no old people around, no infirm, no nervous middle-class people wondering how to get safely—emphasize safely—home. Some of them were likely on the buses that moved through, stuffed full, not stopping for pickup or drop-off. And then there it was—like a magic vision stopped before him in the middle of the avenue, near 41st Street—a maroon double-decker tour bus, absolutely empty. Every bus that had gone by, public buses, had been full, then suddenly this—amazing. Look at it. No one went near it. *Tavern on the Green* stenciled on its side. Newly reopened, the restaurant was sending double-decker buses around Midtown like that old steakhouse, what was the name. Perhaps that would stave off the next bankruptcy. George approached the open doorway.

Not taking anybody, the driver said.

That's crazy, George said. It's an emergency and you have an empty bus. He climbed on.

Driver said, I'm only going to 67th by the park, leaving it there.

That's fine, George said, as long as it's out of here.

He made his way toward the back of the bus and immediately behind him perhaps forty teenagers followed, shouting, quickly ascending the stairs to the top level, calling out destinations, *A hundred twenty-fifth street and Saint Nicholas!* Kids laughing, jostling. Modern piracy, a forced boarding of the ship. Once the bus was past the traffic at Times Square, 45th or 46th Street, they moved pretty well, there were no traffic lights and the only delicate maneuvering required was at Columbus Circle, in the primeval blackness. From the circle the driver went straight up Central Park West instead of going the legal way, around via Broadway—he wanted away from this scene. They pulled into the Tavern on the Green entryway at 67th Street, the driver parked and the multitude of teenagers flew off the bus as quickly as they'd come aboard, asking no questions, making no demands. They spread into the night. In thirty seconds they were gone. George left last and stopped to thank the uptight driver, a not terrifically intelligent-looking guy about thirty years old, who looked pissed off his double-decker got hijacked. As if he could have stopped it.

≡

THAT SUMMER ANNA was cat caretaker for a professor of classical history and his wife who were in Rome and environs on a Fulbright grant. Their apartment was a gorgeous, nicely air-conditioned place on the fifth floor of a building on Morningside Drive. It would be for years to come the model in her mind of how to live in New York City, floor to picture rail bookshelves and warm carpets, even a grand piano that shamed her, for she had given up lessons at nine, when Mark did, imitating, and did not dare now to play it; big windows staring northward across 121st Street and east into the trees of Morningside Park, sycamores, maples, oaks, and elms. Mornings, the place flooded with sunlight from the east; afternoons, it cooled in the dusty indirect light. And tonight, in the east, the glow of fires, fires, fires.

Every spring and summer produced its own boyfriend—most winters she'd been without, it must have been some biological program her body enacted on the world that she was unaware of—and this summer she was with Francis for much of the time, a sharp-boned, board-thin, tawny-haired boy from County Kerry in Ireland, with white skin that in certain lights looked almost blue; for such a cardboard build, a surprisingly substantial member. It sprung pink from a light brown bush of hair. It was the only hair on his body other than what was on his head and a few gallant strands in his armpits. He was always ready for sex, eager as a dog for a walk, but it also rather terrified him, she could tell. Every new sexual foray created a kind of palpable nervousness in the process and afterward left him in awe—even the first time she sucked his cock, the first time he fucked her from behind. Simple things, she thought, but she was no Irishman. His cock was a heavy cock, she noted this every time she took it in her hand. On this overheated and hazy night they were on the roof of the building looking at the fires burning just across Morningside and from there eastward, all the way to the far side of Harlem and up into the South Bronx; she counted twenty visible fires, with no other lights, no greens or reds at the intersections, no yellow lights in stamp-sized windows, all black on black; occasional sirens with the flashing rising and falling of redness from the roof lights; she had Francis's cock out of his cutoff shorts and stiffening under her fingers. He was wearing sneakers with brown socks and she was wishing he weren't.

Take your shoes off, she commanded him, lightly stroking him. He did.

And socks, she said. His feet white as two cave fish. She took the socks from him and balled them up and tossed them over the side of the building into the alleyway between it and the next building to the south.

Apparently you don't like a fellow's socks, he said.

Apparently, she said. She was wearing a cotton print skirt and she pulled her underwear off but did not throw it over the side. She climbed on top of him, with him still in her hand:

she was facing the short parapet, which had been enhanced with a chain-link barrier atop it to keep one from toppling or tossing oneself down to the street below; she fucked him as she watched the fires. He slid his hands up under her T-shirt and onto her breasts, pressed her nipples between two fingers.

Pinch them harder, she said after a minute, and he did, and she moved faster on top of him and he groaned and she whispered, Not yet, not yet! and looked down at his face; it was funny, and she wouldn't forget it, he gritted his teeth to keep from coming. He looked with his teeth gritted and his red hair like a Dick Tracy gangster going Grrrr! It was not an ejaculation-control method she thought would work so she held herself above him for a long count until his breathing slowed; then she started again. Now it was better and she gripped his chest tight and dug into it through his shirt with her nails, really dug, hoping the pain of it would hold him off, which it seemed to do, until she speeded up and he speeded up from below her. She used her fingers on herself and came and then he came with five or six growling grunts—she'd been almost silent—and then they slowed and, with him still in her and her fingers spread again across his chest, rocking a little, she watched the fires, these almost shapeless dancing beasts on the landscape. People would speak of the blackout and she would remember fucking that boy on that rooftop, digging her nails into him and the bruises on that alabaster skin of his, which shamed her a bit, but only a bit, in the sunlight of the following day.

11

Winter came. With a special vengeance after the Hades summer. Record snows. January 1978, a day before registration: almost everyone was back. George, in the swirling blizzard with two black beauties in him, that finest of diet-pill speed, and a half-pint bottle of Jim Beam in his coat pocket just in case, ran into Louis on College Walk; Louis seemed also to be in a state of enhanced enthusiasm, George wondered on what. It was past midnight and they were alone there, standing in more than a foot of snow, which was continuing to fall heavily. Cocaine was George's guess. To go with a snowy evening. This was the opening salvo of what would be the double storm of January 1978, two blizzards back to back. The first was the largest: they stood on the walk with the stuff still falling, blowing, engulfing. There would be by next day almost three feet, a record of some kind, and a few days later another fifteen inches, all of which would then freeze a meter above paving level on all the walkways of the university and become so hard and slick there would be no dislodging it until March. Daily doses of minimal sand, plywood boards to allow cumbersome passage up and down the many steps. Rumor had it a multitude of lawsuits followed, hundreds of falls and injuries to compensate for, the head of B&G went down of course: they didn't clear it in time and once it was on the ground they couldn't move it, they would have needed the Vietnam-era land-clearing bulldozers like those the Montrealers used to clean their streets, plows and blowers the size of alpine chalets. Louis told George he looked dashing in his parka and ski-cap-under-hood, like a good straight New England boy, and the L.L.Bean duck-hunting boots laced tight, with the dun corduroys tucked in.

Louis said, And a new erotic archetype is born! The Bean-boy! The ones in the catalogue are so *not it*—but you—well, yes. Hello Small-boat Sailor!

Give me a break, George said.

As for Louis's look, he was far from a parka state of mind and had chosen an old velvet collared tweed overcoat salvaged, he told George later, during his freshman year from his grandfather's house in Short Hills, before they opened it up for the estate sale. The weekend before the sale, the relatives had come through—most of them early, waiting outside for the agent's arrival at nine—like locusts except picky, they were picky locusts. They had the heart and spirit of locusts but were unwilling to be seen by the other relations as needing the stuff or even condescending to want it. Yet every decent piece of art disappeared before Louis even got himself over there at midday; and every watch and every gold tie pin and every cuff link and shirt stud.

According to Louis, he'd just wanted to accessorize. All the old man's suits had been a little bit too short and a little bit too tight but the tweed velvet-collared coat just fit. It must have been long on the old boy.

For the snow Louis also wore another grandfather remnant, the warmest gloves imaginable, deerskin with separate wool liners. George admired them. They cinched with a little strap around the wrist. On his head, a beret, but that came from Broadway. He did not look French: he looked maybe like a Spaniard—a clerk for a town merchant perhaps, a Spanish Bob Cratchit. Or else he looked like a Swiss writer of science articles, perhaps a onetime school friend of Walter Benjamin, yes, that type, a thwarted intellectual. With the glasses, yes. That was closer, he'd go with that one.

I'm Swiss and ready for a hike, he said. We Swiss are always ready for a hike.

George said he'd been going down to the park to see what it looked like but Louis said, No no no! We're going to go to Fifth Avenue! I'm already on my way! You'll join.

It was a lot of work, it turned out, this trudging through the snow. The trains were slow too, of course, it was midnight and a blizzard. At 42nd they had to wait half an hour for an uptown BMT train, the RR, that would take them to 59th and Fifth.

We'll go to the Plaza and it'll be like Scott and Zelda meet Admiral Byrd, Louis said.

George said, You know we could have walked across from Columbus Circle and been there already.

No, Louis said. Then we'd be tired. I want to walk down the middle of Fifth Avenue. I want to take pictures!

He pulled from the pocket of his coat a little Yashica automatic camera.

I'm going to give it that Arthur feel, lots of tonality, abrupt composition, you know, low-impact high-impact the way he does. Except they're all going to be crooked and *gay*.

You're going to have trouble with that coat, George said.

What? Why?

The tails are too long, They'll drag in the snow. Look, they're already wet from walking across campus. You're going to be wearing a thirty-pound wet wool coat soon.

Louis thought about it and took off his belt and said, Here, hold this. Then he hiked the coat up and told George to pass the belt around his waist.

Who do you think I am, Mr. French? George said.

Help me, Louis said. He stood there like that until George reached around him in an unmistakable embrace and passed the belt around the coat.

I should have said nothing, George said.

You know you wanted it, Louis said.

No, I don't know that, George said. He got the belt tip through the buckle and let Louis pull it tight.

You look like a banker Robin Hood, George said.

As if there ever would be such a creature, Louis said. Someday I'll have to invent him.

At 59th Street the stairs up out of the subway—there were no stairs, essentially, just a long, ruffled, steep embankment of snow. George grabbed the railing, which was perhaps eight inches above the snow line, and felt with his feet but to no purpose; each foot, dug down, found only snow, so he proceeded to yank himself up by estimation with Louis hard-breathing behind him. Up to the top and out onto 59th Street, the park in whitecapped darkness behind them.

They dragged their legs through the snow to Fifth and gazed down it, empty and miraculous.

Falling faintly, faintly falling! Louis sang into the whiteness.

For George the shock came from the softened lines of everything and the diamond glitter of the streetlights on the crystalline powder. And the silence: the silence: the silence.

The trees bent like old crones looming behind them. Or—like spirits descending. Elms with white wigs. Everything so white, with night sky above and dark meer below, as yet unfrozen, the charcoal gray matte bordering it all.

Louis took a few quick shots—the camera apparently did everything for him, aperture and shutter speed, and he kept it focused at infinity so he could just hold it up and shoot without even looking through the finder.

George said, God, I love this place.

It's a field of angels, Louis said, and shot some more.

You have more film? George said.

One more.

Well, take it easy then, cowboy. You won't want to miss Bergdorf's and Saks, laced with white.

Be still my heart, said Louis. All this beauty! Let's walk.

But he stopped and turned back to his angels. More shots. Then they walked—out in the middle of the avenue, where the garbage-truck plows must have come through an hour or two before. Here there was only a foot or so of snow; the curbside banks were five feet high already from the first run of plows, the parked cars like strange white burial mounds.

They shuffled past the Plaza on their right, the GM Building on their left; then FAO Schwarz; then the Grace Building with its curved sweep into the sky, aptly white with snow-dotted dark glass. Nothing moving, not another soul to be seen, a gorgeous post-apocalypse-empty Midtown. Louis snapped here and there; George said nothing. Louis too was silent—what seemed to George a hard labor for him, saying nothing. The silence, though, was of religious proportions; it filled the space. They labored through the snow and the loudest local sound was their own breathing.

Louis, at 55th Street, said: This is exhausting. Beautiful but exhausting.

You gotta get in shape, George said.

Are you in shape? Louis said.

No, George said. My fucking legs are on fire.

Let's go to 50th and then, I know, we'll catch a cab!

George looked at him.

Okay, we'll walk over to the train on Seventh, Louis said.

If we make it that far. Otherwise they'll find our remains, after the spring melt, leering skulls with matted remains of hair, huddled in some filthy massage parlor doorway.

If we die, said Louis, I want to die in the doorway of Tad's Steakhouse.

Do as you will, George said.

I need to perish ironically, Louis said.

Louis said he was impervious to the cold, which was not his usual thing. He complained about it endlessly most of the time.

I guess beauty alleviates discomfort, he said. Adrenaline. Joy. Good to know.

He stopped. George looked at him.

I just need to stand here for a minute, Louis said.

You okay?

I'm more than okay, Louis said.

And goddamn if he didn't start crying; the tears were dropping from his eyelids and rolling down over his cheeks and that, George believed, *had* to be cold.

Hey, man, George said. He clamped a hand on Louis's shoulder. He was aware of being notably manly about it.

I'm not sad, Louis said. This made them both cough out a laugh.

Yeah, said George.

Louis said, as if reading aloud, *I'm not sad, the chubby playwright gurgled.* Then he started laughing for real, with the snot and tears running down.

And I'm actually *not,* he said, when he'd collected himself, used his handkerchief.

Sometimes, he said, you feel the irreplaceability of a moment in time—its perfect ephemeral uniqueness. Yes? You know?

George said he thought he knew.

Maybe *that* is timelessness, Louis said. That recognition. A soul-photography. But you're caught on a time train racing past it. All this beauty. In a few hours the plows will come and the cars will come back and the curbs at the crossings will turn to gray lethal slush, and men in bad hats and women in bad coats—because believe it, the fashionable people will still be inside or down on the islands and it will all be the usual ugly driven thing, the blindness of life as we actually live it. Look at all this—

And he swept his arm from left to right across the street scene: the façades laced with snow, the snow in little mounds on the hoods of the traffic lights, three each, red, yellow, and green, the snow like pencil erasers on the tops of the light poles, and at street level, the immensity of it, two and a half feet or more of snow—final count, thirty-four inches—dumped as a child would dump a sand pail over the center of one of the most populous cities on earth, stilling the place, silencing all. The brightness of the night when coated in blinding white. The colors. The muted foggy darkness beyond. Three in the morning.

Let's walk, George said.

Do you think St. Patrick's is open? Louis said.

You're asking the wrong Protestant, George said.

≡

It was, in fact, open, the Cathedral, because of the snow, and the people stranded, and the people who needed to offer prayers against an icy apocalypse. And there were people in it—the first humans they'd seen, more than a dozen, perhaps fifteen or twenty, spread around, many of these with heads back in the pews sleeping. People curled up, scrunched up, but no one, that they could see, lying down. Getting prone in the pews was discouraged apparently, even on long nights snowed in. The air in the place was somehow as damp as that outside, but with a sense of old stone and wood, candle smoke and bodies. Dark too, unlike all the blinding white of the avenue. George and Louis walked the length of the nave to the apse, ran their hands along the brass of the altar rail.

I can see this moving people, Louis said.

I can't, George said.

That's because you're a Protestant, Louis said.

If that means not medieval then yeah, I guess so.

He was lying though. The quality of quiet here was different from outside. Out there it was exotic, here it was intrinsic. A place to kneel where prayer had been valid.

I want to light a candle, Louis said.

C'mon.

I've always wanted to light a candle in a church, Louis said. It's like porn, for a Jew. Do you have a quarter?

You have to *pay*? George said.

Oh, honey, Louis said.

≡

Louis got George into bed, quite how George never remembered, but he would forever associate Jim Beam in a pint bottle with his only male blow job. George was in a state his mother's generation had called *tight,* but not in the way they meant. The alcohol had merely beveled the edges of the speed, and the speed made him horny to a degree he was always surprised and delighted by. Louis, a wise move, had rubbed his cock extensively before trying to kiss him. When it got down to business George wanted to shave him before he fucked him in the ass; George did his back and ass and told Louis to cup his balls and started to do his legs and the Norelco gave out, choking on all the hair.

Oh my god, look at my leg, Louis said, twisted around to see. He had two long tracks of white hairless skin down the back of his left thigh, all the rest hairy.

And you broke my Norelco!

George lay back.

Clean it and it will revive.

Like you, Louis said.

He traced his tongue down George's torso. Then up from bed and back with a bottle of oil, warm.

George raised his head. How'd you get the oil warm, he said.

I keep it beside the radiator, Louis said. Smart, right?

He worked George's cock.

You really are a good-looking white man, Louis said. Big beefy white guy.

Shhh, George said. His eyes were closed.

Don't come yet, Louis said. I still want you to fuck me.

Afterward Louis said, I've always been a little in love with you, you know.

I thought you were in lust with me, actually, George said.

Well, that. Umm. Yes. But I do actually feel fond of you too, he said.

That's not love, George said. That's genial lust.

After a lingering silence. They were looking at each other. Louis said: Are you freaked out lying here with a guy? In the *after*glow?

A little, George said. Less than I'd expect. Probably because I'm a little stoned and a little drunk and speeding my brains out.

Yet for a few minutes he slept; it wasn't like sleep but like a trance state with dreams. He came out of it with his cock in Louis's mouth. Louis was better at sucking a cock than anybody he'd ever been with. Meaning women. It was like a whole other experience. On the other hand, George looked down and saw a man's head bobbing toward his belly. With what was called, without malice, a Jewfro. And a hint of bald spot. Just a hint. The smells weren't right either. He had to look away quickly to suppress his dismay. He closed his eyes. Just felt the feeling. Hands on his thighs. Interesting. It was more intense somehow—more intimate? Not exactly. He was being distinctly *served,* out of admiration: that's what he felt. He felt Louis's hands appreciating his legs. He didn't sleep with women who behaved that way, who were into servicing a man or into the distinct erotic possibilities of his body parts—who were erotically gratified by touching him, or by looking at him, as a body. They were gratified by these things socially, emotionally, but not erotically. *He* was gratified by those aspects of a woman; it was never anything he detected the women feeling. They responded to some core of his masculinity and identity, to its foreignness, perhaps to its fearsomeness, or to the genuine affection that they had managed to elicit from him but had never won from their fathers, who feared them. Louis's affection was simpler: it was almost entirely unpsychological. There was something so direct and uncomplicated about it. Of course the potential for complication is always there. Like hair.

≡

Lavender smoke bombs at graduation; Gay and Lesbian Alliance. A glaring hot day in May. Media was there not for the Gay and Lesbian Alliance action but for a larger threatened demonstration, a walkout protesting the university's investments in South Africa. In frustration, looking for some kind of attention and response, Louis threw a half cup of tepid Chock's coffee at Jane Pauley—he hadn't managed to reach her with it but security nonetheless hauled him off campus. George had the duty of reporting it for the *Spec*. According to Louis he said to the guards, I'm graduating!

Not in there, they said. She's not pressing charges so just get lost . . .

He went to Chock's for more coffee and snuck back on campus half an hour later. One of the local news channels spotted him and interviewed him: Why did you throw coffee at Jane Pauley, are you in charge of this demonstration—are you demonstrating for divestment? No, we're demonstrating for equal rights for gay and lesbian people. End of interview. They couldn't turn the camera and mic off quickly enough.

Louis told George, It's funny. All that but—a phrase came into my head. After that nothing mattered. This is what writing is for me, a phrase comes and I feel compelled—sometimes I feel compelled—to create a system of other phrases to hold it. Today it was *dreams of a rising sea.* So then the Gay and Lesbian Alliance had one of its raucous and jargon-happy meetings—after *the action.* And all I wanted—I was the star, I threw coffee at Jane Pauley—and all I wanted was to get back to my apartment and work with *dreams of a rising sea.*

12

Autumn 1978. A sublet on Claremont Avenue. Anna told James, her current half boyfriend, about her childhood friend Nancy. Except there was no Nancy: Nancy was her but she didn't want the story to be so raw, so direct. In this story Nancy was a cute and fleshy twelve-year-old, already developing, with dark hair, and she was walking one day to the market—why had she not taken her bike? We don't know . . . Anyway she was walking to the market for her mother, to get milk, and there was a man sitting in his car, just sitting in his car. He said, Hey, hey. She stopped and looked at him. He said, Come over here a minute. She wasn't sure—it didn't feel right, that's for certain—but she couldn't just walk away, she wasn't brought up that way. People were regular, people were nice, grown-ups were responsible and had authority that you didn't question, it was a regular town, a nice town, working people, a factory town—they made *candy* in this town, for god's sake—she went over to the car, and he said, Look honey, look at this, and his pants were open and he had his penis—yes, his penis!—in his hand and his hand was rubbing it, god it was big and purple, the most awful-looking thing she'd ever seen. Look, baby, he said. I'm gonna put it in your mouth. She turned then—she'd been frozen there a minute but she turned and she ran away! Ran and ran and turned down Cedar Street and then Poplar to get away, though she had to double back over on Elm to get to Willow Street, where she lived.

Oh, Nancy. Oh, Nancy. She came slamming into the kitchen.

Her mother had said, What's the matter?

Nancy had stood there, getting her breath.

What happened? said her mother.

Nothing, Nancy said. I was just running.

Where's the milk? her mother said.

Milk? Nancy said.

I sent you out for milk! her mother said. Oh, Nancy, for heaven's sake!

That's what Nancy's mother said when she was mad: for heaven's sake.

Nancy said, Oh. Oh. I forgot.

Her mother said, What *happened* to you? Because, you see, she knew something was wrong.

Nancy said, Nothing. I don't want to talk about it, and she ran upstairs to her room.

The End.

Anna always said *The End* at the end.

James said, What about the milk?

Her mother had to go for the milk.

She left Nancy home?

Oh no, Anna said. No, Nancy was too traumatized to stay alone. When her mother left she ran after her and went with her in the car. They passed where the man's car had been parked and she looked for it but it was gone. Or he was gone. Her mother said, What are you looking at? but she didn't answer. She couldn't actually remember what the car looked like. Her mother bought her ice cream. Her mother knew. She knew.

James, who dealt on campus and elsewhere, speed and acid and possibly worse, she tried not to know, was not a student, he lived down in the West 50s, and what she liked about him at this particular time was that he was depraved.

This really happened to you, didn't it?

Oh, no, Anna said. Nancy.

Sure, James said. She smiled at him, a kind of admission. She didn't tell him that his cock was kind of purple and ugly like the one in the story. That was what had reminded her.

≡

It was never a good idea to fuck your girlfriend's roommate; and not merely your girlfriend's roommate, but her friend; and not merely your girlfriend's roommate and friend, but also the lover of your own roommate, who was not merely your roommate but also your friend. So what should she have been called, this woman whom you should not fuck: your friend's lover and your own lover's friend? All roommates, more or less. Fucking that person and she eager, with ligaments and tendons taut and voice low-growling, fucking you back—you could look this up under *not a good idea*, it would be high up on the list. Top fifteen at least, after Don't cut off your pinky finger with poultry shears, at least not for love—advice once offered ironically in a letter by William Burroughs to Allen Ginsberg, who knew that Burroughs had done just that thing. A bad idea. But at a certain moment the roommate fucking was irresistible. And there he was, wrong place, right time, the moment caught him. Morning, mild winter sunlight, 116th Street, his girlfriend's dorm apartment but his girlfriend, Marianne, was still sleeping; Eliza had let him in, he'd followed her into her room. Her nightgown; the light through it. It was quite early for him, a little before eight, he'd been up all night as he was often up all night, he'd taken some speed, again, which put him in a state of ceaseless arousal, again. He rose from the chair near the foot of her bed and went to her side: May I sit down? he said. He was already half-hard and getting harder, looking at her.

Yes, she said, about as quietly as it was possible to say it. After he'd identified himself on the intercom downstairs, she had come down that hall to the door and let him in, wearing only that nightgown; Marianne still asleep, unhearing. A long corridor with five bedrooms. Eliza had looked at him in the doorway and said hello.

Hello, he'd said.

They'd walked down the hall and chatted, she in the nightgown with her black Irish hair in a braid down her back. No, she hadn't been asleep. She was reading for Spanish. Juan Rulfo. Did he know Rulfo? He did not. You should, she said. *Should.* She had thin ankles and strong feet, very strong-looking, but the nails too long, slightly frightening. She'd gone into her room and left the door open, him right behind her, so he'd followed, more talk of Rulfo—a Mexican, the first of the magical realists, he makes García Márquez look like Dr. Seuss—no, that's not true. But you know, she said. She knew he was enamored of García Márquez.

Axolotl? she'd said.

He'd said, What?

Cortázar, she'd said. Then: Never mind.

Now this. Somehow sitting on her bed. Unbraid your hair, he said.

I don't want to, she said.

He held it in his hand.

Please, he said.

She sat up and stared at him and kept her eyes on him and pulled apart the strands, then shook her head back and forth like a stunning horse and lay back again. He arranged it around her, the dark hair against the white linens, and let the front tresses fall onto the lace at the breast of her nightgown. Such sheets she had; like his mother's sheets. She just looked at him. In her face, permission. Some prevailing percentage of willingness. And dread: because she knew. That was the difference between some people and other people, some people knew where it was all going and, god help her, she was one of these. He touched her cheek, her neck, stared at her. Like a duchess from a Sargent painting, he said. Her eyes examined the compliment, liked it a bit, then pushed it aside: the eyes showed him her fear, her amusement, her defiance: he could see all of it. A woman's face. Like a river, so many elements, unified but always moving, never the same one moment to the next but governed by underlying structures and contours of personality: a rockscape under the moving water that determines the riffles and eddies above. The absolute and ineffable, made fluid. What did his own face show? Awe and desire. And fear, a fear to match her fear, the two fears like puzzle pieces that one wants to put together but they won't go, there being no comfort in fear.

I dare you to kiss me, he said.

Jon will be here soon, she said.

He put his face close to hers and whispered it: I dare you.

She came up slightly to bring her face to his. They both had eyes open, searching each other. Her breath was a little thick with morning. Their tongues touched; then she pulled away, turned her head from him, and lay silent on the pillow. He assumed she was angry. He touched her hair again. Her neck. She didn't move. He was about to get up when she surprised him, came back to him, grabbed him with her arms around his neck and brought her face quickly to his and kissed him again, harder than before. His left hand moved down over the light warm cotton until he had her breast cupped; and found her nipple hardening under the cloth; and then her eyes closed and the kiss became more urgent and he smelled her skin, always that shock—the new smell of someone's skin. The taste of a new mouth. He continued to watch her, watching her as he pulled her up to kneeling and watching her when he put his hand under the nightgown to feel her ass and her stomach and her leg and make his way between her legs where she was wet, her pubic hair was wet around her cunt—watching her until they pulled apart and undressed—she had nothing on under the nightgown. It was stunning to see her there naked: why was this always so amazing, such a gift? He pulled off his boots and his pants and then went for her with his shirt open and his coat still on, a thrift shop cashmere overcoat. He'd never fucked in an overcoat before. She was glorious against the sheets and she pulled him into her, she was gleaming wet, he saw it on her thighs as she lay back and opened for him, and she held him with her legs and ground against him from below. Her arms were around him inside the coat, legs outside. He moved right into her, all the way, and there was a moment, just then, when neither of them could breathe, mouths open, faces wrought, that look of agony that is not agony but a pleasure so close to pain it was largely history that guided the mind in knowing which was which, a pleasure beyond any other physical pleasure we know. They said heroin was better but he didn't believe it. That moment when desire gets to burn on, right next to its fulfillment, instead of the usual hollow thing, where fulfillment kills desire dead. The unreal pleasure. He tried to fuck her hard but she clung tightly to him so it was a bucking and grinding without the long in-out of it. They wanted it over quickly, the conditions demanded it and so did their bodies, and it *was* over quickly—he came and he felt as if his head were exploding but he couldn't cry out, she'd seen the howl in him and put her hand across his face, forcing the heel of it right into his mouth. He would remember as much as anything else later about their sex that morning the taste and feel of her hand in his mouth, a thought that drove him imaginatively right back to the moment, right back to the intensity of desire for her. She held him in and he stayed hard in her for a minute, maybe more. They breathed, he half on top of her. He asked her, Does Jon usually ring the buzzer downstairs? He meant, will we get a warning? And she said, Yes, most of the time.

So he moved down her and she said we can't do this, he could be right outside—but she opened for him and she slid her fingers into the piles of his sweaty hair. This hair of yours, she said.

That hair of *yours*, he said from between her white thighs. He slid one hand up her body and took some of her hair and he put the fingers of his other hand just a little bit inside her and his tongue lightly on the hood of her clit and started slowly, circling with the fingers there in the wetness and circling with the tongue above. He felt her body give in to it. He built speed. He could feel his semen in her, smell it, taste it when his tongue ventured downward, so much it started to lather like soap as he went harder and faster with his two fingers and she let out a short sound more like a bark than a scream, a gruff shout, and put the pillow in her mouth biting it and growling, her hair, her hair, her hair on the pillow, and so much pubic hair it spilled from her vulva onto each leg uninterrupted. She was bucking and pulling him around on the bed and turning on her side and then she was done and she pulled away from him and pushed him off as hard as if he were an overbearing house pet. She let go of the pillow which retained its bite mark and wet stain and she lay panting and he too was sweating and panting. But—he needed to get away before they were caught: so he rose quickly and began to dress. He wiped his hand on the back of his shirt. He knew he would remember that. Funny, how you know. She put on her nightgown.

He looked down at the mess of sheets and pillows and straightened them a little and flipped the pillow with the bite mark, to hide it. He went over to look in her mirror. He had his back to her, and he ran his fingers through his wet hair.

Jesus, she said.

I am not he, George said. I am but a voice crying out in the wilderness.

She rose up and tried to hit him, not hard, but he pulled back. Then he returned and put his arms around her and he said, That was beautiful, and you are beautiful.

Beautiful and wrong, she said. She was not resisting the hug but not yielding to it either; more like she was nullifying it. George didn't mind that, he was feeling elated and full of affection—love, it was, really, this was how easily he could fall in love—and he could see the darkness start to close in on her, angle across her face as if a cloud had passed before the sun.

Maybe so, he said, but, you know, compared to bombing Cambodia, it's not that bad.

You're not a Catholic, she said. She was getting angry, he could tell.

No. Thank god.

This darkened her face further. Oh man, Jon was in for it, a scalding. A raking. A raking and a scalding.

You'd better go, she said. He looked at her to say goodbye and she was sitting on the opposite side of the bed, back to him. She meant it.

Open the windows, he said.

She was fortunate, on a corner.

Air the place out.

She didn't answer or move. He went and opened them for her. Then he left her, closed her door behind him and went down the hall of the suite in his long coat and used the collective bathroom and washed his groin and dried it with his girlfriend's towel, as he'd done before except before it had been her body that he'd been washing off himself; washed his face twice, it had been slick with her. He sprayed around himself some powdery deodorant he found beside the tub, and took up a comb one of the girls in the suite didn't bother to keep clean, little gatherings of darkish gunk between each tooth; long light brown hair trailing from it. He used it anyway. He looked at himself: such an adventure that was, looking into one's own eyes, knowing he existed but not being able to decipher the fact. Then he went to Marianne's room and knocked, and she opened the door, sleepy-looking, and smiled to see him. In the bathroom, and now here, he *should* have felt guilty, he *should* have felt awful and panicked at his sins, which is how he'd usually felt before about his sins, his terrible sins, but he didn't, there was none of that: it was as if he'd lost a thousand pounds, he was buoyant, he was bouncing on the surface of the moon. And he was horny again: he would fuck his girlfriend now, and god, with the speed he was already getting hard again. Amazing stuff. But oh, how he wanted back into Eliza's room. Outside Marianne's large window the sky was a pale winter blue, the sunlight glittered on the bare tips of the silver-brown trees, and he felt better than he'd ever felt in his life, with the day full of gleam and promise and the future floating near him, touchable, graspable, light and easy as a child's balloon.

That night, Eliza canceled Jon, who was going to a movie with some other guys and a girlfriend or two—she made some shit up and went to the apartment on Claremont Avenue that George shared with Jon and another friend. George was there alone.

She said, I felt you all day. I felt you inside me all day, an ache up into my spine.

I bet it made you mad, he said.

Oh my god, she said. I was so *fuck*ing mad at you. Why did you do that? Why did you have to go and *do* that?

He looked at her.

It was there, he said. Sitting right between us. It has been for a long time. It was like a big red—

If you say *apple* I will scream, she said. That's a certainty. Count on it.

Like a big piece of cake, he said.

You brought the fork. The cake could have gone in the fridge.

Too much goes in the fridge.

You know what, we've taken the cake metaphor as far as it needs to go. You could have left it alone and you didn't. What was there, yes. It was there.

Is it absolutely necessary that sex be attended always by this army of shoulds and shouldn'ts?

Yes, she said.

Why? he said.

Aside from the religious and moral considerations? Which universally discourage rampant indiscriminate fucking? Biological survival—rules of attachment and commitment? Because otherwise who would take care of the children? Provide? Because otherwise the men would just eat them is what would happen. Like guinea pigs and grizzly bears do. You *should* have left it alone.

My memory is that *you* could have left it alone too. My memory is that you turned away and I was about to get up—

You should have gotten up! That's, that's what a— She stopped.

What? he said. Go ahead, say it.

A gentleman would have done, she said.

A gentleman wouldn't have been there in the first place and in any case it's 1979 and there are no more gentlemen.

You are so full of shit, she said.

He was holding her by her hip bones, swinging her slightly, twisting her, so that his cock, growing prominent in his jeans, would be dragging across her front.

What's this called, he said, this slightly convex piece of territory down here? The pelvic yoke?

You're misinformed, she said. That's actually ridiculous.

He'd heard it somewhere.

He thought of it later when he was sitting on the bed and she stood on the mattress above him looming and inviting him to pull each of her legs over his shoulders, which he did; she balanced herself with her hands on the top of his head, and he put his arms and hands up her back either side of her spine and with her feet planted against his back she leaned back on his arms and pulled his head to her, and he used his lips and tongue on her and let her grind on his mouth and chin and there it was: he was yoked. The affair lasted less than two months. She was a harrowing, angry woman and it was the most powerful erotic experience of his life thus far, subduing her, feeling her come. The air ionized with hostility. A month before graduation, the affair already over, she nevertheless told Jon, as George had figured she eventually would—she was mean that way, nothing held back if it can be a lash; Jon had broken up with her immediately and he would not speak to George, who meanwhile was breaking up with Marianne since she was going for the summer to India, then doing a year at San Diego. Some marine biology thing. Graduation ended it all. Jon he eventually made up with but he never saw or heard from Eliza again. He did not miss her but he missed the sexual potency, the power he'd felt when he was with her. It had been as if he'd discovered the perfect prosthesis for the limb he had never admitted had been severed from him earlier in his life. He would figure out that this power came from the absence of fear; he knew she had no real interest in him. He thought she found him cavalier, glib. Shallow. And a moral danger. So she didn't like him—not all that much. Which was all right. It meant she couldn't destroy him.

13

Some two weeks after graduation in 1979, the Sunday of Memorial Day weekend, Anna needed help moving into her new apartment. She remembered a scene in a Joan Didion novel, a woman's electric unease at a cocktail party, being in the same room with two different men she's slept with. Anna now was with three—she had solicited in the absence of other muscular alternatives three exes to assist. It was indeed peculiar, as Didion had written it. More so that each of them knew quite well about the other two. A certain amount of posturing was inevitable. Razzing over issues of dexterity and strength.

Three former boyfriends to help her move. Testament, she said, to the loyalty and affection she inspired . . . There was Gregory, the actor and aspiring playwright of the gritty American kind, an Ivy League Sam Shepard, a straight Edward Albee: he wrote grueling scenes of injurious intimacy. He was the most handsome of them, really striking, one of those men you could tell would be handsome his whole life; he was, too, a sweet man. He spoke in a half whisper and the rest of his personality was as vague and slightly unreliable as his voice. With an impishness, an arched eyebrow at the world.

There was David, parents with a lot of money, the kind of newish money that showed on his face and in the way he walked and what he wore. From Miami. He kept saying how his mother looked *just like* Janet Leigh in some later iteration of Janet Leigh with a frosted helmet of hair that Anna had trouble perceiving as desirable. These boys and their mothers. Younger, he'd been an awkward guy and had a bad temper, easily aggrieved, a nurser of perceived injuries, but with a certain thing he had, a gleam, a sense of manners, a constant hum of desire: he was one of those guys who, you could tell, *loved* women, loved pussy. Which he did. To a distracting degree, so that by the time he was finished enjoying it with fingers and mouth and even once, stoned, whispering to it in Spanish—yes, he did—she'd felt so isolated to her cunt that it was as if the rest of her didn't exist. So they'd stayed *friends*. That thing. He'd take her out twice a year to very good restaurants downtown and give her an excuse to dress up a little. She'd kiss him on the lips as reward. No—she shouldn't say that. She would be genuinely grateful on such evenings, affectionate, he was always pleasant, even a little funny, he treated her so well . . . she wanted to give him that, acknowledge that in him and that between them. But still. It was a reward.

And George. The important one.

She was important to George as well, she could tell he felt this and had regularly displayed a kind of devotion to her as a body on the planet. It did not make him enjoy bumping the two big bureaus up the stairs one after the other with the annoying David, heading off to law school at NYU in his pressed jeans. At one point George said to him point-blank: You iron your jeans.

I send them to the cleaners, he said. They do it.

You dry-clean your jeans?

Yeah. I don't want to have to deal with them.

You realize before Paco Rabanne and whatever, Calvin, these items were manufactured as suitable pants for men who, like, drove mules and waded in manure?

The culture has transformed them. Now they're for people like me, who know all the doormen's names at Studio.

He meant Studio 54. The regulars were on a first-name basis not only with the staff but with the institution itself.

Her apartment: run-down but with ancient exposed wood. George liked it. It reminded him of certain boats he'd worked on. The wood looked like mahogany, hints of luminous gold and pink under the finish, which was stained and dried out in many places and here and there ruined entirely. He wanted to get his hands on it. The bathroom was down the hall and shared with other tenants; the building had once been a mansion, ended up a boardinghouse and then SRO and now was lying in wait for reclamation by a rich person. It was enormous, the bathroom, and spectacularly tiled—jade color background with some scene of chinoiserie with flowers and a lord of some kind. It was part of four floors of cheap ill-kept flats, most of them badly divided, but not hers, which was at the rear, three intact rooms in what had been a beautiful brownstone. No lease. The apartments were month-to-month and, a few older ones, week-to-week. There was a nail in the bedroom which they had painted over, the landlord's crew, okay, a cheap rush job, painting over a nail, that's par, no big deal, except here was a paint-over none of them had ever seen or heard of before: a hanger had hung on the nail and did still, a wire hanger like for a shirt. It was hanging on the nail when the painters arrived and they had just painted over that too.

She told them this on the sidewalk as they were pulling things out of the U-Haul. George walked in and took a look and there it was, a hanger form in bas-relief against the wall, high up and a little right of center, nearer the door than the window.

That's amazing, he said. There was a small can of red floor paint in one of the closets and a stiff old brush and later he outlined the hanger in deep red, making it a hat, and painted a clown face below it. With the clown's usual creepy smile and unreadable eyes made up to appear sad. It's your personal homunculus slash circus entertainer, he told her.

She said, Your choice of the word *slash* is unfortunate, but thanks. Very helpful.

She left it there for the year and a half she was in the apartment. She looked at it in many different moods. There was something in the way George smiled at her that day: something actually *in* it. And she could see it in that clown's face. Something intimate and true that went through her. And of course those shoulders of his, laying into the sides of her larger pieces of furniture. And the sweat. But they all had bodies, these boys, these young men, bodies that were not unappealing, and they all sweated: so . . . it had to be faced in the end, that two of the sweaty bodies she would shy from now, and one she would want. She had to conclude later that what had compelled her was all that sat between them, unfinished. Unspoken. Some acknowledgment that had to be made—that they loved each other, yes, why was this so hard to come to? To *say*, even silently? She didn't allow the word to pass through her mind until well after. But it was okay, they could love each other and go their separate ways, knowing at least that each knew what the other felt, even though they didn't say it in this dispensation, this period of attenuated relations. That night after the move, when the others had finally been shaken off, when he'd stood ready to go but looked at her and she stepped into him and put her arms around him and he'd kissed her. They'd *looked* it at each other—and looked it again while they were having sex and then later, yet again, talking. They'd acknowledged it and needed to do so because both sensed—both knew—that they would fall out of touch—now that school was behind them, now that they were embarking, moving to a new stage of creating themselves, changing neighborhoods—now that they wouldn't just run into each other on the known paths. The *known paths*—every neighborhood in this city that she would ever live in—Upper West Side, Harlem, Lower East Side, Prospect Heights for a while, Fort Greene briefly, and then back to the Upper West Side—would have its known paths, where she would or would not be likely to see or run into or be able to enjoy or have to endure someone or something. The doorway where the men pissed at night. The bad-smelling burger place with its exhaust fan out over the street. The flower shop. A certain boy or a certain man, whom she would run into or wish to run into or then, later, not wish to run into.

≡

AFTER, THEY SHARED a cigarette, then a joint. They talked. Plans. Hopes. The past. They now officially had *pasts*.

She said, There was a story you were going to tell me. Back in sophomore year. Before we broke up.

He knew what she meant. And she could tell he knew. He didn't say anything. Then he said, Oh man.

It was about your mother, Anna said. I've always wondered.

Oh man, George said again.

She said, Well, it's your mother . . . so you're the only man involved.

Huh? he said.

Oh man is you, she said.

Oh man is I, he said, repeating back to her with a stunned sound.

He looked at her with an expression she could only think of as panicked and begging.

It's okay, she said. Never mind.

He said: Oh man is the universe. I mean I've never told anyone this.

I know, she said.

I mean I haven't told anyone I know personally. There were . . . He paused and waved his hand slightly. Professionals.

There had in fact been a social worker and Wyndham, the cop, and then a therapist he'd gone to for a while, paid for by the state.

She touched him. Hand on arm. She kissed that shoulder, still bulging out at her as on the night they'd first met. He breathed.

He told her. He called it, in his head, the intolerable night. It was the memory of it, the *fact* of it, sitting like a stone or a dam, something that fell there, that he didn't want there, that made it intolerable. His mother, some period of time before the culminating event, had begun coming to his room while he slept, not that often—he'd guess, looking back now, once every few weeks, more than a few weeks? Hard to tell—coming to his room to kiss him, to touch his shoulders and chest.

With shoulders and chest specifically named out loud as zones of violation, Anna felt a bloodrush of alarm, absolutely a physical terror, a terror of her own desire specifically for his shoulders and chest, now and past, an instant of adrenalized shame at pleasures already taken there—and only the sharpest sense of the impermissibility of her pulling away from his body at that moment kept her against him.

He felt it. He felt her body tense up there but instead of pulling away she'd pulled herself tighter against him. Her muscles needed to react and they'd pulled her toward him instead of pushing away. He would realize all this not in the moment but after, later, looking back, would realize too her reaction was a measure of at what cost he told this story. It—the story—carried around it an atmosphere of shame that was noxious, that one yanked back from, despite all affection and commitment. Despite sympathy and love. It was good to know this. He would later admire her ability to pull closer to him there, at that moment, *not* to jump back but to embrace him: it would become a memory like a sword.

He told her the basics, with some details, but not all, no single telling of it could fit it all, all the ways he felt, all the moments recorded in a heightened sensibility, emblazoned as such on his psyche. He didn't know, couldn't say, how long it had gone on, his mother's visits—some months at least. He had, he told Anna, admitted none of it to himself until later. What he thought was that he was having exciting dreams, a woman's caress in the darkness, a woman's deep, desiring kisses.

She knelt beside the bed, he said. She knelt as if in prayer. I can see this—but *how can I, how do I know this, when I was asleep?*

Anna waited.

It was in his head, he told her. It was in the dreams, but in the dreams as he remembered them. He never saw a face, or a body, though he knew she was kneeling there. He saw but he didn't see. A dream-not-a-dream, like something he'd imagined but imagined so well, so clearly and over so sustained a period of repeated imaginings, that it was virtually the same in quality of memory as something seen—seen though he'd never *known* himself to have seen it. Through these nocturnal visits he'd lain, adamantly still, adamantly closed-eyed, converting everything to dream, to a series of dreams, which he experienced over the course of those months, even close to a year, when he was sixteen and seventeen years old. They were still in there like that, like a series of dreams remembered even though he knew later they were *not* dreams, remembered like the tidal-wave dreams he'd had in the eighth grade—he could still say, *I remember what those dreams were like*. She might have begun when he was fifteen. He'd been big early, muscular of back and shoulder and arm, thick in the chest. Man-sized. He always thought in this regard about how she'd opened the door once to come into his room when he was fifteen and he was spread-legged on his bed jerking off and she'd seen him, seen all of it at once, and said Oh! and closed the door and tried to apologize later. Perhaps this had caused what came afterward.

Part of the horror was that the dreams—of kisses, of hands on him—these sensations felt almost supernaturally good. And he would be hard—and this became part of it later, this awareness of his cock and her interest in it. The best sex dreams of his life—the best sex dreams of anyone's life because the sex was real, even if up to a certain moment unconsummated.

Ah, but then. But then she couldn't resist, could she—telling it now to Anna, his hatred of his mother rose in him, hate and hate and hate and beneath that a pain like fury, a boiling cauldron of pain—*of course* she had to touch it of course she had to stroke it through his sweatpants until the night she lowered the pants and stripped her panties, which moments later he, on waking, really waking, horror-waking, saw there on the floor, as obscene an image as he could have invented: and she was pulling up her nightgown and trying to climb on him. He woke with that—even he couldn't sleep through *that, that* was too much even for his repressed and starved sexuality. He shouted—he remembered it in a palpable way, could still feel it in his chest and throat, this shout, like a roar from some depth of self-knowledge and anger he hadn't quite known existed but recognized as his own—and he rose up and pushed her off him as if he'd been attacked by a monster. She flew five or six feet and then was on the floor and saying oh jesus my shoulder I think you broke my shoulder jesus christ and he stood over her, his pants pulled back up, barely able to keep himself from kicking her. He snatched a flannel shirt from the chair and left, it was autumn, he had no shoes on, he was accustomed to that from the waterfront, he walked the half mile to the middle of town, to the Town Green, which was by Town Hall, the name maintained as if this were the eighteenth fucking century—then again, the town was founded in the seventeenth fucking century so who knew—there was a heavy dew, a mist along the ground, the wet grass in this small park wetting his feet and soaking the trailing bottoms of his sweats so when he sat he turned them up to his shins and the air chilled his wet skin and then he listened, trying to empty his mind, to the late crickets who in song foretold a fall that had already arrived. The sound of crickets had been, his whole life, a comfort to him, though portentous too, for the fall, a new school year, and who knew what was coming? He thought about this sitting there. He was a senior now, there were no more surprises left for him in Saybrook, certainly not *now*, after what she'd done, that was the ultimate surprise.

Some time passed. He sat. The cold air, the sky, cloudy, above slightly to north and west behind the clouds a moon pushing through its pale light. He tried to slow his breathing. It did slow, eventually. Then a police car came by, U-turned to his side of Main, stopped. Out came the cop. Walking over with more stride and energy than was comfortable for George at this time of night and in his frame of mind.

What's up, son? the cop said. Kind of late.

George pondered how to answer this.

The cop said, I'm going to need you to look me in the eye.

George looked him in the eye, as requested. He said his mother's name. She was not unknown to the police, a heavy drinker, a woman of high temper.

There's probably been a call, he said.

The cop went back to the car, spoke on the radio. After a time he replaced the radio, walked back to the bench.

She called for an ambulance, the cop said. She reported a fall. They took her to the ER.

It wasn't exactly a fall, George said. Again looking the cop in the eye. Something familiar there. He wanted to drill into the poor man's brain, with its cop wariness, its ambivalent cop half-curiosity.

George said, I found her climbing all over me in my bed. I woke up, threw her off. She was drunk.

Cop stared at him then shook his head. That's not a good situation, he said.

No, said George.

Now you're out here in the cold, said the cop. He shook his

head again. He was a young guy, not much beyond his early twenties. George thought he recognized him. The cop had the same realization.

Do I know you from the boatyard? the cop said. You work for O'Connor in the boathouse?

I know your boat, George said. The thirty-foot sloop? From Holland? That's a beautiful boat. I used to look at that boat every day.

It was my grandfather's, the cop said. He bought it in Denmark, not Holland. He sailed it to Belfast and then to Plymouth and then to here. Crossed the Atlantic in fifty days, with a crew of three.

Wow, George said. Shit. I didn't recognize you with the hat on. You sail with that blond woman. She's good. I mean, she sails.

You watched her, huh? the cop said. That's my wife.

Sorry, George said.

No, the cop said. I'll tell her you said she's good, it'll make her day.

Tomorrow, George said.

Yeah, tomorrow, the cop said. I used to work for O'Connor, back in high school. He still got the crucifix in the office and all those skin mags on that shelf right underneath? And industrial-size jar of Vaseline in the head?

Yup, George said. He could see it dawn on the cop that O'Connor's pornography might be a dangerous zone of conversation given the tenor of the evening.

[illegible], well, the cop said. You're George? George Langland? Toffh[illegible] Road?

That's me.

Anyone I can call for you, George? You can't stay out here.

Technically the green is closed and you're underage and it's three in the morning.

George sat forward, gripped the front of the bench on each side. No, I'm good, he said. I'll just go home.

Hop in the car, the cop said.

I can walk, George said.

Hop in, the cop said.

It seemed like something close to an order. George followed him and got in the passenger door, which the cop was holding open.

What's your name? George asked him when he was behind the wheel.

Wyndham, the cop said. Out here, Officer Wyndham. In the boatyard you can call me Teddy.

Teddy, yeah, I remember hearing that. Officer. Officer Wyndham.

Wyndham smiled at that. I'm hungry, he said. I'm due for my break. You hungry?

George said, I don't have any money.

It's on me, Wyndham said. He lifted his radio, looked at George.

You also don't have any shoes but I can take care of that, I think.

Then he spoke into the radio: This is one-eight I'm going seven-seventeen at . . . he looked at his watch. Oh-three-twenty-two, he said. Over.

Roger that, one-eight. Disposition of the Langland kid, over?

Wyndham looked at George. Kid's with me for the seven-seventeen and then I'll drop him at his house, over, Wyndham said.

Roger that, Mother Teresa, over.

And out, said Wyndham.

Wyndham took him to the Eden Roc on the Post Road. When they got out of the car Wyndham told him to wait, opened the trunk, and pulled out a pair of black cop shoes.

Here, he said. Put these on. They'll be big. Just flop in them.

Three thirty in the morning and there were some people there that George knew and that he knew were *not straight*, not at that hour in that place, and they sat up almost comically rigid and brought the volume and hilarity down sharply when the cop walked in behind George. He would have some heavy explaining to do. *It was about my mother.* He could hear himself saying it. They'd get that. Mumble something and look away. Shit, man . . . The diner had, to the right of the entrance, a large room, three glittering glass chandeliers lighting it, with tables and round-backed wooden chairs with red leather trim, and to the left a long counter with booths along the windows, which is where George and Wyndham and anyone else local and young and sensible would sit. One of the booths was open. The waitress flirted with Wyndham, called him honey. He ordered grilled swiss and bacon on rye, cup of tomato soup, fries.

What about you? he said.

I'll have the cheeseburger.

Get the deluxe, Wyndham said.

Cheeseburger deluxe.

How you want it cooked, baby? Wyndham was honey, he was baby, and they were a neat little happy family.

Medium.

American cheese?

Yes, said George. Mayo on the side, please?

Sure, baby. She whisked up the menus. Iced tea?

Wyndham: Yup.

George said that was fine.

Wyndham sat and looked at him. You didn't realize how much shit a cop had to wear and carry on him until you saw him distributing it on a booth bench and table in order to sit down. The radio looked like it weighed eight pounds. Wyndham had knobbed it down to low static and murmur.

What I'm supposed to do, Wyndham said, is report you and get you to a social worker.

I'm eighteen, George said.

No, you're seventeen, you'll be eighteen in a month.

George looked at him with the question of how did he know.

They have it in the files. I got it on the radio. In any case, you need to be eighteen but if you were eighteen you could be looking at assault for your mother though that wouldn't likely go anywhere. It would get on your record and make life difficult later. Colleges and jobs. Have you ever been arrested for a felony is what they ask you. Not have you been convicted. You'd have to say yes. So better to be in the social work category.

I don't want to be in any category.

Wyndham pointed out—in circumspect language—that people who break their alcoholic mother's shoulder ex-post that alcoholic mother trying to climb in bed with them don't just shrug that shit off and go scrape and rewax the hull of some rich guy's sixty-eight-foot yawl. He should find a friend to live with for the rest of the school year and that's where the social worker would come in.

How much of a shit storm if you live somewhere else this year then split for college?

A shit storm, George said. I don't know how big.

Well, see, the social worker and someone like me or a

superior, some cop, we tell your mother this is the way it's going to be and she has to accept it. It can be done all voluntary and nice and not change your legal status which is a big fucking deal.

After the food Wyndham took him home; his mother was not back yet from the hospital. In his room, the underpants were gone. In pain and incoherence, she'd known enough to pick them up. Crazy like a fucking wild boar. Not a fox: something that ate the fucking foxes. He tore all the sheets off the bed and put the spread back on and lay down on top of it. Put the radio on. Vin Scelsa overnight out of New York—Allman Brothers then the Band, okay, but then Pink Floyd came on—first the heart beating and then the laughing man and the screaming woman and with that last he twisted himself around to turn it off. Then silence; he stayed in the dark on his back. Wind blew the oak branches outside his window, they scratched the roof, and the yellow streetlight beyond the tree cast pale shadows on his ceiling and walls, shadows of the leaves in undulation, like penitents in a ritual dance.

He told Anna a lot of this, not all, of course—there was too much. It was hard to hold back, he had every detail in his memory, all the moments and images, live as rats.

Before school ended the following June she was dead, of liver cancer. The final months were bloating and jaundice and a kind of toxic dementia from the poisons left roaming her bloodstream . . . He wasn't with her then—he was staying in a basement bedroom, with black light and lava lamp and Hendrix poster, a room abandoned by the brother, away at school, of his friend William, whose family lived down by the water. He went fitfully to see her. He was profoundly aware—aware in a ghastly and irredeemable way—of abandoning her.

Quickly she was dead. Her final weeks were another story to tell, later. At the end, she couldn't speak: she stared at him with large imploring eyes. Among her legacies, or his inheritances, was that for a long time he didn't get women his own age—with their uncertainties and mixed messages and essential fear, which translated itself to him as rejection. From early on and nearly ever after he would feel the greatest sexual urgency and intimacy with women of sexual experience far beyond his own, the further beyond, the better. This part he didn't say to Anna. She wasn't crying full out but her face was streaked with tears, which she wiped away. She kissed him: yes, on the shoulders and chest and lightly on the mouth, he could feel the mix of salt and cold from the drying tears and the warmth of her wet mouth.

I'm so sorry, she said. Her head now on his chest. So sorry.

Thank you, he said. It's, I'm surprised, it's actually enormous, to tell it. It's like wow look at the size of that iceberg, once you turn the sonar on.

She coughed a laugh at this.

Thank you for telling me, she said. Her voice muffled by the pectoral muscle her mouth lay on. They were still naked. Inevitably he got hard and inevitably they ended up joined again; it was slow, they grazed against each other like two sheets touching breeze-swayed on the line, until the very end, when he and she were both finished, neither of them having come, which made it a little sweeter, more tender, without that loud crescendo.

They were on her mattress on the floor, a cotton blanket over it, nothing over them, nothing on the windows, quite a show when they thought about it.

You want to go out and get a beer? he said. It's not that late.

Sure, Anna said. She slowly removed herself from his body. They rose and dressed.

Do you ever wear underwear? she asked him. I seem to remember you did sometimes.

Not much, he said. If I'm wearing something thin or if I think I'm going to get sweaty I might.

Didn't you think you'd get sweaty here?

He looked at her with a funny smile.

I mean *moving* stuff, she said.

I don't know, he said. I don't know what I was thinking. He started to laugh. She started to laugh too.

They would not spend the night together. This was it. The mattress on the floor was not that accommodating. And they weren't together in that way. He would walk Broadway for two hours after leaving her, before going home, letting himself be transformed by his telling, by his reliving of the story. Before that dropping her back at her door, on the sidewalk he held her, kissed her forehead and cheeks and finally lips and said, not quite sure where it came from, *I never won't be thinking about you.*

Oh my god that is such bullshit, she said. Such a total lie! She pushed herself back from him. Why do men lie so much?

We're trying to make something pretty to give you, he said. A big pretty version of the world. A big pretty version of *us*, as noble heroes in this big pretty world we're giving you. It's kind of like chivalry in the age of public relations.

Well, thanks. I mean, it was nice even if untrue. Here's what I'll say, to mark the occasion—be good. Be strong and brave. You are that. So be it.

You're strong and brave too, he said. Plus you're kind and smart and good-looking. So you'll go far.

She laughed at that but still felt that rush of intensity about her future—she *wanted* to go far. He touched her cheek and was turning to go and she said, Wait! She hugged him really hard.

No crying, he said.

No crying, she said.

Then one more kiss outside a different doorway from the first soft kiss outside the Carman Hall entrance three years ago. Very similar kiss, he noticed. Short. Full of something that back then he hadn't known but which now he did. It felt now, as then, almost too much like the kisses of the dreams he'd told her about, such a haunting feeling to be kissed now that way—the tenderness of it—and only *she* had ever managed it, to kiss him that way. This was a realization he would store for later study. He looked at her and gave her a small smile, an unextravagant smile, a smile recognizing all the sadness of the evening—and then he turned and walked away.

≡

The world is charg'd with the grandeur of God . . . All the thoughts that were unleashed by telling her. He heard in his head the voice of his great-aunt, sometime in the months after his mother died, before he had moved to New York:

Your father, god bless him, I know how much you miss him, dear, your father was a saint. He was a saint. What he put up with from your mother—I'm sorry, it's true—what he put up with you'll never know. You have no idea, dear. I wouldn't want you to know. He put up with the worst. The worst. More than anyone should be asked. You know, he did it for you. He loved you, he was crazy about you. It killed him. She killed him—she was like a disease and she killed him. I'm sorry, I have to say it. You have no idea, dear. This is what she did.

This was his father's aunt. Grandiose and destructive in her own way. But one part was true: his mother lived as a kind of intimacy terrorist.

Early in freshman year, still September, maybe two or three weeks in, he'd had a dream: A Jungian cunt. Large, wet, disembodied, belonging to no woman but to the universe. Then, a bright light. He could hear his own voice as if on a resounding speaker, exhausted, portentous: *I assign this light to all of them . . .* And then he dreamed he was having sex . . . on a foosball table? No, impossible. He had by then in his life been with two prostitutes and one girlfriend, Carrie. He felt himself very inexperienced at the time, but here he was in front of the world. Not foosball, idiotic, how could it be—it was the hockey-puck bowling-lane thing they'd had in The Gold Rail, a bar and burger joint between 111th and 110th. An enormous crowd there, the bar packed, beyond it the restaurant full, every table taken, he could see all the faces, everyone he knew, professors now and teachers from high school and friends from high school and a few of the new college friends, and his relatives, he could see them all at their tables and booths laughing, smiling, talking—seeming to laugh and smile at him—while on the gently sloped bowling machine, which was near the bar, on the slightly rising surface of the white wood lane, he fucked this creature with a perfect body—it was the body from *A Clockwork Orange*, the scene after Malcolm McDowell has been reprogrammed, they bring out this naked woman and he is unable to touch her, psychologically indoctrinated to the point that if he attempted it he would get sick—that kind of body, with prominent hard nipples and large perfect breasts and lean strong slightly rounded stomach and legs like a jumper, thick and ropy with muscle. As from a comic book; he was humping some Stan Lee fantasy—and he was large and extremely hard, she was splayed out on this table-like surface before him, and he was almost slicing into her with this dream-cock of his, slamming against her with contemplative force, bang in and slowly out, and bang again, he felt a calm fire. His eyes traveled slowly up that movie-perfect body from rich wet tangled pubic hair along belly and over breasts and shoulders and long neck and there it was: the face, glamorous, haggard, staring back at him, his mother's face, aged and harrowed and grotesque—he looked up to the crowd, all looking back at him. And then the dream went black.

≡

Telling Anna had been the first break in the dam wall. He'd had flood dreams all through his teen years, tidal waves that were warned of and arrived and towered and crashed over him while he gripped lampposts or some other unlikely dream-objects; or else the dreams were of rising waters, flat, reflective, inexorable, he'd watch as the water approached the window ledges. Now he knew what the water really was: the water was the facts. He wanted to find some version of himself that was not complicit and he kept failing, kept remembering with gutwrench in the delicatessen, at the newsstand, awaiting the train, the sensations, the sudden overwhelming horror with what had been in front of him—her—and what was within him, himself. It cut his breath off short, made his stomach hurt, literally, made him want to hit things, made him want someone to hit him. Never leaving him, that half second, before he *fully* understood (he'd always primitively understood) the knowledge, the memory, that moment of *wanting* it. He'd been hard for it. Jesus. She'd raised him to want it. The memories other than that moment so vague. He was asleep and *couldn't* have heard these things, seen these things: he'd been asleep: he'd been asleep. She must have come in and kissed him—kissed his lips, kissed him with a yielding, infinite intention, while he slept but was not asleep. And his cock hardened, as it would then, and his desire rose, as it would then, like floodwaters. The lips. This was a sweet, sweet dream he kept having, the loving kisses, the desire and comfort of it. There was tenderness in it, love, more than she had showed him in her strictly maternal relations. Oh, look at you. Then it was her hand. He kept his eyes closed, a deep tunnel of dark, not asleep but actively believing he was asleep; and as on so many nights, but this one more so, he felt every sensation in a granular way that dreams never provided. He was seventeen. He *had* to think it was a dream, what else could it have been? And many times in the years since when a woman took him, tenderly or brazenly or hungrily or with bawdy lewdness in her hand or into her mouth, he felt behind his arousal and even occasionally his love a stirring anger, a desire to fuck her throat and drown her in a biblical flood of semen. Then came the night his mother went further—pulled off her nightgown, he'd heard it, felt her movements, he didn't know what. But that was when he'd opened finally, finally, finally, his eyes—to look at her there, standing two feet from his head, naked, her dark pubic triangle and her world-knowing cunt mounded there, visible beneath the hair, the rest of her pale as rice paper in moonlight, and while he was paralyzed trying to process what this was, she climbed on top of him and he finally proved himself awake by shouting—roaring really—he had never felt such an anger before or since, he could have killed her—goddamn you goddamn you and throwing her off him, onto the floor. She landed on that shoulder and broke that collarbone, she never got over it that he'd broken her, and she hollered and wept, lying there, naked. Her hair like a rumpled silk cloth covering her head. He got up and left, left the room, stepped over her somehow, left *her* most importantly, didn't know where to go, he went out the front door in sweatpants and flannel shirt, barefoot, coatless, early October in New England, and began to walk, but where to go? Where was it safe? There was nowhere to go that solved this problem, that walled it off from him. Where was the absolution, where was the forgetting, where could he have gone in the end? He was almost eighteen, she was forty-three. He walked into town, the town dark, nothing open around there, he went around the village green and sat there on a bench for a while—until the police car came—he had lifted her off him as he might have lifted a child, hands across her ribs on either side and up! And now he could feel the skin still against his palms and thumbs. He picked her up as if she were a child and threw her down as if he were a child abuser and now he could feel her skin on his hands and the weight of her flesh gathered above his two thumbs, his extended fingers. Goddamn her. Goddamn her again. The sound of crickets, the exhilaration of autumn, the promise of hearth and harvest, and of death, loss, mysteries.

After a time in the green, waiting there on that bench, damp-footed, feeling the air but oblivious to the chill, falling into a capsule within himself, with the calm of the gravely wounded, the more clearly he felt he could see his life. As it was and, in some hazy but definite way, as it would be, in his adulthood. All those years to come. He felt oddly strong, he knew suddenly that he would win and she would lose, he didn't know exactly that she would *die*, but he knew that she would lose, and the price, the price, well, he didn't know yet that things such as this, such victories and all that sudden, radical change, crashing into adulthood from a fiery plane, came with an enduring price, a weekly shakedown, daily even, the screaming unrelenting vig of his life, his broken self; he hadn't realized that the enormous shame wouldn't diminish as did guilt about some misdeed, fading into the past, but would multiply and take on the shape of his daily life, the shape of himself, like clothes that require a bit of time to fit. And the phantoms came and slit the tires and sugared the gasoline of his psyche and his history. He hadn't slept that night or so it felt to him but he must have dozed a little because after, when he rose at close to six, he had found her downstairs in what the family, including his father, had called the sun room, which was full of plants that various housekeepers took care of. She was lying on the couch in there, dressed more or less: a shift on, she had no bra, quite plainly, and she said, You broke my collarbone. And he said, Whatever is broken in you, you broke it. He went back up to his room, dressed, and left. The big meal with Wyndham meant he wasn't hungry; he walked again to the center of the village and back to the Eden Roc, took a place this time at the counter, ordered coffee. This was the new him: he had stepped into a semi-permanent costume of near-adulthood and aloneness, an enforced solitude. He remembered, always would remember, walking back into that house in the predawn morning, four a.m. or later, while she was still at the hospital, and finding this place, the only place he'd ever known, too conflicted a place to call home in any but casual ways yet a deeply felt abode: he knew the place, and it was as if he were coming back to it after years and years away, to find it oddly transformed, reduced, the way spaces known in time past are always smaller when one sees them again. That was the way this was, only the time here so much shorter, the evidence of lived reality sitting before him from only eight hours before—a half apple, now browning, that before bed he'd left on a dish in the kitchen—everything now was cast in amber. The whole place was like a memory, an eerie dream. It was as if the familiarity of the objects, once known, long forgotten, made them inherently strange. He never lived in the same house with her again; he barely spoke to her until she fell ill after Christmas. Dead that April, before he graduated from high school. In his life he had told this only to Anna . . . He had told her all this and watched her cry for him, but he had not cried himself, ever—he hadn't shed a tear about his mother, but Anna could see it in him of course, grief caught inside, trapped in glass, behind some door with bent latch that would not open to let the stuff out. Anna held him and then he stood, walked, tested his breathing, like a man recovering from a confusing and frightening dream, and said, Hey, let's go get a beer. Sometimes he thought he was a monster with no feelings at all. Several other women had thought so too. He drew people in and then pushed them away because being loved was not safe; it was being wanted and needed and it was a dangerous thing and it was not a place that promised him well-being.

There was relief in death. She died. It was as if he had killed her dead—he had killed her in order to be rid of her leaden needs and terrible legacy—he had always felt that way, but never admitted it out loud. Whatever death was working inside her was sprung into high force that night when he'd thrown her onto the floor. He felt guilty of it, as if he'd committed a crime, murder, but he felt no remorse. He didn't wish to be caught or punished for it—he'd do it again and should have done it sooner. You should be a lawyer, she used to say: unrelenting and logical, he could argue her into a frenzy. Then it was over. Early in the morning hours of April 1, 1975, well before dawn on Easter Tuesday, his mother died. He was eighteen, two months from his high school graduation. Despite her long illness George had not known, not officially, that she was going to die from what was ailing her, until the Thursday prior—Maundy Thursday, the Episcopal service that featured the washing of the feet—when her doctor took him aside in the waiting room, took him out of the waiting room in fact, where he was sitting with his grandparents, her parents, who hardly forgave her and would be even angrier in a short time when he told them she was dying; she'd lied not just to him but to them, to the last. His grandmother, his mother's mother, with a hard-set mouth and tears down both cheeks—furious. Her father, numb, selfish, mean, he had ever been so and would remain so; what was worst in her had probably been delivered in seeds from him. George followed the doctor out of the lobby; this doctor was a kind man, it became clear, he took George into a curtained-off area largely unlit, they stood near a glass door in the light from the lamps outside so the doctor could tell him that his mother had a badly diseased liver and would not survive very long, a few days more at most, that despite what she'd been telling everyone (that she was merely anemic and just had to rest in order to recover her strength) she had been very ill for months and now was going to die. That final evening, Monday, George saw her, tented, tubed, unable to speak, face hollowed, forty-three years old going on seventy, large eyes watching him, never leaving his face as he moved around her bed, fixing her covers, her IV, eyes in which he saw sadness and regret but also something enormous and new—fear, he saw fear writ large, he had never seen her afraid before. She was bleeding internally and on the way out and now, now, finally, she'd encountered something to be afraid of. George touched her arm, through the cotton blanket, this is how he remembered it, touching her or trying to touch her though she was inaccessible behind tent and tape and tubes and the double blankets, those hospital cotton blankets of wide white weave, slightly rough to the touch, raw. He did not remember saying anything to her. What skin of hers he could touch, her arm and hand, was dry like powder. Yet the room—a corner of the ICU, no one near her, again the darkness, darkness at the corners lighting only in the center of the frame—the room and the darkness itself were loud with his anger and his good-bye. She knew he was angry—perhaps that, and not death, was what frightened her so, to depart without forgiveness. She had committed a series of crimes in raising him and now was committing a last one in leaving him before he was grown.

And when he got the call, from that same kind doctor at two in the morning, phoning his grandparents' house where George was staying as if in vigil, the doctor said he was sorry, and George had said, Thank you, thank you for all you've done. When the doctor said finally that she was dead, relief filled him like light, a relief so encompassing and powerful he was shocked by it, shocked by what seemed to him its naked immorality, which made him feel ashamed. But not sufficiently ashamed to dampen the feeling, to put a halt to this overwhelming relief.

The pieties of her dismissal from the world—the wakes (afternoon and evening), the funeral, the party after the funeral, all the bullshit about how much she loved him. She loved me all right, he wanted to say. Instead, good Episcopalian boy, he smiled, he said thank you, he said, to all of them, You're kind, she spoke of you, yes, she liked you a good deal, she admired you, yes, thank you, she was a remarkable woman, yes. One of the village elders said to him, Well, I know there was some trouble between you at the end but none of that matters now. But wait, actually it rather did matter . . . George nodded, half smiled at the man. You're kind, thank you. Thank you. If I need anything, yes. Yes, I know, thank you. You still feel her spirit, I think I know what you mean. She was full of life, yes.

His sexuality. Her. On the sofa, leg crossed, one tucked under her, the other with shoe dangling, the evening's first drink with its lipstick crescent below the rim. The cigarettes similarly stained.

And then his bloody aunt on the phone after she died. *Your father, I'm telling you, he was a saint. With the lions in the den he wouldn't have had it worse. Nothing could be worse than what he put up with from that woman—you don't know, dear, you'll never know. She was your mother, God bless I shouldn't say, of course you love her. But what he put up with was* the worst. *The. Worst. More than any man should even have to imagine. She couldn't control herself, or she wouldn't. He stayed with her for you. He did it for you. Until he died.*

Of course George doubted this. His father had stayed with her because she was an erotic addiction. So there it stood: this salad of the forbidden and the catastrophic that was his sexuality.

He thought of Anna frequently, mainly when he was not involved with anyone, wondering where she was and what she was doing. She lingered in him in the way of a religious idea from one's youth, a sense of faith that, while not practiced, one never quite abandons.

14

For Anna the hole left by George was more ragged, like a sudden tear in a skin of steel. She took a job that summer as a paralegal, met a couple of unreliable and handsome young men—one she found in line, buying sheets in Gimbels on East 86th Street, his were navy blue, she should have known to avoid him—got a roommate, lost a roommate, got another, somehow managed to live peaceably with the second one, and the autumn passed. She went home for the minimal two days at Thanksgiving and again at Christmas, got through the winter, and in springtime met a boy, a year younger, still an undergraduate, who thought for a short time he was in love with her.

The affair began in April and ended that August, 1980, just after the middle of the month, on a night that happened every year, when one felt summer break—air gone soft suddenly, without its previous brutality. Anna, out on the street, after the human heat and smoke and close quarters of a party she'd been at, accompanied by this boy, this young man, this future success, one of those upper-middle-class white boys whose lives are written on their faces, who will have the same haircut at fifty as they had at twenty, his name was Evan, and having escaped that room, she found herself willing for a moment to call the weather, the evening itself, kind, though she knew it wasn't. She and Evan were walking. The Young Businessman as she called him: he had an off-sequence semester left still to complete in college though he was her age—he'd taken two years off to work in France, la-di-da—another few months before he would graduate and commence his Young Businessman life. There had been no Young Businessmen, it seemed to her, four and three and even two years ago: So where had they all come from?

Her feelings for him had burned through the hard cured wood of desire and faced now the moist green facts; almost a relief, he was about to end it. After they escaped the party they rejected the subway for the sweetness of the cool air. She could feel him calculating there beside her. She pushed back her hair, which smelled like cigarettes. For almost half an hour they walked, out of the Village, into Chelsea, along Sixth Avenue through the grim 30s and 40s, not talking much, finally stopping to sit on the stone ledge of a reflecting pool in front of one of the silver towers across from Rockefeller Center. Time & Life Building.

Well, there you go, she said, that covers it.

What? he said.

She gestured at the steel Helvetica letters that stood over the nearest entrance. *Time*, she said. *Ampersand. Life*. Covers the gamut of possible discourse.

Oh, he said. Yeah.

Sometimes hitting his intellect was like running your small car into the side of an elk. He came from out west, where irony baffled.

And he was nervous, she could see.

The pool they sat in front of ran the width of the building along its Sixth Avenue side, separating the humped swirl-patterned plaza from the building's plate-glass façade. The traffic lights along the avenue reflected in the black liquid like flames on the water, except every few minutes they turned from red to green. She and Evan had walked a long way, more than two miles. He had asked her just now if she was all right, with her nice shoes, and she'd said yes, she was fine, which was true for once; they were that rare thing, comfortable shoes, sandals with little wedge heels.

Let's sit down anyway, he'd said. The formality gave him away.

Off and on there had been a slight breeze, and it rose now. She wore a pale pink dress with a gathered waist and thin straps, like a sundress but a little dressier than that, and over it a small white cotton sweater that she'd draped around her neck, sleeves hanging down in front of her like the two ends of a man's necktie come undone. People had begun, after the disco and preppie phases, to dress on a regular basis to go out, to parties, even for movies and a drink after, a fact she both enjoyed and was, politically speaking, wary of: it boded ill for justice. Her dark hair fell behind her, cascading into the sweater's folds and at one point along the way he had reached over and flipped some of her hair out from amid the sweater. Where had that been? In front of the coffee shop near 14th Street? Crossing 23rd? The skirt's stiff cotton bustled upward when she sat; she smoothed it against her legs. This might have been the gesture of a happier woman, of a woman luxuriating in the little self-deceptions that accompanied falling in love. But it was not that kind of night, not a night when this man was endeavoring to make her happy, when he was doing his best to make her laugh, when she was waiting to see what he would do, or what she would do, as she was a woman who never knew ahead of time what she would do. Looking back across her growing history of desirable men, she never understood what, aside from the unpredictable tides of lust, made her say no one night, yes another. So far, her instincts had proved more or less trustworthy. They were not all good men, not by any means, but there were no really awful nights, a fact for which, on hearing the stories of her friends, she felt grateful. This night, however, was shaping up badly. She sat, she pushed down the skirt, and considered, in a moment of solidarity, all the women that had been here before, generations of them, sitting somewhere on the avenue late at night with a man, while he readies himself to get rid of her. Thousands of them there must be, tens of thousands! It's a long tradition, like sewing your first hem, baking your first pie: getting dumped near the end of summer.

You are incredibly valuable to me, Evan said.

Oh no, she said. *No no no, please.*

No, really, he said.

You *have to* be able to do better than that. I went out with you.

What's wrong with saying you're a valuable person in my life?

Besides that it's a lame cliché? she said. I mean, okay. How valuable? Can you give me a figure? A year's starting salary, maybe? Do you have another cigarette? I'm at least that valuable.

He gave her the box. She took one out. He struck the match, she leaned over and inhaled, and then sat straight again and blew the smoke above them.

Thank you, she said.

I'm not an ogre, he said.

No, you're not an ogre.

She had to struggle with herself not to say aloud what passed through her mind, that ogres were more interesting than he was.

Relationships, he said, then stopped.

Yes? she said. Go on? I'm dying to hear your wisdom on this topic.

You don't have to make this so difficult.

Oh yes, I do, she said. That's my job. If you don't go home bloody and in tatters I haven't done justice to the occasion.

Relationships have to progress, he said. They have to change and go somewhere new, and where ours will go next, I can't go, not now.

Indeed, she said. And when is Marianne coming back from California, exactly? This woman Marianne was doubly a bane; George had gone out with her for almost a year when they were juniors. A visibly sexy woman but, it was widely known, difficult, demanding, subject to fits. Why did men go for this?

Evan didn't answer her spoken question or her silent one. Anna smoked her cigarette. She was remembering certain scenes. On an earlier evening, about a month past, he had actually wept; she'd told him she planned to end their little affair, since he had another girlfriend with whom he had actually at least once, by his own admission, discussed marriage—a fact that he couldn't deny was fundamentally dooming. They *talked on the phone*, for god's sake, two or three times a week. But oh oh oh, he cried: he loved her so much. What an asshole. Anna didn't believe for a minute he loved her. He cried because he didn't have the balls to tell the girl across the continent about his wandering soul. Or his wandering other parts. Now she was looking at his hair, which was thinning. He knew this himself, certainly, but she was oddly pleased by the fact that she'd never mentioned it, never indicated that she'd noticed it. Her restraint now made her feel noble. She had cried too, of course, how could she not join him? She actually did love him after all, a little; or at least she had been in the pleasurable high dive of convincing herself that she loved him, even while she had seen clearly that he would never belong to her, and that she found distasteful certain aspects of his being. The whole mess was the usual idiocy that one believed one had outgrown, but never did; it was embarrassing to remember, and the embarrassment made her suddenly so angry she could have slapped him in the face. Then it passed. At least she had the satisfaction of being able to situate her own tears in the universe of the authentic: he had cried because he couldn't have her, and she had cried because she was causing him this sadness. And of course she had backed down; and of course the backing down had been arousing and voluptuous. They lay in bed for hours after, talking, each returning to the other's body, taking from the supply of erotic satisfaction that had almost been withdrawn. Even at the time she must have known he was a complete fake. Here was a new rule: the moment, the *second* that you sensed something fake, that you smelled some kind of fakery, that was it—know the man is a fake. Continue fucking him or whatever but never be fooled again.

She exhaled a gust of smoke. I mean it, she said. When is she coming back? Tomorrow? The next day?

No, he said. I don't know exactly. Like ten days, two weeks.

Leaving yourself a nice gap there, aren't you? Time for a little pussy in between.

Oh Christ, he said.

I know how you think. That's exactly how you think.

Whatever you say.

Let me ask you something, she said.

I'm going to break up with her, he said.

You're probably not, but that's not what I want to ask you, she said.

I just have to do it in my own time, in my own way.

Yeah, yeah, sure. Whatever. She's a ballbuster, I have reason to know. But no—here's what I'm asking—you're going to vote for Reagan, aren't you?

This stopped him for a moment.

What do you mean? he finally said.

What do you think I mean? she said. I'm asking—are you going to vote for Reagan or not?

Christ, I don't know, he said.

Yes, you do, she said. You're going to vote for Reagan. I'd stake my life on it.

It's not like Carter is so great, he said. He's incompetent. The Iran thing is a total fiasco. The economy is in shambles.

Of course, of course, the problem is Carter, she said. You have to save the country from Carter by supporting a barely sentient, third-rate, right-wing actor. It makes total sense. A man who, to the degree you can credit his intellect with actually holding on to something close to a conviction, believes in spreading wealth among the wealthy, where it belongs. He believes in strength—as in, I have the money, I buy the gun, I shoot you, I win. You know, I'm at peace with this little breakup here. I agree with you, we can't go on. You're released. You're free to go. *Vaya con Dios.*

Anna, he said.

She dropped her cigarette onto the sidewalk, put her pretty shoe on it and firmly ground it out.

What?

What we have—

Had, you mean? Briefly? *Very* briefly?

What we have, it can't be touched by things like politics.

Oh my *fucking* God, she said. That's the most idiotic thing you have ever said. And believe me—it has competition. It *is* politics. *You* are politics. For instance, you know how, at base, you're a good person, but you have no courage at all, and so will always choose to be a self-serving bastard? *That's* politics—

You're just being nasty now, he said.

You haven't seen nasty, she said. Now, with Reagan, you *know* you're not going to have to fight against the social grain anymore to be a self-serving bastard. Because this culture and Reagan and his crew will open the doors for you, they'll make it easy and rewarding, they'll market assholes so they look like patriots and scholars. And so the moment has come in which your inevitable next step has been presented to you. I wanted to know if you're taking it. And you are.

At this he looked down; he took her hand and squeezed it, as if they were in this together, as if they faced together some shared grief, the loss of a grandparent or the sudden, dire illness of a dear friend. She couldn't get over it, how false he was at this moment, and how much he believed in his own falseness. She saw suddenly, with a forceful clarity, how successful he would be, what a nice life he would have. And what would become of *her*? How was *she* to function in a world in which these fucking guys would thrive? She supposed they had always thrived.

She pulled her hand from his. I want another cigarette, she said.

They walked again for a bit and then she said they should get a cab and go home.

≡

THEIR DRIVER, WHO had the look, Anna thought, of Frank Zappa meets the doorman on *Rhoda*—even though you never saw the doorman on *Rhoda* you knew this was what he looked like—started chatting as soon as they'd given their twin destinations, first his place and then hers, two blocks farther uptown. A talker. Then he held a fat joint in the open window of the bulletproof divider:

Do you guys get high? he said.

Yeah, sure, Anna said. I mean, I will. I don't know about him. He's voting for Reagan.

No shit? the driver said. He turned around—didn't use the mirror but did the full turn—to look at Evan before turning back to the road.

You're voting for that dickwad?

I don't know *who* I'm voting for, Evan said. Maybe I'll vote for Anderson.

Casper the friendly fuckin' ghost, you mean, the driver said. Well, whatever turns you on, man.

He lit the joint, inhaled, and passed it over the seat for them to take from him, which Anna did. She pulled in a short toke, to get the feel of it, then a larger one and held it down. She handed it to Evan.

When the driver blew his smoke out it curled from his open window and blew directly into Anna's. Evan handed the joint back over the seat, coughing slightly.

That fuck is going to win, the cabdriver said. They were in Central Park, alone with no other cars on the Park Drive, rattling through the crossing lights both red and green. It occurred to Anna that if they got stopped they'd all go to jail. That would put a crimp in Evan's career plans.

People are just stupid enough to elect that guy, the cabbie said. They all think he can make them rich. I mean, all the white people.

While he was talking he waved the joint around like a baton. Anna leaned across Evan, who was looking glum and silent, and poked her head into the driver's little window. She smiled at him and gently took the joint from his fingers.

Good dope, she said.

Yeah, he said. I got it from this American Indian dude. I can't remember what tribe he is, Apache or some shit. Anyway, a cool guy. Sells some prime weed. He's got these sinsemilla sticks that look like little veggie kabobs, man, you just want to eat them.

Cool, Anna said. She pulled on the joint and wondered why she'd said *cool* in that way, as if she were seventeen and living in Santa Cruz. Some sudden reversion to high school stoner-speak: one more social pose for the repertoire. She pulled herself over onto Evan's legs so she could continue leaning into the opening—she put herself onto Evan's lap, essentially, and it felt good, which annoyed her. His hand was on her hip, keeping her balanced; slowly it moved to the top of her thigh. She opened her legs slightly, because of the pot, because the weight and warmth of his hand there made her want to, because she was curious to see what he'd do, and because now that she didn't care about him, unlike an hour ago, it was quite possible to fuck him. She pulled herself out of the driver's window with the joint; Evan's hand moved inward. She took a second hit, turned herself sideways, leaned into Evan's face, and started blowing the smoke slowly into his mouth. Grudgingly his lips opened; she was staring at his cheek, clean shaven, as it always was and as it always would be, world without end, amen. Imagine that. For the entire rest of his utterly predictable life. She wanted to do something to him: she didn't know what. She blew the last of the smoke into his eyes.

Aaagh, he said. Stings.

Serves you right, she said.

The problem with getting high is all the thinking. Why had she let herself be smitten by this child? He was certainly handsome. He was ambitious. He was decent in bed, athletic and durable if not terrifically sensitive. Then he had cried. That about wrapped it up: he was intellectually not her equal and tonight, in particular, she could see—even better, now that she was stoned—the bedrock cowardice that would dominate his life. So it—they—wouldn't have lasted even if it *had* lasted, and all her fantasies once again were dried and flat, ready to be folded and put away with the pile of other bad romances and embarrassing hopes that she was collecting for her trousseau. Plus—his hand had stopped well short of the goal line. What a putz.

She looked him in the eye.

You're scared of me now? she said.

No, he said. He gave her an unconvincing smile, a basic unit from the interpersonal tool kit.

Sure, she said. She pulled up her skirt and pushed his hand down right onto her wet spot. There you go—he seemed to be able to figure it out from there.

By the time the cab veered out of the park at 110th, there

was no doubt she would go upstairs with him. After the joint was done she had turned herself again on his lap to face front, leaned back against his chest, and, pulling his head toward hers, managed to get her lips onto the corners of his. He had begun to kiss her, and she had taken his hand and put it again between her legs. They made out in this way, her squirming in his lap, feeling him hard beneath her, keeping her hand over his as he pushed it up her leg and massaged her. He kissed her neck. Zappa the driver was glancing at them in the rearview as he drove, and really, who wouldn't? Once or twice she stared right back. Her brazenness amazed her. It was new.

When they pulled up to Evan's place on 106th Street, half-way down the block to the river, she hopped from his lap and straightened her clothes.

Cancel the second stop, she said through the acrylic opening. Evan had taken out his wallet.

I'll pay, she said. He looked at her and put the wallet away; she tugged a twenty from her tiny bag and got out of the car on the wrong side and went to the driver's window.

Thank you so much for a wonderful ride, she said, blew him a little kiss.

Hey, he said. No problem. The ride was four seventy-five and she tipped him five plus the quarter. She had never tipped a cabbie anything close to five before. She was stoned, seductive, angry and rash. Evan stood on the sidewalk watching. She felt like an assassin.

In the elevator she pushed into him, put her hand on his pants, kissed him. This is new, he said. She detected his nervousness and so continued, amused, even going a little harder. His face looked like something made from dough—he was afraid.

Up in his bedroom, she executed it all ruthlessly; she pleased him ruthlessly, straddling him, running her body down along him, letting her breasts fall against him, her hair, moving downward, taking him in her mouth briefly, feeling his breath suck in, feeling him rise—funny the way men almost levitated when you did that. Ruthlessly, she provided this tandem of brief pleasures while he lay there, and then, ruthlessly, she fucked him—that phrase *ain't no pleasure but meanness* flicking through her mind. He seemed so small, so insignificant to her, even while he lay beneath her and was inside her. She pushed down roughly on him and she thought: So this is what it's about, this is what it is to feel powerful, this is what it is to feel like a man: what one needed, to experience power, was to find an advantage and use it, to abandon the idea of equality, or justice, or love. In the flush of that thought she began moving much faster on top of him, as if she were a guy, and her orgasm rose up strong and fast from a deep heat in the middle of her, up her thighs, down from her abdomen, usually this happened slowly and often it hung there, not arriving or sometimes arriving, but not here, not now: she came in two short explosions, fell upon him for a moment, and then she rolled off him. He followed her, as if he would now get on top, but she shook her head, pushed him back and rose from the bed.

What? he said. Clearly, he was shocked.

So was she, though in a more pleasant way. She quickly had her underpants on and then was hooking her bra. She could feel that her chest and cheeks were still flushed. She was breathing hard.

Whew, she said. What a strange, unreliable gift orgasm is.

He glared at her, an angry disbelieving expression—she

would remember it later with a trace of sympathy but for now it only annoyed her, that he still, after his performance, had expectations. She lifted her pink dress above her head and let it fall over her body like a curtain coming down at the end of a play.

And you're just leaving? he said. He sounded like a bratty twelve-year-old boy, and the particular note in his voice was so familiar that she knew, though she'd not acknowledged it before, that he frequently sounded like a bratty twelve-year-old boy.

Her little sweater, her shoes, her bag: all there. She would straighten her hair in the elevator.

I'm not *just* leaving, she said.

I guess I'll call you, he said.

Don't, she said.

And then she walked out.

≡

In the outer hall she stood, slightly nauseated, waiting for the elevator in the dim landlord light. Ah. Here was the flip side of power: isolation. She felt as if she were in a capsule of some kind, autonomous and untouchable. Power was a disease—it cut you off, like leprosy. What a vista of solitude. Until now, even to be aware of such a state had been completely outside her nature, not to mention her convictions, which were flimsier things. She was utterly still, almost frozen, feeling herself change. All the narrative trajectories she'd sketched for her life—sexually, romantically, professionally, even spiritually—pointed to some relatively nice ending that as of this minute she didn't believe in anymore. Maybe she would again tomorrow. Maybe not. Maybe from here on everything would be different and she would remember this night, this sex, this emptying moment in the hall, as the point when everything was altered, when her life went off in a new and not necessarily better direction. Now—here it was, right in front of her, making her dizzy, this *change*, she felt it, a part of her, but also not, something alien—this was the unmooring of American life. Now, anything was possible: any form of false promise, any form of blindness, any form of savagery, destruction, cruelty or ruin. And why not? After all, it was the beginning of a new decade.

|| PART TWO ||

all exit in silence

15

Among other innovations the new decade introduced was the practice of New York City landlords driving people out of their apartments with dogs. It was the rents starting to climb. Koch was mayor; there were tax abatements for creating luxury apartments out of run-down SROs and now everybody loved real estate. People a year or two out of college actually *talked* about real estate as if it were world history or Chinese art.

Which made life more difficult. By 1981 Anna wanted to live on her own, she had lost her cheap rental on 108th when the building was sold, moved in with a couple of semi-friends from Barnard. She was working at *Newsweek* as a researcher, she shouldn't need to live in a share apartment. Yet suddenly everything decent was, minimum, six or seven hundred a month. She found a place, finally, a small one-bedroom on 98th Street, just east of Broadway, rent-stabilized, old landlord with old lady wife as his secretary on East 42nd Street, she went in to sign the lease, the old man's hand shook over the signature lines. It was a little noisy, an open kitchen set off from the medium-sized living room by a counter; the living room faced west and the small bedroom north, at the back of the building, just higher than the buildings behind her, just higher too than the ailanthus tree that was almost six stories tall and that despite its aesthetic poverty she came to love; nice light, pleasant light, not the kind that would heat the place up too much. It was five twenty-five a month, a bargain but almost half her take-home pay, which was insane, but it made her happy. Two blocks from the subway. And there on Broadway was Fowad Discount Clothing store, with the racks of crazy polyester blouses and skirts out on the sidewalk, no, not *forward*, but *Fowad*; and Comidas Criollas y Chinas, the Chinese-Cuban place for rice and beans and maduros. There were a slew of these on Broadway: La Tacita de Oro, La Bella China, a Citibank on the corner of 96th with six new cash machines. She loved cash machines with their crisp twenties and tried to have balances allowing her to withdraw from them but sometimes she didn't. She bought herself a modest stereo at the electronics place on the west side of Broadway. If she'd needed a washing machine or refrigerator she could have had that too, along with televisions, fans, air conditioners, all at 99th. At 100th Street the renovated Metro Theater, former porn hole that even the guys she knew hadn't gone near, now a pretty little revival house with seats rising two levels, elegant old décor repainted and restored. Every Wednesday a Japanese directors double feature: Ozu, Mizoguchi, Kurosawa. At 95th Street the Thalia—another revival house (go ten blocks south she'd hit a third, the New Yorker, then the Regency), the Thalia the most rugged of them all, so ancient some thought it predated the medium of film. Holes in the seats and a curious construction in which the floor sank from rear to mid-theater then started rising again, with seats in front higher than those behind. It worked in that you were looking uphill at the screen so no one in front of you actually got in the way. She learned never to let her hands wander under the seats. Gum of Neolithic era and yesterday too, layered on the steel seat bottoms. That sense of encroaching human fluids. She went by herself but wished she didn't have to. She saw *Paris, Texas* there, and came out and walked forty blocks south to Columbus Circle before taking a slow bus back home, just to have time to absorb the thing.

And at the Embassy a *special* (meaning scandalous and semi-forbidden) screening of Oshima's *In the Realm of the Senses*, which disturbed her and then, for a time, obsessed her. Certain images—the oral sex at the beginning, among others, she wanted to make a man come in that deliberate, quiet, almost cold-blooded yet servile way—such images clung and appeared in her mind's eye throughout a typical workday. She read what she could find about Sada Abe, on whom the story was based—she'd killed her lover via erotic asphyxiation, cut off his penis and scrotum and carried them around with her in her kimono. This violence was not the appeal—nor was the obsessional love that drove Abe—but the bloodlust was, and that mysterious abasement, which builds up as an annihilating power. She wanted to know what it was, to feel that kind of obsession, that kind of erotic pull, enough to make you lose your sense of self. Like a surfer longing for the largest possible wave, though it would swamp him, possibly kill him. She didn't believe she could actually be induced to do such—she was too proud. But for a time it fascinated her. The men she was meeting, young white men, did not have that pull; they were weak magnets, all wearing crisp white broadcloth shirts, hoping their crisp white broadcloth ships would come in. What had happened to the dangerous ones, shirtless, dirty, untrustworthy, alive as fallen wires snapping at the curbside?

She thought about the wires snapping at the curbside. Good snake imagery, girl. Not surprising. And she could listen to the Clash and Talking Heads all day. She needed to go downtown and find the punks, but she rarely ventured there and never came home with anyone. Such skinny boys.

≡

A RECESSION CAME and lingered into '82, more than a year, and for a long portion of it George was living on forty dollars a week—which he got for one day of work in a photographer's studio—just office work and bank statements and the like; the photographer had no work either. George had, starting at age twenty-one, two hundred dollars a month from his mother's estate, which was from the sale of the house and some stock, and which just about covered his rent and utilities. In the strange heat of an early spring, there was a transit strike. He'd bounced through a couple of short-term sublets and now without his own place he was staying with a girl on Staten Island, her name was Jennifer. It was a miracle for a man of his age never to have gone out with a Jennifer before, there were so many, but she was the first. She went by Jenn, which was unusual then, a new name shortening for a new decade. She had an apartment in St. George, a pretty apartment in a bad neighborhood, a five-minute fast walk to the ferry, three and a half at a manageable run, he'd go in on the car level from the parking lot and not break stride as they were closing the gates. Every single time he rode that boat—especially when he sat on the deck outside and watched the water and the passing Liberty statue, which he almost always did—he thought of his acid night with Anna, her body and hair and lips in that wind, and the fallen tree, and the death of Jeffrey Goldstein.

And there was the statue, the muscular lady; and there were the two monoliths. No matter what time of day or night, this set of monuments, one statue and two towers, heralded one's arrival to Manhattan or saluted one's departure from it, isolated indomitable facts of the harbor geography: one verdigris and forever alight by candescence manmade or natural; the other two lustrous slabs thrust more than a quarter mile into the sky, twin statements of absolute black when in darkness, tremendously grave; or, on overcast days, leaden gray, like the water; or, on lighter days, silver; and, sometimes, in limpid sunlight, magically reflective in pale blue, turning pink or pulsing magenta at sunset. Like the harbor itself, changeable but the same. Water all around. The entire rest of the density of buildings, which is to say, the city, was like a unitary *other* fact, a massive stone and glass palisade. The ferry, on its way to Manhattan, just after it passed the Statue of Liberty, tacked forty or fifty degrees starboard to slide between the Battery and Governors Island and nose its way into the slips of the South Ferry terminal. Sometimes he waited in the stern, abandoned by the other riders, who rushed forward and pressed like sheep at the bow, eager to disembark; and from here he looked back, past Governors Island and across the water to the old Norwegian sailor town of Red Hook in Brooklyn. The Norwegians had called it the Bitter Desert. The Dutch had given it the name that lasted, after its outcropped land and the red clay that formed it—but the bitter desert it remained, just possibly the toughest section of New York City, a rank contested by certain areas of the South Bronx, parts of Bushwick and Bedford-Stuyvesant, and a series of postapocalyptic corners on Lenox Avenue in Harlem where flames burned in ash cans and ghostly young men like Kurtz's acolytes at the nightfire moved through the shadows in a gangly dance, selling dope. All these Dutch-named villages. You could feel this history downtown, where the place had been settled. The log pilings and wooden walls that the ferry banged itself on, slowing itself, stopping, creaking its way to the dock, might have dated from colonial times. If he were looking from the bow he'd see approaching the trimmed tops of the pilings, wooden and haphazard, mossed and algae'd, scattered like teeth in the gray-green water. Some of these pilings supported the plank barricades mounted with tires, which jutted out at uneven angles from the beveled edge of Manhattan, the thirteen-mile plinth on which modernity had been built—all this cheap old wood added a homey touch.

They lived together, he and Jenn, for four months on Staten Island before he found himself a place on Henry Street, just south of the Lower East Side, not far from Chinatown and the fish market. Before that, when the subways and buses were out, that near-two-week strike, the ferries still ran (different contract, different union) so he came into town and walked to the job near the Flatiron, for his forty-dollar, eight-hour day.

All those other days with Jenn in the hot apartment on Staten Island. She worked three nights as a waitress at a bar in St. George so they were both home most days: she was supposed to be working on her art—she made paper, and from it, collages of large size and rough surfaces. He was supposed to be writing: what, he didn't know. Magazine and newspaper pitches. But mostly they read and fucked and listened to music, played backgammon—whenever he took a late lead, knocked her out and blocked her return, and then doubled the cube, she threw the board off the bed. No matter how many times she did this he never altered his strategy. It was a contest, as was so much between them. They went for walks down to the water in search of a cool breeze. She'd been a stripper for a while in '77 and '78, lined her eyes with kohl, and she liked clubs; she pulled him into punk and new wave—he was an altogether too Caucuasian boy from Connecticut and in this scene he'd known only Patti Smith. And, by then, Blondie and Talking Heads. Somehow he had seen the New York Dolls in '74 but wasn't taken, which she thought, given the golden opportunity, was criminal. She got him listening to Iggy Pop and the Ramones (he got the Ramones, he told her: they sounded like the Beach Boys put through a grinder) and the lesser-known Bowie stuff, the Sex Pistols and other bands he never remembered the names of; and if she was feeling rich from a night of good tips they'd meet late and take the ferry to go to CBGB or the Mudd Club, where he always felt out of place.

She was lean, spikey, painted and inked, she loved to dance and was his short-lived pass to such venues; she sweated openly and profusely and liked to embrace him and kiss him in the heat and wet of it. He tried to like this; he tried to yield to the body-pleasure of it but never quite managed it. Sweat in bed was fine but on the dance floor it was testimony to a wordless erotic place that she had gotten to and he hadn't. She was long-limbed and sinewy, her body was a topography of clean lines, small breasted with sharp nipples, a strong, alluring torso and ass, muscled legs as from a futurist mural; her leanness was such that, in sex, everything stood out when she came, tendons like taut ropes down her neck and between her torso and arms, muscles of her shoulders and chest and abdomen delineated, flexed, adamant, while she gripped the sheets on either side hard enough to put small tears into them, leaving a few of her sheets looking as if they'd been attacked by chickens. Sometimes instead her nails went into his back, an intense pain that in such a sexual-pleasure state felt like a distant sweet scream. Later it would hurt. She curled upward and scissored her legs tight against him. Almost always three growling grunts. Four was an accomplishment. Hell, it was all an accomplishment. It was with Jenn that he began to understand that there was a kind of miracle in bodies, in their uniqueness and their gifts. Hers, at these moments, was magnificent and frightening. The muscles of her vagina fluttered on his cock with surprising strength, massaged the semen efficiently out of him as they would one day urge outward an unsuspecting child. The sex was explosive, it had an angry edge to it, knocking bones, it felt as if both he and she were picking a fight, looking to get back at the other for something, to avenge some hurt, to find recompense for some valuable item that had been taken from them. As if each held a grudge, not against the other but against all women and all men respectively; against sex. Against cocks and cunts. He would flip her over and she would strike back at him repeatedly, and kick, really try to hurt him, but once he learned to keep going, to do battle and overwhelm her, she would then arch her back and push her cunt upward to be fucked. The first time, he'd stopped.

What did you stop for, she said.

I thought something was wrong. You were kicking me.

Fight for it, she said. I want you to fight for it.

She kicked him in the leg again. It hurt. She tried to get away from him, he pulled her back. He fought for it. He was much larger than she was, though he had to avoid her legs, which were like powerful hammering machines. It frightened him to subdue her; he felt an anger and a taste for violence that he had buried very early in his life, expressed only two or three times, the last when he'd thrown his mother off him and broken her collarbone.

Later she said, You know what a safe word is?

I've heard the term, he said. She was looking at him.

He said, What's your safe word?

Einstein, she said.

Einstein, he said. Tasting it.

Take off your belt, she said.

So, as he told his friends, *that* was good. He did not say: it was a flickering of good interrupted by his fear, his sense of imminent nausea in expressions of power. He'd shoved her down once and she'd grunted and then said you want to bruise me don't you, you want to leave marks—this had frozen him, stopped him dead.

Aside from the sex, they shared minimal points of contact. She was looking for something, some place in the downtown scene with loud art and raw poetry and multi-pierced tattoo glamour that was already out there but she couldn't quite hook up with, not with her undogmatic collages that invited you see in their textures and shapes what you wanted to see, not with her particular talents and certainly not alongside him, with his khakis and many worn blue oxford cloth shirts. (She'd counted after they did a big laundry. Eight, and she chased one out from under the bed, still dirty. Nine. How can you have nine of the same shirt? she asked him. How can they all be worn, none new?) And not on Staten Island. Her separation from what she wanted to be and where she wanted to be put her adrift in general, in relation to her own life and soon enough, specifically, from him. He was not brokenhearted.

Your problem, she told him on parting, is you don't *want* anything.

I want to survive, he said.

Some years later, near the end of the decade, he ran into

her, she was living in a giant building in Kips Bay, the ink still showing on the back of one arm but she wore none of the metal; she'd had a kid, was married to some guy in marketing. That's what they all had ended up doing—that was the compromise all the women had made with the '80s, with infectious disease and even more infectious consumerism, with real estate prices missile-shot into the ozone hole: they had married some marketing guy. In order that they should spawn more marketing guys and the career-halted women who married them, and the species should in this way go on. At the time he was trying to avoid the knowledge that he too was by then, in essence, a marketing guy. There was still a bit of sizzle, burnt ions, in the air between them; but again as before, though he could recognize it now in minutes instead of months, there was that strong sense that whatever she had going on, he wasn't going to stay interested.

16

He thought, he'd long thought, given his history, that he would never marry. But of course he did marry. In the end almost everyone does, at least once. It lasted eight years, as a marriage, far longer as a friendship and a locus of devotion. They had a son. His wife's full name was Marina Schneider, forebears Mexican on her mother's side, German on her father's. He met her because one night on the verge of summer he went out to Queens to visit his uncle.

This uncle, Ken, was his father's childless older brother, lifelong celibate or who knew, maybe he'd been gay. George thought of Ken as his only living relation, aside from his maternal grandparents, who were in a home in Connecticut and not in touch, but it wasn't really true. Ken lived in Queens and represented for George the working-class roots that his mother and her parents had always abhorred. Besides him, though, there was a sister, in Ohio, whom George had last seen when he was three. There were cousins via the sister, cousins he'd never met. The siblings had basically been blown apart by the early deaths of their parents and by George's father's marriage to his mother, who made no show of affection or regard for her in-laws. But early in June one day he got a card from Ken, forwarded from the Columbia alumni office, George was shocked they knew where he lived. *Maybe got a summer job for you come and see me, Signed, Your Uncle Ken.* Below that a phone number and an address out by Flushing Meadows. What was that—George had never contemplated it before—putting *Signed* before you signed? Wasn't the signature itself the sign that you'd signed?

It was strange but not bad to see the old guy. He lived just off College Point Boulevard. When George arrived, Ken said, Make yourself a sandwich, I got some bologna in the kitchen. The kind with the olives in it. Bread and mayo, mustard. You take mustard? You're sophisticated now, I know. I got the Grey Poupon, it's all there. Look in the icebox.

George made two sandwiches, which, when Ken turned his down, George ate both of. They watched the Mets for a while.

How are things around here? George said.

This is what you asked: the murder rate approaching two thousand a year in New York, wherever you were the first thing you wondered about were your odds of surviving the place.

Lotta Chinamen moving in, said Ken.

They were between innings. Vigorous singing ad for the same beer George and Ken were drinking. *My beer is Rheingold the dry beer, think of Rheingold whenever you buy beer.* Gold drawn from the River Rhine, indeed. Then brewed in the Bronx.

Yeah? said George. Chinamen, huh? It was a word George associated with *Cannery Row*, where it was used in abundance and where he'd first learned it, at age fourteen or so, when he loved Steinbeck. His mother's family, of course, never used such language. They did worse.

Don't get me wrong, Ken said. I got no problem with the

Chinamen. The Japs, that's another story. They tried to kill me. Every day. And they were good at it.

Ken had been a pipefitter for the Navy, stationed in Honolulu in 1941 when the Japanese bombed Pearl Harbor. He'd helped build the base at Okinawa after the war. He'd spent more than four years in the Pacific. For his last tour—he'd signed up for three in all—he was sent to the American sector in Germany, to help rebuild the shipyard at Hamburg.

You can tell the difference, George said. Japanese from Chinese. You're a man of the world.

Oh, no, Ken said. I just assume they're all Chinamen. Smooth sailing from there.

George laughed at this, which made Ken crack up too.

Smoooooth sailing, he repeated and showed his yellow teeth and a dark strip of missing molars on the left side. The gums of old men laughing; they look like children in a horror film.

He said: I mean, why look for trouble?

You should have been a diplomat, George said.

The old man's place, three rooms plus kitchen on the parlor floor of a clapboard rowhouse, smelled like an old man's place, sour, medicinal, needing air. That *fine tang of faintly scented urine* as with Bloom's breakfast kidney. He'd told George over the phone he had asbestosis, a lung disease, emphysema, probably lung cancer too. So the Japanese weren't his killers; Johns Manville was.

≡

THE METS GAME on television. The stadium's glow was visible over the rooftops outside, to the north and a bit west of them, maybe eight blocks away, maybe ten, and they could hear the crowd roar in real time a couple of seconds before they heard it on the television—when there was a hit or a long fly ball, it went roar—crack of bat—roar.

That's weird, George said.

What?

The way you hear the crowd before you see what they're roaring about and then you hear it again on the delay on television.

I can't hear it anymore, I'm too deaf. You can hear it?

Yeah, George said. You want to go over there? I could call a car service. We could probably sit down field level for a few bucks.

Ken stared at the television. I have a lot of trouble breathing when I walk, he said. I get real tired. I got congestive heart failure. Not enough oxygen in my blood.

Where's the phone? George said.

Kitchen, Ken said. Get me another beer while you're there.

George called information from the wall phone. Flushing Meadows, he told the woman. I want a number at Shea Stadium, *not* the ticket office, please. Something like the medical or nurse or sick bay?

Operator said, Infirmary?

George: Yeah, that.

He dialed the number, a guy picked up.

Hey listen, I want to bring my uncle over there. He's got breathing problems, emphysema, he's got an oxygen tank, he can't walk very far. I'm wondering if you got a wheelchair we can use to take him to and from his seat?

Yes, they had that.

From the living room: Where's my beer?

Forget your beer, George said. I'm calling the car service.

They got to the stadium at the beginning of the fourth inning. Mets versus Phillies. Perhaps the best team in the league. Official attendance was 11,275 but there weren't 9,000 people there, a Tuesday night. Ken, set up in his wheelchair, palmed a ten over to the usher who showed them to an empty box among many other empty boxes near third base—here were the missing from the eleven thousand, season ticket holders not shown up. It had hit George as it always hit him going through the tunnel, the beauty of the game, the dazzling emerald of the field under the white lights. The smooth caramel of the infield dirt. The pop of a fastball hitting the catcher's mitt, like a musket fired off in the woods. Not far from here the British had chased Washington's army across the grassy Hempstead plains into the mists and fogs of the forests of the north shore. The British couldn't find him. Washington took the battle up to the heights of northern Manhattan then retreated farther up the Hudson. The British controlled New York thereafter and Washington's army escaped to fight another day.

Nice, Ken said, appraising field and seats. The wheelchair was folded and sat before the empty chair beside him. George sat on the aisle. Ken was a little out of breath, but not so much he didn't catch the beer vendor at first sign of his appearance.

Is it really ice cold? said Ken. The sign on the carrier which held twenty-five paper cups of beer said in all caps *ICE COLD.*

Ice cold beer here! the vendor cried out. It wasn't a real answer: more an incantation stirred by the question, in the way of a parrot responding to a familiar prompt.

Look at Schmidt, Ken said. The Philly hero was smoothing the dirt in front of him at third base.

Great player, George said.

I hate the fucking guy. Looks like Tom Selleck—who I also

hate, because he reminds me of Schmidt. He fucking kills us. *Kills* us.

Next time up Schmidt homered to left with a man on.

See what I mean? See what I mean? He fucking kills us.

Schmidt passed before them as he approached and rounded third. Fucking bum! Ken called out. Fuck you! Kraut! People looked at them. Schmidt did not. Ken coughed once, twice, then for an endless-seeming minute, gasping for breath.

I shouldn't shout, he whispered, when it was over. But fuck him, I enjoyed that.

The car service that brought them home provided an old Chrysler Imperial. In red. With a red velour interior. Ken was tired now, the walk from the stadium portals out to the car, fifty yards or so, had been an ordeal.

You want to make some quick money for five or six weeks this summer, I know a guy, Ken said when his breathing settled.

What's the job? George said.

You go around to these fairs like at churches and shit and run one of the rides. You tow the ride in, between fairs you garage it out here, my guy I think said in Elmhurst. Call him.

George wrote down the number.

≡

ANTHONY DOBRONE WAS the pal of his uncle with the ride he wanted to farm out.

It's called the Basher, Dobrone said. Kids fucking love it. Cars that go around and crash into each other. Two seats to a car they both have dummy steering wheels but the whole thing is run on cables and pinions underneath—the kids don't actually control it. The cars hit each other it seems like at random but it ain't, you can learn to track the pattern. Anyway they love it. They'll line up. You'll roll in the money.

The deal was the church fairs got twenty-five a day plus forty cents on every dollar in tickets. Dobrone paid the twenty-five dollars rent and expected profit on it. George would pay everything else, gassing and parking the car he towed the thing with, the incidentals.

Listen. Are you listening to me? Don't let these fucking mafia priests rob you with the tickets. They want to rob you with the whole ticket thing. You gotta go in with a count and be there when *they* count otherwise they cheat you.

What do you mean? George said. Go in with the count?

The kids pay you in tickets, he said.

He was the kind of guy who sounded exasperated whenever he had to explain anything.

The church or whoever, the, the, the street fair, whatever—they sell the tickets let's say it's fourteen tickets to the dollar. So to ride the Basher is seven tickets. Okay? Because basically you're charging the value of fifty cents a ride. So you get the tickets. The church or whoever cashes them out at the end of the fair. You're supposed to get sixty percent of the ticket value. So for you twenty-five tickets is a dollar. You get thirty cents on every ride they get twenty cents on every ride.

Plus they get the rent?

Plus they get the rent.

You can make money at this?

You gotta hustle. You gotta put in the hours. You run it noon to midnight that's twelve hours you're running the ride. Or ten if you take a couple breaks. Start at nine on weekends. Six seven minutes you unload and load you got eight rides an hour if you keep it moving. Let's say you average eight kids a ride—peak times is better but let's say average. That's sixty-four kids an hour. That's sixteen dollars an hour to you, to us. So ten hours a hundred sixty you make for the day, after my forty comes back it's one twenty so another twenty-four to you on your guaranteed twenty-five let's call it fifty bucks, four days two hundred dollars you can't complain.

Minus expenses, George said.

Minimal, Dobrone said. He was getting ready to go out he said, and George had to talk to him while he changed his clothes: shirt some sort of coffee brown and caramel swirly pattern with the pointed collar, tan slacks, chocolate-brown linen jacket thrown over the back of the couch. He sprayed the shirt and the crotch of the pants with Right Guard after he got them on. Pulled his leg up like a Doberman and really got the spray in there.

That's attractive, George said in a low voice.

What? Dobrone said.

I said, you look like you have a date. You got a date?

Party, Dobrone said. It'll fucking *end* with a date, know what I mean. Come with me, I'm going to take you over the garage and show you the setup and give you the keys. Did I give you the calendar? I got a copy here for you.

The setup, in a garage in a godforsaken dead industrial section of Woodside, not Elmhurst, involved a trailer hitch on which a blue-painted wooden box had been attached. Box was somewhat of a wide load, wider by six inches on each side than the big Econoline E300 van that pulled it. The van carried the generator for the electrical operation of the ride and six minicars that got attached by hooks to the contraption under the platform of the ride, a series of arms.

Dobrone said, I need you to handle the thing, I don't want

to get any fucking grease or shit on my clothes. I'll walk you through. First you gotta drop the trailer to ground level it becomes the base. These levers.

Of course George had trouble with the levers.

C'mon, Dobrone said. You're a young guy, put some fucking muscle into it.

George leaned in on it a little and the lever snapped down. It dropped the frame and lifted the wheel on that side.

Good now the other side.

The box opened to three times its width and twice its length, like an unfolding poster. There were wooden lifts, six big blue blocks essentially, same height as the lowered trailer, and he was to put these underneath the corners of the ride and halfway down each side, to stabilize it. Everything about the thing looked like trouble but not to Dobrone, who showed him how the ride opened up, how it ran. It needed gasoline for the generator. The generator started with a lawn mower/outboard motor–type pull cord. George hated these things, which always acted up when you least could afford the delay, which clamped to a stop pulling one's arm nearly out of the socket. The Econoline looked beat to shit. Three on the column. The clutch was not tight. The whole operation was going to be a fucking nightmare.

Sure, he said to Dobrone. He kept saying it: Sure, sure, to everything the guy said.

Of course the expenses were somewhat above minimal. Of course the van was trouble, of course setup was trouble, of course he almost broke his arm yanking on the uncooperative pull cord of the generator. Of course there were fewer riders than predicted. In the old Italian part of the Village, St. Carmine, they shook him down for an extra ten a day. For *security and sanitation* they said. In three days no one swept around his area and he saw no security whatsoever. The more wily unparented kids started sneaking on, he had to run them off or give up and start the ride up. By noon he was in a fury. There had been some busy points in the late morning but it was plain he wasn't going to be making the money Dobrone had predicted.

Next to his ride was a red canvas tent. Fortunes Told. When George was setting up in the morning and saw the sign he'd assumed this would be a facsimile of the usual Gypsy storefront fortune-telling operation—but then he saw the girl, who did not look the part. She looked more like Princess Caroline of Monaco. She belonged to a particular type, dark hair, bright eyes, not tall, that tended to buckle him at the knees. They had nodded at each other earlier. She spent the morning inside the tent, setting up, he guessed, but she was sitting now in a lawn chair, no customer, reading a thick paperback.

He slowed then stopped the ride and seven children filed off. He spoke to the three stowaways.

You guys got tickets for the ride you just took? he said.

You pulled my shirt, the small one said.

Yeah, because you're too small and you didn't plan to pay. So? Tickets?

Fuck you, College, the largest of them said.

Get the fuck out of here, George said.

After they'd gone, the girl next door, who was doing no business at all, said, I'm sorry for your troubles.

He looked at her. Smiled, looked back at the ride, keeping an eye, then back at her.

Thank you, he said. Unless you're making fun, he said. Then, no thank you.

I'm not making fun.

Then thank you, he said again.

He let another half dozen kids on the ride, started it up, looked back at her.

What are you reading? he said.

She held up a paperback with a simple cover, *Anna Karenina.*

Ah, he said. You can read Tolstoy and still be opposed to the patriarchy—

I can walk and chew gum at the same time too, she said.

He gives you Vronsky to hate, George said.

And Levin to love, she said. Life is complicated. He renders it that way.

Okay, George said. A pause then, which he didn't want to see expand.

So how's business? he said.

Medium bad, she said.

But you're not a bad medium.

Ha ha.

What do you do? Palms, crystal ball?

It's not like that. I look at you.

You look at me?

You, your aura. Your body. I hold your hands. You want to try it? It's fifteen tickets.

When I take a break, he said.

Sure, she said.

She raised her book and settled it again in front of her. I'm here, she said.

≡

HER NAME, SHE told him, was Marina. Her tent had candles inside, even in that heat, hanging rugs and skeins of fabric in various prints. It had a certain look.

Maybe she *was* a Gypsy.

Only a bit, she said. I'm from Seattle. I go to Yale.

You go to Yale?

A semester left, she said. I'm off sequence because of traveling. I'm doing this and a part-time office job for summer money. What about you?

I'm finished school. Sort of.

Sort of?

Incompletes.

How many?

Four.

I've heard worse.

Not at Yale, I bet.

No. Columbia guys mostly.

Ha, he said.

What?

That's where I went.

He sat, she held his hands across a table, looked at him. One of her lights was directly behind him. He watched her eyes circle his face; then stare into his own eyes; then probe at the rest of his face.

Phlebas the Phoenician, she said.

A fortnight dead, he said.

Very good. What I mean is, not that you're dead or dying but you have a lot of . . . water. Ocean. You sail?

I did, he said.

Like a lot?

Yes, it was my job, sort of. Boats were my job. In fact—a *marina* was my job.

It will be again, she said. She said it low and quickly. She looked back into his eyes. In a different way.

What else?

You're going to be rich.

I doubt that.

She ignored him. Still staring.

There's sadness, she said.

Well, that's true for everyone, isn't it.

Larger, she said.

Oh good, he said. Before now? Like in the past—or later?

Both.

Oh double good, he said. What else?

A man is going to come into your life soon. I can't see him quite. He's tall. I see a lot of *B*s.

Bees, like honeybees?

No, *B*s, the letter *B*.

Huh, he said, thinking.

That's it, she said. She dropped his hands from hers. He missed her touch instantly.

That's it? I'm gonna be a rich sad man at the boat show? With some B guy?

Well, I could say nice things about you: you're kind, you're strong.

That's good, I like that.

But mostly yeah, you're going to be a rich sad man at the boat show, she said, and laughed. That's what she called him after that.

Closing up at eleven that night: Good night, rich sad man, she said.

Good night, crackpot Gypsy, he said.

The Gypsy in her closet she told him later was a Romany woman on her father's side, married to her great-grandfather, a scandal in the family back in Bavaria.

In the evening, when she was out again, not sitting in her chair but standing—she'd added eye makeup and lipstick and put her hair up on her head, going for an exotic look for the evening crowd, swaying a little in her fluid skirt.

He'd had several full runs of the Basher; people were filing off, a new line was forming. He moved closer to her and said, Would you like to go somewhere later, get a drink or coffee?

I want dinner, she said. I mean, I'll pay for my own dinner, I didn't mean I want dinner from you—just where to go. I'm going to be very hungry and you don't want to know me long when I'm hungry and being prevented from eating.

So when they were shut down and cashed out they crossed Sixth Avenue to the corner of W. 3rd Street. What were known as the W. 4th Street courts were there, on the corner of W. 3rd, an anomaly having to do with the subway stop right there, called W. 4th, which exited onto W. 3rd and two blocks north at Waverly (which was labeled the West 8th exit), but not at W. 4th itself. *Or* W. 8th. This was New York logic.

I've always wondered about this, she said.

He explained it.

Is that clear now? he said.

Not in the least, she said.

The main idea, said George, is to confuse the shit out of people from out of town. Same with the highway signs. Completely inexplicable.

It was an undersized full court, where there was always a game going on, surrounded by high cyclone fencing—was lit by two spotlights hung at second-story level on the building behind it, plus the streetlights on Sixth and W. 3rd Street. Just enough light to be playing at eleven thirty. If the ball had been dark brown like some, instead of a more vivid orange, they might have had trouble. The game—like all the games here—was fast and physical, and George and Marina stood at the fence watching. As would, it seemed to George, anyone who laid eyes on it, but contrary to this, people passed by, hardly taking it in.

They hung their fingers on the fence, they watched for a while, the players all black, gleaming, shirtless except one older guy with a gut. He wore a gray athletic-department-type T-shirt with the arms cut off. He got the ball and Marina said, Watch, he'll have a flawless shot from fifteen to twenty. All the old fat guys do.

He set and shot: all net, if there had been a net.

Told you, she said.

Yes you did, George said.

She lit a cigarette—Winston 100s. They were too long for her small face.

He probably passes really sharp and fast, she said. That's another reliable skill set for the old guys.

A couple of plays later, he did. It was like a rifle shot and hard for his teammate to handle but he managed.

Check, George said.

Marina smoked with one hand still clutching the fence above her.

Oh my god, she said.

What?

I'll tell you later. Let's eat.

≡

THEY WALKED, FAST, from Sixth east to Second Avenue. At the Kiev, Marina said, I want the matzoh ball soup.

Are you part Jewish?

Why does it matter to you?

I'm just probing, George said. Checking out your medicine cabinet during the party. The usual thing. See what you have going on.

It's a little early for that, she said. We've only known each other for twelve hours.

Everything had an edge now. They knew what was happening, they were going to have a thing, maybe not tonight—probably not tonight—but they'd be seeing each other and going to bed at some point and as if preparation for sleeping together, some head-butting ritual of their unique species, everything now was turning into a skirmish. Push, push back; pull, pull back. For some reason, unusual for him, George didn't feel in the least alarmed by it.

I'm trying to determine the depth of your relationship to the matzoh ball soup. How spiritual it might be.

It's fully fucking spiritual, Marina said. *And* physical. Like Jesus and his sacraments. You never tasted it?

I'm about to, apparently, George said. He ordered that, and a hamburger with fried onions. There was on each table a bowl of ice with half-sour pickles and a ramekin of coleslaw embedded in it. Chipped Formica tables in marbleized bluish gray. Chrome-rimmed. Aluminum legs. Cheap wood chairs. They sat at the window that ran along 7th Street.

Near midnight was a funny hour at the Kiev. Several hours before the club kids came in post-clubbing, an hour or so after they might have come in prior to. There was a lower kohl ratio at this hour, people who wanted to eat after something more mainstream like the movies. Plus the usual neighborhood bridge trolls who might roll in at any hour if they had the money.

This place is heaven, Marina said. She took up a pickle and snapped off a piece with her side teeth.

I die for the pickles.

She was a short, compact girl.

He walked her home and she kissed him there, a wet kiss, hard against his face, he could feel hunger in it but also assertion, she was a force and this expressed it. She lived on E. 5th Street across from an old Ukrainian socialist meeting hall where there was a theater company now. Walking past he saw there would be a weekend at the end of the month featuring three one-acts, one of which was by Louis Pennybaker.

They ate together every night she worked the festival that week, and on the Sunday she brought him in.

She had a roundness to her body, upper arms, belly, thighs, ass—all with the curvature, it was immensely sexy; her skin was olive-caramel-dark-rose, her small round belly and round breasts like some Matisse chalk study of a woman except Matisse's version would be a pinkish color like diluted Pepto-Bismol. He had never been in a woman's mouth like hers. A wet expressive instrument that communicated want. Actual-seeming physical hunger for his cock. Supple muscular lips. Most women George had been with—all dozen of them—had not gone in for oral sex at first, worked their way to it, an act of special intimacy. She was the first who displayed both experience and interest at the outset: another feature of the new decade. She said, after they'd been fucking, I want you to come in my mouth, and he wondered if this was a birth control thing. She might have said something in that case; but, he soon learned, this was her thing, she came this way, a hand between her legs.

Hold my head, she said. Fuck my face. When he was getting close she felt it, she pulled away and said, Wait, wait, and she bit him a little—tap tap—to hold him back; her hand flew then between her legs, her whole arm was moving, her shoulder, her lips just touching him, keeping him on the edge, eyes closed, then open staring at his cock, then closed again, and when she was ready she went at him with that hungry mouth. She started coming and her mouth fell open with it but soon closed around him again, her tongue worked right behind the tip of his cock, flicking hard and fast, and he came as she was finishing. She wanted it all, pulled it into her. He felt as if his head would explode. She kissed him after, as somehow he knew that she would, that what her mouth was full of would be part of it, her lips shining with it. He could feel the slip-slide of his semen on them. She sent her tongue deep into his mouth. He sucked on it as she had on him.

He lay back. He said, That was . . .

Then he was quiet.

What? she said. That was what?

It took him a minute to collect his thoughts.

Profoundly impressive, he said.

Damn right, she said. Her mouth was still shining. Let's do it again.

I need a few minutes.

Profoundly impressive, she said. I'm putting that in quotes on my book cover.

You should embroider it on the duvet, he said.

She hit him in the ribs. With a fist.

Ow, he said.

She said, So how long do you need? I'll set the timer.

Longer now that I'm injured, he said.

Remember the night we met, I said, I'll tell you later?

Yeah, he said. What was that?

Those guys playing basketball were making me insanely horny, she said. That's what I wanted to tell you. The skin, the sweat, the movement. I stop there every time I pass it now. If I stay in this neighborhood, I'll live to be a hundred.

≡

THE BASHER SURVIVED George slightly more than two weeks. He was towing it from a church festival in the Bronx, middle of a Monday morning, when the Econoline's clutch went. He was in permanent neutral, revving the unengaged engine, frantically shifting. There was hardly a shoulder on I-95 where he was but he managed to get as much of the car and wide load as possible into it and up onto the adjoining grassy knoll while the van rolled, powerless, to a stop. The squarish box that was the Basher jutted out crazily into the right lane. George jumped out with his money and paperwork and looked at it and then climbed the embankment and about forty seconds later a truck clipped the corner of the ride and came to a stop straddling the right and middle lanes. A nightmare traffic jam was born—the cars behind all managed to stop and begin going around the truck. George slipped through the fence onto the treed road beside the highway and started to walk. All he could think about the accident was, it could have been worse.

At Gun Hill Road he found a working pay phone and called Dobrone. Dobrone had an answering machine and spoke onto the outgoing tape like a not very smart second grader reading from Dick and Jane: You . . . have . . . reached . . . Anthony Dobrone . . . George waited until after the beep.

Your Basher has been bashed, he said. Busted, banged up, and hammered. It's totaled. It's at the seven-point-three-mile marker on the Bruckner. Basically the clutch went out on the Econoline as I told you it would—

Beep. The answering machine was on a timer and it cut him off. He quartered the phone and dialed again. The five rings and the interminable Dobrone recording. Finally: Go ahead and leave a message!

Yeah, to continue, your fucking Ford long past the date it could have towed anything like that fucking ride lost its transmission and died on ninety-five in the Bronx. There was no shoulder but I got it as far over as I could while it was still moving. Then fortunately I got out to take a piss and a fucking truck hit it. I knew you wouldn't pay me for the day so I split. It's between you and the cops now. It's been swell. Bye.

On his *bye*, the cut-off beep came in, taking away the very end; yet the basic idea, he felt, had been communicated.

A week later George found a note on his doormat one evening, coming home late with Marina. He didn't think he'd given this man his address; he didn't think he'd given it to Ken either, and he had no phone so he considered the nasty implications of Dobrone's ability to find him.

I am going to come after you for this money you fucking punk bec it cost me $500 to get it off the highway + $125 fine a day x 3 days is $875 and the ride itself goes used for five grand. The Ford's tranny I give benefit of the doubt maybe it wasn't your fucking fault but if you'd driven it careful and accel in low gear like I showed you prob it would have been fine there was only 70k miles on the van I will find you—

Wow, Marina said, when he showed her. That's creepy.

George never heard from Dobrone again. He found out

later Ken had paid him, which was infuriating but not a problem he could solve. By the time George had enough money to pay Ken back, the old man was dead.

═

IT WAS AN easy relationship, with Marina. She was mentally acute, she kept him interested and fresh; she was physically active, they did things; she was sound and kept him from depression. Her sexual interests developed and changed, it was like she was studying for a degree in her own pleasure. They did a little wandering from each other, in the first year or so. What was most important, she was totally independent of him and everyone else; she had no need for him, she just liked him. And after three years and a few months, how could he *not* have married such a woman, given the chance? It was sold to her parents that he was a journalist, though by the time they married he'd given that up and was selling coffee off a truck. He was fortunate, he later understood, that she never asked him if he loved her or, when he said he loved her, never asked him what he meant, what *it* was, this emotion he referred to as love. She trusted him and took his word for it and besides, she was too busy for such questions. She'd gone to graduate school for a year, in foreign affairs, and by the time they married, later, in 1985, she was a junior analyst for a risk management firm, specializing in preparing smooth paths, well-informed and protected paths, for overseas development. The kind of thing people with Yale degrees did, as opposed to people with Columbia degrees who worked in cafés and photocopy shops, until they decided to throw in the towel and go to graduate school of some kind. She had to travel, which she was good at.

She had an enormous family—he had almost none. His uncle on his father's side and his mother's parents (his father's both long dead) couldn't travel anymore. He spoke to his grandparents by phone every once in a while but did not see them. They and he were happy with the arrangement. He invited his three closest friends, and Louis, whom he saw once in a while, and his business-partner-slash-boss, whom he'd known for less than a year, but no one, in 1985, the year they married, would go all the way to Seattle for a wedding. Marina's brother Maximillian was called into service as his best man. Her parents were skeptical about him—he was classless and seemingly friendless and had no family, all of which made them uneasy—but when they all first met, that winter of 1983, he managed to hit it off with the mother. Always a good idea. Why, you're all alone! she said, after they'd quizzed him about family. It was cold. She wanted to buy him a coat, as his own coat, torn, corduroy, was clearly inadequate.

I have a better coat in New York, he told her. I promise to start wearing it.

You do not have a better coat, Marina said.

To her mother: He's lying.

I do too! You don't know about it.

Liar.

He would not, however, come hell or gray-hard-frozen water, accept a coat from Marina's mother. Marina slipped him money, which he promised to repay her, and he went out with her and bought his own coat. A U.S. Navy peacoat at a military surplus store which Marina said her mother might not approve of, but her father certainly would, except he wouldn't notice.

17

Anna, having concluded she had no attractive future in a weekly newsmagazine research department, started law school in the fall of 1983, at Columbia, and the next spring when exams were over she left for Europe. The dollar was strong, everywhere was cheap. First Rome, then Paris for two weeks, then she left Paris and drove through the Alps with a girl named Molly and her somewhat-boyfriend named Jack down to the lake district in Italy where Anna and Molly left Jack, who was going to meet his family at a villa on Lake Como which he would not stop talking about but which he never breathed a word about inviting them into, not even for a glass of water. Then the two women drove up to Geneva. It was easier to find a stick shift to rent in Europe and she had to learn to drive one. Molly was better at it and did most of the mountain driving. The violence of the Alps. It took her only a little time being driven through them, along their breaks and chasms, through their small valleys, to understand the violence as an aspect of their beauty. She could see it in the jagged faces and deep shadows of the mountains themselves, that was obvious, as if they'd been hacked out of larger stones by crude and powerful forces.

But it was part of everything, suggested everywhere: not just death but sudden, hard death. How many people in this part of the world fell to their deaths every year? And beyond death: the brutality of every transition. Wounds and blood and water and rocks, and sunlight lancing through the tree cover. It was June but still wet, there had been a late thaw and much rain in May, and everything was in drip, leaking, the wet rocks darkening and at quick angles catching the light. The place was large and close, both; and so erotic she was on edge; she felt as if she were going to be attacked. You could feel it in the earth, see it in the landscapes. You could, most certainly, *smell* it. The cycles, it all represented a contest for control between people, who gained at best a brief foothold on safety and life, and the earth itself, which was the overpowering victor. The earth fed on death. Perhaps this was why these people forever fought with one another: everything was a fight. All those little castles—sometimes two or three in a small valley, or more, you could stand on the hills in Bellinzona and count them, four, five, out on the low mountainsides, at the extremities of the bowl of valley, which had formed with massifs behind it—what were they all there for but to hide in, from violence, and to dash out of, to commit violence. Everything looked weathered from a beating. The high summer pastures filling with the dung of the cows; she saw in her mind all the animal offspring, she envisioned the blood of the pigs birthing, the calves yanked from the milk cows amid buckets of mucus and afterbirth; every farmer spent a portion of his year up to his armpits in gore.

In Geneva she met a man, Joachim. He dressed very well. She complimented him on it, it was something she liked about him, something that turned her on, in fact, that he dressed very well.

Just because you're an assassin doesn't mean you should dress poorly, he said. He was naked at the time, in her bed. She'd always remember that, the way he said it. She laughed, he put out his cigarette on a plate she'd given him for the purpose and reached for her. He had a cock slightly smaller than average but it was the hardest cock she had ever encountered; it didn't feel, when he was aroused, quite human, more like a warm stone extrusion, unyielding to her fingertips, even its bulb stony to the touch. She was in Geneva to take a summer course in international law. Starting the last week in July she had a five-week summer job with a firm back in New York. He dropped by unannounced one afternoon in the days just before her exam, she was studying, and he began undressing her at the door and fucked her with his suit still on, pants draped open over his thighs, two buttons of the shirt open at the bottom, tie thrown back as some men do at meals. It had been a fantasy of hers and he kept it up for many minutes and she came hard twice, once near the beginning and again at the end, the second was sudden, surprising her. After, he just cleaned himself and left. The visit had lasted twenty-six minutes. She sat at her desk slightly stunned and warmed by the orgasms, and realized that she didn't like this man, didn't like him at all, but this would not stop her from fucking him, if he came around again (which he did once more). Indeed, somehow her distaste made fucking him all the more exciting. To her surprise she found she was no longer seeking love and affection from men, or not at first, not erotically: she wanted selfish desire on their faces, even a trace of contempt. She wanted a man to see her as an erotic entity, to want her for his use and to think he was using her. But then she questioned this thought: it was too simplistic and didn't capture the depths of the desire at work. She wanted a kind of sex that was galvanizing but precluded the complexities and dangers of intimacy. Men she loved, meaning her brother, meaning to a lesser extent George, to an even lesser extent two others, or no, one other—well, it was borderline—meaning to a different extent her father too—in essence, they all had walked away from her. She found now that the ones who were interesting to fuck were frequently not interesting to talk to—not for very long and most definitely not after she was sexually satisfied. Their contempt became a buffer: their physical desire for her drew them close, their contempt, which frequently she came to see as fear, masked, kept them safely distant. And except for the temporary arousal their desire created in her, she didn't have to feel anything at all.

≡

SHE CAME BACK to New York and began work for the law firm. She had done well the first year and it was a big firm, very WASPy, Simpson, Thacher & Bartlett, like the pears, a cream-colored firm, cream stationery and creamy walls, with offices on Park Avenue and Wall Street; she was at the Park Avenue office just catty-corner from the Seagram Building, in the headquarters of Chemical Bank, which was their biggest client. Her international law course was helpful: they put her on the team working on loans to Argentina and Chile. *Anywhere we find a nice dictator we send money*, she wrote in a note to Molly. Molly was in Los Angeles and trying to get into the film business, which, she said, was filled with lechers, philanderers and outright rapists. She felt hunted like a carp by alligators.

≡

LATE THAT SUMMER, walking home from work, she took Columbus from 67th after crossing the park. Near 81st Street who came down the steps out of Charivari but George.

You? she said. You? He—she could hardly believe it—blushed. He was carrying a black jacket, a cotton-linen mix by the looks of it, with a shining white lining.

Anna said, You're blushing from embarrassment, it's charming. Caught coming out of Charivari.

I feel like one of my ninth-grade buddies caught me talking to a tenth-grade girl, he said.

I can tell that happened to you. The way you said it. It happened didn't it? she said. Then, while he was considering an answer: Never mind, don't answer. Just try the jacket on. I want to see.

It looked good on him. Sleeves a little long.

Let's show some of that spectacular lining, she said, and rolled the sleeves up twice, to above his wrists. She reached behind him to look at the label.

Willi Smith, she said. Well, look at you. Very Danceteria.

Never, he said. I'm too New England for that. I just liked it and it was on sale.

They looked at each other. She felt—what? She couldn't tell what she felt. Affectionate, amused at the jacket and his passage into the 1980s . . . and slightly stirred. She was cataloguing how she looked: skirt and silk blouse and dress flats. Office.

Your hair's shorter, he said.

I just had it cut. For this job.

Law firm?

Just for the summer. Very white shoe.

She posed and curtsied slightly. Thus the look, she said.

It looks good.

Not like Willi Smith, she said.

Me in a shower of diamonds wouldn't measure up to you in old pajamas, George said.

Oh, please. So what are you up to?

I'm currently unemployed, George said. I have a second interview coming up with the public radio station.

WNYC?

Yes, he said.

I listen to them.

Well, now I do too. Have to pretend it's my métier.

I like the guy in the morning, she said.

Steve Post, George said.

Yes.

Speaking of pajamas. He's a hippie from WBAI. The voice of COMINTERN. He's like in slippers and twenty-year-old flannel shirts. I saw him last time I was there.

What would you do for them?

Write news, George said.

Oh, you'll get that. You'd be great.

We'll see, George said.

You want to get a drink? she said. It surprised her, that her heart came up into her throat.

I can't, he said. He looked genuinely disappointed. I'm on my way back downtown for dinner.

Some other time, Anna said. She pushed cheer into her face and voice.

Yes, he said. Let's. I'd like to catch up.

Then she said: Are you seeing someone now?

Yeah, he said.

Ah, she said. She nodded, as if approving.

What about you? he said. On that front.

I'm currently unattached, she said. No interviews coming up either.

Those are never scheduled ahead of time, he said. And you're never dressed properly.

Yeah, well . . . So tell me about your girl. Woman. Potential mate.

Potential mate, he said. Ha.

He told her about Marina. How they met, briefly. It was funny. Even she thought so, though he had seen the clouds of hostility brewing on her forehead a moment before.

They exchanged their phone numbers and addresses. On the back of her summer intern business card. It stayed in her drawer of miscellany for a long time. Eventually she heard he was married, and knew he must have moved, but the card remained, then got moved with her and placed in a new drawer of miscellany. She could never bring herself to throw it away.

═

A WEEK BEFORE the term started, people were arriving back, she'd gotten busy socially and let the dishes build up in the sink. Mostly breakfast things. Just before classes began, the day after Labor Day, she addressed the pile and near the bottom of it she found a broken glass; she picked the pieces of glass out from amid remnant suds, silverware, a cup and saucer; she finished those and then, washing the sink itself, she wiped straight and hard across an invisible shard that was left, jutting up from the small drain. It cut into the pad of her middle finger deeply enough that it looked as if she could have peeled the chunk of finger right off with a quick jerk. That feeling—shock, and the expectation of, rather than the immediate suffering of, deep pain, the kind of woozy hope that it wasn't true, that it wasn't so bad, that it wouldn't hurt; seconds of that. Then the pain began. The blood was biblical. Finally, with the thing wrapped in a cloth, throbbing, she took herself to the ER. St. Luke's Hospital. Not too crowded but there was a drunk or fucked-up or perhaps quite ill young guy, almost a kid, toppling over in his seat . . . A cop—there were usually two or three cops around the ER—tried to get him to respond. He had apparently arrived without registering at the desk. The cop asked him, What is your name? No answer, a gurgling moan. What. Is. Your. Name?

A few slurs and murmurs, in Spanish.

Anyone here speak Spanish? the cop said, looking around the room. There were only six or so people waiting, it was 10:30 a.m. on a Tuesday.

A black kid stood up, walked over. Yeah. I speak Spanish.

The cop said, Ask him his name. Anna's finger was wrapped too tight, the pounding was going to make her faint, but she didn't want to unwrap it.

The kid looked at the listing man, leaned a little toward him, and said, in a loud high tenor voice, El cop-o wants to know your name-o . . .

She laughed. Dirty look from the cop, before he turned to the kid.

Siddown, you clown.

The boy just stared at him.

The cop pointed.

I said sit.

The boy walked back and sat.

The cop said, What are you here for anyway?

The kid said, What?

What's wrong with you? Why are you here?

They told me I might got strep throat. My throat hurts.

Then I got some advice for you. Keep it shut.

Her doctor was a resident, maybe thirty, she thought, a Caribbean man with that accent, light brown skin, freckles across the nose. Stirring gray-green eyes suggesting amusement and a mischievous intent.

Anna Goff, he said, before he put aside the form they'd filled out for her at the desk.

Yes, she said.

What do we have here?

I cut my finger. She unwrapped it.

So you did, he said. She liked the way he held her hand. Then he flirted with her while he examined the cut, and while he sewed it. A funny curved needle. She watched and said ouch, but only once.

You're going to have quite the middle finger for a few days, he said when he'd put the last bit of tape around her bandage.

I'll flash it at my professors.

What are you studying? he said. With his accent, mild, the *studying* ended on the upnote, emphasis on the last syllable.

I'm in the law school.

Impressive, he said.

You went to medical school, so it's not that impressive, she said.

You're right, you're right, he said, it's really nothing.

The way he said it, cheerful tone and timing, made her laugh.

He instructed her on how to keep the bandage dry, how to check for infection, how the stitches would come out.

I can tell you to come back here for us to remove them

but really there are only two stitches and it's easy, once you feel them moving around and there's no pain, in about four or five days, just clip them off and pull them out.

She would hear that, *clip them off, pull them out*, in the way he said it, for days and days. It came back to her sometimes even years later when she would go to snip some thread or string. From their first date and into the years his voice had a way of coming to her, being present in her head: it was part of his beauty, a kind of resonance and rhythm made in the body.

He asked, after all was finished, for her phone number. She was only a little surprised. His name was Bertrand. Full name, Bertrand Christopher Edward White. What Muhammad Ali had called a slave name, he said, a true one. Each of the three names after his first belonged to a British sugar plantation master along the way and was now carved into his family history. He took her to dinner on the Thursday night—he had called her that first night and asked her out for that week but she had claimed to have other plans, so they settled on the following Thursday. She was surprised at herself, suddenly coy, suddenly playing the game of making him wait. She made him wait for sex too, kissing and groping in doorways until their fourth date, when she invited him to her apartment on a Saturday afternoon before his midnight shift at the hospital. They'd spent the afternoon together at the Botanical Gardens. He had that British thing for gardens. She wanted to make him a British-style tea, strong black tea and cakes and clotted cream. She'd bought the cakes and looked up how to make the cream. They didn't really get to them until well after the dinner hour. He was taut in sex: tense in a way that vibrated; she liked it. She loved his smell, his skin, and she loved his body, not tall, not big, but tight-muscled and almost perfectly proportioned. He had beautiful legs, which was something she had never given much thought to. His tension and his distance were exciting without being contemptuous, or so it seemed; he liked her, he treated her well, he was interesting when she got him talking about the hospital or about growing up outside Kingston, his life on the water as a boy, fishing for snapper and pompano from a raft on the flats. He was perhaps what she'd been looking for, a man she could bear being with, and still find intensity sleeping with.

And after that, it appeared he was in love with her. She enjoyed him with a thrill—the same feeling, she realized later, as you'd have over an extraordinary car someone's given you. You'd say: I love that car. She loved to look at him. He had very little hair on his body, just his tight-coiled pubic hair and a small patch in each armpit. This was luxurious, with that skin. And if he became aroused in a particular way, aggressive, harsh, as certain passing comments on the street, certain larger insults led him sometimes to be, she didn't wish necessarily to like it, but she did.

They were married the following May, 1985, a week after her second-year exams. She still had a year to go so they intended no major changes, he was doing his residency in internal medicine, she was going to school, they would live together, that was all. No furniture and china, no new curtains. And no families, she said. The simplest possible wedding. He complied, perhaps (viewed in retrospect) too easily; a few friends, City Hall, a nice dinner. She sent her parents a note. They sent back a weird card, a Hallmark wedding gift card, and a check for one hundred dollars.

But well before that she had learned him, socially. She learned that he *used* his accent, turned it up and turned it down to meet the needs of the moment. It took her a little while to detect this, to hear it and see it in his affect. This should have been a warning sign. It's the kind of habitual posing that can drive you mad in someone you're close to, have to live with, once you *know* it. She didn't think of it that way until she'd married him. With her friends he played it strong, with his own he played it down. When the company was mixed he was at his most volatile. The distinctions were subtle but her ear for it became beyond fine-tuned. Not long and it was pinpricks tuned, third-degree-burn tuned. At the hospital he used it as a bedside-manner technique to charm or amuse or seduce a patient. As he had, she came to see, with her.

The peculiar name he'd been given, the first name of Bertrand, was his father's idea, after Bertrand Russell—the father an intellectually frustrated owner of fishing boats who wanted actually to be an English writer and thinker.

Well, Anna said, the career of V. S. Naipaul must drive him crazy.

Bert made the funniest face in response—

Oh, he said. My lord. You have no idea, man! No idea!

Anna laughed.

I swear he gets up in the morning and if Naipaul is mentioned in the paper or on the BBC or even just comes into his mind he starts to shake and tells my mum, now I have to go back to bed. Of course he doesn't go back to bed, he goes to his boats, you know. But with a look on his face. I call it grouper face. He looks like a grouper. You've seen a grouper?

No, she said.

I'll show you a grouper, he said.

Promises, promises, she said. He never did show her a grouper.

≡

Come the end of that summer she invited her parents to New York, got them a nice hotel suite for three nights, bought them theater tickets, she even went with them to one of the plays, while Bert was working. She didn't do musicals, she told them, but they knew this already about her. They of course were from Pennsylvania and were perfectly happy to do musicals. One night she and Bert took them to a traditional sawdust French bistro in the Theater District, Tout Va Bien, on 51st Street. Another night, Bert dined with them then went to work at midnight; it was traditional Italian, La Strada, on 46th.

These places opened after the war, she said.

Which war? Bert said.

They all looked at him.

Oh, that war, he said. They laughed.

These restaurants—plenty of them around town, a bunch on the Upper East Side—were already passé in a way she liked. She was pre-nostalgic.

Guys came back from France and Italy, she said. I guess some of the people who emigrated capitalized on the new familiarity. Can you imagine, this was exotic.

No one, Bert said, coming back from England would have been demanding an English restaurant, though. No no.

Why not? her father said. It was his conviction that the highest moral achievement was to be pleasant when in public, and largely silent at home.

Well, to put the matter in the simplest terms, Bert said, English food is disgusting.

Well then, her father said. That certainly explains it.

You were in France, Anna's mother said, to Anna. It was almost an accusation.

Yes. Italy too for a few days. We flew to Rome.

We? her mother said.

A friend and I, she said.

The friend in question was Molly but Anna would not give her mother the satisfaction of being assured it wasn't a man.

On their third and last night Anna took her father for a nightcap in the hotel bar, a too-modern room with a curving bar in black and red. In its favor was that it was almost empty.

Bert had gone to work his monster shift at the hospital, she had attended *Tom and Viv* at the Public Theater with her parents; she had little interest in contemporary theater but this play she had actually wanted to see. Now it had put her in a rage.

That T. S. Eliot wasn't a good man, her mother said after the play.

The play totally distorted their history, Anna said. That's why it feels so good and so right for the moment: it's a bunch of sentimental lies. And the actors were all wrong.

Her mother, an early sleeper, went up to bed; her father was a lifetime member of the insomnia club. Anna at sixteen and seventeen and eighteen, coming home late, used to encounter him in the room called *the study*, kind of a funny room with a TV and couch and big mahogany desk with leather top and a desk chair of green leather brass-tacked to a cherrywood frame. The desk and its chair were exclusively her father's territory, only he was allowed to sit there; but the couch and TV, if he wasn't ensconced at the desk, were open territory. He had a painting on the wall, an oil he was rather proud of, depicting a bear up on hind legs, teeth out, gripping a tree. They shook the trees to impress females, he told her. When she was little she wondered what female bears found impressive in this tree-shaking bit. An odd picture for her mild-mannered father, not only to have but which to give pride of place—perhaps he had longed for that kind of wild virility. The thought was amusing and poignant.

You want brandy? Anna said. We should have a brandy.

Well, it's a special trip I guess, her father said. What a vague man he was. Never yes, or no. Some sentence pronouncing an unwillingness to be full-fledged in willing or not willing. In her youth she hadn't realized how often this vapid quality manifested socially, though his capacity in their relationship actually never to be there, or to say anything with force or conviction, these she had known well.

She ordered them each a Martell. A little cold water on the side.

I'm really angry at you guys, she said, after her first sip of the cognac.

Well, I guess we knew that, her father said. He took a sip and quivered.

You know, it wasn't easy for us, he said after a silence.

She was glaring at him, she felt it but couldn't quite stop it. Perhaps if she stared into the amber-brown Martell.

We lost *both* our children—Mark, then you, her father said. What did we do? What did we do that made us deserve that?

She wanted to say, you're small-hearted people, but that was vicious and not entirely true, for look at him now. Look at the suffering in his face, after all these years. Christ, why did she feel for this man? This was what men did to you, fathers, husbands, lovers, all of them. Showed so little emotion that you yearned for it and then when you finally got it you forgave them and wanted to comfort them. Fuck that. *Fuck that.*

She said, When Mark took off, after the calls, when time stretched out, measured in Mark minutes, Mark hours, Mark days, Mark months, and then Mark years—

He went to say something. We—

No, she said. No. Let me finish. It was normal and it was inevitable and it was suffering of a kind I found terrifying. I still find it terrifying. I still don't have a family because of it. I had to get away from it. I had to insulate myself while I was there and—

What could we have done—

You could have wrestled that grief out of you over time or worked through it and not so deeply *embraced* it. You could have, I don't know, begun to fucking *live* again. Or try, for your child, to live again. With me as your actual living breathing daughter, the new center of your world, not just a reminder, not just a place holder in a landscape of sorrow. But that's an impossible thing to ask, really, isn't it? Mark didn't *die* or get kidnapped and he wasn't left brain dead after a drunken teen car accident; he walked away and didn't call and made you wait. For twenty years.

And then before she could properly resist, it came up and swept over her and she began to cry, gulping sobs, tears soaking her face, falling into her lap, her nose running, her mouth open but unable to articulate the sentence she needed to say, it was playing in her head, over and over and over: I love my brother, I love my brother, I love my brother. Where has he gone? My beautiful brother? She never did say it.

═

A HONEYMOON, BERT had a week, a full year after the marriage. Back to *la bell'Italia*. Starting in Rome for her (she had more time, Bert was meeting her in Florence), ending in Venice. It really was an extraordinary place. Anna had expected something more concocted, less authentic, but no: the light was like a blessing. It was the essence of physical beauty, really: light on forms. The forms were largely stone and masonry, the colors infinite variations within a certain range, from sandy yellow in Rome, through red brick, terracotta, charcoal farther north, to pale mauve and dried blood on the crumbling walls of Venice. They had taken the train from Florence to Padua—they stayed in Padua to save on the hotel. Nothing was cheap in Venice but everywhere else, with the dollar at near eighteen hundred lire, was cheaper than cheap, nice rooms in a pensione for twenty thousand lire, full meals for two with three courses, wine, fruit, coffee, a little cheese, for thirty-five. Less than twenty dollars. They came into Venice one day by train, one day by bus. Some Italians they'd asked told them, oh take the train, the bus is twice as long, and other Italians told them, you must take the bus, it's half the time of the train. Each took about thirty minutes. It was remarkable how assertively the Italians gave you directions that were wrong in every crucial respect.

On their way to Padua from Florence: the countryside in Tuscany and Emilia and Veneto: well, it was famous and it was famous because it was so fucking beautiful. She wanted to see it all, own it almost. Not own it as in proprietary ownership: own it as in *know* it, internalize it, have it. Live in it. She wanted to see Ravenna and the Palladian villas in Vicenza. More. She wanted to see where Joyce and Svevo had wandered in Trieste. She didn't have the time or the money. But she loved what was in front of her. To walk in Venice. You figured it must have been a cliché, the beauty of the place, and unendurable with the tourists, but it wasn't, it was absolutely vivid and self-renewing. The tourists were like the fifty thousand pigeons in the Piazza San Marco, a slightly unpleasant but remarkable aspect of all that made the place so astonishing. You went down the narrow alleyways and wider *calli* or along the minor canals, your eye accommodating a new palette for the universe, the thousand shades of ocher and red, the buildings peeling to reveal abstracts in every grade of sand and taupe and rose, sepia and sanguine, all breaking away in the constant moisture, one revealing the other beneath it and a third shade beneath that. And overhead, spilling from the windowsills, lush geraniums in scarlet and crimson and ruby and cerise, all reds, only reds, and such narrow walks the windows opened on, how did they get the sun—but the Italians could breathe and produce flowers. Down every shadowed way you came quickly to an end, had to turn right or left, and you saw chalked on the wall a childish simple arrow, to the right or left or occasionally both. It took Bert and her a bit to figure out the arrows. They referred to one of two destinations, depending on which direction you were walking: going one way, the arrows pointed to San Marco; going the other way, to the train station.

Bert one day wanted to see an exhibition she had no interest in—*Gli Atroci Machini di Tortura nella Historia*; Atrocious Machines of Torture in History, translated literally: it was the biggest hit in Venice and was held over.

I take a medical interest, Bert told her.

Yeah, sure, she said.

He went off, she walked. They had seen some paintings that morning in one of the old palazzi. Everything a crumbling wreck yet you knew it would all still be there, would endure another century, or two or three. Longer than her own country's experiment in violent capitalism run amok. She came upon the Grand Canal and followed it a short distance to the Ponte Rialto, where they'd agreed to meet, and sat down at one of the café tables set up at canal's edge on the pescaria, what the Venetians called their quays, or this one anyway; it was a café next to the stone steps leading up to the bridge. A German café, so she ordered a beer first, it was excellent, dry, just cold enough but not too. She had a sandwich with it, thin prosciutto and a sharp cheese. Then a coffee and then another. She had a book—the Blue Guide, *Northern Italy: From the Alps to Rome*—she opened it to the proper pages, Padua–Mestre–Bassano–Venice, but she did not read it. She simply sat there, back to the tourists passing up the pescaria onto the bridge, and watched the water, which seemed to move in several directions at once, catching the light; she watched too the gondole and gondolieri maneuvering them, boats clapping against the quayside with the sound of tight lumber on smooth stone, or up against each other, like stringless guitars knocked together, that sound of hollow wood; the gondolieri took on passengers at a short stairway perhaps ten yards down the cobbled walkway from where she sat; and at a table beside her there was planted an ancient-looking couple, clearly not Italian, English in fact, though she wouldn't know it until they spoke, after an hour of silence. In the meanwhile they stared into the half distance and smoked filterless cigarettes one after another down to the nubbin before ponderously mashing them with the toes of their shoes against the stones. They were both angular thin, desiccated, slightly stooped from a shortage of calcium, pale in the way of northern Europeans. They wore the bleakest possible expressions. Their unhappiness, sitting in total silence for so long—while she waited for Bert, read a few lines, looked at the water—it fascinated her. How does one end up there exactly . . . what sort of tortured emotional isolation would be required. They moved each limb slowly, like two tortoises in the sun, to lift to lips their glasses of white wine (of which they consumed a great deal), to meticulously place the glasses back on the table, to bring cigarette to mouth, eventually to drop cigarette and lift foot to extinguish it, leaning over slightly with eyebrows arched in interest at the forceful procedure, making sure the thing was done completely—grind, grind, grind. They'd been given an ashtray but did not use it.

Finally, the woman spoke up, out of nowhere, addressing her partner with the driest of dry upper-class English accents:

What *are* you going to do with all your *money*, John?

A longish silence while she (and Anna, and the universe) awaited the answer.

I don't know, he finally said, shrugging his face, if such is possible, a grimace of uncaring, a flicking of his cigarette, brushing a bit of ash from his pant leg, not looking at the woman, though she, it seemed for the first time, was clearly looking at him.

Invest it, I suppose, he said.

After which they returned to their sunlit rock of silence, two lizards. It seemed to Anna they must have needed the warmth to bring their blood up to an operable temperature.

Anna paid with her newly acquired VISA card. The Italian trip would put her in hock, by perhaps eighteen hundred dollars, maybe a little less. Added on to the law school loans, which would total about twenty-five thousand. She wanted on graduating to do nonprofit work. Nonprofit should be her middle name.

≡

Back in New York, she found Bert in the kitchen one afternoon when he was home, a rare event, him being home, his hours so long—he was rearranging the dishes in the dishwasher. He seemed furious. He was furious.

It looks like you're tossing the dishes in here from horseshoes' distance, he said, hammering the rack back into the body of the machine.

I can't believe you're actually angry about this, she said. You're never fucking here and when you are here, rare of rare days, *this* is what you get up to, emotionally? What's the matter with you?

She found out soon enough what was the matter with him. Monogamy and domesticity and the need sexually to roam was the matter with him. He was, she discovered (it wasn't that hard to discover, after a few suspicious moments and then two days of painful urination), a serial cheater. She threw him out after twenty-three months.

He said, We can get past this. I don't want to be divorced.

Of course you don't want to be divorced. That's a *condition* and you're a doctor so you don't want to have a condition. Except being married to me is a condition too and not a label. You think you want the label, but what it really is, to be in a relationship, it's not symbolic. It's a living organism. It bleeds and shits on the floor. It requires attention and care. Now it requires two shots and a round of antibiotics. You'd know all about that.

Don't, he said.

Do! she said. Do! And I will! The relationship of two people—it's work. You don't have a fucking clue. It's been obvious for a while—I started to see what it meant, what it is, this relationship, and I watched you not seeing it or caring to see it.

I thought—but he will! Except he won't. So fine. I didn't know how long I'd be able to hold out anyway. The quicker we end it, the better. Find someone who lives as much in the gesture and the symbol and the label as you do. A trophy wife. You'll need a higher salary but that's in reach. So move out and go find her.

You're a cunt, he said. That was all he said; he just looked at her with a molten anger.

He continued the look. The moments in life when men frighten you: this was one. He finally rose and grabbed a jacket and keys and slammed out.

When he had moved out completely and she'd reconfigured the apartment so that it felt like hers, she made it her business to sleep with one of his colleagues. She'd really wanted to. A sweet man of preternatural good looks, on an exchange from Italy. It didn't last long, just a few weeks.

I feel bad about this, he said. He gestured. What we're doing.

Oh don't, she said.

If she'd known someone she could trust to do it, she'd have enjoyed being photographed in bed with the Italian.

I'd love to have pictures of us, she said. I'd send them to him.

Oh my god, he said. Please god. You won't do that.

Do you see a camera? she said.

He yanked himself halfway up in bed and looked right and left, up at the ceiling. She laughed. He flopped back down.

The last time she saw Bert, outside the courthouse downtown, near the Serra wall and Foley Square, he looked at her and said, I'm sorry, you know.

That's great, she said. Thanks. You might change one day.

But no marriage can survive if it involves one person sitting around waiting for the other person to *change*. That's for fools.

She was getting shrill: or no, she was about to get shrill and wouldn't permit it.

But thank you, really. I wish you the best.

I wish you the best. Jesus fucking Christ. It was like she was a polite HR executive putting the finishing touches on his dismissal. Then an awkward hug and her life in marriage was over.

And of course she wondered: what was happening with George? She had heard he was engaged, they must be married by now. To Marina. Like a boatyard, funny.

18

After nine months and two weeks George quit his job at the public radio station, writing news. It was a grim place, joyless, competitive for no reason as there was little to compete for, and he'd wearied of trying and failing to get difficult stories into the six-minute newscasts. They in turn had wearied of his weariness and let him take unemployment.

Unemployment, he could pay his rent. Plus he still had the two hundred dollars a month from his mother's trust. Something in fact had bumped it up—he wasn't clear on the details. It was two hundred and nineteen now.

He was adrift, his schedule was askew, he was not sleeping most nights. Marina was in Washington just finishing her master's degree in foreign affairs. She came back to New York most weekends. They would marry when she was done with a last summer course, in September, in Seattle. For now, he walked.

Fulton Street to the water, east of his apartment a few blocks. Down by the fish market. You could smell not just the fish but the mob around the place. Large men inappropriately dressed standing around not looking like they had any good reason to be standing there but who were standing there anyway, not concerned with good reasons or the lack of them. They seemed purposeful. They spoke to one another in groups of three or four with restrained animation and sour looks, like the bettors at an OTB parlor. The reason: never enough payoff. The standard payoff was not enough.

The market proper was a long two-story metal-awning'd structure on the waterfront with stalls inside, belonging to the various fishmongers. Outside a large parking area for the trucks, cobblestone and wood. Three in the morning, it was hopping, which was why George walked there when he'd been out and sleep was a long way off. The buyers came between two and five.

Mr. Langland! Greetings!

The voice came from behind him, his recognition of it a half second behind the shock that made him jump: it was Arthur Townes. He bowed, with his old tongue-in-cheek formality.

You scared the shit out of me, George said. Jesus fucking Christ.

Four in the morning on the waterfront? You're nervous? Yes, yes? Whatever for, Mr. Langland? There's nothing to fear. Look at those nice men there. They'll help you.

They'll help me overboard, George said.

Well, yes, that is the case.

What are you doing here? George said.

Well, I have a camera. So yes, I am taking pictures. With the camera. Or—but wait—it would be reasonable to conclude I'm taking pictures, yes? Right? Uh-huh. You however do not have a camera. So what are you taking?

I'm taking the air, George said.

Fishy air, Arthur said. And these stones of the roadway. Do

you notice how greasy? Animal fats so saturate the atmosphere they precipitate onto the cobblestones and macadam. You're breathing the stuff now.

I did notice that, yes, George said. What are you shooting?

I am trying to shoot the fish, the men with the fish, the piles of ice with the fish strewn upon them, yes, very cool stuff, uh huh, okay? Very cool. The fish. But the problem is, or I should say the repeated problems *are*, the large gentlemen with heavily voweled last names who frown upon such goings-on. They don't want anything *recorded for posterity*, shall we say? No pictures, right? No pictures, *pal*, that is. Don't forget to say *pal*. You can understand. So I move through quickly and shoot surreptitiously but one of them just promised to tear my arms off and take my camera if he saw me again so I'm engaged in, in, in—what should I call it? Strategic withdrawal. Like in Vietnam.

Wise, George said.

I tried to explain I'm testing a new film for Kodak. It's true. A superfast film for low light. Thirty-two hundred ASA. It's pushed, of course. The film's actually more like between eight hundred and a thousand real speed but still. Thirty-two hundred on the box. A whole new world. I'm one of the people they've given it to with all the specs, shoulders and whatnot—

George thought about asking, but did not ask, what a shoulder was.

So the gentlemen of the vowels were not moved. This place would be ideal, I said. Not moved. Kodak! I said. Rochester. This was when he threatened to pull my arms out of my sockets, which was, I said, you know, extreme. That's extreme.

He was likely aiming for extreme, George said.

Uh huh, uh huh, he was, right, yes, Arthur said. Just so.

Very extreme. You know you need your own longshoreman-type hook to work here? Yes, indeed. It's true. I tried. I came down one night to get a job and perhaps take pictures around that. But no no. You must have your own hook. The requisite hook as it were. Strict requirement.

Like an ice hook? A short gaffe? With a handle?

What you say, Arthur said. From your mellifluous tongue.

You need to have one or two? George said. I remember seeing guys with two of them carrying blocks of ice to the fishing boats.

Oh, only one.

Of course I have no idea where to get even one.

Marine supplies, Mr. Langland. Marine supplies. Or your professional-type hardware provider. I recommend Point Lookout. If you want me to pick one up for you I'll be going out there to take pictures, I should say relatively soon.

I'm okay, George said. No cargo hook for now. You want to get a coffee?

Get coffee? Yes. You have a location?

Up Fulton, George said.

Oh, that place, yes.

They set off.

Arthur said, Note *you're* a New Yorker now, but not I, I'm still from the Midwest.

How's that?

You said *get* a *coffee*. But I said, would say, will say, *get coffee*. Or more like, *have coffee*. You and I will go out *for coffee*. No *a*.

I'm trying to think Connecticut.

That's the distant past, Arthur said. And you're from an interesting location linguistically. The linguistic group breaks at the Connecticut River, you know. East of, west of. East of is New England. West of is still largely Middle Atlantic. The Franklin Roosevelt accent. Buckley has it. And everything else too, Bronx, Brooklyn, Queens, Long Island, and that funny Philadelphia-to–Maryland Shore accent where they say *new* for *no* and *wutter* for *water*.

I grew up on the Connecticut River. Astraddle it.

Sounds uncomfortable.

Only mildly. Until the teen years.

Indeed.

They sat in the diner. No one associated with the management or service staff moved a muscle to attend to them.

What are you up to, Arthur? George said. Arthur's beard had more gray visible in it. And he'd gained weight, he had a significant belly. All of it fit with the man's otherworldly strangeness. The bizarre internal logic of his speech.

I take pictures. Largely at night. Days I'm in the photocopy business still. But I'm to have a show! Did I tell you? No, of course I didn't tell you, I haven't seen you.

He told George about the feet. He'd spent a year taking black-and-white pictures in the subway, of women's feet. One of the shots, one of his first in the series, before he had really decided it was to be a series, ended up on the cover of *Aperture*. A woman's somewhat dirty feet in sandals. Now it was to be a show. Probably in early '86, possibly as late as April. Gallery in SoHo, none of this Avenue A nonsense. He was working on the prints now.

Exhibition quality, he said. Quite difficult. The art is like thirty percent in the taking and seventy percent in the printing and the printing is harder. W. Eugene Smith, you know, Gene Smith? I mean, c'mon, Gene Smith—he spent a week on one print. A week! And they're large! Sixteen and eighteen and twenty inches, by twenty-four. That size. So would you think costly? You would be correct. The gallery pays. And then takes it from the sales of course. Come to my studio I'll show you some prints.

He gave George the address, the expectable hours. A second-floor studio on Franklin Street.

Near the towers, George said.

Right there, Arthur said. Did you know there's a man recording them? A sound artist. They have artists' spaces in there, you can apply to the New York State Council on the Arts. Yes, yes. Because they have two gigantic buildings with a hundred stories each and the Port Authority can't rent the space. So this one guy has wired up the windows and records the creaks, the groans and sway. I've heard it. Distant whale calls, right? Like that.

Then he pulled out a notebook. This was what it was like hanging out with Arthur: George had forgotten.

I've been collecting adjectives ending in *ly*, Arthur said. Contrary to the notion that such words ending in *ly* are all adverbs. They are not. These are adjectives.

He began to recite from his pages:

Burly curly jolly silly chilly smelly, let's see . . . willy-nilly. Now, there was a tough one. But yes it was, it was yes, an adjective. Also an adverb. But an adjective yes. Qualifies.

Otherwordly, George said.

Well, that's really worldly you don't need other but okay.

Okay, George said. No willy-nilly contradiction from me.

Very good, yes, Mr. Langland.

That would be churl . . . ish.

Not so good, Mr. Langland. You mean surly.

I mean contumely, George said.

Arthur practically jumped. Mr. Langland! The rare noun! Chaucer called it a sin, you know. Contemptuous speech—yes. But it reminds me of comely. And lovely. You are brilliant. Wasted on the fish market clearly. We should discuss your future.

No way. It's almost five in the fucking morning, what do you want? George said.

I want it all, Arthur said. All of it. Don't you? As long as it doesn't require money. I refuse to make money.

An interesting question, what George wanted. He contemplated answering it and his first thought was that his life was suspended in amber at the moment. He'd been going uptown on Friday mornings that spring and summer to have late breakfast and play softball well into the cooling of the afternoon with some of the old *Spectator* crowd that showed up that summer to play in the pickup games down by the river in the park. When he could, George claimed first base, or third. Sometimes he was forced into the outfield. Older black guys, young Dominicans made up the rest of the crowd. The Dominican kids in particular often were *serious* ballplayers. They had bat speed, the line drives came singing off their swings like cannon shots. The games went late into the afternoon, and the sunlight over the Hudson became deadly in the field. Playing short center George once saw a line drive contact the bat and instantly disappear, a black dot that within two feet of launch was obliterated in a blinding white light of the sun; he moved to where he thought it would be, not many steps from his position, and he didn't see it again until it was about four feet away from his face; he got his glove up in time to catch it, a feat accomplished by what he privately considered a miracle of adrenalized self-defense, but for which he quietly accepted kudos from his team. The muscular kid who'd hit it said, Nice catch, man. It's blind out there.

≡

One morning in late May, Marina back from DC, they walked west from his place, then down and around the Battery, to an ongoing gathering on the West Side called Art on the Beach—it was on the gritty sand landfill behind the Trade Towers where he'd seen the fireworks—where he'd met Anna—and so here he was again, this time in daylight. Marina knew about Anna, she knew more about his exes than he knew about hers, a lot more, and she had more exes than he did; she knew he'd met Anna here on July Fourth that year; now he was with her, Marina, looking at oddball sculptures and tableaux vivant, including one with a young woman in an evening gown and some chunks of concrete. Probably from the old highway, which the city had finally gotten around to tearing down.

How long do you stay here? George asked the woman.

She adjusted her gown, pushed her chin higher in the air. As long as I can, she said. Six hours sometimes.

Food, bathroom?

I'm a camel, she said. A slight turn of her body indicated she didn't wish to talk any longer. This was art after all.

George and Marina wandered off.

It demeans the art, to have to explain it, Marina said.

I was asking more for her to explain herself, George said.

Same thing. Or worse. She must have friends who bring her food and water.

She's a camel, George said. She doesn't need food and water.

George liked best the arrangements of metals and wire that looked just slightly more intentional than trash. A pyramid of sand dotted with used shoes, like an overcrowded shoe burial mound. Various jerry-rigged weathervanes, scrap metal pinwheels. Art imitating toys.

If one could manage to be puerile and angry at the same time, George said, you'd have this.

What you're describing is a tantrum, Marina said.

A tantrum in black jeans, George said.

19

That July, George met Burke, answering an ad from the *Voice* classifieds, a guy looking for help running a coffee truck. Promised *signif cash inc. wknds.* Burke was a tall guy, about six two, giving off a sense of energy and amused cynicism. The thing he was not cynical about was coffee. He had big plans for coffee but he needed capital and the way to make it was to do a couple of years of selling off a truck. He had the truck. Low overhead, high returns. He had to garage the truck and gas it and, with some frequency it seemed, fix the engine; those were his expenses outside buying the coffee and bakery items and on weekends sandwiches and fruit. George accompanied him to the scorching Brooklyn ball fields on Saturdays and Sundays in July and August. The day started at six to prep the truck and be at the ball fields by 8:30. Generally done at four. He gave George Mondays off but he worked seven days himself; weekdays, he worked outside various outer-borough city office buildings, schools with summer classes in session, near City College: places where it would have been a hike to go get coffee and a piece of pound cake.

I have a two-burner Bundt, he said, and an old espresso

machine from one of the *criolla* places on Atlantic Avenue. They have them uptown on the West Side. You went to Columbia? Plenty of them. Floridita, you know?

George knew most of them but couldn't remember that one.

Where's Floridita? he said.

Up like 127th Street, Burke said.

I know that place, George said. It's gigantic, huge.

They make money, man. Weekends at one, two, three a.m.? That place is filled, man. To the brim. They got like ten waitresses on the tables, another twenty staff going, still making money. Anyway I got the machine for the Brooklyn and Bronx crowds and the uptown people, make a lot of cafecitos. You know the Spanish?

Yeah. I even know cortado—

Cortado! That's good. Anyway the Bundts are for the American coffee. It's a good roast.

It was quite possible—likely—Burke was on speed, it occurred to George later.

Cubans take the most sugar, he said. You see a guy using a lot of sugar, really a lot—you know, Cubano. We're also gonna get for Saturdays and Sundays some pork and chicken sandwiches and plaintain chips and ices and a case full of cold soda. We'll get potato chips for the Irish, a lot of Irish in those games. The Italians will eat the ices. I brought out beer one time, made a lot of money that day but it was illegal, I was fucking on edge the whole day looking for cops plus fights ended up breaking out so I killed that.

One of the idiosyncracies of the business was that Burke had landed on a supply of ten thousand coffee cups and no lids.

I paid thirty-five dollars for the cups, he said. Guy wanted fifty, I got him down. I said, I know it's ten thousand cups but they got no fucking lids, man.

Eventually he found a supplier with the right lids; he bought a thousand at a time—for twelve dollars. That the lids were costing him three and a half times what the cups cost made him a little insane. He spoke of it frequently as one might a recent epidemic or invasion by an occupying army.

The cups came secondhand, George said. The lids didn't. Seems pretty straightforward.

Do you even understand what it is to have a lid that costs so much more than the cup? Burke said. He addressed this question with a look of horror, always. There were other horrors as well: they carried in the truck four big sugar dispensers but soon were down to three, having discovered that if you filled them up someone would steal them—sugar had gotten expensive. They'd had to chase a guy down for what would have been a second dispenser loss. So they only filled them up two inches at a time and had to keep filling them through the day. This was George's job. After writing news for public radio. Burke yelled, Sugar! when one of the steel-topped glass jars neared empty.

Burke was obsessed by the coffee. He wanted better and better brands. They'd stay at each field a half hour or an hour or right through if the business stayed good—these fields generally ran three or four games a day from nine in the morning with the last game starting at four p.m. Burke had the schedules for the leagues and planned out the day on a Brooklyn map he had to replace three times during the season, they took such a beating. He'd pencil in the fields and times and figure out whether it was worth it to drive around or stick to one big field for the whole day. If he picked one field and it was slow he had the map ready and could move on. There were licenses and permits he was supposed to have; George came to understand he had none of them.

They made a lot of cash, which compensated for the dangers involved.

I'm looking for a kind of partner, Burke told him at the end of summer.

George had been saving his two hundred and nineteen dollars a month since he'd been working plus he'd collected unemployment while being paid in cash, and he wasn't spending much: the advantage of working so many hours being that he was either unavailable or too tired to spend what he made.

I have two grand in the bank, George said. About. If we keep making money I can go in on something for five thousand by next spring.

Okay, Burke said. I'm guessing now that will be like a ten or twelve percent share. Plus you are part of the sweat. We'll negotiate it. Maybe fifteen percent whatever. I'm going to open a string of cafés. They *will* make money.

≡

MARINA WAS BACK in DC, prior to their wedding. Burke invited George to a party at the edge of Carroll Gardens/Red Hook—a mixed group, that new thing, the art/ghetto party, urban pioneer black jeans people raised in the suburbs, hanging with street kids, feeling cool. They drove around Carroll Gardens looking for a place to park; George, who hadn't seen the neighborhood before, expressed amazement that there were cars parked in the bus stops, in front of the hydrants, everywhere. Madonnas and saints on the twelve-by-ten-foot front yards.

What's with the parking? he said.

They don't bother giving tickets here, Burke said. It's all mob. Nobody gets a ticket. Waste of time and plus you might get your arms broken. Or your head.

So we can park anywhere, George said.

Oh no, not us, Burke said. They'll know this piece of shit is from out of town. Or anywhere north of Atlantic Avenue or south of Ninth Street. Which is out of town as far as they're concerned.

≡

THE EAST VILLAGE had a red cast to the light—all the brownstones and red brick—whereas the Upper West Side was always gray, with a hint of lavender that became a purplish sky at night; where George now lived, lower down past City Hall, there was almost no light at all, just slivers of the stuff in the cracks among the two centuries of poverty and soot. Sunsets involved a seeping loss of light. Nights were black.

Burke, it turned out, had a child, a daughter, seven. Burke was thirty-one and George was twenty-seven.

She's *seven*? George said. Where have you been keeping her?

She lives with her mother in Brooklyn, Burke said. Midwood. Near the college.

So that's why you park the truck out there?

Yeah, said Burke.

When do you see her? You've been working every day.

Burke said, They were in Maine a lot of the summer. Which is nice for the kid. My ex has an aunt and uncle with a place up there. Before they left I was going out to Brooklyn nights, taking her out for supper. Few nights a week.

That's hard, George said. See her as much as you can.

I *want* to see her as much as I can, for Christ's fucking sake, Burke said.

No, I mean take some time off. I can handle the truck.

Really? Go solo?

Sure. I used to handle the fucking Basher, remember? I told you the story.

Oh yeah, that fiasco. Where'd you leave it, on the New England Thruway?

On the Bruckner, George said.

Same fucking thing.

On the way to, you might say. Anyway, I wouldn't do that with the truck. I *like* the truck. Take Wednesdays and Sundays. You can go get her on Saturday nights once you have a place.

═

GETTING A PLACE had become a little tricky. People lined up in Sheridan Square at the newsstand there to get first copies of the classifieds in the *Village Voice*, which was delivered about midnight on Tuesdays. Burke, though, didn't mess with lines. He sat at eleven a.m. in the Red Bar on 7th Street with the three daily papers laid out like menus before him.

He said: These old Poles and Ukrainians survived three armies and every kind of wartime famine and plague and made it over here to work in some leather factory and feed their nine cats—they're dying like old people die, in large numbers. The apartments will only be on the market for a few days. You have to move move move. Wait—here's one. Irina Mikhaelevna Malagovina. Beloved grandmother and great-aunt to Ronald, Evelyn, blah blah. A fixture on her East 5th Street block.

He looked up, checked the pay phone was empty. You got a quarter? he said.

You don't need a quarter for information, George said.

Oh right. And up he went, ankle-boot long-legged strides to the pay phone. Frantically waved then, for paper and pen . . .

Just remember it, George called. For chrissake.

He returned to the table. Three nineteen East 10th, he said. So much for her East 5th Street blah blah dee blah blah. That was meant to throw people off. These people are fucking animals.

That's east of here, George said.

No shit, Sherlock. It's across from the park.

That's good, you won't be killed for a few weeks at least.

It's all cool, I'm cool with everyone around here, said Burke.

I love your narcissism. It's the most charming thing about you.

From early on, George and Burke behaved as equals, giving each other shit, but George found himself having that thing that had come up in New York now, as rents rose: real estate envy. Equals except one was the owner and one was the employee. One had more money. Marina would be looking for a larger place for them, probably uptown, but George actually liked living over far east, on Henry Street, he liked his apartment, it had a full bathroom unlike a lot of the places over in the East Village with the tub in the kitchen and the shared toilet in the hall. Still, this was where it was all happening now, where he spent most of his time, and it was a long walk from beyond the courthouses especially in weather. Not to mention the taxis home at night.

They walked three blocks up Avenue A, cut to the right at Tenth Street. The building was halfway down the block between A and B.

There was a bell marked *Super* which they rang. Repeatedly. Finally a woman came and let them in the front door. She was built like a squat rectangle and wore a housedress.

What? she said.

We wondered if you have an apartment? A lady Irina who lived here has died.

How do you know this? She didn't seem concerned, just curious.

I'm friends with her cousin, Burke said.

Only a few days, she said.

I'm Burke.

Hello Mr. Burke.

What's your name? he said.

I'm Magya.

Are you the super?

I manage building. Two others.

So this apartment?

Yes. Landlord will rent it, said Magya.

Who's the landlord?

Don't worry, said Magya.

What do you mean?

Don't worry. You talk to me. What you do for money?

What's my job?

Yes. Job.

I sell coffee off a coffee truck. Good money.

You not a lawyer? No rent to lawyer.

Not a lawyer, no. What's the rent?

Three hundred seventy-five. Five hundred for lease. No paint. You paint.

No way. That's impossible.

Two bedrooms! You think someone else don't pay? You stupid boy. Go away.

Magya! Five years ago the landlords paid *us* to move in. Free rent for two months.

Magya turned toward him. This time is over now! Poof! She waved her sledgehammer arms. New times, she said. Now you pay. Or someone else. Next year five hundred then seven hundred, eight hundred then a thousand. You'll see.

She turned again toward her apartment door.

No, wait, fine. I'll get it.

Back she turned. When you get?

Burke looked at his watch. Two o'clock.

Make sure not too late, Magya said. Two o'clock. Otherwise you don't know.

Maybe two thirty, Burke said. The bank could be crowded.

Magya waved at this as in, two, two thirty, whatever.

Can we see it? Burke said.

Not now. Family not finished. I talk to them. Tomorrow you see.

What floor? Burke said.

Third floor. Easy for you, you strong boy.

Then Burke did the Burke thing. He bent over and hugged her—she looked shocked and then uncomfortable but she stood it.

He said, Magya, I'm so grateful. He took her hands, both. Shook them up and down once. Grateful to you. Thank you. Thank you.

He appeared to choke up.

Is okay, Magya said. She took her hands back and looked glad to have them.

Burke straightened and took a deep breath, as if he was collecting himself—Thank you. I trust you. You are my friend.

Good boy. You are good boy. Her face said: *That was interesting but don't do it again.* You come back tomorrow you see. Another wave of the hammer arm.

They walked down the dirty hallway, out the two slamming doors. Into the light. Into the non-cat-piss air.

Down on the sidewalk and turned back toward Avenue A.

That was fucking brilliant, George said.

Burke looked at him, shook his head, started walking. It just came to me, he said. I needed some way to lock her down, to commit her.

Three seventy-five is high, George said.

I'll get it down, Burke said. Once I have the lease. Go to housing court. Probably the legal rent is like one fifty. Maybe less. I'll get it for two and a quarter.

In fact, when he went, he showed Magya the papers and said he'd drop his claim for one hundred and eighty-five dollars. They settled at two thirty-five. No hard feelings. Turned out Grace Jones lived in the building; a very polite woman though never cheery. Burke asked her, when he was in the midst of this operation, what her rent was. She was paying a hundred and five a month.

I've been here for eight years, sweetie. See the lock on that front door? There was no lock. There was no door.

Even when she laughed Grace Jones wasn't cheery.

Burke said later, You can afford to be Grace Jones if you're only paying a hundred and five a month.

From the new building they stopped in Bar A on 7th, a long U-shaped bar, afternoon hours just a few kids in the place, some neighborhood guy sleeping in one of the booths set as far back into the darkness as possible.

The old guy: Well, once I saw a fellow who'd read most every book in his city library and he knew just about all there is to know that you can know in English. Scads about scads. Horse breeding and black holes and the birth of metaphor.

That's only the *B*s, George said.

Burke had been talking to the bartender, hitting on her basically, but now they stopped to listen.

What? the old man said.

He knew all there was in the library, but that's just the *B*s. Breeding, black holes, birth—

Yeah, you're right, the old man said. That's just the *B*s. He also knew the *C*s—for all the little cocksuckers and cunts. Like you. And the fucking *D*s, for dickwad and douchebag.

The bartender and Burke laughed. George raised his glass to the old guy. Regarded him enjoying his moment of barside celebrity. The missing teeth of an old drunk's mean grin.

Now you buy me a fucking drink, he said. You buy me a fucking drink.

Every sentence he liked, he was going to say twice. Another stage in the brain rot of a drunk.

George nodded at the bartender, pushed a five out of the soggy bills she'd left on the bar. One for him, one for me, George said. She gave him two back from the five, he tossed one as tip into the trough where the coasters were stacked. She palmed it.

This was happiness and would forever be: half-empty bars in the late afternoon. He loved his whiskey. He loved its brown-gold color. To him it was the color of sex. A little water and you got the swirl, the movement. One ice cube, or two if small, to cool the alcohol. His mother. Red lipstick on the glass, cigarettes. Jesus fucking Christ.

He ordered a draft Rolling Rock. Boilermaker time. His father's people drank that way: shot of whiskey in a jigger and a pilsner glass of beer. The draft was seventy-five cents and he had three seventy-five left. Two whiskeys and another beer. He searched his pockets for an extra single, for the tip.

Soon enough it was six and Burke's flame went off duty, a new bartender came in; Burke's was tall and blond, the new one shorter and dark. The tall ones loved Burke, he was six two and physical, skinny like a rock star but substantial across the shoulders and chest. The two of them retired to one of the dark booths to continue their deep negotiations. Last George saw they were making out with Burke's hand up her shirt. George weaved home. It was a long stagger to Henry Street. George lived down at the bottom of Chinatown behind the courts and City Hall; he always said, on Henry near Catherine. He liked saying that. *Henry near Catherine.* He wished he were near some Catherine at this moment, whee. Catherine not far from St. James. Made him think of the infirmary. Cab Calloway. He should take a cab. He made jokes about it but they began to take on characteristics in his mind, these fictional people, Henry, Catherine, and St. James . . .

Burke's daughter's name was Clarissa. Her mother, Allison, loved the Richardson novel. George pointed out that in the book Clarissa was, essentially, raped; he was not the first to have so indicated, Burke made clear, and, he further made clear, it pissed him off every time.

I actually like the name, George said. It's a lovely name.

Burke patted him on the shoulder. He was given to these

patronizing gestures of superiority whenever he felt vulnerable.

One day, with the smell of the future around his face, the scent of their future success, George told Burke: It's almost impossible to have a conscience in this country and still function. The money makes it impossible. It's the center of everything and everything it touches, it corrupts.

Burke said, Bullshit.

20

So they were in coffee.

Chock Full o' Nuts was the first coffee chain, Burke said. Of course it wasn't—but for him and his friends it was.

And it was all about the women, Burke said. In Europe the cafés are for men, or men and women both, but here they're for the women. The men are an afterthought. Schrafft's. White gloves. A respectable piece of pie. Sandwiches with the crusts cut off. And you know why the Chocks mugs were so thick of course. Not to keep the coffee warm, no, no. A big ample mug: not a lot of coffee inside it. That's a win for both sides, baby.

One day that fall Burke sat down, filled out two years of tax forms, federal and state, making up the expense numbers, the gas and cups and coffee and sugar et cetera, et cetera, expensing the cups at full price, the additional lids he'd never acquired, paid all the taxes and fines, and then took all the cash he had left after two years—amounting to more than thirty thousand dollars—to the local Manufacturers Hanover bank and told them it was all theirs if they'd open him a business account under the name Brown & Co. and provide revolving credit sufficient for him to open and keep operating a café. He'd filed papers of incorporation with the state of New York under that name (later this corporation would be dissolved in favor of one created in Delaware because that's how corporations roll, baby) with a board comprising himself, his second wife with whom he did not live, George, and his mother, who lived upstate in Monticello so that it required a day trip to get her signatures on the various papers.

Can't you just send them up there? George said. Have her send them back?

Oh my god no. They would disappear into a Collyer brothers nightmare morass, from which they would never emerge. I'm not even taking them into her house—that's how powerful I consider her magic, her juju of disappearance and chaos and destruction. I respect that shit, having learned my lessons years ago. I told her she has to meet me at Denny's.

A New York City café born at an upstate Denny's, George said. I can already see the piece in the Living section.

Damn right, Burke said. She was like, oh, I love Denny's! That I'm starting a new business and that she's nominally on the board she doesn't give a shit about. In many ways she remains the dumbass simple shiksa teenager my father married all those decades ago.

Your father was Jewish? George said. He'd never inquired into issues of Burke's background. As far as Burke ever was heard to tell, life began in New York in 1972 at Max's Kansas City.

Bernstein, said Burke. I changed it at twenty-two. People in New York were always asking me if I was related to Leonard. Which would have been okay if they didn't look so plainly fucking disappointed that I wasn't. You want to know big? That fucking guy was big.

Muhammad Ali was bigger, George said.

Yeah, but nobody asked if I was related to him. Anyway I changed it to Burke.

After Mike Burke of the Yankees? After Edmund Burke, the father of rational conservatism?

Mike Burke, what, with the sideburns? No. No, no, it was after this character Gene Barry played on TV. Named Burke.

Burke's Law, George said.

He drove a '62 Rolls Silver Cloud, Burke said. Or didn't drive. Was driven in. That car is still out there. I'm going to own it. I mean the actual one from the show. Before the decade is out. Are you listening? Are you setting this down? It's like John Kennedy with the moon, I will get that car.

It's good to have important projects in life, George said.

Thank you.

What about freedom and justice and such?

Those are in there too, Burke said. A little behind the Rolls but they're there.

You see what you did though, right? George said. You see that they asked you about Bernstein because not only the name—you look a little like him. A lot taller but similar cut of face, the wavy hair. The mouth. Right? So you change your name to Burke after Gene Barry and his fucking car but guess what, it circles back around because you picked an actor who looked basically like Leonard Bernstein.

Fuck, Burke said.

The modern human mind, George said. Who can explain it? Who can escape it?

Fuck, Burke said. That's fucking me up.

He looked directly at George, pointed his finger.

I never should have told you my secret, he said. You fucked it up.

≡

THE LOAN, THE finding a location, the renovation: the café opened in August 1986, on Avenue A between 7th and 8th Streets. One of those places, it turned out, that popped up in your neighborhood while you were away. It was scary dead for the first three weeks and then it picked up quickly. Burke let various musicians and bands play when they wanted to, built a riser as a stage in back for them to play on. He could fit three tables on it in the mornings and any other hours no one was playing there. On the bare brick walls (they would miss the insulation come winter), which were in such bad shape they evoked Italian ruins, he hung the local art. There was a little Greco-Roman revival movement on that year, he had some clumsy-looking big oils of classical statuary with broken arms and wild eyes. What George called Crayola-Neoclassical, later shortened to Neo-Crayola: gaudy Apollos and Aphrodites on vivid red or green or blue backgrounds. Wide brushstrokes and notable genitalia. A few good pieces. Burke favored large furious pieces of art, purchased locally or on loan from neighborhood galleries and artists: Salvadoran guerrillas in red jungles, screaming children, that sort of thing.

Any of the painters they'd bought pictures from who started to get known and whose work started to be worth real money, Burke sold the work, sowed the money back into the café.

I don't want to pay the insurance, Burke said.

All this art, both classical and political, was tinged with an irony that showed in the crudeness and comic book character of the figuration. The irony of skinny-legged suburban children who had populated the neighborhood and adjoining ones, people brought up in a world that could commodify any conviction or idea or style. Some of the work had rage but most of it worked best without rage: these artists were largely refugees, white suburban kids or no longer kids but still in Converse and 501 black jeans; their rage tended to look childish and calculated and was infuriating to some people in the way calculating, badly behaved children always were infuriating. Caustic skepticism worked. It was how they felt about their parents, and it ended up being the attitude they brought to the rest of the world, including, quite often, what they painted, or filmed, or depicted in their writing. One local woman painter did nineteenth-century landscapes with modern military scenes at the center, government commandos killing peasants being the subject of the painting Burke bought from her. Her name was Tess. Her boyfriend they called Dr. Bedhead.

Running a café: you knew all these people. Eventually, some of them—apologetic at first, then not—ended up back in the suburbs raising their own children. But plenty of others stayed, toughed it out, had families and did the city grind with the public schools and bad services and the double strollers on the subway stairs. The café hours were insane. Six a.m. bakery deliveries or earlier, other suppliers, someone had to be there from five thirty on, to accept. They opened at seven thirty—it could have been later, in that neighborhood there was little point, no one much rose until ten, but Burke was loyal to the working guys and the white girls with jobs in Midtown who came in on their way to the subway for coffee with skim milk to go. Latecomers among the plumber and carpenter crowd. For that group you'd have to open at six thirty and there wasn't that much profit in the coffee alone. The café closed at one in the morning. Burke hired good people. Musicians, painters, actors but with practical intelligence, something he could pick out with the accuracy of a shaman. But either Burke or George had to be there at opening and the other at closing because this was retail and you could not trust anyone with the money. Every night it was seven times what any of them made in a week. Sometimes if for one reason or another the same one had to do a night followed by a morning they came in and closed out the day's sales at eleven or midnight and carried the rest over to the next morning. Soon they were doing three thousand a day in business, more on the weekends. Thick leather and canvas pouches with padlocks. A device for sorting and rolling change. A tiny back office with file cabinet, small desk, and two squeaky chairs found on the street, just like the old desk chairs at *Spectator*, gray aluminum frames, green vinyl leatherette seat back and covers, each with a dooming tear in it someplace, there must be an army of those motherfuckers spread across the land.

I grew up with no money. Did you grow up with no money? Burke said.

Money was an issue, George said. We always had less of it than we were supposed to have, but that's not the same.

I cannot tell you the satisfaction—it's like a deep physical well-being I feel, like I'm settled down into my own self, my own body, it's really *physical*—when I have a lot of money. When I'm carrying a few hundred bucks and I have like ten thousand in the bank. It's like a drug.

How much would be enough? George said.

That's an interesting question, Burke said.

Made particularly interesting in that he never answered it. To George, after a time, this lack of an answer was the answer: the figure was literally unknowable and would always be unknowable because no known figure, put in front of the man, could ever be declared enough. Money was like Circe's potion, like the Sirens' song, like Calypso's magic: take a taste, just the smallest bit, and it owned you. In college once, he was flirting with a girl on his floor, he was a sophomore, it was spring, they were in the lounge, a larger discussion got going on the topic of money. High '70s. Emphasis on high. Whether money had real value. George ended up taking what money he had, around twenty dollars, collecting from some other people, sitting down on the metal plate outside the service elevator, and setting a hundred and six dollars on fire. People went batshit crazy. People were nuts about money. They associated the actual paper currency with some kind of morality—this was the American lesson. Money *was* morality. It was a core meaning. The scene changed them physically, their bodies became frantic. The ones who went most nuts were of course from the most well-off families. Prelaw assholes. Utterly predictable. One of them said, We could give that money to the poor!

George pulled a bunch of bills out of the flames. Here, he said. You want to give it to the poor? Let's go out and give it to them right now. I'll go with you.

The guy turned and walked away.

You don't even want to talk to the poor, never mind give them money, George said.

Oh, his pride. Oh, the power. This was power—to show you were above even this, which gave meaning to American life. His wounded glee, burning the money. Like take *that* motherfuckers.

And there was in the 1980s in New York a lot of tasting going on. Not in smallest bits either. Burke's name for the café, long established in his imagination, was Brown & Co. Some questioned the wisdom of it—Marina said brown was the color of death, rotting in the soil—but George sensed what Burke was after. This would be his skill. What Burke really wanted, despite the Loisaida feeling of the place now, with the overstated art and hacked-up brick, the unmatched, used-furniture-shop tables and chairs, what Burke was after really was the comforting elegance of Edwardian club rooms. Brown & Co. sounded like the rest of the sign could read *Importers of Fine Comestibles. Estb'd 1783.* Inside this idea resided the chain's true identity: a place for educated white people. They were twenty years in before anything felt *wrong* to them about this situation. More immediate and practical was the problem of how to make this kind of thing modern, fast, diverse, and adaptable.

There was a bookshop east of Avenue B called Neither/Nor. With a large performance space. A lot of space all over because even the bookshop portion wasn't filled up, featuring exclusively self-published and hand-made booklets and comics sold on consignment. At night it was very dark—you could hardly see the texts—and various volunteers, many with no talent whatsoever, played music to no one in particular in the back room. George had gotten to know the couple that had opened it. Eager and skinny. The woman was from France and wore fishnets and electric-purple high heels. George brought Burke to see the place. As it happened, no bad music: instead a poet was reading, who was very good—George had seen him before, at ABC No Rio. For his last poem, a sonnet, he lighted a book of matches, the whole book—held it aloft, and let it fall to the floor and die with the dying words of the verse. The floor, George couldn't help noting, was wood, beaten, broken through in places, chairs arranged around the holes, frightening openings into a black void, the suggestion that at any moment one could fall through to a kingdom of darkness and rats.

I think we should open a café in back, George said. This place is cool.

This place is deadly, Burke said. What has it got that we don't have on Avenue A except a lot less traffic? And less light?

George looked around. Fishnets? he said.

Core mission, Burke said. Core mission. Plus we got some fishnets going on. We are not absent fishnets.

They're not part of the genetics of the place, George said. What George wanted, he realized, was for the enterprise, their café business, to be avant-garde. Burke said, This bookstore is avant-garde because it has no books in it. Hard to make a café truly avant-garde, Georgie. You'd have to refuse to serve coffee. *Georgie* was the cheerful Burke. It raised his spirits to say no to things.

≡

Marina and George's baby was due soon. They had found a place uptown, Upper West Side, 105th Street—I want some space, and high ceilings, Marina had said—and they would deliver at St. Luke's eight blocks north. Marina was not a tall woman, she was most compact through the middle, and her pregnancy saw her grow to a prodigious size. In the final weeks, middle and late December, she was showing signs of toxemia, preeclampsia, high blood sugar. *It was coming on Christmas they were cutting down trees* . . . Marina's ob-gyn was heading to the Caribbean for two weeks; therefore, she had Marina in to the delivery room a week before the holiday, on a Saturday, and the residents and nurses spent Saturday and Sunday trying to induce labor; just the days, Saturday night they were sent home, but for nine hours both days Marina lay in bed hooked up to a Pitocin drip. Nurses came and went every half hour or so, adjusting the flow of the bag. Every couple of hours they changed the catheter bag.

This is how the Mossad tortures PLO guys, Marina said, halfway into the first day of brutal, unproductive cramps.

You wouldn't say that in DC with your state security colleagues, George said.

Discretion is part of any foreign-service career, she said.

They were released at six, with Marina's cervix still shut tight as an uptown jewelry shop at midnight, and tramped back again the next morning, volunteers in their own beheading. George was taking time from the café to sit in a dark-beige room with her. It was that color of beige available only to institutions in the 1950s, '60s, and '70s, a hue that had some red in it and some yellow in it but somehow everything combined to dinge. The room was run-down. At one point he decided to open the blinds: he thought he'd let in some milky winter light. One pull and the entire enormous blind structure—the upper portion behind a false wall at the top of the six-foot window—came tumbling down in a cloud of black soot accumulated over the previous several decades from the truck exhaust on Amsterdam Avenue. It crashed, things on the windowsill went flying, broke, it was an explosive event. The soot mushroomed up into his face, into his mouth, then settled again everywhere on him, in his hair and on his clothes, across his brow like Al Jolson halfway ready for his set. The crash brought them all running from the four corners of the obstetrics ward.

Oh my god, you're covered in soot, Marina said. Her hand was over her mouth like a nineteenth-century etching of a woman saying *eek*.

Now I know how to get the nurses, George said. He had

a wad of tissues from the bedside table and was spitting black stuff into it.

They tsk-tsked him but really couldn't quite blame him—why shouldn't he open the goddamned blinds? Well, because the shit of the ages falls out of the walls if you do that. No risk of infection though: she hadn't opened even half a centimeter.

The end of the second day they walked home again with their pillow and paint roller (for back labor) and focus object, a small painting by their neighbor, a gift. Paris, the Seine, in ink and watercolor. The blue-gray river led a pathway between the stone gray-brown walls.

Marina gave birth finally in early January '87. It required more than thirty hours of labor and concluded with an emergency cesarean section. At some point in there, during a slow period, Marina's mother, having flown in to be on hand, spelled him in the birthing room and George went out and got a hero sandwich and two bottles of beer. He downed them on a cold bench in the middle of Broadway. That was his sustenance over forty-two hours or so. Later, rolling the paint roller down her lower spine and across her coccyx—they were fifteen or twenty hours in at that point—he concluded that no physical feat he'd ever seen accomplished by a man matched this. He couldn't fully grasp it. Twenty-five hours, twenty-eight. Somewhere in the thirtieth hour and Marina's cervix just reaching the tenth centimeter, the baby's heartbeat had started to slow, his oxygen levels were going down, and off they sped on a gurney to the OB-GYN operating room. One of the nurses helped George wash and suit up and brought him into the room, which was not, given the rush, properly set up for an observer: they sat him in a simple chair like from a kitchen, at the end of Marina's arm, and he held her hand, which grew frigid because of the epidural, like a refrigerated hand. Early on he made the mistake of turning his head toward where the business was being done and he saw far too much of the inside of his wife's body, red pink yellow layers of skin and fat, clamped as if in a sandwich, elevated to allow the obstetrician's hands to explore the womb and extricate the baby, and she was in there up to her forearms. This was his next revelation then: you do not want, ever, to see the inside of a loved one's body.

Out he came, then, Nathaniel they'd decided to call him: first Apgar score of nine. Valiant fellow. Once the baby had been cleaned and wrapped George looked over the nurse's shoulder as she was suctioning his lungs, a tube up his nose, down his throat, pulling out the amniotic fluid that the vaginal walls had not had the chance to squeeze out of him, as a thousand moms over a thousand sinks squeezed clean a thousand sponges on a thousand quiet evenings. The baby was remarkably awake, clear-eyed: there was a nobility and endurance in his face that George could see already, not the kind of strength that changed the world but the deeper kind of strength that refused to allow the world to change it. He was moved by the endurance he saw in that face.

Birth and death, there was always a story. All this would become the folklore that so many birth stories became; she was overhydrated and her hands in the recovery room were blown up like the Stay-Puft Marshmallow Man's. He thought they would have to saw off her wedding ring but the anesthesiologist said no, the swelling would go down shortly, and so it did. Finally it was over and she was asleep and the baby was where the baby was and he left, thrust out of the hospital doors into a dim dawn in which snow had begun to fall: gray-white world of an empty Amsterdam Avenue, sky swirling. He went back to their apartment on 105th Street where his mother-in-law was asleep in the spare room, and opened the fridge and emptied into a tall water glass the white wine that had been residing there; he drank it down. It wasn't nearly enough. There was an alky bar on Broadway that opened at seven as the law permitted (of course noon on Sundays), didn't close till four a.m. when the law required, and by 7:15 that morning he was sitting in it with a Jameson and a small glass of beer. He'd never drunk in the morning and never would again but this was an exceptional day and, besides, when you'd been up for close to forty-eight hours, what was morning anyway? It was all night as far as his body and his psyche could measure. The pre-workday business in such a place was an education: men—family men, hello—came in on their way to their jobs, jobs clearly hated, downed a drink and left. The champ was a red-faced guy in his thirties, already shot-looking, face raw from a bad shave, collar too tight, bad tie, JC Penney–type imitation British trenchcoat—a lifetime of middle management awaited the men in those coats—and when Joseph, the bald and pot-bellied day shift bartender, saw the guy come from southward past the windows and toward the door, he pulled out the house scotch from the well and poured two doubles, to the brim. Fellow came through the swinging door, placed a ten on the bar—probably four apiece for the doubles and two for Joe, for being daily and quick about it. He put the drinks down like two small sips of cool water. Out the door again. Forty seconds in all, certainly not a full minute, and then, only then, was he ready for the first few hours of his day. Barely. He likely would need a booster by eleven and the evenings at home must be an unending bad dream, filled with dreary meanness or worse. In George's inner dictionary, where the mind catalogues its words and phrases, this guy's red face would for years thereafter pop up under *fucking miserable life*. It made George a little sad, in the midst of this grinding melancholy, to be in his exhausted way so happy. Oh, the feel of a baby in your arms.

When the baby—Nate—was six months old they took him out to Seattle to be baptized and to see her people. In church on Sunday: the foreign land, slightly ominous, of the Roman religionists. The smoke of incense and a touch here and there, still, of Latin. Ten words of Latin left in the Mass, perhaps. It was like a vestigial tail. The old priest who gave the sermon had a thick accent. He was, George found out later, a Basque; his mouth looked like it had been pushed around in a bad fight and the English words came out of it pre-mangled. His bald head, with chin and ears and cheeks and forehead, looked like a series of lumps he'd taken in that same bad fight. He said, in his sermon, George remembered only the one line: that if we wish to lead satisfactory lives, we would be required to conduct ourselves with dedication, joy, and tenacity. Three words, he remembered them ever after: *dedication*, *joy*, and *tenacity*. Afterward Marina's mother introduced Marina and George and the baby to the old priest and he touched and smiled at and blessed the baby, who was fussing, needing to nurse. There was a rustic beauty to this face, ardent and authentic, brown-eyed. He went by the name Father San Sebastian, having taken his religious name from the largest city in the Basque region of Spain.

He said to them, while the baby fussed, Little children's lives are very hard. At night the dark comes and they do not want to go to sleep. They are afraid they are going to die. You have to help them. Not now, he sleeps and eats, but later, later he will be afraid.

≡

THAT FIRST YEAR George was still working seventy hours a week in the café, which was hard on Marina, but she had friends and her mother stayed for two months. Burke was preparing to expand the business. Late 1987 they had four or five good managers to work with. To keep them in it Burke set them up to make a piece of the business over time. George and Burke went and bought themselves good suits at Barneys to wear to the bank. George wore his tie that afternoon, Burke went with open collar and his Ray-Bans. He brought a neat portfolio of bank statements and press reviews of the café. They got the big loan, three hundred and fifty thousand dollars, all they owned on collateral, plus two co-signers, and aside from weddings and funerals George never wore a tie again. They opened the first of the chain versions of Brown & Co. coffee shop on Fifth Avenue and 22nd Street, across from the Flatiron. One of the design elements George, whose official title was Executive VP, Management and Marketing, insisted on: large bathrooms. Two of them. In every store. Soon they had four shops and an office (an *office*, for chrissakes, George had said) so that neither he nor Burke would see the inside of a store for a week or more at a time, which meant he could control his hours better, even stay home some days. When Nate was three Marina decided to finish her foreign affairs degree in Washington. It meant she was down there three or four days a week for three and a half months in the fall and three and a half again in the spring. They had enough money to hire someone to live in—they moved into a three-bedroom with maid's room on Riverside Drive; this was the building in which George would eventually buy a co-op, a larger five-bedroom on the seventh floor, and where he'd stay. The nanny's name was Lourdes. Nanny and housekeeper. A three-times-weekly cleaning service as well. Lourdes ran it all. When, one day a few years later, he and Marina decided to split, she would stay in DC, he in New York, Nate would split the time, each parent would visit the other city, it wasn't that much of a change. For middle school, when Nate was eleven, he moved back to New York. Washington's a drag, he said.

≡

THE LATE '80s lessons of Burke: to the degree the café has or is creating and promoting a larger sense of design and culture, in other words if the place has a sensibility, American men are either embarrassed and hostile in relation to it or they don't notice it. In any case they aren't affected by it. For attracting the women, cheap does not help. It doesn't confirm that they are who they wish to be. As for the men, there are exceptions of course. The unemployed poets with the notebooks. A couple of gay men. That's it. Writers and painters. A few composers. These are the icons. Like Hitchcock, him you don't put on the wall. Or Francis Ford Coppola.

And how did we go from coffee to communications? It's a natural connection. Back to forever. Coffee and friends. Coffee and talk. Being together. We have to make it comfortable. Everyone is nervous and confused about what they're supposed to like. So we're well situated not only to exploit the unease of the consumer but to exploit it in order to alleviate it. People who spend all their money and who are not sure they're spending it on the right stuff. That's our market. We push up the prices to make the coffee thing a necessary luxury belonging to a certain class, not just thirty-five cents in a Parthenon cup on the way to work. It's class unease that we're alleviating. Here you can sit. Here you know the bathrooms are usable.

Eventually the stores were decorated by printed wallpaper: images of James Joyce, James Baldwin, Etta James—all the Jameses. But George continued to buy for himself. Here and there. Eclectic. No dealers, no advice, he just went to shows.

21

Three years into another new decade, which looked not much more promising than the last. Anna didn't like her job, she didn't like the weather, which that summer was unrelentingly hot, and she'd moved uptown to Harlem. She loved her apartment—but getting to and from it was soul-compressing. Which meant some days, the worst days, she didn't even want to leave the house. Or the apartment: she would likely always call where she lived *the house* but no. The apartment. It was enormous, on Eighth Avenue and 121st Street, with two bedrooms and a room that was circular, or octagonal, really, with built-in bookshelves on each wall and even over the doorway. If she lived to be a hundred she'd never have enough books to fill it. It was costing her nine hundred and fifty dollars a month, which was a bit above her budget but not too far: she was making sixty thousand—low for a lawyer but okay for a nonprofit and quite good for a human—doing governance and nonprofit finance. She brought home around three thousand a month, and the apartment, utilities, and law school loans took up more than half of that. She was single, her other expenses were low. She saved a little, she always saved a little, and in recent months she had been spending her money furnishing this enormous space. Two bedrooms and a library, with light from north and west, which made her feel she should become a painter just to take advantage of it—the high ceilings and suffused, charitable light. There was an IKEA, a miracle store from Sweden, that had just opened by Newark Airport, and she rented U-Hauls three times to go out there. She paid the super twenty dollars each time to help her carry the stuff up. Then followed multi-week projects of putting the pieces together. Frequently she got two-thirds of the way and had to undo it all and start again—something would be off. When your furniture puts you in a fury . . . she hurt her wrists and bruised and cut her fingers, screwing and rescrewing with those little fucking hex keys.

≡

THERE HAD BEEN, that past winter and spring, a man; she had thought for a time, only a short time but long enough to leave scars, that this was *the* man. His name was Colin. He was, if such was possible, both kind and neglectful. Physically rugged—dark, bearded, very into nature, not meant for New York at all, though his work for a national conservancy had brought him here. He was not beautiful but he had enthusiasm and energy and, physically, a magnetism that she responded to on an electrical level—she felt him in her nerves, even right into her crotch, a small ache and swelling whenever she used to see him and even now when she thought of him. He had nothing but good intentions but the good intentions were spread over wide territories and did not include steadfastness or reliability. Of course, when had she ever liked anyone reliable? (Ah, her brother—there he was again.) It soon became apparent he could not concentrate for any length of time on anything except the world of his environmental work, animals and habitat, that his excitements were constantly stirred by new conflicts, new places, new outrages against people and rivers and mountains and species. He would never settle down, as, sure enough, he didn't. He'd departed for the Pacific Northwest. Some work he was going to do there with native peoples. Indigenous cultures. Her brain said Indians but she always corrected it. Because of him.

What could emphasize loneliness like a large and lovely apartment that one lived in by oneself? She would dedicate herself to it for weeks at a time and for days after that she would love the place, luxuriate in it—then a crash would come.

And bad days. Days such as this one, when it was bad because of the day before. Yesterday after dealing all day with John, one of the foundation directors, who poked his head into her office at every opportunity and who managed to keep *running into* her in the halls and who kept insisting she go out to lunch again, even after last time, when he'd tried to kiss her outside the restaurant and she'd told him that this was not acceptable and was in fact insulting and that they were professional colleagues and that's all—yet here he was, still at it, until she wanted to say to him, *John, you have a wife. Get a life. Or throw yourself into your work. Don't you have actual work to do? Ever?*—and, *Do the words* lawsuit *and* public humiliation *mean anything to you at all?*—after that kind of day, which at this point with him every day was shaping up to be, then came today and more of the same, until finally a little after six she left to go home and make ramen noodles and broccoli, one of her standard suppers. She was on the subway—always its own little adventure—and a guy passed behind her, not rubbing against her or anything but a little too close, given the space available, and she swore to God he smelled her. She heard it, behind her head, sniff, sniff, with the second sniff elongated, really taking in the aromatic scenery. Of course she immediately and self-consciously (because she was nothing if not that) started cataloguing in her head what such scenery included: the shampoo of morning and the "organic climate-control" hair product that smelled of geranium and coriander; and the morning's dab of perfume and other things; and of course her skin itself, the smell emanating from clothes being dropped into the hamper, a kind of parboiled, slightly peppery smell, like a mild meat with a dusting of coriander and a hint of cumin, all those smells plus—if he had a developed nose and probably he did, or why else would this be his *thing*—the other smells that must have been hinting their way upward by end of day from all the landmark bodily locations, various sectors along the front lines in the battle against actual mammal life . . . And at this point she was really tired, and she was thinking about Colin again, which she'd been trying *not* to do, and she just wanted to sink to the floor of the train and weep. Then she got really pissed . . . *really* pissed. And first thing, because god forbid this guy actually be forced to pay for his crime, she took it out on the woman in the seat in front of where she was standing, who had kept her legs stuck out for three stops so far and no relief in sight. Finally *this* was what she couldn't take anymore, so when the woman kind of bumped into Anna's legs for the ninth time, Anna bumped firmly back and forced the woman to pull hers in. The woman looked at her, looked at her straight and not really hostile, just sharply, with a look that said, I know what's going on here, I saw it, I heard it, and what are you taking it out on me for? So Anna felt bad.

Sorry, she said. The woman nodded.

And of course she'd been fundamentally invaded, a boundary broken, and she felt bad. This made her, when she took it in, furious. She wanted to turn on the guy who by then was down the car but still checking her out and just start screaming, YOU'RE A FUCKING FREAK and WHAT THE FUCK IS THE MATTER WITH YOU and DON'T YOU THINK I COULD HEAR THAT FUCKING *SNIFFING*, FOR GOD'S SAKE?

And, ultimately, here was the question, as far as he was concerned, or the director John was concerned, or any of these assholes was concerned, like that vicious overbuilt guy with spaces between his teeth at the really bad salad-bar takeout place on Eighth below 125th Street ("You and me go on a date? You got a hot date tonight?" until this woman who was his wife or his mother or some other relation, it was impossible to tell, but who in her own way was also kind of awful, said something harsh to him, at which point he made a gesture at Anna, as if *she* had rebuked him); or like these two cops that she saw outside the church meeting hall on her block a couple of times a week, she could never figure out what they were there protecting—one of them, a smallish blond one, said all these things when she was walking home—the other night it was, Hey, miss, you got lovely tits, you know that? Miss, you live around here or what? And the other cop, this tall guy, laughed and said, Cool it, but without any teeth in it, which only made it a little worse, so the shorter well-built one called out, Oh, I'm so sorry, miss, I hope I didn't offend you, miss, while she speed-walked down the block, her face going red and wanting to cry. So to all of them, to this one and this one and this one, she wished to pose the question: *Just look at me, gentlemen, go ahead, here I am, I'm thirty-three years old, look at me—no, not* there, *you dumb shits, up here, up at my eyes, boys, take a look and tell me this, you goddamned motherfuckers: DO I EVEN FUCKING EXIST?*

This last being the question that kind of stuck with her through the next morning, and into the afternoon. This was how yesterday extended into tomorrow.

≡

SHE WORKED AT a nonprofit. A profitable nonprofit, they liked to call it. It managed the endowments of other nonprofits, a kind of investment bank for the all-cotton, blue-button-down-and-corduroy set. Wire-rimmed glasses, frayed cuffs and collars, knit ties. As for Anna, she was making her sixty a year, no bonus, seven years out of law school—abominable for someone in finance with a law degree. Every time she thought about it she decided to think about it later. For now, she was satisfied.

Except for John of course, whom she would have to mace and kick in the balls and probably get an order of protection against and leave her job to free herself from, to get him to leave her alone, if that even worked. And except for Colin, who, sure enough—as she cleansed him from her system, or tried to, except there were electronic instant communications now—had emailed her from Seattle today. He was on his way up to Vancouver to take pictures of the Indians slash Indigenous persons slash First Nations people, doing their salmon fishing. Something about their religion, they have the right to use these ancient nets woven like wicker from fine long sticks of river trees to catch the salmon when no one else is allowed to use nets, and all the local white fishing industry people and their cohort plus the local white people in general hated them for it and were going nuts. All super enthusiastic and cheerful on Colin's part. He'd gotten some kind of grant, as if he needed it. God, what an absolute asshole and motherfucker. He had this area along his side, just a spot really, one on each side, where his ribs ended and his side dipped down to his hip bone, that she couldn't get out of her mind. It was soft on the surface and hard-muscled beneath and very pale, just beyond where the dark hair on his stomach ended, back of that line, the skin so smooth and white, and it sloped down (when he was lying on his back), drawing the hand toward the unreachable long muscled valley of his spine. A couple of little brown moles. Jesus Christ.

Next day she was scheduled to have a meeting with a new agency that had been established with a four and a half million-dollar endowment and too much overhead. They had great dreams of the income they could draw from this. It was kind of sad. She guessed they hadn't been reading the papers for the last what? Three years?

≡

AND YES, SHE was writing back to Colin, just some blather about her job and she hoped he was well and gee that's great about the fucking salmon and the fucking nets made out of fucking hemlock sticks and deer tendons and whatever, and let's not forget the herring and the cormorants, and do the bears up there have attorneys? She had to admit she used to be an environmentalist . . . then she fell in love with one. Then he left. So she was sitting there at her desk writing away, pretending to be his cheerful old pal. She felt like typing, *Well, things in New York are just great, I still have a job, nothing's collapsed for a long time, no fires on the trains, I'm hearing less gunfire up in the neighborhood and no one puts the police beatings in the papers anymore, which makes it easier all around,* except suddenly she thought she was going to throw up. She stared at what she'd already written. Then she reached out fast and clicked on the delete button—and confirmed it, yes, yes, she wanted it gone—before she could change her mind and send it and then have to feel like a fucking pathetic idiot for the next week and a half waiting to hear back from him. Then she speed-walked to the ladies' room and did throw up. Still, she was proud of herself. Kind of.

There was a man upstairs from her apartment whom she was convinced was beating his girlfriend. Maybe all that thumping and outcry was sex and maybe she was sobbing all the time because of their deep and unbridgeable philosophical differences, but Anna doubted it. Funny thing was, he seemed like a nice guy, seeing him on the stairs. She thought he worked for the MTA. He looked a little like Wesley Snipes but not as scary-looking. Except now she thought he was as scary-looking.

So somebody else always had it worse, right? That was comforting.

≡

Lucy, Anna's most lasting friend from law school, called her.

Anna said, Oh, hi.

Lucy said, What's the matter?

Anna said, Nothing's the matter. Just busy.

Don't lie, I can hear it in your voice.

Oh, Anna said. Well.

Yes?

Where to begin, Anna said.

You need a new job, Lucy said.

Yeah, there's that. If John the Hard-dicked Director keeps bothering me I can retire for a while on the settlement they're going to owe me.

Ha, Lucy said. Better just to get a new job.

Yeah, okay, Anna said.

And as long as I'm offering advice—

You always offer advice—

As long as I'm *offering* advice, Lucy said, you should live in Brooklyn.

Fuck Brooklyn, Anna said. I love my apartment.

Nobody lives in Harlem, Lucy said.

Excuse me?

White girls don't live in Harlem, I meant.

That's not true. There are a few of us. We eye each other knowingly on the C train. You know, that little nod thing, like undercover cops or rival photographers.

Right, Lucy said. I assume you're mooning about Colin.

A little, Anna said.

Don't, Lucy said. Nothing would make him happier. Meanwhile, I want to talk about Mick.

She frequently wanted to talk about Mick, her ethereal and drug-addicted boyfriend, whom Anna sort of liked, except for the drug addict thing, which always tended to be a problem. He was interesting and smart and fairly kind, a rare combination. Anyway, problems galore. Lucy endlessly troubled. They were currently having no sex *and* no talk, the worst of both worlds.

Heroin has that effect, Anna said.

Have you ever tried it? Lucy said.

No, Anna said. I have not tried it. I haven't been able to fit that into my busy schedule yet. But I've heard.

After that a silence.

Lucy? Anna said. Lucy? Tell me you're not doing heroin with Mick, okay? Even if it's a lie.

I'm not doing heroin with Mick, Lucy said, rotely. He doesn't shoot up, you know. He just snorts.

Great, Anna said. She didn't say she was having a second date tonight with Eric—from Brooklyn! It seemed in poor taste to bring up a hopeful note on the love-life front just then. Plus Lucy would have buried her in inquiries and assertions.

≡

THE DATE WITH Eric ended badly. They went out for drinks and then saw Fellini's *8½* at the Film Forum, which was funny and interesting and partially insane, and she ended up going back with him to Brooklyn for a drink where they talked about the movie for a while, he had this whole thing about Fellini's view of women, men's view of women, and she didn't tell him that she had gotten to the point where her ears glazed over, if you could say such a thing, when men talked about men's view of women. But she ended up of course in his place and they were kissing and making out on his couch. He had a nice Siamese cat. After they were at it for a while, he told her that if a man has an erection for a long period of time his heart can explode or something, which made her laugh.

Women have other reasons their hearts explode, she said.

Still, given the opening, and one was always curious, she put her fingers around it, through his pants, just to see what he was talking about, which she should not have done since in the end she knew she wasn't sleeping with him. Lucy always said she judged by their hands, which was pretty common but wasn't in Anna's experience all that dependable—or big hands were pretty dependable but smaller hands could go either way; another friend, from college, Maya, swore she was always right and she could tell by the lines around a man's mouth, a kind of ampleness, she called it. Anna thought this was ridiculous. She had never found a pattern. So there it was, Eric's manhood—that she thought of this word was the first signal she wasn't sleeping with him. It was thick and certainly long enough and he kind of arced and moaned when she took it, and then he said, into her neck, "Mmm, do you like that, baby?" in this grotesque porn voice and at that point it was all over. He had spent forty or fifty on drinks and food, so she'd paid for the movie, and after the ten-minute conversation about why she wasn't sleeping with him, and his bitter *Fuck you* to end the evening, she spent twenty-eight dollars on a car service from Boerum Hill up to 121st Street.

She thought next day that the evening was really over before it started, when she got to the bar a few minutes ahead of him. There were these people there, a group, three women and two guys, all in major outfits, corpies Lucy called them, very corporate and not long out of college and the types where you knew they were not going to stay in New York for that long after they married and you wished, badly, that they weren't here now either, and four of the five had what looked to be the newest Motorola cell phones on the bar—this was like twelve grand in cellular technology sitting amid the seven-ounce vats of Cosmos they'd been served, Anna figured the phones had to have come from the jobs. One of the phones buzzed and began to wriggle across the zinc and the woman who grabbed it up practically shrieked: Oh my god I can't believe he's *calling* me, oh my god! And so they passed the fucking phone around, one to the other to the other, looking at this poor fool's number in the readout and laughing and screaming and making comments. It was one of the ugliest little social moments of recent months; it had the bitter taste of a city and a society in deep decline; it was, if she was still allowed to use such words, immoral and poisonous, and at that moment she thought to herself, what exactly am I doing here? But of course she stayed.

≡

NOT MANY WEEKS later, she was coming home after dark one evening—she'd gone to HR about John so she figured her days were numbered and she'd celebrated this beginning of the end by having drinks with Lucy and Mick. The two of them were into going to this club later where some blues band was playing but Anna had wanted to go home and shower and change. She was walking down Frederick Douglass from the station at one-two-five, as Lou Reed called it, and four kids were making their way down the street ahead of her, boys, walking that walk, stiff kneed and shoulders dipping, that put-on young-male self-confidence, little guys maybe twelve, learning their moves, T-shirts down to their knees, shorts hanging mid-shin, sneakers untied, and one of them was carrying in two arms a black cat whose rump hung heavily over the crook of the boy's left arm, tail dangling down and twitching like Beatrix Potter's cat watching the goldfish pond in *Peter Rabbit*. And Anna, walking faster than they—people around here walked so slowly it drove her insane—approached the boys and the cat's tail flicked back and forth, dark cat, dark night, that cat the blackest thing on a charcoal street. She was passing them and one of the kids was saying, *Yeah well the cops come, tell him, aight? Cuz tell him the cops roll up on you no reason and they fuck with you . . .* It struck her as a Norman Rockwell scene if Norman Rockwell had had a clue about this other side of American life. But no, it was more than that: she perceived it internally then, one of those occasions when one realized this scene, this here-and-now, this reality, was exactly what it was and what it had always been intended to be, and, for now, it was gentle and numinous: the present moment. And what surprised her was how happy it made her, just for a few minutes—how filled with joy.

≡

Brown & Co. issued its IPO in 1994 and was opening stores in Canada and Europe and George was invited to the opening night and after party for Louis's new play, which had already in previews become a big deal. It was making his old friend famous. He had been known before this but now he was on the cusp of Very Big. The letter arrived at George's office with a wax seal and promised two tickets at the Will Call window. George examined the seal and then got a loupe from design to look closer: some kind of Mughal-era pornography, the two-backed beast, but very hard to see. The Post Office would be appalled.

George was at a moment: he liked himself in his expensive clothes. In his suits and black cashmere shirts. Nate was still mostly in DC with Marina. He went out frequently, plays, films, exhibitions, etc. He was in an easy relationship that he knew wouldn't last. At this party, after the play, Louis approached him. George was standing alone with a drink—he'd come alone, some instinct told him to.

Oh, look at you, Louis said, in your gorgeous suit! Bespoke! Are you bespoken for these days? Is that a hint of gray at the temples? Are you almost forty like me? Don't answer all at once.

I'm younger than you, as I recall, George said. Suit's made for me in Bogotá. I have a son, an ex-wife, occasional lovers, so go ahead, give it your best shot. Since I don't go for men I don't give you good odds. But hell.

Shot indeed, Louis said. George smiled and nodded and took a large sip of his wine.

I got there once, Louis said. Remember? 'Twas a dark and *stormy* night.

I remember no such thing plus it didn't happen, George said. Plus I'm not high and drunk and feeling warm.

Straight men are such liars, Louis said.

You still want to die in the doorway of a Tad's Steakhouse? George asked.

Tad's! Louis said.

I thought about that for years, George said. Made me laugh every time. Whenever I saw one.

Are there still Tad's Steakhouses around anywhere? Do you eat there?

I *never* ate there. *You* ate there.

Only once, Louis said.

That's not what you claimed. You said you loved them.

I exaggerated, Louis said. It's still a flaw. The idea, the existence and proposition of Tad's Steakhouse, it held ironic appeal. But the meat was inedible. Anyway I don't eat meat anymore at all. I'm really, really healthy. I work out. And you, you look great as always.

I make it to the gym once or twice a week, George said. Just enough to fight the flab to a draw.

You don't have flab, Louis said.

Yes, I do, George said.

It's well hidden. Oh no, speaking of—have you *seen* Arthur?

Not in a long time. Five or six years maybe.

He's big as a house. A big house. It's so sad. He's a great photographer, you know. I mean really fine. But he's so fat now I don't know how he moves around.

Several people came by and greeted Louis. He dealt with them, giving them a few Louis-y lines each, then turned back to George.

I would have introduced you but I can't remember who they are, Louis said. Back to our snowy, snowy night.

George looked at him. It's a very good play, he said. Congratulations.

Thank you, Louis said. You may change the topic on a dime *if* you're complimenting me.

The ghost of Wilde at the table, I was almost out of my chair. And the assistant, he's so good. Anyway. People were crying.

I know, Louis said. Not you though.

I don't cry at plays, I cry at movies, George said. I cried through the whole Sid Caesar documentary—

But it was funny, Louis said.

I know, I know, George said. But think of all that's been lost. Anyway some people around me were crying. Not at Sid Caesar—tonight.

Don't you love that? Louis said. Crying in public? There should be more crying in public. I was on a train out to Long Island the other day to see my mother, who still speaks to me, unlike my father, and on the train the conductor, a woman, she came to take my ticket. I held it out to her, then she shook her head and walked into the door area and I couldn't really see her but she seemed to be leaning against the doors face-first and—I *assumed*—crying. She came back for my ticket after a couple of minutes and sure enough, teary, red eyes, the whole thing, a slightly younger than middle-aged woman, a little chubby, weeping at work. On the train.

What about? George said.

Did I ask her? I did not, Louis said. We'll never know now. That's what I thought too—I want to know but I never will. So I said to her, I gave her my ticket and I said, *Oh, I'm so sorry*, and she said, which amazed me, I think only a woman would say this, *It's not you.* Yeah. Du-uh. Of course it's not me. You just met me. Women are insane, aren't they? Like why would I think it's me. So I said I *know* it's not me but I'm sorry anyway and she went on to the next person and another and a few feet away I heard her say *it all gets to be too much sometimes.* To another woman she said this. It was almost as if she were talking about the weather but I wanted to say, honey, it's not every day the conductor lady is weeping on the Long Island Rail Road. Bernie!

He reached for the arms of a friend. Bernie! This is George! From college! Bernie and I roomed together in the East Village circa what?

Like '83, '84, '85, Bernie said. I know in '86 I moved to Bennington for two years.

Those years, Louis said. Of dying. And later years, of dying.

Well, your play.

We had fun though, didn't we? We had fun!

Bernie said, Fun's not really in your repertoire, Louis.

That's unfair. I love fun.

Fun's not really in your repertoire, Louis . . . George would hear this in his head later.

When Bernie had gone off, George said, Bernie seems something of an imperious bitch. But maybe it's me.

No, it's him, Louis said. Once you get close to him he gets even worse. Overwrought and vicious. A termagant, a virago. Queer men have to start owning these terms because why should the harpie women have all the fun.

The Play—he would forever after call it The Play, would never use its title as he did with his others, as opposed to his others—was to be released in two parts. Part I opened in London, traveled to San Francisco (the San Francisco audiences were outlandish and rowdy and emotional, shouting at the stage and weeping, which Louis said he didn't wish to be moved by and struggled not to be, but was) and finally opened in New York considerably revised. They cried in New York too, but not like in San Francisco. He'd been working on it for five years. And even before that, before he knew what the play would be. One short act of it had played at that church on East 5th Street across from Marina's old apartment, more than a decade ago. George had seen it there. The final play kept the same title—*God's Beautiful Men.* An updated story of Lot. The three angels who destroyed everything. Except it was set in 1986. In the earlier one-act the three angels are invited to dinner with Abraham; he takes them to a restaurant. The destruction was AIDS. Which was not to say there weren't explosions. The final Broadway production had convincing explosions, bombs depicted onstage. Frightening the audience. It had made George jump in his seat.

Louis left to make the rounds. Someone tapped George on the shoulder. It was Anna. She looked sophisticated. Beautiful shoes, he noticed. Running cream to yellow. Makeup. Hair.

Wow, he said.

Wow yourself, she said.

You've stayed in touch with Louis?

I did some work for the GMHC. We reconnected.

What kind of work? George said. This is my subtle way of finding out what you're doing.

Nonprofit governance, she said. How to establish a board, by-laws, that kind of thing.

George looked at her.

Legal work? she said.

Right, right, George said. I got lost there. I kept thinking, holy shit, it's been ten years.

Eleven and a half, Anna said.

Well I guess you passed the bar, he said.

I did. That and I found some jobs too. You've built some kind of empire that's part of the language now. *Soy half-caff latte.*

George covered his ears—It burns! It burns! he said. I'm personally responsible for most of that.

It's an achievement, she said.

So is designing a prison, I guess, he said.

Anna looked at him. A moment's pause.

I heard you got married, she said.

Yeah, I did. We have a son now. We're divorced. My ex lives in DC with him and I go down to see him. Or she brings him up.

Hard to read her face.

What's his name? she said.

Nate. Nathaniel—but we call him Nate.

Good sturdy New England name, she said. Like you.

I'm sturdy? George said.

Well, you're New England anyway, Anna said, and they laughed.

And if I remember correctly, she said, you're sturdy enough.

She eyed him. He felt a little jolt . . . *if I remember correctly* . . .

What about you? he said.

I married a charming handsome cad, she said. Sent him packing. I just held on to the most charming and handsome memories and let the rest go.

And so?

Now I have a cat.

Probably better, George said.

In some ways, Anna said.

Would you like to get a drink? George said.

Now?

Sure.

Anna's eyes were lowered. About to his chest level. As if she were staring deep into space, except right through his breast bone. She remembered the sting, that day outside Charivari. She wondered if he did. Memories swelled in behind that one—came up and seemed to crowd into her throat. She looked up from his chest into his eyes.

No, she said. I don't think so.

≡

ONE DAY BURKE announced he wanted George to fly with him to California to meet what he called *these people*.

Montecristo Coffees of San Francisco, Burke said, sounding more reverent than he usually managed, although if anything made him reverent it was the coffee business. He said, They're like the gods of coffee importers.

The red-eye and an early check-in, at the Drake, no less; Burke was feeling a little grandiose. Each lay down for a couple of hours before showering and gathering for a ten o'clock meeting at the Montecristo offices about three blocks north.

Montecristo's head of sales: We are in touch through the year with virtually every farm in our network, that's six hundred farms. Not all of them get to sell to us in any given year, it depends on the crop outcomes. Right now—example—we have a farmer, Gustavo Haberman, he's in southern Mexico, near the border with Guatemala. Beautiful estate. Fincas, the estates are called. Except this is Chiapas, there's a rebel group in that part of the country, the EZLN, informally known as the Zapatistas, you've heard of them. Gustavo isn't a big landowner, it's cooperative-style management with profit-sharing, he's married to an Indigenous woman, so he's essentially safe, but the district is surrounded by the Mexican army. You can't blame the EZLN, the government is as corrupt as they come and has broken promises over and over about land reform and Indigenous rights. But the conflict keeps interrupting the traffic down to the coast. So we have approved Haberman's shipments and we have paid him an upfront percentage to help get the coffee out, about seven thousand dollars, which is not much but it goes a longer way there. We have no guarantees anything is going to make it out or if they'll even have a crop. There are a dozen situations like this in the coffee-growing parts of the world. There are a lot of gambles.

The sales guy said: Small-batch roasting. Delicate process depends on the bean. And when you get it you grind it medium coarse, not too fine, and put it through a drip by hand. You prime the grounds with a little water then a slow regular pour, water at ninety-three or ninety-four centigrade—never boiling. You have to make these coffees by hand. You can't just dump them into some monster urn from hell and shoot the boiling water through. You have to make them in a drip—Chemex or some other glass pot, ground and dripped by the order. The coffee has to have a set amount of time in contact with the water, not too much, not too little.

Burke nodded at the guy, rapt. George was thinking, Oh yeah? Really? Make a kind of show of it then, the drama of your coffee. He started considering outfits.

I don't see how you can do this at the scale you're trying to work at, said the sales guy. Then he took them around for a little tasting. The coffees were in fact superb, each with a slightly different feeling in the mouth. Burke was in a religious state: transcendence and conversion.

Burke's idea, laid out on the plane: he drew small careful pictures with his mechanical pencil on the yellow-brown endpapers of the novel George was reading, showing a medium-large store site, counter midway into the space and on the left from the entrance, with seating up front as always, a few more tables beyond the regular food and drink counter, and against the rear wall a bar, with small circles for stools and, depicted as ovals, two baristas behind it.

Burke said, We can have the normal counter as always—urns, paper cups, plastic lids, you can be in and out in two minutes depending on the line—and then we can have the coffee bar in back, literally like a bar, one to two tenders, ready to take the specialty orders. They can hand out tasters when they're not busy.

You know how expensive this is? George said.

We'll charge for it, Burke said. The four-dollar ceiling will be breached.

Which lowers the volume so I ask again do you know how expensive this will be?

We're gonna sell the beans, man. The beans. We shall become purveyors of some of the finest coffees in the world and be a standing example of how those coffees should be handled.

They opened their first coffee bar in the West Village, appropriately enough, in the space where their third store had been. They had to close for two weeks to adapt the place. It was large enough. Or so they thought. There was a surprising amount of publicity, the *Voice* covered it, some of the free weeklies. The *Times* had called but so far no one had come.

And it was a success. It had been a loss leader and a heavy one at first but Burke was right: when they got the beans the net slowly, grudgingly turned positive.

This was George's introduction to Mexico. In 1996 after the first peace agreement he flew down and visited the fincas in the Soconusco region of Chiapas, the rich coastal lands with the Pacific on the western edge and the shaded mountains on the east. The big city on the coast, Tapachula, was a smaller version of Marseille and Bari and other coastal crossover towns, roiling with illegality. Immigrants, drugs, other goods traveling between Mexico and Central America. You could almost smell the blood on the knives. George managed to find a good guide (the fellows in San Francisco made an introduction) who took him up into the mountains. The roads were rough even in the dry season and even with a Jeep; they were stuck a few times. Haberman, it turned out, was a native of Chiapas, born in La Concordia on the other side of the mountains, moved to this estate when he was two; he'd gone back to Europe to attend school and university, returning to take over the finca. You could see the German in him, he was a head taller or more than everyone around him, deep-tanned, bald, blue-eyed. In his midfifties. Rangy with a slight stoop.

He had a twenty-seven-year-old daughter, Isabel, part Tzotzil Maya, from her mother's side. Fairer and taller than the others, than her mother certainly, but not so much that one didn't recognize her as from that part of the world. Her mother and other women on the finca wore traditional dresses or wide pants and the embroidered blouses made locally, with much red and deep purple; Isabel was in boots, fatigues, belted military shirt-jacket. George checked her for a gun but she didn't appear to be carrying one; just a sheath with a knife, typical for the place. Typical for the *men* of the place, that was to say. She was something else altogether. Neither friendly nor unfriendly. Not in the coffee business, it seemed clear.

Three days he stayed with the Habermans and saw the workings of the finca. It was early October and the harvest was full on. Bringing in the cherries from around the finca, sorting them for the ripest, laying them out on drying beds, keeping at them every day, turning and raking to make sure there was no fermentation. Once the cherries were dry the outer husks broke open and were easier to remove, leaving the beans. Some cherries were cultivated for more bushes, taken into the greenhouse, kept in shade, nurtured along. Every bit of it was labor intensive. George thought about what they were getting per sixty-kilo sack of beans and wondered how in hell they kept it profitable. The family all spoke English with him, the mother least well but adequately for informational purposes and sometimes he could make her laugh. He didn't understand her name and so couldn't retain it—her husband and daughter had a diminutive nickname for her, something like "Credi" but not quite—so he called her señora to stay safe.

Hot water was in short supply but so was cold water so it worked out. The shower ran just hard enough to wash and rinse in. Which was good because the humidity was such that he needed two per day, rather than be soaked with sweat that wouldn't dry. After each he coated himself in DEET. The spray became like a cologne. He'd brought only four shirts but the servant—another unpronounceable name—washed his. They came back lightly starched and pressed. Life wasn't hard enough, she had to starch and iron the linen—his shirts included. At dinner the first two nights Isabel had been seated beside him. She warmed to him a little. He found her breathtaking, almost literally: every time he had to talk to her directly his throat felt like it was closing on him. On the second night, as on the first, the dishes were cleared by her mother and, George had been startled to see, her father, along with the lone servant who'd done George's shirts, who besides her house duties cooked and served all the meals. There was a dorm for the workers (that's where his guide was staying for three days) with its own mess provisions. After the first meal George had tried to help but he'd been sat down with dispatch. On this second night, before the coffee, which was superb, served black, small cup, sweet with its oils and saccharides and particular acids, Isabel leaned over and said, You know about our revolution, yes? Our struggle against the corporations and the neoliberal servant governments?

Zapatistas? he said.

We say EZLN, she said. Ejército Zapatista de Liberación Nacional. But it is more than that. It is a movement of the Indigenous people. Against global capitalism.

I wish you luck with that, he said.

You are a global capitalist yourself, she said. No?

Well, no. I'm not rich enough—we're not rich enough. We just have a chain of cafés. We're not looking to move production around the world in search of cheap labor while strong-arming governments to drop worker protections and environmental protections and the usual tariffs on moving goods in and out of the country. So no. I'm not a global capitalist.

So you get it? she said.

He was silently amused at her use of *you get it*. The colloquial had a slightly comic feel when delivered, even with a mild accent, in a foreign place.

If not approving of all that qualifies as *getting it*, then yes. But I'm still a rich northerner who has never suffered as a result of these things.

Do you vote for the Democrats?

If I absolutely must, he said. I often vote third party but we don't really have any effective third parties.

You should have voted for Perot! she said, and laughed. Anti-global, yes?

She pronounced *global* as GLOW-bal, the last syllable rhyming with the name Al.

Yeah, but there was some other crap attached to it that didn't look so good. You know the word *crap*?

Mierda, she said.

Yeah, basically, he said. *Crap* also means just *claptrap*—which is junk. The kind of things that fall out of your closet when there's too much stuff in it.

Claptrap, she said.

Yes, he said.

EZLN are not claptrap, she said.

No, I don't think so, he said, looking at her. Her eyes were tea-brown.

We need your support, she said.

We? George said, gesturing around.

My parents too, yes. They support. Some of the coffee money goes there. The government does not like it.

No doubt.

She looked at him.

How much are you looking for? George asked.

Twelve percent of the coffee price.

I can't have the company paying. It's totally illegal. Which means it endangers everyone who works for us. What about ten thousand dollars right now, from me? Personally? We have to leave the company out of it.

Twenty, she said.

My my, he said. You're something.

I am what thing?

You're very—remarkable, George said.

Thank you, she said. So it is twenty thousand.

You can't take a check, I assume, George said. Obviously I don't have the cash. I'm going to have to call the U.S. to set up a transfer to a bank here. You tell me which one.

In Tapachula, she said. I have a bank. But it cannot go into an account here. You have to get it in cash.

Call your bank and get the information to transfer the money, then we'll go to pick it up.

When she had the information he called, and after some muscular, New York–rich-asshole finagling got the manager of his banking group to promise the money in twenty-four hours. He rode with her next day in one of the ranch's Land Rovers, which handled the terrain better than the Jeep had done. It was a drive of an hour and a half or a bit more, down to the coast. She knew the bank; she knew which banker. Something illicit, clearly, and well established. It was not, on the Mexican end, legal to turn it into cash, but they did. Anything for a price. George never set his hands on it. A sum less than twenty thousand—mostly in dollars, he noticed—was put in a yellow envelope. The peso was losing value by the day, so dollars in an envelope offered the best interest rate around.

How much did you have to kick back, he asked Isabel on the way home.

Three thousand, she said.

He whistled.

It could be worse, she said.

He asked her, Did you go to university?

Of course, she said.

Mexico City?

Yes.

What did you study?

You will laugh, she said. Poetry. You yanquis always laugh at poetry.

I don't laugh at poetry, he said.

Do you know any Mexican poetry? I mean know of it? Not to say out loud from memory.

I know Octavio Paz.

Octavio Paz is very great, she said. You should know also Jaime Sabines. He's from here. From the capital, up north. Tuxtla. You know Tuxtla?

I had to come through it to get down here, George said. Big town.

Sabines was born the year they opened the library in Tuxtla. The first library in Chiapas. He wrote love poems.

Ah, said George.

The best love poems.

Why are they the best?

Because they are mystical and, how do you say it . . . Of the earth?

Earthy?

Yes, earthy. They are mystical and they are earthy.

I'll read him. In English, I'm afraid.

Better than nothing, she said. Then she said: *un olor a tierra recién nacida, a mujeres que duermen con la mano en el sexo, complacidas . . .*

George looked at her. She had a particular smile. Throwing erotic lines at him in the Land Rover.

She said, *Y se van llorando, llorando, la hermosa vida.*

That's crying crying, George said. The beautiful life.

Si, profesor. You could read the poems in Spanish.

I'll get a dual-language copy, he said.

Okay, she said. She said almost nothing the rest of the ride, nothing that night at dinner, and early in the morning he left with his guide to see the fincas farther east in the mountains. As they drove off the ranch he saw her standing outside the gates. When she saw them coming she turned and walked into the forest. No wave, no smile. He got the message: she had waited there to show him she was carrying in the money.

Coming home, the guide drove him to Oaxaca, where he got a direct flight to Houston. Arriving he'd had to fly to Veracruz, hop to Tuxtla on a propeller plane over the mountains, then hire a car to take him down to Tapachula. He couldn't get the place out of his mind: the mountains, the clouds topping them, pink skies, the deep sounds of the rain forest, and how the birds and insects and other animals, the monkeys and anything else that could make noise at night, did. He kept wondering why the Europeans had to come and fuck it all up—but then he wouldn't be standing there taking it in, would he.

When he told Burke on his return that he'd given her twenty thousand dollars, Burke almost jumped out of his executive desk chair.

You what? You *what*?

My own money, George said. A bank transfer.

Oh man, you must have a thing for this woman. You left a trail as wide as Sherman marching through Georgia. You're fucking crazy.

It was a charitable donation to the poor of the village around the ranch, George said. I was very moved by their strength and nobility. Nothing wrong with that.

Yeah, wait til the SWAT teams arrive at your house. It'll be way worse than if you were giving classified information to the newspapers. They'll probably just shoot you.

And you'll mourn, George said.

Yeah, Burke said. Right.

≡

New stores planned: Denver, Portland, LA. In the east, Charleston, Georgetown, New Haven, Boston (three), Burlington, Portland. Discussions about whether to go into the malls. George's position was that there was no other way to reach the suburban market. Small local malls. Separate structures in the parking fields. Burke was against it but not ironclad so there continued to be meetings. George accused him of snobbery.

High-end branding relies on this thing you call snobbery, Burke said.

Cold drinks: iced regular tea, iced medium-roast coffee,

iced Americano (espresso with cold water). Iced herbal teas, a rotating crew of them.

Hot tea and various roasts of coffee with steamed milk, foamed milk, warm milk (skim, 1 percent, whole and half-and-half), soy milk, almond milk. Or, as George and Burke had always taken it: black. Cranberry tea, lemongrass and mint tea. Chamomile, the preferred herbal tea of Peter Rabbit after he's eaten too many vegetables from Mr. McGregor's garden. George never forgot Mrs. McGregor having baked Peter's father in a fucking pie. The kids hearing the story never reacted to this—after he read it to Nate he started asking around. They completely took this in stride.

George brought in linden-flower tea. It was seasonal like the pumpkin stuff. A big hit. Iced and hot.

Where'd you get that? Burke asked him.

Our nanny makes it, George said. Picks the flowers in the park in June. Though she told me—she was very grave on this point—she's Ecuadoran but linden tea is *not* Ecuadoran, it's Cuban. She had a Cuban *tía abuela* who used to give it to her. With sugar.

Within a few years, linden tea and all the rest would be in seven hundred stores in sixteen countries.

≡

SOME GIRL'S GONNA *see that dress and crave that day like crazy . . .* It was mid-1990s and she was near forty when she decided she had to accept the fact that she would be childless: she had not expected to be so; had not expected to marry so briefly and so badly; she had been, back in her college days, visibly ambitious and, it seemed to some, smart at a level that was intimidating; but she'd never been doctrinaire about men or marriage or family . . . It turned out that everyone was *so conventional.* At twenty, at Barnard, after the thing with Susan and her boyfriend, which she did not repeat despite entreaties, she'd had an affair with a woman, a graduate student in philosophy who, as far as Anna could guess, had likely still not finished her dissertation, something about phenomenology, Teilhard de Chardin seen in the light of Heidegger or vice versa, she couldn't remember. Now Anna was doing so again; it wouldn't last long, she knew. She'd have to remember to have another affair with a woman at sixty. Which would be when, 2017. An unimaginable year. She would work on keeping her figure; there were hot women at sixty. That's what she wanted at the moment. Since there would be no child. This woman, Helen, was six or seven years older than Anna and had achieved early greatness by being put out of her prep school in 1970 for refusing to remove her black leather gloves and sunglasses in class and then raising the Viet Cong flag during the national anthem at a football game. She drifted across country. Hitchhiked as bait. Men, cars. She had been one to keep her psychic bruises fresh back then. And physical and sexual bruises. She made some use of it all: for half a dozen years or a bit more, she'd made a living as a dominatrix in Brooklyn.

You get your underwear at Target? Helen said. Helen was kneeling and Anna was standing before her holding her head: funny as she heard the voice to feel with her fingertips the words vibrate slightly in Helen's skull . . . It's the vowels that vibrate. Uuuuhhhnn-deeehhr-weaaahhhhrr. Helen had begun to roll Anna's underpants down. Standard bikini, black, lacy waist, cotton and Lycra.

Anna looked down to her underwear. Do they look bad? she said. I don't think they look bad.

No, I like them, Helen said. Of course I like them *better* rolled up on the floor. She pulled them down to Anna's feet and Anna stepped out of them, first left foot, then right.

But I mean, Target.

They're *fine*, Anna said. Don't be so fucking bourgeois. You were a revolutionary, weren't you?

The word *bourgeois* sent a bolt of aggression through both of them. Anna felt the arousal like waves rising and receding and crashing back and, not quite regular, rising again and crossing paths at the shore; and there was this strong pull like the undertow, a pull pulling at her, as if Helen's whole mouth were pulling something out of her, and she tried to let it go, to give it, but she couldn't. Not yet. They stopped, both heaving. Helen's face shone, wet; she left a trail up Anna's belly, kissing it.

It all had started because she'd looked up voluptuous Susan on the Internet at work. Voluptuous Susan from that night against the wall of the library, the wind, the wind, she'd felt it running up her legs like a strong hand. A reference in the Barnard magazine class notes. Susan lived in the city. They had a drink and it was clear what Anna was thinking about; but Susan was married and not looking for that. She insisted Anna meet Helen. You'll like Helen, she said.

But she always went back to men. Some habit: some goddamned unabated longing—for her marriage? For her lost brother? For her absent-even-while-present father? Some recuperation. But she hadn't really meant it, any of it, in a while. Just the company. She liked the sexual companionship, needed it, from a certain kind of man she had trouble finding and, with them being that sort of man, would never be able to hold on to; nor should she ever want to hold on to them if she knew what was good for her. They had to be smart and they had to be aloof to the point of granite incapacity for emotion; they could not feel need, they could only feel want. Then some nice man would come along and, sure, she'd give it a try. She *should* like such men, after all. But immediately they took everything more seriously than they had any reason to take it, which was a drag, and not really a surprise. Men yield so easily to their grandiose dreams, their romantic visions of themselves. And so now, here was a three-month relationship destroyed by a man saying "I love you"—after sex, the worst time, although, with him, there would never have been a good time. In the moments when he built up to it, just before he spoke, she felt it coming. She thought, No, no, don't do it. Her *Don't—!* coincided with his *I lo—* so that no further discussion was needed. She rolled away from him, onto her back, covered her face with her hands, as if she'd just seen a friend die.

I wish you hadn't done that, she said.

I didn't! I didn't finish! I stopped.

Effectively, you did, I heard it.

That's so unfair, he said. Men are impulsive. You must know no one ever means it, not really, except maybe your grandparents. It was just, you know, a feeling I had. For a few seconds.

She'd taken her hands off her face and now she looked at him. You know, she said, in your idiotic way, you're brilliant.

Paralysis is my revenge, he told her. What else have I got? What real power?

And Anna thought: There, that explains it. Why the nice men bored her so. They never believed in their own power.

22

Nate had spent most of his early childhood in DC with Marina and various au pairs until he was ready for middle school and Marina had taken a job with State. He'd spent plenty of time in New York with George, liked New York, and was amenable to a move up. George's job meant some travel and Marina became very busy too but they had Lourdes living in and she took good care of Nate when George was away and Marina couldn't get up for a day or two. Sometimes when she did come up George would return to the smell of her perfume in his bed, even after a change of the sheets. Little things. A pair of panties in the bottom of the hamper. A long black hair.

The school they sent Nate to was Darcy Prep, not quite as elite as Collegiate or Trinity but close enough and more modern in approach. Enlightened good intentions in schools turned out to be a heavier burden than the strop and the switch. The former, which George understood even if they pre-dated his own schooldays, were tools to force compliant behavior. What you believed, your worldview, made absolutely no difference to the school, the teachers, etc. Now the school wanted the children to *actually believe* what everyone else believed, which was a different matter. Nate was a not particularly popular dreamy near-genius, a bored student in most subjects but languages, music, and the complete works of Monty Python and J. R. R. Tolkien. In eighth grade, like any red-blooded male American of thirteen, Nate had started to explore pornography: it was just that his favorite works of filthy abandon happened to be in Latin. He built his own website devoted to the material. Until the school made him shut it down. What if his name's not on it? George had said. The other students will still know, he was told.

And so George found himself spending more time than he would have liked with assistant heads of school, inept psychologists, and Nate's advisor and only advocate, a ghostly figure of monastic austerity, Dr. David Miterello, head of Darcy's well-known classical languages department.

Later in eighth grade, they called him in again to the school to *discuss Nate.*

George called Marina and said, Why don't you come up and deal with some of this bullshit.

Oh no, she said. I dealt with the K-through-five bullshit.

George said to Nate, What did you do? This time?

I brought them apples, Nate said.

You what?

I brought each of them an apple. Like a living cliché. I put the apples on their desks and took pictures of them and I put the pictures up on Myspace. You know, with commentary. Quotes from the specific teachers and such.

That's very helpful, George said. I'm sure you painted them in the best and most subtle light.

I'm not from fucking Delft, Nate said.

At this George snapped his fingers, as if he were at a Village jazz club in 1957, appreciating a solo.

Very good, he said. I'm glad all those visits to the Met have stuck with you. But watch your mouth.

Later, George asked Nate, couldn't you just fake being cooperative and sound? So I don't have to go to any more of these meetings?

I try, Nate said. Then I let my guard down, and boom!—I've said something kind of innocuous during social studies discussion, like *If women want abortions so much and can't get them why do they get pregnant?* Next thing you know I'm waiting in the outer office looking at last week's *New Yorker*.

═

Brown & Co. The restrooms. Burke was obsessed with the bathrooms, the daily despoiling, the flow of street people through the stores morning and night to use *his* bathrooms, and the effete barista hipster wannabes who in general refused to clean up adequately after them. A constant problem—he was providing the fucking public bathrooms New York had been talking about for fifty fucking years; shit, he was indoor-plumbing the whole fucking country. Brown's and McDonald's. This wasn't company he wanted to keep. He was toilet paper and running water for every down-and-out in the cities, he was Dorothy fucking Day for these people, and the shops were in constant danger of befoulments. He hated the old men and the women, these he saw frequently in his stores when he popped in for a macchiato and a look-see. People even slept sometimes, with their heads down on the tables. He never believed that the associates did anything about the incursions, the bathroom usage, the sleepers, despite twenty memos to store managers over the last three years, most of them written in a rage by him personally and toned down by the corporate comms people before they went out. The stores were supposed to be, and largely were, comforting upper-middle-class showrooms, workrooms, parlors, refuges, the dining room between mealtimes where you did your homework: they were governed entirely by a white aesthetic, hanging just between the urban and suburban brands. They morphed as your needs changed, regularly spaced across the landscape, retreats from the street—but the fucking street, which once they'd had running in defeat, was creeping back and Burke, keen as always, said he could smell it, even in his fucking office sometimes he claimed he could smell it. The stores were out there at the vanguard of civilization; hell, they'd brought civilization up to the front lines almost single-handedly, they were the fucking outposts of progress with the ivory piled high (except the ivory was coffee beans) and when the shit started to go bad again, as he knew it eventually would, he believed they were only two steps away from becoming the filthy junkie-ridden 14th Street doughnut shops of the '70s and early '80s . . . where Burke and George and their friends, drunk and high after the Mudd Club, had gone to sober up, where they'd watched the junkies pouring as much sugar as their takeout cups could hold and listened to the last of the old Lower East Side Jews in bad clothes and pockets stuffed with newspaper clippings arguing as always the cruel corruption of money versus the essential truth of classical, labor-empowered socialism. Their largest, most divisive arguments concerned whether the *New York Times* could ever, under any circumstances, even occasionally, be trusted to tell the truth.

What made it worse of course was that in some essential

way Burke wasn't even the boss anymore. The whole fucking thing ran without him. George and he would go into the shops and only rarely did anyone working there recognize Burke. People who read the society columns, mostly. He was one of the hundred richest men in the world (number 37 last year) and he went to the White House and he got on TV and they had no fucking clue. He told George to make a note—more pictures of him, just him, on the web page. He said, And let's hire a publicist.

You always fire them, George said.

Yeah, well I can't fire another one until we hire him. Or her. Maybe a her this time. Yeah.

He ended up in the store in one of the two bathrooms terrifying the manager and the baristas after they *did* know who he was, cleaning one of them himself.

You see, you see? I am not above this. He put on the gloves, he took the large sponge—George could tell he wished there were a camera crew there and made a note to have LeAnne the communications VP do something with it in the next profile of him, there being no actual lived reality that is not narrativized—he leaned over the toilet, and his tie swung out in front of him. Don't wear a fucking tie, he said. They laughed. The frequency of Burke's tie wearing had increased in tandem with the widening of his social and political ambitions. Here, tuck this in for me, he said to the manager and opened his arms to create an accessible plane of his chest. She dutifully did so. Between third and fourth button, with adept hands. Immediately George wanted to kiss her and take her clothes off. Surprising how little it took. Burke started slopping water over the toilet, squirted the cleanser, scrubbed it with the brush, swabbed with the sponge, did the sink and mirror with a separate set of cleaning cloths—never mix the toilet with the sink! he shouted—and then mopped the floor, rinsing the mop in the big tin pail and squeezing between wood dowels several times, again and again and one last time. When he said, Done, the staff applauded, which made George wince and Burke hold up his hand.

Unless you're gonna start applauding the poor schmucks among you who have to do this five times a fucking day, Burke said, don't applaud me. He checked his watch. He said: Six minutes. Seven, okay, seven minutes. Did I do a perfect job? Far from it. But now, now it's not a shithole. The kind of traffic you get, you're going to have to do this every two hours. Make a schedule. Spread the pain.

He peeled off his gloves. You need better gloves than these, he said.

The manager looked at him.

Is this what we send you?

Yes, sir.

I'll look into it. For now, everybody, wear two pair. Double them up.

≡

A WOMAN, A poet, George and Burke had known in the East Village was now making a name for herself with a literary blog: sexy-voiced reviews and commentary on books and authors and the general scene. She had several contributors besides herself but she was the spine of it and a growing mini-celebrity of the kind the Web was starting to produce.

See the thing about Iris? George said. I emailed you.

Yeah, Burke said. Did you ever fuck her? He was looking at the Mexico report, which bored him.

Not my type, George said. He tried to imagine it: that wispy six-foot woman, hipless, with the fluttering eyes.

It would have been like fucking a butterfly, he said. The wings beating wildly, this strange dust all over you.

You're a case, you know that?

George's father had used that expression: you're a case.

What she's doing with the website is interesting, George said.

Ah, the website. The website. Leading, as you clearly intended, to my asking what goes on with our own largely unimpressive website.

It's interesting how the Web rewards the individual over the corporate, George said.

That won't last, Burke said. A skeptic of late consumer capitalism, Burke nevertheless served it and foresaw only growing victories for it, against all ideas, all reactions, all entreaties for justice or even good sense. It would grow and win until it finally exploded, like a goat left alone in a grain silo. Eating until it died.

Right now she can use all this dramatic photography and whatnot because she basically steals it and no one stops her, George said. We'd have to pay.

You're making excuses, Burke said.

Yeah, well.

So really, what's happening?

We've got editorial copy, nice graphics. Stories from plantations in Uganda, Mexico, Peru, worthy children of the earth finding nobility and meaning getting paid to grow coffee for Greenwich Village playwrights and the social workers of the Upper West Side.

That's nice, Burke said. You have a good attitude about our business model.

I speak in jest, George said. Partial jest.

And the traffic for such inspiring material?

Minimal.

What's next?

I don't think we can use it for sales in any but a decorative way. The shipping costs make the price point prohibitive or force us to lose money on it. Or most likely both. We're shaping the online shopping program to be for high-end coffee- and tea-makers and accessories and a couple of the really limited-edition brands. With a special price for four-pound bags of Mount Washington beans for fans of the everyday who'll use a lot of it.

And grind it themselves?

Yeah.

No, Burke said. No. Four-pound bags of beans or four individual pound bags of ground. The market, whatever it is, quintuples once you grind it.

Cost, George said.

Try it, Burke said. Tally the losses. Then we'll revisit. Same with the LEs. Make sure nobody clicks off the page because they don't use a coffee grinder. Convince them to buy a fucking grinder sure but sell the ground to the schmendricks who will never bother to grind it themselves.

The LEs, it's a shame, George said. These coffee beans should be ground and brewed immediately thereafter.

Tell them that. Explain it. Better, do a video showing how it should be done. Flash them a good cheap basic grinder. In fact tell them we're selling the grinder at cost just to introduce them to the beauty of the thing.

I'm making a note, George said.

Burke stood and began his stretches. Once an hour, when he was in the office, he did seven or eight minutes of stretching.

You should stretch, he said to George.

I'm going to the gym later, George said.

Burke's head was between his knees. That's not the same, he said. He rose slowly, like a giraffe standing for the first time. Spread his arms. He brought his hands back to meet behind him.

You can't go to the gym for an hour to undo the damage of sitting all fucking day, he said. He sat down again, took up a sales sheet.

So did *you*? George said, when Burke raised his head. Fuck her?

Who?

Iris.

Yeah, a couple of times, Burke said. And you're right. It was like fucking a butterfly. Why are we selling Ecuadoran coffee in Mexico? Shouldn't the house blend in Mexico be Mexican? Wouldn't this make sense?

Costs less, George said. It would cost us more to sell the Mexican blend in Mexico than it costs us to sell it here. Don't ask. They have all kinds of red tape for selling there and all kinds of rule-waiving and subsidies you get when you export it. For the currency. We export theirs they make money, we import Ecuadoran they make money. See?

Too bad, Burke said. The Chiapas beans are good quality at the price point. All the fucking plantations are closing. But you know this. Your friends down there are running short of money, I presume.

They never had money, George said.

How much have you given them, I wonder, Burke said.

George said nothing.

Hm? said Burke.

Yes, you wonder, George said. I heard you.

Ha, Burke said. Well, I hope you're hiding it well from the old U.S. government.

I take it off my taxes as a charitable deduction, George said. It's a purloined letter thing—hide the secret in open view.

Have you ever FOIA'd your FBI files?

God no.

You don't want to know?

Never. I never want to know.

I got mine, Burke said.

When?

About a year ago. Your shenanigans were in there.

I don't want to hear about it, George said.

The girl was in there.

They always are, George said. Those guys are nothing if not condom-sniffers.

Ah, so you slept with her?

Never. The matter never even—

Don't say entered your mind that's always a lie. It always enters the mind. Other places it doesn't enter maybe but the mind, always.

It was never even remotely something I would have done or could have done, George said. It was never in the realm of possibility.

Isn't that romantic? Those might be the most romantic kinds of encounters.

Fuck you.

Okay, never mind.

In Chiapas there were few sons or daughters who wanted to take over these businesses, which were difficult, subject to wild fluctuations of weather and totally unpredictable pricing, based on a market dominated by a dozen large global sellers—Brown was now one—whose volatility was hardly comprehensible even to them.

Burke looked up, closed the Mexico report.

She had a thing about her ass, he said.

George said, What?

Iris, Burke said.

Oh yes, George said.

She was terrified you'd try to go there, she'd jump ten feet if your finger even got near it or if your cock was pulled from home and wandered south on the next thrust—

You mean her asshole, George said.

Yeah. It happened not once but several times, said Burke. Enough to know it was a thing. He looked at the report again, picked it up, and threw it across the room. Her ass*hole*, he said. Yes. That sweet puckered little coin. I'm getting to the point I can't run this company anymore except as some sort of Zen exercise. I should quit, sell out, open a little tea-and-coffee place in the countryside somewhere. Like in the Sonoran Desert, near some old copper mining town on the road the tourists take. Fuck the waitresses if they're willing. Sit and watch the lizards.

I'm not seeing this, George said.

It's been another bad year for love, Burke said. I've just had my chart done. Yeah, don't look that way. You should do it. And yes, this is to be a bad year for love.

Perhaps he meant with the various girlfriends; or he meant with Marta, his wife, she with the matte black hair. Eight years married to her. Knowing Burke well and Marta somewhat, George often wondered how they'd possibly stayed together even that long.

George asked him directly: How have you managed to stay married, considering . . . you know.

How much I fuck around?

There's that, George said.

Tolerance unto blindness, he said. Who can distinguish all the reasons behind marital longevity? Self-punishment. A kind of cruel stasis. A fight to the death. The comfort of being known, and not alone. What was the Hassan-i Sabbah expression Burroughs used all the time? Nothing is true, everything is permitted. Something like that.

The wife, Marta, was sharp-boned and neurasthenic, with extravagant taste. It was, apparently, an open marriage though George heard only about Burke's exploits, never Marta's. She looked as if she might once have been a tigress in bed but now—skeletal, leather-brown from too much sun, heavily made up and lacquered and processed—the idea of her reenacting such moments struck George as horrifying beyond the possible boundaries of the kinky; she'd passed through John Waters territory and was on her way to Blake's woodcuts for *The Inferno*. On the other hand . . . Having once thought of her this way he could never again think of her without a light-flash of jagged pornography. He would look at certain features: her overly managed feet, for instance, tan, tendoned, veined, and pedicured to a childlike cherry red; her small breasts, which hung below her gym-hardened pectorals and, as she was often braless, her tack-like nipples. He could imagine her—and imagined Burke liking her—in latex, growling and wielding a whip.

═

In the office the next week, Burke said: Do you still care if you kill a squirrel? Driving? Run one over? I used to care but now I live in the suburbs and I'm tired of the motherfuckers. They're everywhere.

Do you actually aim for them? George said. Do you go after them?

Not in the Silver Cloud I don't, of course not.

He had actually purchased the Rolls from the old TV show. Spent a fortune bringing it into prime condition.

The 735, maybe. Just kidding. No. I just realized the other day, one ran in front of my car, the BMW. I was on my way over to the Y to play basketball, the squirrel didn't get run over, but I went to brake, to steer, and I realized I didn't give a shit so I just drove. What the fuck are they always scampering across the street for? What is that? Can't they go by tree limbs and electrical wires the way they used to do and as God intended them to do?

That's harsh.

Very harsh, Burke said. But liberating. Oh my god. It's so liberating.

Own it, said George.

I do, Burke said. I do. I own it.

Burke's ideas: the music. He was listening, rather compulsively, to Gould playing Liszt's transcription of Beethoven's Pastoral symphony, struck particularly by the first movement: *Allegro ma non troppo*.

He loved the phrase and wanted a coffee drink: allegro ma non troppo. George's job was to figure out how actually to present this drink. A little strong a little sweet a little rich. The signage. The friendly explanations and background: what the fuck are we talking about? Well . . . this. One sign for the windows on introduction:

ALLEGRO MA NON TROPPO:

According to the Grove Dictionary of Music: An Italian phrase used in music signifying a tempo that is lively but not too much.

According to us: a coffee drink perfect for afternoons. A doppio half-caff espresso, a half teaspoon of sugar and a teaspoon of sumptuous heavy cream. With a complimentary almond biscotto. Perfetto—ma non troppo!

They paid forty thousand dollars to Grove for world English rights, all variations on this one-purpose use. Oh, how the sales and franchise teams wanted biscotto changed to biscotti. Oh, how they all clamored.

Burke backed George. It's biscotto, he said. Otherwise we'd have to give them two. We use the words correctly or we don't fucking use them at all.

Speaking of which, he said to George, there are no degrees of perfect. Either it is or isn't.

That's the play, said George. It's a little joke, a tease.

Hmm, Burke said.

Plus the U.S. Consitution, George said. You'll recall that it cites our efforts to form *a more perfect union.* So tell it to Madison.

Hmm, Burke said. Actually it's not clear Madison wrote that.

Burke was an American history buff. It was part of his political ambitions.

The preamble, he said, came out of what was called the Style Committee, I think. Very modern touch, the Style Committee. I'll have to look it all up.

Perfetto—ma non troppo!'s days were numbered.

And, in short order, sales and George's own marketing people got their way, the products people developed a cellophane packet of two super-mini biscotti and so they were able to restore their precious *i*. Of course that didn't last. The drink proved just popular enough to keep on the menu, morphing over time into the simple *allegro*. They abandoned the free biscotti altogether. An allegro was essentially a half-caff double espresso (doppio) with your choice of warm dairy (not steamed), and you then added your own sugar. A soy allegro with Allegra. It was a nightmare if you actually cared.

In some ways a typical product journey at Brown & Co. The corporation formed its personality and then, from personality, its style, over time, just as a person might. This was Burke's theology. From this grew what he called a *culture*. What George didn't say was the company's culture was essentially Burke and his fantasies of twentieth-century white mercantile wealth, writ large by people like George, who understood how to write it. Why one chair worked and another didn't. Why the workstations with the library lights with green lampshades. At least they didn't have oil paintings of hunting dogs and stags and such. The art was more post-Impressionist. The Upper West Side version of oil paintings of dogs and horses. There was a sentimentality, George didn't mind calling it that but wouldn't have so named it to Burke, about a life of cultured ease that was at the core of Burke's vision of himself and of his company. It didn't go with the destroyed bathrooms or the peanut butter and honey in the squeeze tube, not exactly, but those things were never permitted to encroach dangerously. Personality altered slightly over time, it *matured*, it *developed*, it *responded to the world*, it was *sensitive to history*. Burke actually spoke in these terms. Of course throughout the years the company's style changed, it had to. To be in the world and to remain appealing demanded that; but it changed manageably, consistently, and always, *always*, in keeping with the corporation's true and firmly guided, *muscular* personality. So you could say—it was true—that culture evolved. But it evolved—here Burke was insistent, though George said his insistence was contrary to the evidence—it evolved along the lines of its original moral formation.

We have shareholders, George said. That's now our moral formation.

No, Burke said. No no no—the shareholders are sharing—that's the word, sharing—in something that has a prescribed moral shape, a set of principles, they know this or ought to. It's in all the paperwork, the prospectuses. It gets repeated. It's part of the mantra.

This was how he slept so well, rose at five, and worked out in his gym. This belief that what ought to be actually was.

Watch the fucking bankers, George said. The fund managers. They don't know shit from moral shapes and sets of principles.

≡

ANNA HAD FOUND an online dating site, on Nerve.com, more sophisticated and openly sexual than the usual. Yet—still—listing after listing, the guys wanted to spend Sundays reading the paper, walking in the goddamned park. She had decided that anyone who put that shit in his profile was just out, executed for banality. Was there not one guy who wanted to spend Sundays fucking? What had happened to men?

She went on some dates in Williamsburg. You could see

the retail money machine coming in, the new restaurants, as destructive as napalm in the jungle. The problem with Williamsburg, she told one of the hipsters, who was her age but playing it eight years younger: One either lives in some kind of solidarity with the poor, or one is against them, an enemy. They are not specters, or colorful characters, or badges of one's bohemianism. They are human beings with distinct lives united not by custom, institution and choice, like other communities, but by the fact that all the forces of a monied society have been arranged against them, with predictable and deadly results.

He objected of course. She had already given up on him.

They are colorful characters to you, she said. Or pains in the ass, depending on how much urine you have to smell, depending on your mood and on how mad and intoxicated and intrusive one or another of them chooses to behave toward you. You are not one of them even though you've decided to share their space, take up their space in fact, import the expensiveness that will follow you your whole life. They are prisoners on this street and you are not.

≡

NATE HAD MOVED up to New York in sixth grade, and it would be a while before they felt comfortable letting him go down to DC by himself on the train. Marina came up once a month—usually on a Friday morning train, returning Sunday; and more than once, probably a dozen times though neither would have wanted to count up the occasions, she and George met in hotels at midday. She had a career that was moving forward and, she told George, a series of chalk-striped lovers, guys who felt in tune with the universe on days they were wearing the same color tie as the president. None of them interested her for very long. Her career interested her and that was enough. George and she had known from early on that they couldn't live together but they'd known too that they still very much liked fucking each other, a pastime they had yet to give up, despite the quality of an extended *coitus interruptus* it had given to all other affairs of the heart over those half dozen years.

Burke, like Shrike harassing Miss Lonelyhearts, called Marina *that succubus* and spoke of George's diminished life force.

Marina settled on a hotel for a while, for two or three visits, and then moved it around; she preferred the very good ones. She loved sex in hotels; whereas for George, something about good hotels sent him spinning in a different direction: he walked into a nice hotel suite, and within minutes found himself thinking either of prostitutes or suicide. The first worked for her.

After the sex, one day in 1999, Marina in her robe, they were drinking the wine he'd brought. George was rubbing his wrists and she said, I have to go out and get you a new shirt.

Things had gotten dramatic.

There's time, George said.

She was sitting on a red upholstered chair, wearing the hotel's pale gray robe, black hair, red lips, one foot beneath her, like she was a painting. Her hair a little wild, her eyes dark and burning, a low warm fire. Her free leg hung down, brown and bare. It was likely because of this face and that leg that George had not been able to sustain any other serious relationship for the prior decade. A sadness began to fill him like air coming into a balloon.

How are you keeping your tan? George said. Given it's, you know, February?

I'm spending a lot of time down south, she said. *Down south*, between them and among other professionals involved in the profitable domination of the place, meant Mexico and certain nations in Central America—Honduras, Guatemala and El Salvador, nobody had much to do with Nicaragua anymore, or Costa Rica, either, for opposite reasons; and the northern part of South America—Colombia, Panama, as far down as Peru in George's case. For all the countries south of that, one used their names: Chile, Argentina, Bolivia, Uruguay. North of that: down south.

Are you still a sixteen? she said.

What?

Your shirt size, you're a sixteen, I recall. Thirty-four sleeve.

Depends on the store. Sometimes a sixteen and a half. Where are you going?

I don't know, she said. Paul Stuart?

Then sixteen will work, he said. Then: Paul Stuart, the hotel suites—where is it again that you get all your money?

From you, she said. Don't you remember? I sold all that Brown stock at the height of the market, back in summer '98 I think. Anyway, I have it in municipals now. A nice steady three percent tax-free. Easy to cash out.

Later they arrived at the apartment, she in her Washington suit, he in his New York suit. She looked a little plump in those suits, not in an unappealing way, but it amused him because she didn't look that way naked.

Nate came into the hall, saw them.

They have been *fuck*ing, he said in a singsong.

Jesus, Nate, George said. His mother took off after him: he dashed down the hall and slammed the door to his room.

That was nice, she called to him. That was very nice. I'm

glad to know you have that kind of soul, that you'd say that. About your mother. You're not even thirteen.

The door popped open. You didn't deny it! Door closed again.

I'm going to kill him, Marina said.

It pleases him, George said.

What? Who can even think about that, their parents having sex?

It means we're close, we're almost a family.

Ha! That's a laugh.

≡

George sometimes still took the subway to work. That Monday, Marina gone, he saw an empty ad rectangle on the subway, just a white board, someone had written in block capitals:

WE ARE BEING LIED TO . . .

On his Palm Pilot, he had a file from the office—a story about Burke. The communications VP must be walking around like a rooster.

> *Brown and Co. founder and CEO, Steve Burke, started in the coffee business with a van and a stack of stolen, lidless takeout coffee cups; his great lament now, on the cusp of a new millennium, is his woeful position in the list of richest people in the United States. This year he was ranked thirty-second but, he says, he would like someday to break into the top ten. He knows he never will.*
>
> *"Banking, software, and health," Burke says—everyone calls him Burke. "These are the only real growth industries. And very few own enough of health to get into those reaches of the list. So it's hedge fund and software kings all the way."*

He goes on, in what might be called his mercantile-philosopher mode:

"Wealth at this level is a story, a fume, a tantalizing odor. It's a set of symbols and fantasies. It's a magic number before which special twigs, gathered by shamans at dawn, are burnt with precise rituals and little known prayers."

Are you going to start giving your money away, he is asked.

"I have to," he said. "It's deeply corrupt not to. Just help me get my mind off this list first . . ." Burke laughs.

"Actually that's not it," he says. "I'm looking for the right thing. We have a foundation and right now the foundation focuses on helping the people who plant and grow and pick the coffee we sell. A lot of those people are living right at the edge and if they go down we go down. If the workers all leave—the young people are going to the cities—if the children of the farmers abandon the land or sell it to commercial developers, we go down. So it's a close-focused operation."

One essentially aimed at Brown and Co.'s continued profitability, he is reminded.

"That's true too," he said. "Now I feel like a sinner being reprimanded, quite sternly, by the local preacher."

Burke lives in a large house in Connecticut, gets driven to work daily in a deep green BMW 700-series sedan, has a wife and a grown daughter, and says he is studying Buddhism.

Studying Buddhism? George said.

Well yeah, I'd like to. I'm thinking about it.

Plus you want to make the ten-richest list? These things go together?

Human beings are paradoxical, Burke said.

I'll say.

Burke seemed in a good mood, a mood George attributed to the article, which was well done and—most crucially—about him. He looked good in the photograph, it managed to hide what could be severe and gaunt in his aspect.

Burke said: Look the other, the list, I'll never make the top ten obviously, those are all finance and tech people, not retailers. But it's about winning. It's about being at the top. And people knowing it. Even now, they *bow*. I swear, literally, I watch them, they *lower their upper bodies, visibly*, when I approach them in a room. I find this both insane and gratifying. Then they stand up straight again, as straight as they can, in order to measure up. I love all that. Call me craven.

You're craven, George said.

But I want *not* to love it, Burke said.

Thus you're a craven Buddhist, George said.

Now you get it, Burke said.

So we've reached the point where the fact of merely having a conscience makes you a religious seeker, George said.

This made Burke look sour. George put his hands up.

No, no, not the face. Don't give me the face. I'm teasing. I admire your conscience, I really do. Not many men in your place *have* a conscience. I admire you. You know this. I wouldn't work here otherwise.

Now Burke looked happier. CEOs were like toddlers, George had long ago concluded; he'd been grateful he'd had one, a toddler, to guide his way in dealing with the larger corporate world.

The wisdom of Burke: You couldn't really unset the thing, dial it back to have it be *less* profitable. Especially once it went public. Systems were in place. Every point earned on invested capital, above what they did in increased demand on the product, i.e., higher sales, came by cutting something somewhere, finding a way to increase the margin by some decimal point of a sliver, which writ large, eventually across more than twelve hundred stores, amounted to real money. Eventually you looked at labor costs. You had to. The banks forced you to and the market forced you to . . . the whole system, the whole gigantic American consumer capitalist machine, was focused without deviation on suppressing wages, avoiding taxes, and lowering the cost of goods. No wonder the whole fucking country was falling apart.

23

The year had turned to 2000 and they'd all survived the date-change calamities. Anna knew she should have been happy with her new job. She should have been excited. Aren't you excited, her friends said. *Yes it's great I'm really looking forward to it . . . Yes, it was time. Time for a change. Ha ha ha. I really felt it was time to make a move. Why not. Not having money wasn't a moral condition that was improving me ha ha ha.*

To make a move toward money. Real money. That moral condition thing, she wasn't so sure. Every molecule in her body was dreading it. A high-powered job, chief of the compliance office, on the sixty-second floor of the WTC—she should have been excited. Her friends said, Aren't you excited?—meaning *this is your social obligation, to be excited—to endorse and internalize, to authenticate and affirm, this choice you've made! To allow this choice and the life you will build around it—your home, your vacations, your clothes, whom you date, the restaurants you go to and the objects you buy—to define you. And your affirmation will help us to continue to affirm—because we must affirm, again and again and again!—our own choices.*

This was the nature of most adult conversation among the

professional classes: if not work, which is its own moral justification, then lifestyle affirmation. She tried—but often she had the feeling of a drill being held to her head, that kind of threat and that kind of calm-tearing noise. It was important, in fending this off, to hold that territory on which no one could be induced to admit defeat. Anything beyond the routinely comic in the failure department was inadmissible. Such as the outward acknowledgment that history and culture had forced them into lives their souls could not abide. *That* she knew not to say . . . Instead, *Yes it's great. Of course the money but also . . .* Also what? What else? A sense of importance? Of being a grown-up? This is how people talk now. No one made her finish the sentence: *Also of course having a career you love!* Little word packages like those packets with the cheese, the plastic spreader unit, and the crackers. Or the prepacked lunches from Brown's with the fork and knife, the sliced kiwi and hard-boiled egg and peanut butter. Airtight. Long shelf life. Nothing could get in to infect, to alter, to ferment.

Foment.

Moment.

Her dread did not involve the tasks, which were engaging enough, in the ways she'd always found the law engaging, a narrative jigsaw puzzle, making the story meet the reality and vice versa; or the people, though they might prove tiresome. But there was the culture. The absolutely unquestioned assumptions. Human rights? How they had quizzed her on this, her professional involvements in it, her personal history. There was always a question mark. Like, had you meant it? Did you still? You've given that shit up, right? We don't believe in that shit around here. Except the gifts office, they paid attention to that shit. You could take a job there at a fifth of your pay . . .

The attenuation of identity that would inevitably be required because you could fake love but you could not fake action. And actions—nobody liked to admit this—changed you. She did not want to *be* what she would become. She did not want to dress as she had to dress. It was not much different from how she'd dressed before except now it was a governable issue. She recoiled at the word *money*. But that's what it was. There was no other conceivable reason to take this job but for the assured draw of fourteen thousand dollars per month and a low six-figure bonus. Likely three hundred thousand a year, now she was in her first full year. She owed very little on her apartment, liked it and had no need to move. She could bank the bonus and then some and quit in a decade and do anything she wanted. Make next to nothing helping poor people. There would be even more of them by then than there were now—she worked for the people who were going to make sure of it.

It was so great.

Unlike when she was nineteen at the bicentennial getting stoned with George on the sand down by the river—it was a little town now, that sand—one could get into the towers from the subway station and depart likewise and never really see them or deal with the size of them. They were, in the immediate area outside, a challenge to one's sense of scale. Approached on the plaza, so near the base of the buildings, one understood them as massive office buildings, unique for, if anything, their breadth; you'd have to look far up to sense their true height and from there you couldn't really see it. Only at some distance, a couple of blocks at least, could they be understood. Thus it became clear to her that the people who worked in them did not understand them: it was a kind of family dynamic, everyone too close to see the true dimensions of the public person any one of the family might be. All the talk of the elevators, of where to go in the concourse, and then back by the elevators, the elevators, the elevators. People were obsessed with the elevators. This was because they were dangerous and inhuman, they were too large, they moved too fast and from time to time they actually banged and shuddered to remind you. Anna had been here only since autumn 1999 but she'd twice heard someone scream in the elevator. Twice. Hard bang. Rattle. Seeming to accelerate. You couldn't believe you were going to stop. Take a dangerous animal home as a pet and soon enough it becomes the ongoing center of attention. Either way you were secretly afraid of being killed. Secret even from yourself. The elevators—they all talked the elevators, yet no one mentioned the bombing in '93. That was off limits. That was actual danger, not merely its evocation. A different building then, really. All this fucking money had moved in since. Four investment banking firms and their attendant enablers such as herself, heading up compliance with the firm Morgan Stanley hired to supplement its legal team. Morgan Stanley wanted to comply the way a safe cracker wants safes to go digital.

The man she was seeing after the New Year, after the worst of winter—Henry, an editor, a man who in his online profile had written (yes indeed, though she'd sworn not to accept such, and without a tinge of irony either, she couldn't fucking believe it) that he loved Sundays in bed with the *New York Times*, but she'd liked his glasses and a witty quote he'd thrown in—now, predictably, he bored the shit out of her.

They walked in the park—it was early spring. She fully expected walking in the park in spring to appear in his Nerve .com listing now.

After they walked, they ended up, for a late lunch, in a bar called Smoke, a jazz place on Broadway that served brunch on weekends. It was well after brunchtime and lunchtime and she and Henry had the place nearly to themselves. There were a couple of friends of the bartender's at the bar, and two waitresses, and eating a plate of grilled vegetables and a pasta bianca at the table beside the one they'd been seated at, André, the owner, who introduced himself and soon enough jumped up to get them a particular wine, a peppery Tuscan red to go with the sweet sausage and rabe frittata they shared.

André was the sort of man from whom Anna picked up an immediate vibe, an electrical current of sex. He was probably in his early fifties, wearing what she noted was an excellent gray houndstooth jacket, black shirt, charcoal pants; he was short, but well built, an active face that passed from expression to expression with an almost digital speed and ease. Within ten minutes, or perhaps five, she knew she would come back to the restaurant alone and she would sleep with him. It became obvious to her that he at least suspected this feeling. Henry—a man who was, in a fashion typical to New York men, almost but not quite genial, a relatively nice person who always had his antenna out for a grievance, who thought his grievances were interesting—Henry was not in the least aware of any of this.

And so she claimed work and headache—both!—and dispatched Henry and after nearly an hour went back to the bar. She smiled at André and took a table; he joined her immediately.

He said, You came back.

I did, she said.

He sat. They talked.

I own a restaurant, he said at one point. It's a lot of work. It's like having a wife who's always sick and mean.

Are you married? she said.

Why do you ask me? he said. You already know I'm not.

You have been, she said.

Everyone has been, he said. He said it in that Mediterranean way that you can't contradict because it comes with a who-cares shrug-off already built-in.

A drink? he said. It's on me.

Some tea, she said. Earl Grey. No milk.

No wine? Maybe something—

No, she said. Tea.

He nodded toward the bartender, who came around to see them. There was only one other couple in the place. The waitresses were off duty until dinner, she gathered. Or new waitresses were coming. He told the bartender to bring him an espresso and Anna the Earl Grey tea, which, she was pleased to see, came loose and in a pot. The cup was scalded. She said she was impressed. He said, These are basics. But she could tell he was pleased. Pleased to please her.

A little more chat. She went in for a minimum of it.

You know why I'm here, she said.

You like our restaurant, he said. He gestured around at the room.

She laughed.

And? he said.

I thought we had a connection, she said. She looked at him. Tea in hand.

Yes, he said. I thought so.

She told him she lived close by. He could have taken her out right then, might have asked for her number, she wasn't sure what he'd do, whether he could even leave the restaurant. He took her number.

Do you stay up late? he said.

Not unless I have to.

Suppose you have to.

Then, sure.

I'll call you when I close. Like to walk, it's close?

Two minutes, she said. Maybe three.

Two, he said. Maybe a minute and a half!

So—he closed the place himself. She wouldn't stay up—she never stayed up in such circumstances or any other in which she was home and could sleep—she'd wake when he called.

When she got home she fed the petulant cat.

Okay, she said. Be that way.

She left him there in the kitchen nipping at his food. She thought about Henry, whom she was about to betray. Or not betray. Merely crush. She'd made no promises, she never made promises. Henry lived in a straitjacket of received wisdom . . . Such and such was the next big thing. This or that was interesting. Have you seen the Gauguin show? It's fabulous. Except it wasn't fabulous in the least: the walls were dark and the rooms underlit and the paintings in particular, seen together, lost their exoticism. Gauguin's colors in that light: a mess. The paintings came off on the whole as a little amateurish if anything. They were not formally interesting and they looked dead. His woodwork stuff was gorgeously ornate and crafty, like something one's secretly talented, perennially strange cousin might produce a few of. The wood itself was deeply alluring: looking at his various tropico-baroque carvings Anna found herself wishing she had not the carving but the wood itself. Perhaps made into something smaller, more human, more primitive. Something she could hold in her hand, feel its density and polish and beauty.

If she challenged Henry with such opinions he would say, Well, I thought it was good, I found it interesting . . . He had no capacity to argue with her because the thoughts themselves were decals stuck onto his brain, not products of its actual workings.

She said to the cat, Fatty Arbuckle, the Fat One, Fatboy—oh Little Fat One, someone's coming over tonight and you are not going to like him. I *know* you won't like him.

She rubbed the cat's neck and behind his ears. He tenderly snatched up bits of his food, as if more from necessity than passion. That was how he always did it. He was a figure of classical ambivalence and disdain.

Her cell—she remembered to put it on her nightstand and washed and got into bed to read. She was asleep by 9:30, the cat along her thigh, his tail sneaking between her legs so she could feel it, bone and fur, through the duvet, each time he flicked it until she was asleep.

When André called she woke instantly, knowing who it was. She said hi, he said hi. He sounded a bit tentative, without his earlier certainty. It was always this way with men, the closer they got the more they seemed to feel the ground tremble beneath them. She preferred the certainty.

What time is it? she said.

One thirty, he said.

She raised her head, squinted. Her clock said 1:47. He was one of those guys. Always put a trim on the facts. Had to. Couldn't not.

I'm closing the restaurant, he said. Locking up.

She gave him the address; he was surprised it was so close. She suggested that he wash up a little, so he wouldn't have to when he got there.

He said, What are you, a schoolteacher? Or what do you call it, the school nurse? I have to lock up, check the kitchen, I'll be there in ten minutes. She murmured a vaguely positive sound, indicating her warm presence in bed, awaiting him, like a fresh bun wrapped in a napkin. He hung up. She liked him sounding irritated.

She lay in bed mildly masturbating, rubbing her nipples, twisting a little at the waist, waiting. When the buzzer rang she banished the cat to the small room, closed him in, and intercommed the man into the building. She listened to him climb the stairs—she was on the fourth floor, he preferred not to use the elevator apparently. All she had on was a black silk robe, nothing beneath. Her skin tightened in the coldish breeze through the foot-wide opening of the door. When he came in he smelled only faintly of the restaurant but strongly of the chilled spring air outside. His short leather jacket. She put her hands against his knotty shoulders and let him see her, in the dim light from the kitchen window behind her and one very small lamp around the corner in the living room. They kissed and he opened her robe, explored. His hands were not rough, despite his work. He put them on her face, moved them down her body . . . She pulled his belt open, managed the button on his pants, pushed her hand in until she had his cock. He kissed her neck. After a minute she slid off his hand, away and down, squatting, and yanked on his pants to free his cock. Everything about him was compact and hard, even his protruding little belly was taut and dense, with a small bit of fat beneath it and then a pelvic bone that jutted out rather cruelly—he even had the bones of an angry peasant. He had a thick cock, sturdy, not quite short but almost. She licked it, drew it between her lips, and felt him transform. It was amazing the way they did that—

this thing that happened to them when you took their cocks into your mouth, always a slight surprise, this secret power, all these years it still amused her. It was like having a jet pack.

He was good. He liked women, it was clear. Used his hands very well; when he'd come, and then she, with his hands, they dozed.

Later, the pale lightening of the sky perhaps an hour before dawn. He was hard and pressing against her. She felt something else too.

Jesus motherfucker. He jumped from the bed. There was the cat. Tail high. And there was the welted scratch rising red and diagonal on the back of his hand. She laughed.

I'm sorry, she said but she still laughed. Meet your competition.

She removed the cat, chastised him but didn't really mean it, he looked at her from the floor of the little room as she closed the door; perhaps she hadn't latched it before. Then she was back in bed with André, and he had her down and was between her legs doing nice enough things with his tongue and lips, but this usually bored her after a while, she'd been with virtually no males who were able to turn her on that way, so after not too long she gently pulled herself away and brought him up into her arms and kissed him to taste herself on him. He was not hard. She used her hand lightly, felt a stirring.

It was well after five in the morning when he stood up from the bed. I'm late, he said. I have to go to the fish market.

You're kidding.

No.

When do you sleep?

I sleep maybe four hours at night and a few hours in the afternoon. Or like eleven o'clock some days in the morning, everything will be set up and I'll sleep then until two. I let the girl handle the lunch, which isn't so much. Some days though I don't sleep.

He went to her bathroom. He had a flat ass that formed two near rectangles where they met the tops of his legs. A moderate amount of hair. His back was wide and slightly curved. His body screamed peasant. She had already decided to call in sick, work from home.

I can use the shower? he said.

Sure, she said. After a minute she rose, holding the cat, and stepped into the bathroom. He'd used his hands on her again and made her come, two fingers and a fist, in and out of her, and now every part of her vulva was swollen from the pounding she'd taken, the lips, the mound, the hood around her clit. It felt as if it was affecting her walk, as if she were holding a wallet between her legs, but she doubted the effect was visible. She watched him in the shower, refracted flesh-colored gestures behind the glass. The cat didn't like the steam and slid from her arms and darted out.

The yellow towel is fresh, you can use that, she said. You want something to eat? Some coffee?

No time, he said. Usually I am out by five o'clock.

This was a lie. It was so funny with them, it was so plain, as if bells clanged every time they lied, bells that not only you heard but they heard too, yet they did it anyway, and no one ever stopped them. She'd gone to the bathroom at some point after the sex last night and hung her robe there; now she put it on. He wasn't so bad. When he was at the door, she kissed him and said, That was nice. If you want to fuck me again some night call me by nine or so and I'll let you know whether it's okay.

When he smiled, you knew he hadn't grown up in the U.S.: the teeth. Okay, he said. Okay okay, and went off down the stairs. Men departing: they always looked to her like little boys, leaving for school. A little cocky, sure, energized, but always, too, a little guilty of something and happy to be getting away with it.

≡

ON THE PHONE with her credit card company. She had transferred money from her bank, it was not being credited. They were holding the money and meanwhile charged her a late fee. She said to the person at the call center, They never had to hold the payment for six days before. Why do they have to do it now? It took more than fifteen minutes including about eleven on hold to get the money liberated, the fee undone, her soul eroded by bureaucracy, no explanation—the banks and credit card companies did this kind of thing because in a percentage of cases they wouldn't be challenged, probably some algorithm that did this to a random set of accounts each month, when the money arrived a day before the deadline. She quieted her fury. Why be furious? This was capitalism.

When she was a little calmer, the buzzer rang.

Who is it?

Henry.

Henry?

Can I come up?

More fury to surpress. Clueless men shortening her *fucking life*. She buzzed him in, opened the door for him. She knew what was coming. The last time she'd seen him she had broken up with him and then fucked him and sent him home. Admit it, she said to herself—she could hear him on the stairs—you confused the poor man.

We have to talk, Henry said.

No, we don't, she said. We talked already. And then we had sex. Remember? So we're covered, aren't we?

She didn't know how not to be slightly nasty. Being only slightly nasty was the accomplishment, in this mood, of a desire to be kind.

But it means something, he said. I mean it's not just some random event. You said we were breaking up and then we went to bed, and now—

Now what? she said. Now *what*? You remember what I said? The last thing I said? That we fucked doesn't mean we're not breaking up, which I then said I was telling you because I didn't want you to be confused.

But I am confused, he said.

Why am I not surprised, she said. Okay, look. It felt good. That day it felt good. Breakup sex. Standing there. Dressed. Minimally exposed. Skirt pulled up. Don't you love that sound? I love that sound, the lining of a skirt against stockings. Very sexy. Today, I can tell you, that's not where my head is. I've just been on corporate hold for an hour. Don't go all emotional on me, Henry. Life is hard enough. It's sex. If we like it a lot, if we like it too much, then perhaps it gets complicated. But frankly this is not what happened and this is not going to happen. Between us. No offense.

No offense? he said.

Yes, quite truly, she said. No offense. Again I'm talking about my frame of mind, not your personal qualities. Or your sexual capacities. Or your cock.

He stood, looking forlorn. Grimaced a little at the word

cock. She felt pity, a little wave of motherliness or niceness, it irritated her that he could elicit that. He was not a bad guy, he just suffered from being a not-even-vaguely interesting guy. She sat down on the ottoman next to where they were standing. You have a handsome cock, she said. I do not disparage it.

And he did. It amazed her how the scrawny, bony guys often had large muscular cocks and the large muscular guys so often didn't. She put her hand on it: there he was, ready Freddy, swelling beneath the prewashed denim . . . of his *boring, light blue, unstylish jeans.* He dressed like Woody Allen. And talked like one of the characters in Allen's stupefying dramas. She pulled her hand back.

Henry, she said. Henry. You're forty-six years old. We've been going out for a month.

Seven weeks, he said.

Seven weeks then, she said. She doubted this but it wasn't worth figuring out. You don't cry. You don't *cry,* Henry. Not here, not anywhere. Jesus.

I'm sorry, he said. I keep thinking of the word *conventional.* You said I was conventional.

Well, you're not conventional for New Mexico, she said. But for the Upper West Side of Manhattan—

I'm sorry, he said again. That word, it plunged me into an abyss. Of gray. A gray abyss.

Henry, see, now, that's the most interesting thing you've ever said.

Maybe you should just give us some time, he said.

No, Henry. Time will not be our friend. Time will just infuriate me. Let's stop before it gets toxic.

This isn't toxic? he said.

Oh no, she said. Not even close.

≡

What goes around et cetera: André later: she found out he was fucking not one but two of the waitresses at the restaurant. Often after closing.

Jesus, she said. Then you come here and go to bed with me.

No no, he said. His hands came up like miniature shields to block this assertion. Not the same day. Other days.

What was it about certain men? He wasn't that good-looking. It's like some animal scent comes off them and women hit the floor on their knees. He didn't have any doubts or misgivings about his desire to fuck you. He showed it in his eyes. He wasn't sizing you up as a piece of meat. He looked straight at you and there it was: desire.

≡

That her firm was basically fucking evil could not be denied. It had only taken the first month to see it whole, though of course she'd known it all along. Morgan Stanley being three-quarters of their business was the first dead giveaway. Indeed, they had their office on the floor beneath Morgan's banking regulations group in the WTC. She and others on her legal team had swipe cards to enter Morgan's floors. Her firm supported Morgan's compliance team. Their job on paper. What they complied with was Morgan. Early in her career, in entirely another context, representing someone in an EEOC case, she'd been in Morgan's offices in Midtown one day and, departing after a meeting with the human resource people and their in-house counsel, she'd been on the elevator descending when some crusty partner had gotten on with four minions. After the doors closed and a second or two of silence had passed, he'd said in a pissed-off voice, I don't pay the goddamned lawyers to tell me what I can't do. I pay them *to find a way to do it*.

She had regarded the man from the side, and slightly behind: he couldn't see her. He probably wouldn't see her even if his face was pointed right at her. He was shorter than all his lackeys. Hair the color of pale slate. A look of permanent distaste on his face, for everything and everyone, carved there as by a sculptor. She understood him the way an oncologist understands cancer, not knowing its cause but recognizing its extent, its effects, knowing that it was incurable and that he was incurable. At that moment too, she had understood the firm—it too was incurable. It didn't even know it had a disease that needed curing. It had to move and it had to eat so that's what it did, and the larger it grew and the more kinds of business it swallowed, the more it had to move and the more it had to eat, and by mid-1999, when she'd negotiated a contract to join up with its near-subsidiary downstairs, to do compliance, it was moving in dark places and eating some bad shit; compliance was like a dash of mustard stirred in with all the shit that got eaten, hardly a thing. What mattered was money. For some of the money, a small dance was required, a certain knot of the necktie expected by the government. Little people took care of it. That was she, a little person, and she would be paid three hundred and twelve thousand, a little more, by the end of her first full year, after her bonus. *What are you going to do with all your money, John?*

24

After Henry and after André she spent some weeks in isolation. She was busy enough with the job to be absent from among her small group of friends. She was not interested in dating again. She tried to keep some healthy food in the house, sauté some vegetables for herself, make some brown rice. She read books, watched films at night—Japanese mainly, she was again becoming obsessed with Japan. And Korean. The Korean films were wild. But some nights she thought about the options, fed Mr. Arbuckle, and found somewhere to eat out, alone. So it was this night. A busy place, on one of the side streets around the corner from Columbus Avenue, bearing Thomas Edison's middle name for reasons unknown, Alva—good food, no tables available by the time she arrived, after eight, but room at the bar. So she took the seat, had her book with her, a little novel by Kawabata, about a writer and the younger woman with whom he'd had an affair when she was sixteen. The woman went on to become a well-known artist but the writer had, in traditional terms, destroyed her life: yet her life appeared to be not destroyed but singular, because of the control as a woman she was able to exercise over it. After her writer-lover, she'd refused to marry. She'd become an established painter, and she had living with her a young woman painter, her protégée and her lover. The scenes between them were delicate as razor wire. Kawabata loved a distorted eroticism—distorted by grief, abuse, modernity. Anna ordered a piece of fish—branzino—with pistachios, shallots and thyme, rice and spinach and little mini squash things. Fish being something she never bothered to obtain and cook for herself at home. A green salad, a piece of good bread and butter.

And so she sat and so she ate and read about Kyoto and Tokyo in the 1960s. And at some point she became aware, off to her left, of a broad, almost tall man, a man that gave a sense of height in the way he moved but was under six feet, she realized; her age, not bad-looking from a quick glance: appraising her. Would she ever be able to understand? What it meant to them, when men looked at her? She'd had more than three decades of this kind of attention now and it still unnerved her, or delighted her, or infuriated her. On occasion, frightened her. She wanted the world to be so ordered that the *right* to look at her, the right to assess her beauty, her class, her erotic potential, was hers to grant: some allowed, some not. Of course it wasn't. And wouldn't be. But the eyes were almost always rapacious: she could feel them down side streets half a block away. From windows. It was an unerring sense: if she felt it, she knew it was there. One was constantly tugging at one's sweater, righting one's skirt, pulling up one's jeans, against those eyes, which were forever trying, like some perverted schoolmaster's hands, to make their way inside one's clothes. Younger, she had tried for a time to give up caring: wear no bra and a loose-buttoned sleeveless blouse and let 'em maneuver for the side view. This was liberating for half a day, then a source of rage and shame. Shame at the rage because that's always where rage ends up when it can't be shown some viable release. She really wanted to kill sometimes. Perhaps this was why half the women of her mother's generation seemed furious and bitter. Not to mention insane, which outcome might, okay, have had other causes, like the systematic eradication of their identities.

And now at this late date, she was forty-three years old for Christ's sake, some fucking guy was staring at her, she could feel it, standing down the bar a couple of seats, she would *not* turn and look at him, only had a rough sense of him—but then he came toward her and spoke:

Excuse me, he said. I believe we used to be in love once.

She turned to level him, to tell him to get lost, to denounce him as a clueless asshole, but some familiarity of the voice and a faint chemical foreknowledge, and her processing, too, of what he had just said, all this told her, mid-turn, that it was George. Then she saw and confirmed the fact. This half-second head start of cognizance was not enough to keep the shock and dismay from her face.

And by then he was actually *crooning* at her, low-voiced: *Well I'll be damned . . .*

She realized she had literally gasped—she heard with horror her sharp intake of air, like Brenda Vaccaro wheezing on that old bra commercial. She put her hand over her mouth.

. . . here comes your ghost again—he finished the line. He laughed at her. You're blushing now, he said. I'm sorry, really.

She was angry. Goddammit, she said. Goddammit. Shit.

I'm so sorry, really, he said. He reached out to touch her but, wisely, didn't.

For fuck's sake, she said, don't stand there looming over me, fucking sit down. I was so about to let you have it. Goddamned asshole staring and singing at me.

He hid his face in his hands.

She looked at him. That's a horrible thing to do. To a woman in her mid-forties. She thought but did not say, who actually *did* love you once.

She reconsidered and corrected herself—almost mid-forties, she said.

You don't look a day over thirty-five he said. Or really, thirty-two. Three. Thirty-three.

He was scrambling to find the right number. Always dangerous territory.

Yeah, sure, she said.

I did apologize.

So you did.

I apologize again. I said what came into my head, verbatim. Often not a great idea.

That's one of the things adulthood is supposed to train you out of, she said.

There's only so much adulthood any one person can handle.

Any one *man* can handle you mean, she said. More males should admit this fact about themselves.

A pause. He said, How about this weather?

It's the not the heat it's the humidity. Actually it was early June and not hot and the weather had been spectacular. She didn't mention this.

Yes, he said. Right. Winter kept us warm, covering Earth in forgetful snow.

He delivered the line flat but with a flavor of affection.

You remember, she said.

I do. You loved it so. I almost memorized it.

You apparently *did* memorize it. It's oddly touching.

They looked at each other. He started to smile, then looked away, looked back with his face straightened.

What are you reading? he said.

Kawabata, she said, and held up the book for a second. An old paperback she'd found used somewhere on holiday. One of the stores on Cape Cod, she suspected.

It's strangely compelling, she said. A society that values art.

He said nothing, watched her.

I didn't recognize you, you know, she said. Last time we met, you were neat as a pin. Louis's play. Now I saw this grizzled floppy-haired guy in jeans checking me out. I was like please God no, but then, what the fuck, there you are, coming over. I wanted my shoulder as cold as I could get it.

It did look—I'd say—lethally cold.

You have a killer opening line though.

Well, I didn't want to kill you exactly.

You aren't here alone, are you?

No, he said. I'm with some people. They're nice, funny. I'd ask you to join us but I can tell you wouldn't and really I'd prefer to politely depart from them and come back and talk to you.

Ha, she said. Well, you're right about not joining. I'm not really up to that. I stopped in for a quiet . . . a quietish drink. I've never seen anyone here I know, before tonight.

She had picked up a guy here one night but she didn't say that. Nor did she say she might have done so again tonight, given the opportunity. The last one had invited her to eat dinner and she'd leaned toward him and said, I don't like to have sex on a full stomach. Now George was the opportunity, a near-paralyzing thought.

George said, Read your book, give me like five minutes.

Or eight. He turned away, turned back. As if to make sure she would wait for him.

Really. I'll be right back.

I believe you, she said. Go.

At his table he drank off his drink and made excuses, went around a bit, there were some laughs, she could see him explaining. People looked over, she averted her eyes, not wanting to look at being looked at. She was doing as requested, reading her book.

He sat next to her.

They looked at each other some more.

Remember—he started to ask, then stopped.

Yeah, hold that, she said. We'll have none of that. That road is closed during the off season. Too much snow. Danger of avalanche.

You look good. Prosperous and everything.

I'm fine, she said, and felt instantly, as always when saying it, that she was lying.

I'm finally making real money working for the bad guys, she said. Are you still . . . what you were? Not spiritually. I mean professionally. A coffee guy.

Not really, he said. I'm transitioning out. We're not really creating anything new, haven't for a long time. It's just about growth now. I'm not that interested.

What are you interested in? she said.

Ah, he said. There's the question. I'm interested in my son, who's thirteen and lives with me.

She looked at her watch.

We have a live-in caretaker, he said.

Funny, she said. A pause. Then: You weren't one of the ones I thought would get rich.

This is something you thought about?

Some people struck me as headed there, yeah, she said. Her first thought was of Evan. Reagan-boy. He was a banker somewhere now. Didn't matter where or what rank: he was rich. Not as rich as George though, certainly. So ha-ha Evan. Should have worked on a coffee truck and skipped B-school.

After a pause he said, We—I mean the men—we identified the already-rich but we never thought about whether a woman was going to *get* rich.

Yeah? she said. The remark infuriated her. Think about what that means, she said. Really dwell on it. For a few days. Or years.

Yeah, I was acknowledging that, he said. Anyway in answer to the question. There are a couple of aspects of it that are interesting—I'm interested in Mexican coffee growers for instance—and many aspects that are definitively not interesting. Where to open a shop in Copenhagen being a recent not interesting example. Also, *why* we should open another shop in Copenhagen, since we have two already.

Three is a stronger number than two.

My god, you sound just like Burke. That's exactly what he would say. Might have said, in fact. These days my ears glaze over. As it were.

You're seeing someone now? she said.

Not really, he said.

She laughed. Not really. Of course. Don't tell Mommy! Mommymommy I only peed in the bed a little and it wasn't my fault it was Frankie's fault, Mommy no really—Mommy!

She did the child's rhythm but an adult tone, without pitching her voice higher. Looked at him, hung between amusement and irritation.

I'm going to try this again, she finally said. Are you seeing someone now?

There is someone I see every week or every couple of weeks . . . Like every ten days, say.

Three times a month, you also might say, Anna said.

You might. God knows what *you* might do, I haven't really talked to you in like ten years.

Seven and a bit, she said. But go on, let us not digress.

Neither of us is committed in any way. I am not breaking her heart and she is not breaking my heart, we're busy with other stuff and basically we like the sex. She has terrible taste. She's forced me to go to not one but two musicals, which I told her is the limit, for the rest of time. I'm fairly sure if she ran into a fabulous-looking old lover in a bar, she'd have no compunction. Is that sufficient?

More than, she said.

How do you know I'm telling the truth? he said.

Oh god, you were always such a bad liar, Anna said. Completely transparent. I doubt you've become that good now. So order one more drink and then maybe I'll invite you up to see my etchings.

Haven't I seen your fucking etchings? he said.

I have some new ones, she said. Then, after a moment's pause, hinging her right arm directly toward him, while he was lifting his glass to his mouth, she put a solid fist in his ribs.

They kissed in the car he'd had waiting, when it took them to her place; she was intensely aware of the unmoving, blunt-cut brown-haired head of the driver up front. She would have taken George home but while she had a cat to look in on, he had a thirteen-year-old son.

Run up and get the cat and come home with me, George said. It's fine. Lourdes can give him some tuna or something.

Not tonight, she said. Plus, he'd punish us all very badly for that. Her body wanted him but her eyes kept landing on the driver's head. What was it this head reminded her of? Her entire life, somehow. Everything that had brought her to this point: a bad haircut in the front seat of a car. And something in it felt cataclysmic. Now she'd spend the next few days wondering if her phone would ring. She wanted to head that off, foremost.

Is this another in our historical series of one-offs? she said to him.

No, he said. Not if I have anything to say about it.

Call me, baby, she said, and moved to go.

That's what you say to all the boys, he said.

Oh no it isn't.

We'll get together tomorrow, George said.

Friday, Anna said.

That's three days, he said into the side of her neck. He felt good.

I'll die.

You so will not die, she said.

What about your etchings? he said.

They won't die either.

One more minute, George said.

One more minute, she said. At forty seconds or so she jumped from the car.

Of course she thought about him into the night, she thought about him in the morning. Not just about him: about what she'd bolted from the car to avoid, the things she'd run away from. She had been alone for a long time, was accustomed to it, attached to it, but it was a wound and she didn't know who she would be without it. He was older and unattached; she was older and unattached. They would not, this time, just glance off each other like two molecules in a heated system. They would stick. She knew this, and feared it.

25

Friday they went to dinner and back to her place. He'd warned Lourdes he might not be home. She raised her eyebrows at him.

Did you tell Nathaniel?

I will, George said.

Nate did not raise his eyebrows or even take his eyes off his laptop screen. Okay, he said.

I'll see you tomorrow, George said.

That would be true in any case, Nate said.

You're very helpful, George said. Thank you. You're like a thug for reality.

Good one, Nate said. George turned to leave his bedroom.

Close the door please, Nate said.

No, George said, over his shoulder.

Anna told him later, in bed, about the last night they'd been together. Not the meeting at Louis's show, but the night in 1979 after he'd helped her move. Twenty years. More.

I went home and cried that night, she said. I cried and cried. Not just for you, not really for you at all or over what you'd told me, though there was that. But also because I knew something was lost.

He stared at the ceiling.

So long ago, he said. He was looking at the memories as if at an old film.

How are you different? she said.

Jesus, he said. How are you? It's too big to think about. Every single thing changes you and we have more than twenty years' worth of things.

Give it a try, she said. As an exercise.

Okay, he said. He waited. She waited.

Well?

Okay. First of all I'm a father and that changes you. Being a parent. I won't go into a whole description of it because everything I would say is a cliché and you've heard it before. Everyone is always the same on this. But from the minute they're born you're changed.

More dramatic for women, I've heard, Anna said.

For women it can be a neutron bomb, George said. The landscape looks the same but everything that is living and familiar has been removed. But a man can hold on to his essential identity and just accommodate parenthood. It's still a change but it doesn't throw you back to square one.

What else, she said. Second of all.

Second of all is money, George said. It can change you and damage you and even kill you—though having none at all will kill you a lot faster. Imagine there's a little fish—a year old maybe, but the big mating fish are three and four years old. He's in the babbling stream and rushing around and eating the bugs and minnows and chasing the larger older female fish who slap him away because they don't want him seeding their eggs but sometimes he sneaks in and bombs them anyway; but then he ends up in the ocean and he becomes, like, a large salmon—

What is this fish thing? she said.

Yeah yeah—now it's the gigantic ocean and he's been hit by a propeller once and just escaped from a tuna once and his ocean-y city has turned into a Manolo Blahnik advertisement with banks and drugstores on every corner, it's like a huge outdoor shopping mall on Long Island, and all the other fish changed colors except him; and he divorced fish wife one and never married fish wife two; and you say, Do you remember the nice stream, and he says, Yeah I remember it well but that isn't where I am now or how I am now.

Where are you now?

He said it without thinking: Swimming in a daze. Thinking about life. Getting ready to die.

That's not true, look at you, you're terrific, you take great care of yourself, quite obviously. You're not even forty-five.

I am not far from forty-five, he said. Spiritually I'm fifty-three. I didn't mean it the way it sounded. I meant: what do I want to do now, who do I want to be now? And I look at these questions from the perspective of someone with twenty years left, or twenty-five, whatever, of active public life, and I have no ambitions, none, I don't want to prove anything to anybody, I don't want to convince the world of anything anymore, I don't want to work. I want to be as peaceful as possible and think and read and maybe write a little, just journals and notes, you know, like a blog. But on paper. I'll tell no one about it. I'd like to sail again—I will sail again. I'd like to paint, to learn to paint. In which case I'd first have to learn to draw. Big decisions.

Now it's sounding like a retirement community, she said.

Exactly, he said. With a Zen garden. I look forward to shuffleboard before lunch. Mainly I look forward to quiet. Do what I do privately. Travel. Quietly. I'd like to live in Mexico, on the coast. Except I'd also like to live in the South of France. And Hong Kong.

And quietly get laid at least once a week, Anna said.

That's a bad thing? I want to take photographs, I want to sail, I want to travel, and then write about what I've seen. I have no other plans. I have a thirteen-year-old son. Fourteen in January. I can feel him departing. Not in a bad way. A natural way. He knows I'm not the point anymore, nor is his mother. So it's just me and the forever now. I've made a lot of money.

I would imagine so, she said.

That's it. That's the ocean. Money. It changes you.

Aha, she said. So that's why I don't swim like a fish.

≡

THE SEX WAS awkward at first—it surprised them both how the years could change people erotically. He was muscled from the gym but she remembered him young: the muscle was there as a natural occurrence underneath a soft layer of youthful disregard.

Awkward largely because of George's faltering erections: he would be hard and then, suddenly, not. Or he'd not get hard at all. Sometimes it went fine but in those circumstances often rushed because, Anna could tell, he feared losing his hard-on. Maybe one of ten times or two of the first dozen had they been able to take their time and enjoy each other's body and enjoy their own bodies in relation to each other's body. Once or twice too she felt him take her with full desire, with actual urgency. These were the only times she had an orgasm in the early days—when she felt he really meant it, and when she felt him with real force. When she didn't have a sense of him up above, watching them as if from a high window.

She told him that part: that she felt as if he were watching from above, was not actually present but thinking about being present. George kept trying to explain it to her—and to himself—what was going on with him, this thing he had learned about himself: he told her that he had lived, was still living, his sexual life in memory: he was unaware now, maybe always had been, in the midst of the act itself, of the moment he was living in. At the beginning, with someone new, he was lost in anxiety; once past that, he was lost again, buried in a desire that was a memory of desire, lost in the sensations, in the images that fed the memory, he was loyal always to the memory, to the feeling of being inside someone as a sensation of having been inside someone else, at some other time; fucking to images he didn't know he had once focused on, images that he couldn't have the full pleasure of when they were part of the reality before him, only when they came up again later, sometimes much later, when he was with someone else in some other place and time. Something would get lodged in his memory, a very precise moment, the way a figure on top of him and facing away would turn, look back, while riding him; hair on a shoulder; the curve of a woman's side, the belly and hip and beginning of limb; then, having not really experienced them when they were *there*, he would be haunted by them, they would appear to him while he was having sex or while he was masturbating, again and again and again.

So, why did it work with the woman he'd been seeing before, sex three times a month? she asked him.

She was fundamentally an actress, he said. She took real

pleasure in the pose. She'd wanted to do videos, photographs, but I wouldn't do it. I mean I hardly really knew her, who needs to be blackmailed.

But the imagined camera, she said. That you could perform for.

Yes. No. Well, maybe. But the point is, he said, this is real. That wasn't real.

If any principle guided the hierarchy of what from his erotic life lodged in his memory, it was to the moment, or the accumulation of moments, of the woman's wanting, of her eagerness for him, her urgent offering of herself. The way her hips rose to him. In a hotel room once he'd said to a business acquaintance—a married woman from out of town who had invited him for a drink, which both knew meant sex—after they'd been at it for a while, pausing, going again, he hadn't come, and late in the evening he said to her I want to fuck you in the ass—and he would never forget her face: the flush of affirmation: she turned away and offered it to him, her ass, broad, dark creased, willing. He came fucking her ass and he had come two dozen times since buried in the memory of that affirmation, that offering; he didn't remember the fucking, he remembered the offer. Or years earlier, that summer of Fridays with Suzy, in his humid room on 110th Street, no curtains, she didn't care, taking her dress off, a sundress, flower-printed, reds and yellows, up over her head, no bra: and she knelt on the bed and put her mouth around his cock. They had sex for two months, but the only actual intercourse he remembered was fucking her from behind in her childhood bed, frilly comforter and white headboard, in her parents' house when she'd invited him out there and her parents were away. So often in recent years, he told Anna, he was reenacting, recording, recording what was already recorded, until at last he would finally come, in the white-hot blindness that forced him to let these memories go. It wasn't merely semen he poured into his partners, but a pornography of memory.

When it was over, he would have to pull it all back to find the humanity in it. He saw now that the intimacy of the act was an aspect he barely accepted, something he had been trying, for a while, maybe always, to keep at bay. Of course: intimacy was an abattoir. He had to look back at his sexual life—and occasionally on his capacity to love—as one would on a vivid and chaotic crowded dream, so many images in the sex, so many disparate narrative directions, in which everything was tangible. He could hear, see, smell, taste, feel. At such times he was not experiencing intimacy but instead some kind of flesh-driven sensual aesthetic event, high-art erotica, close-ups in black and white, the weight of breast in his hand, the nipple, the shoulder, the armpit, the neck. All those beautiful lines and curves. The strangeness and allure of a body other than his own body, its smells and tastes and textures. A woman's buttock cupped and lifted as she lay on her side with one leg drawn up. Her cunt wanted his cock, he could feel that, but he could not feel *her*. Or no—actually this was not true: he could feel her, if he worked at it and cared enough; over time, he could learn to know her in this way, he could at the end hold her and kiss her and take in her smell and feel the force of her reality. What was missing was not his feeling for her, but for himself. The missing figure was him, always him: he was only there to have the experience of her. He saw himself as if on film. So intimacy—intimacy evaded him. He had learned early to fake it well. But he was always protected. And he was always ready to flee, always desiring flight. Intimacy left him lying in his bed at sixteen hearing his mother's boozy voice coming up the stairs singing, *Ohhh we ain't got a barrel of monn-ney, maybe we're ragged and funn-ny* . . . until her footstep fell heavy and dreadful outside his door.

But here it is, he said. I can't fake it anymore, not with you, now. I've lost those chops. I'm defenseless.

To me? she said.

To you, to this, to us. To a different life. To a certain kind of vulnerability I haven't had to feel for a long time. Maybe ever. Or not since you and I were together twenty-four years ago.

Anna wanted to know if he'd been faking intimacy with her back then.

He thought about it.

No, he said. I didn't know what it was, what all this was. I didn't know where we were going. It was pure romance. Then, you see, I discovered I was vulnerable. You might recall I ended the relationship at the drop of a hat, essentially.

It was slightly more than a dropped hat, she said, and he laughed. I mean, it seemed like a pretty big deal to you as I recall.

Yeah, but you knew it wasn't. I could see on your face you knew it wasn't. Which made me furious. What *was* a big deal, what you couldn't see, was suddenly I was staring into a raw wound, into vulnerability, and I didn't like it. I didn't want to feel hurt, not ever, not again. Only loved and desired and served.

With this he wanted to hold her. He pulled her close to him. I'm sorry, he said.

Men, she said. One wearies.

Yeah, well, he said. That was all he said.

≡

After this conversation, it got better. And better and better. There was excitement in it, romance, a fulfillment of a neglected hope. But it prompted in her as well a sense of jagged break with sandy layers as when you snap a piece of halvah, a dissociation from her own life—as if her parents had arrived to live with her—as if she'd contracted and then been cured of a difficult disease—as if she'd found her brother. Some frightening thrust into the past, that common fearsome dream where you're back in school naked and late for an exam. He called her *at work*. Nobody called her at work. She said to a friend at lunch, Remember when lovers used to call each other at work? That's so great, her friend said. Anna could hear her chagrin. But it *was* exciting, in the past. The phone would ring and you wouldn't know who it was . . . maybe H.R. Maybe your doctor's office. *Or your lover*. Someone at the intense diving stages just before you become lovers. Someone you wanted to be your lover. Now she had caller ID and she knew who it was, so the little thrill came not with the voice but the digital display of a number. And if she was busy, a little bit of *ugh, not now*.

They were together two or three evenings a week and later four or five: dinner, movie, maybe drinks, eventually more evenings of supper in, Lourdes's cuisine, a little Ecuadoran (her own), a little Mexican (her husband's), a little bit contemporary New York. When they stayed in, Lourdes got to go home to her husband. If they went out George would apologize and she always said, No worries. Now that Nate was older and her husband had come up from Mexico she had ceased living in full-time. But if George was out she'd go home and give her husband supper and come back and stay over with Nate.

George told her to have her husband come over. She could feed him at the apartment and they could watch television together but even after almost fourteen years she was shy for that; or perhaps he was.

≡

For George the relationship was the strongest of the recent tugs against his attachment to his job. He negotiated with Burke a new role, part-time, slightly vague, he had an office and an assistant and one of his chores now was to find something for his assistant to do. Her name was Katrine; about thirty, very smart. He sent her to all the meetings he didn't go to and increasingly took her when he did go. She represented him with crisp authority; or so he was told and, dealing with her, so he could guess.

What do you do now? Nate asked him one day. For a living?

I'm still with Brown, he said. I'm senior vice president for strategic initiatives.

You don't do marketing anymore? Decide what to call the drinks, what kind of furniture to put in the shops?

No. I'm out of the jargon-and-chairs business.

Mainly you hang around with Anna, Nate said.

Yes, George said. When she's available.

George was sitting with his laptop in his office at the back of the apartment. Or office/den: computer, desk, couch, chairs, TV. Nate was standing in the doorway. He often stood, just so, in various doorways. He offered no full commitments, such as would be implied by coming all the way into the room.

Is that all right? George said.

Yeah, sure, Nate said. Does Mom know? Or do I have to keep quiet?

I happen to know you've already not kept quiet, George said.

Oh yeah, Nate said.

Anna worried that Nate didn't like her. He'd turned fourteen at the beginning of the year; boys that age, she hadn't dealt with them since she was fourteen.

George said, He happens to like you very much.

How can you tell? Anna said.

He told me.

He seems alienated when I'm around.

He's always alienated, George said. Or no. He always seems alienated. It's a kind of pose. He's very skeptical and detests enthusiasm of all kinds. He's what we used to call a sourpuss. But he definitely likes you. He wants you to move in with your cat.

For me or the cat? Anna said.

Thirty percent you, George said. Seventy percent cat.

≡

THEY TALKED ABOUT a future together. Or he did, when she let him. She had her heels dug in spiritually, she wanted to move slowly, slowly. Talk about vulnerable, she said. You had a lasting relationship. You had a child. For me, every single attempt has been a disaster. She noted that his job was becoming easier but hers was getting more difficult, more demanding. Some days, openly hysterical. Morgan was looking for new avenues of profit after the tech bubble. The regulatory maze was not one maze but a catalogue of mazes and she had access to a library of maps that were supposed to work if you found the right one. Morgan's strategy, a compliance nightmare, was to create, almost weekly, new kinds of financial instruments and throw them out on the market to see what or who would bite. The prospectuses were like those impossible British crosswords. All the large firms were doing the same, copying and revising one another's Byzantine inventions. It would take the feds years to catch up to it all, so let's all worry about that later. She tried gently to remind her legal colleagues who were actually in Morgan's employ that this might be a shortsighted attitude, that the future didn't merely hold the fed but actual consequences. *I don't pay lawyers to tell me what I can't do . . .*

George knew she liked her professional identity, she liked having a staff and standing and she even liked the bigger money, but she hated her actual job, what she had to do, the people and the values she had to accommodate. And over all the nights they stayed together, mostly at his place after she'd fed the cat, but sometimes at hers, with him turning woozy on Benadryl to fight his allergy to the feline, he kept hinting to her that she could, if she wished, quit; and he would quit, and they would travel together, and the world would be new and beautiful. He suspected she couldn't quite take it in, the idea that they could live to be a hundred and not spend more than a fraction of what he was worth. She couldn't see it: freedom of that radical kind. He managed to dislodge her for ten days, finally, and they flew to Mexico, with Nate in DC for his spring break. They stayed for almost a week in Quintana Roo with its astonishing beachfronts edging the rain forest; and then down for a couple of days on the opposite coast, in Chiapas, with a day trip inland to visit the Habermans. Then Oaxaca and on to Mexico City to fly home. He knew she had once had some feeling for Mexico, akin to his own great affection for the place and he could see it being rekindled. But she was eager to get back to work as well. He could feel it, in the day or two before they caught their flight home.

Back in New York, he told her he loved her.

I know, she said, her head on his chest. I know. I'm going to get there soon.

≡

8:12 ON A Tuesday. September 11, 2001. Anna had taken to coming in early, by 7:30 usually, clearing things away, this allowed her to leave when she felt like it, knowing she would clean up in the morning. It gave her a start on the day; she'd found coming in to a clean desk left her not remembering what exactly was the *next thing.*

8:35, she thought of calling a realtor. She was practically living with George now; she was ready to bring the cat but she had not yet been able to accept the idea of selling her apartment. What in the world, where in the world, would be *hers*? But it was a note on her desk: three realtors to call, recommendations from colleagues and friends. Things had gotten easier. The sex had gotten better: whatever he'd been scared of he didn't seem to be scared of anymore. And she really liked Nate; she even liked Marina when Marina was up in New York. Marina seemed happy for them. Marina mainly was busy. Everything this family said to one another had an edge, what might seem like meanness but really was their own form of intimacy, insulated by humor. She felt more alert than she had in a long time. She even had moments, looking at George, most of the time when she was looking at his enormous uncomplicated back, like a bricklayer's—she had moments when a near-tears feeling of love for him came up in her throat and hurt her eyes.

She'd force it down again. She wouldn't say it yet. She wanted things on the lowest burner possible.

8:46. Her coffee flew off the desk at her, scalded her arm, she flew then, the coffee fell all over some papers, the papers danced to the floor: all facts that she took in a split second before she'd aurally processed the noise, the enormous crash. Her first quick thought was *earthquake*: such a huge earthquake to happen in New York. But then no. After that things got murky. The lights went out, emergency lights came on. A piercing alarm. Behind which there was a lot of screaming. Announcements were made that couldn't be distinguished from the other noise. After the alarms cut out they heard they should stay at their desks awaiting further instructions. This was bullshit, they all knew it was bullshit. For one thing, the smoke, it was already crawling in from every available opening in the skin of their suite of offices. For a second the heat: the building was getting hotter. With co-workers, people hugged, touched, people said we're going to be all right, people said my phone has no service, and together they made their way to the stairs—sixty-two flights, hard to contemplate.

And moving down them, one flight, two, five: a vapor of uncaring: like a gas seeping into the air she breathed. She could feel it, an anaesthetic slowing her down, slowing her down, slowing her down. Something different from the smoke, which was acrid beyond acrid, like burnt plastic knife blades in the bronchi and lungs, a serious poison that made you think if you made it out you'd die of this shit anyway. People choking and sobbing on the stairs. But still moving. The ones who stopped stayed against the walls on the landings. Some she saw entering the floors they'd reached: she wondered what they thought they'd find there. She continued to descend with others, no one spoke, just made noises of despair, weeping some of them, she looked at them as if from another time and place, already historical. And by the time they were down fifteen flights or so, every half minute a firefighter shoved past them all, then her, then the next one, going up, men become mute aliens with tanks and monstrous masks, Otto Dix's stormtroopers advancing in the poison air, the charred air, which she breathed. She was getting sicker from it but she paid as little attention to that as possible—or rather it mattered to her less than she'd have found conceivable before today—all she cared about was going down down down. She had descended so many flights: dropdropdropdropdropdropdrop turn dropdropdropdropdropdrop turn—over and over spinning down down down in a circle. She would have taken off her heels but for the heat and the broken glass. Suddenly she knew what the people were doing who were entering the other floors, suspending their escape. They wanted out. They must be breaking open the sheath of glass that ran up between each decorative beam along the skin of the building, they must be jumping. Of course. The air alone would be a relief. She couldn't see the numbers on the doors, the emergency lights were too dim and the smoke was too thick; she tried to keep track of the flights, but she lost the count. She'd descended twenty, maybe twenty-five flights. Which would put her where? Fortieth floor? Thirty-fifth? Possibly she was underestimating, perhaps she was only twenty or twenty-five now from the lobby. It was hot—it was getting hotter. The firefighters up and everyone else down, no one speaking, people crying but no screaming, at least she thought not, or if there was it was almost undetectable because the other thing was so present, an ambient roar, so it was like an enormous roaring silence—this is what hell would be, perhaps, the roar of flames, sound as torment, at the same time human speechlessness, the ultimate silence—like a meat of silence, a raw substance, the people in front of her and behind her: *all exit in silence*. She wanted to stop, it was time to stop. She felt the building was trembling now, she stopped on the next landing and stepped out of the way, she could feel it swinging and lurching, just a few inches back and forth, caught between wind and flame and the unmeasurable forces of concrete and steel and human horror. Quaking. A deep ongoing rumbling like an earthquake rumble. But the uncaring was like a drug: all was alive, but shrinking down, tunneling down, and she knew that there was nothing left to care about, to worry about, to fear: an all-enfolding mercy: freedom. Freedom and mercy were the same thing, the inside of the moment, once you were allowed to step into you were forgiven. She was overwhelmed. She was glad, suddenly, sickeningly, that she had never had a child. No child. But of course. Because if she'd had a child it would now be orphaned. This was how she confronted her own death: if she'd had a child she would be leaving it. She was breathing in little sputters, she was about to break. But then there *was* a child, present in her mind: a moment of confusion and then clarity: it was herself as a child, standing and waiting for something. Oh god how she suddenly loved that child: tears came. So vulnerable. Children were so vulnerable. Look at the people, so frightened, moving through the smoke and ash. All children. What do we do to them? And then the rumble grew louder, fast, and then an immense roar, a second only, a sound like no sound that had occurred ever before, so huge it transformed physical reality, so loud it took possession of *everything*, so large she began to feel herself escaping, sliding out from her own body to evade it: the air was fumes and dust and smoke and the noise was a force that lifted her and she was in the air: oh god this was it. She opened her mouth, she was forced forward and everything was being let out, everything in her and right there the building just broke around her and split and she saw a flash of the sparkling sky, just a flash and then—time is a supple thing, it expands outward at a push—before the darkness she thought of her parents, she thought of George oh George if I'd just had a half hour more I might have made it out but now she was inside the end of time flaring outward like a musket—and then then: she was smashed. She had an enormous eighth-of-a-second's self-knowledge of being snapped, crushed, a monumental assault, a disposal of her, too fast for pain, though somehow encompassing the pain, then nothing but darkness and blinding light . . . And here was everything and here was nothing: in the midst of everything, nothing, and in the midst of nothing, everything. Oh the sound, the light. Then no more light. Then silence. True silence. She loved the silence. And darkness. She loved the darkness. Here was the child. It was waiting for her. She knew this child. It was her. It was her but not her; it loved her. It was love itself. The soft weight of the child, the soft darkness of the silence, and the simple will to disappear into that. All was soft, soft. The child, silence, darkness. Pinpricks of light. Love. She hadn't known—oh but yes, she had—she *had* known and she *knew*. Always. It was always there, just outside the mind's grasp. This. The silent love of a silent child silent in darkness. Love—not merely from without but from within—the love had been her love and her love had been the same as all the other love.

All that love. All that darkness.

It took her.

═

And what was it? Consciousness lingered after the body went. A half second or a second in regular time, containing infinities, telescoping parentheses, an unimaginable refinement, a half second you stepped inside of and disappeared . . . She did not miss the sand or waves of oceanside or the slats of sunlight angling in the woods. The sharp air of autumn. The faces of children. The urgency of love, the rush of ecstasy. Not eros, hunger, pain, relief; not the taste of coffee or fresh lime or late-summer tomatoes, the little strawberries in Rome in June; nor the myriad colors, they were all inside her now, seen in a perfect light—she did not have to miss anything at all because everything was present. Everything resided inside the shell of a moment and the moment never ended and here was the same as there and everywhere else. A thousand years, a single day . . . She still felt every touch of desire, without need. Was it true that no one had sufficiently loved her? It was not true, manifestly not true—look how plain it was, that she had been loved with love both infinite and specific and these were expressions of the same love just as any two words in the language are expressive of that one language. She had been loved from before the beginning of time and she had been loved in time. She saw her brother—oh how broken. He loved her. He thought of her daily—of course he had and he still did. Some southwestern city in midday's merciless light, broken by shame and pointless sense of failure. Pointless because what was there to succeed at, after all, that could touch or change all this? She saw George, who loved her, who had finally said it and clumsily showed it—he had never in fact stopped loving her—he was wandering there in the smoke and ash. She saw his longing and his grief. The longing, the longing one carried around hour to hour, day to day, the grief, the sense of loss and hopeless need, she could see his, could see her brother's, who was so broken, could see that of her blind, willfully clueless parents—but her longing was no more. In this present, nothing was missed, everything was known, nothing was longed for, everything was, here, now, always: a condition of complete simplicity. This moment would never give way to some predicted next moment—and so longing was not even possible. She could see it, the world's longing, like a ribbon of stars, like a widening band of debris on the dancing surface of the sea, a widening crescent of suffering racing away toward an indefinable horizon: endless human longing, endlessly fulfilled, if only they knew it. But they could not.

|| PART THREE ||

far from the twisted reach of crazy sorrow

26

God gave them a day of supreme beauty in which to lose their city. The sky was a depth of blue, pellucid, pure, that could occur only by special dispensation, with not a cloud visible, not a hint; nor would there be clouds for days. That morning, shortly before the first plane hit the North Tower, George had stepped out of his building's doorway to go downtown and everything visible before him on the street stood out in this special light; the visible world was giving full expression to its three dimensions; every object, every person, every stone cornice and metal grate and human gesture, almost every breath (as if he were tripping and could see human breath in the air) insisted on its own place in eternity and he couldn't doubt the reality of anything, including, when he learned of it, destruction at the scale capitalism had finally made both possible and, through the numbing violence of its entertainments, eerily familiar. This was what people said when they saw it on television, that it looked like a movie they had all seen before; but the people who saw it from nearby didn't say that. From where he watched on the corner of 23rd and Fifth (the Seventh Avenue train had finally given up at the 23rd Street station), by the entrance to

Madison Square Park, he could make out every ridge and detail of the towers' silver exteriors and every jagged edge around the enormous lusterless black holes from which flames danced and gray-black smoke hurled, lower on the South Tower than on the North. The North's was much larger—the entry wound. A super-matte black, absent light—totally without radiance—to such a degree as no one, he believed, had ever before seen in the natural world. An absolute black, an unimaginable flat lightlessness. With flames licking out: these were the gates of hell. He was looking at the South Tower. She was in that tower. He knew it. Since a little after nine, when he'd first heard the news he had been trying to reach her on her mobile and at her desk, at first busy signals—who got a busy signal anymore?—now there was simply no service. People stood around him dazed; a woman wept. People kept trying their phones, putting them away. He wondered if all of them were trying to reach someone they believed might be inside the building, as he had been.

And then it fell. People screamed. The muted roar of it reached them a second or two after the fall itself. All around him screams, shouts, as in near–slow motion the building sank massively—but *massively* hardly did justice to what he was seeing, they were all seeing, the size of it, the gigantic collapse—and disappeared in a monumental burst of dust and debris. A man to George's left kept saying, Oh my god oh my god oh my god oh my god. George felt a blanket of horror and beneath it a shattering of the nothing, the no-feeling, that had resided all his life where grief should have been. Like a low flame of agony had been lit and was finding its fuel. His stomach did a flip, he thought he would vomit but he didn't; he was too paralyzed to vomit. Oh my god oh my god oh my god, the man continued to say. Finally: There must be five thousand people in there!

He was shouting, the man, he was momentarily unhinged. As were they all, but almost all were silent, except this fellow. Five thousand people!

The dust rose as if from a bomb. He thought, couldn't not think it, that we'd been doing as bad as this to people around the world, virtually weekly, for decades. The debris flew up and outward into the sky like a flock of millions of birds taking off in panic and determination—and the birds, the pigeons and gulls and starlings typical in such light, where were they? All gone. Replaced by paper—terror origami—white pages diaphanous and brilliant, confidential memos, reports, the mountains of accumulated unnecessary bullshit on 20-pound 92-rated bright white photocopy stock—floated out over the harbor; they would be gathered up that day and the next and for a week or more thereafter from the streets of Brooklyn across the harbor. *We from the streets of Brooklyn and you know we good-lookin'.*

≡

LATER, ARTHUR TOLD George it had all felt to him at first like a wartime catastrophe scene, working downtown that morning—cops, roadblocks, fire and emergency services, ambulances on the backs of which sat people getting oxygen. Debris. People wandering. Lights flashing. This was all in the pictures. Arthur had been forced to duck the cops—the last thing they wanted to see was him and his camera. Then it changed: everywhere and toxic, like something in the desert, a sandstorm during a gas attack, he saw the dust rise and begin to roll up Broadway, he tried to protect his Nikon beneath his sweatshirt and he started running north. Arthur was a big man, stocky with a gut, but he'd lost weight from a decade earlier: he looked as if with enough impetus he could move with dispatch. Before the wave overcame him he ducked inside a Chase Bank. The bank ATM foyer as sanctuary from the bombers, that was a twenty-first-century American construct. The House of Morgan. Darkness—the power was out. Pale red light with little reach coming from the emergency lights, two on the front wall over the doors, one on each side going back. Bless the manager, he hadn't locked the place up yet. People just standing, some sitting on the floor up against the tellers' banquette. It would come to mind many times later, after the fever of militarism and policing and security and the wealthy getting wealthier at the direct expense of everyone else, he would remember that day in the Chase Bank on lower Broadway, that there were no cops, no visible guard that he could remember though there must have been; all that money and nobody gave a shit.

He was worried for his camera: he'd bought two years prior a refurbished F4, an auto-everything camera and was shooting with it the 28–105mm AF lens. He had a manual-focus 20mm with him and would use it. He had twenty or so rolls of Kodak 400 color print film and he knew it wasn't nearly enough. The F4 loaded automatically: if he could get it out of the goddamned dust. Wasn't there a Calumet down here somewhere? Maybe they'd let him in and give him a can of Dust-Off and some more film . . .

He never found the Calumet.

But god bless Nikon, the camera still worked. He took some shots out the windows including one of a man bent over, one arm slung over his head trudging northward in the storm of destruction like some old-time blizzard shot you'd see in the archives. He had a contact at the *Washington Post* he wanted to call to say he'd have the pictures but he knew there'd be no service down here, land or cell. He'd have to get himself uptown to a landline before too long—though if he left he would not get back in. In the end he just walked into the offices of the *Times* and the *New Yorker* and gave them pictures. It worked out.

In the bank no one spoke. Some, he could see as his eyes adjusted to the light, were quietly crying, or had been. Others just stared into space; that expression on their faces, like Bobby Kennedy's in the picture of him at JFK's funeral, a blank mask, no one home, whoever lived there had moved away—far, far away. He would see this expression on people all day. Stunned into silence.

≡

PEOPLE WANTED NUMBERS. How many? The mayor that night, normally to George's view a vicious and small-minded man, a definite prosecutor and an old-school Catholic priest rolled into one, with similar sexual peccadillos it turned out later, somehow found within himself one evening of grace and responded: *Whatever the number is, it will be more than we can bear.*

This was the difference between cities and nations. People outside the city, Americans, responded with love of country that turned within hours to hysteria and ignorance and militarism and destruction; conspicuous flag-flying, which always, in George's lifetime, signified the desire that Americans go somewhere distant and kill large numbers of brown-skinned people. This time would be no different: the president threatened and the jets flew within days.

New Yorkers, though, responded with affection and grief

for their city and, for as long as such was permitted in the general clamor for war, they created a community of the most loving and generous kind, an expression of a civic personality like nothing George had seen or could have imagined. He didn't hear a word about revenge, retribution, patriotism. This terrible event had happened: in many ways they all knew, but didn't say, that it had been inevitable, that they'd all at one time or another expected something like it, though not on that scale; that American foreign policy, like Malcolm X's famous chickens, had come home to roost. He heard kindness, he heard help, he heard encouragement with emphasis on the actual root word, *courage*. People reached out for one another in extraordinary ways.

═

THE FIRE BURNS as the novel taught it how . . . Beneath the rubble the fires burned for weeks, while men clambered around the surface looking for survivors. In the early days the steelworkers were going through a pair of boots every day, the bottoms melting down from the heat beneath their feet. Sometimes, and with less frequency each day, a set of two sharp whistles would go up and people called from all sides *Quiet! Quiet!* and everyone would stop—a thousand men some days would stop—the machines would stop, everything, and the deepest, always-shocking silence befell them; most of the men would remove their headgear, their helmets, and wait, while another body or part of a body was carried out on a stretcher. Every time.

No one George knew had been deeper in it than Arthur, not just that day but for weeks after—and whenever Arthur thought about it later he would lose his shit, yes, break down. But while he was there—he put in ten days or so done up to look like one of the workers, shooting with a borrowed Leica he could keep under his shirt—he shot the pictures. He shot the pictures of the men carrying out the stretchers, of the men above him high atop the mangled peaks of the rubble, silhouetted against the magnesium-white light of the construction kliegs and ghostly in the dust. They looked like astronauts and soldiers and Spanish Conquistadors.

≡

THERE WAS NO describing the smell downtown in those weeks, poisoned, sharp, vicious, it felt so tangible you thought you could cut it up into acrid squares and wrap it in butcher paper.

Yet George wanted it. Brown was providing coffee, tea, and food to the workers, so George was able to get himself onto a list of volunteers doing overnights three times a week at St. Paul's Chapel, which was their respite center. He didn't wish to leave this place. That smell was his, it was his pain, it made real as the eerie white light made real the dream of the towers falling, shown over and over, falling, falling, falling.

St. Paul's was just north of the site, which everyone now called *Ground Zero* though he would not; a rage was building in him at the comfort people were taking in all things military. Even those who disliked it hardly dared whisper against it. Patriotism was all, the Correct American Response, but he could not share in it. He could not understand a culture, a society, a country, that had so opposed war twenty-five years ago and so loved it now. He had never seen a flag enthusiast who was against war, who did not in fact approve of killing, the browner and more distant the victim, the higher the rate of approval. Anger was spreading in him like a virus and making him sick.

He could not take in that she was gone. Could not apprehend it. Or he could understand that she was gone, that he wouldn't see her again, that his grief would entail split-second memories, flash images, followed by suppression and pain; what he could not internalize was that she was gone in *there*, in *that*.

The hole—not a hole actually but an unimaginable topography of rubble—was like an alien landing site: planetary-strength white light radiated from it—metal halide lights of such size and density he could not believe the world had ever seen such before, glowing across town to Wall Street and westward out into the river, allowing the dredging of the steel and glass and concrete piles, peppered with tissue and bone of twenty-eight hundred humans, to go on night and day. The metalworkers employed in this physically, psychologically, and morally toxic task received food, massage, rest, clothes, podiatry, acupuncture, and other nonmedical doctoring and bodily comforts, even psychotherapy, at the chapel, which had almost been hit as the towers fell and as the surrounding buildings burned, but which had survived and so remained the oldest building in Manhattan, where George Washington had once sermonized. Even having put in time on his high school football and wrestling teams, George had never seen gathered a group of men so enormous as the metalworkers brought in from around the country to work at the Trade Center site. Not one had smaller than a fifty-inch chest and many exceeded that by a dozen or more inches. They ranged in height from five feet six or seven to perhaps six feet, but not much more. Height was not an advantage for them. The church had stacks of clothes, sweatpants and sweatshirts and the like, they were coming in by the truckload from around the country, sized from normal small to normal extra-large and if you had doubled the extra-large size you might have been able to fit a few of the men, who walked around where the clothes were stored, in the upper galleries of the chapel, held up the shirts, and laughed. Useful and in demand were the Timberland boots, provided by the company: again, multiple truckloads. In the early weeks, too, meals were coming in four times a day in vans from the Union Square Café, Café Daniel, and other high-end restaurants. The whiteness of the light in the streets around was made even whiter by the dust in the air, a permanent white smoke hovering two stories or three or four stories above the pavement. He helped unload the food, chatted with the other volunteers, he was in a state of mind such that ten minutes after speaking to someone he could no longer remember the person he'd been talking to or what had been said; he twice, in the span of an hour, introduced himself to the same woman—a thin, practical woman in charge of the late meal that the men came in for at eleven p.m.—and just barely stopped himself from doing it a third time.

I'm sorry, he said. I'm in a daze.

Did you lose someone?

He'd not answered this question before. It hadn't been put to him directly—not did you know someone or is your family okay but Did You Lose Someone?—and the answer made bile rise in his throat.

Yes, he said.

I'm sorry, she said. There are so many. So terribly many.

Yes, he said. Yes.

Death had undone them. He was a full-grown man; even, in some circles, an important man, a man with authority and responsibility; he did not wish to weep here at the chapel of

St. Paul. He wanted to work and then walk, since he had the authorization, not otherwise to be gained, to walk around.

I'm from Brown and Company, he said. We do the coffee and tea.

Oh, she said, perking up. Thank you.

We're working on doing some more on other fronts.

Now he was on stable ground, now he was talking the company, now he was talking business, he could function. He was existing in ten percent of himself; the rest was a stunned, beaten prisoner, the prison itself having suddenly descended all around him, leaving him to stand before a cracked graffiti wall of injuries and grief.

Certain moments you know right then will change everything; other moments slip by you and you realize later, there it was, that was it. Over and over it comes back to you. This was both—a first.

≡

In the days after, once the subways opened again, but for the farthest downtown stations, which wouldn't be opened for months or even, in the case of Cortlandt Street, years, with the lines all switched around for reasons no layman ever understood, so that the F was the D and the N was the Q and nothing was what it was supposed to be, a city rearranged as if it had been spilled and too hurriedly restacked—in these shredded days, you could go to Times Square station and see the tiled columns covered, completely, with flyers, overlapping, double- and triple-layered, mid-shin to overhead, masking-taped appeals seeking the lost, the unaccounted for, the not yet legally dead. Estella Dominguez Stuart—worked at Windows on the

World—last seen 8:10 a.m. Sept 11 2001—any information please call . . . And gathered on the concrete around the columns at first a few candles and flowers and soon enough scores of them and other trinkets and small treasures, a primitive culture's strange gifts to the gods who'd struck down with fury and fire the two mountains at the bottom of the village, an act of unimaginable destruction. Staring at him day after day were all the photocopied faces. Smiling mostly, snapshots at family occasions. Some of the signs were done with graphics software and some were in a desperate scrawl.

After a few days and into the next week he had felt compelled to find her family. He knew so little. This was the atomization: they had loved each other like ions, or like particles that attract but don't join. They ended up in a kind of orbit around each other. He didn't know their first names; he couldn't remember the town they were in. Somewhere in Pennsylvania. He and Anna had hardly talked about their families; he talked about boats, she about books, politics, work a little bit, almost nothing personal, except perhaps her brother and his music collection. Which filled specially-made low shelves that ran the length of her living room—something like fifteen hundred vinyl albums. The Goffs. But, the town, the town. Finally it came back: Hershey. She was embarrassed by it. The chocolate town. But back in the day she was embarrassed because everyone used to say Hershey highway. This almost bent him over, the Hershey highway. An explosion of erotic imagery in his brain and the near-tangible presence of her essential shyness, her vulnerability. Boom, like a bomb. Oh my god, it took him this long to learn how to love somebody, love somebody really and deeply and painfully, and now it was being carved out of his flesh like some enormous tumor hacked out with a hunting knife. This hurt was the collapsed star of all his hurt, all the hurt he'd never allowed himself to feel, come back to say, *no matter how many years you wait, we're here, we don't die on our own; you have to find a way to kill us.*

≡

AND THEN: HOW long should death really take? Anna had no will that George knew of. She had him, she had a small group of close friends, three or four; what other lesser friends, ex-boyfriends, other connections she might have had, George didn't know. Back in Pennsylvania, she had parents she didn't have much to do with. She had a minimal mortgage. Her expenses had been low, she had banked over two hundred thousand dollars in the twenty-two months since she'd taken this job, the job that killed her. A life insurance policy equal to her draw was part of her benefits package. So the parents were going to come into more than half a million plus her apartment and the equity she had in that, certainly another four or five hundred thousand. And beneath the gravity required by the situation and beneath their actual sadness, George could see their secret excitement. All they needed was the death certificate. How long it would take, no one knew. Eventually, at the suggestion of a lawyer George had hired, they filed affidavits from everyone they could find—leading with George and including even the building super, who'd seen her leave for work that morning—attesting that she had a job where she had a job; that she'd gone in that morning, early as usual; and that she hadn't been heard from since. Her beloved cat had been alone. She'd left two unwashed dishes in the sink.

How eerie it was in the first days to go back to her apartment. He'd spent many nights there with a sense of safety and happiness and freedom he'd not felt before, not for any prolonged period; now it was harrowing. He'd been going to feed the cat and water the plants. Enough already—he would have to take the cat.

I need you to come with me, he told Nate, and Nate came, not a word of reluctance or complaint. As he was nearing fifteen, this was notable. He'd been nothing but cooperation since the towers fell. In the apartment the usually aloof cat came to them immediately; Nate bent and stroked him. He's hungry, Nate said. Gordo. For Gordito. Fat Boy. The Fat One. None of these his original name but the ones he'd grown into, earned. They fed the cat and let him eat, wandering around the apartment, which gave every sign of being the well-lived-in home of someone who on leaving that last morning had not doubted for a moment that she'd be coming home again at end of day. Mail on the table, clothes on the chair. Two glasses and a bowl in the sink which George had refused to touch, as if it were an art installation, not reality, not actual dishes. He watched Nate wash them; this moved him. George wasn't ready to look through—invade, rifle—the files, her papers, for official documents. Her mortgage for instance. Her birth certificate. Her insurance information. The company she worked for, one of the sucker fish to Morgan, not much of it left, he was betting, did they even have another office? Jesus, when you considered the details, these deaths were complicated and there were almost three thousand of them. Nate squatted and was going through the albums. Wow, he kept saying. Wow.

You can probably have them, George said.

Nate turned to look at him. Really? he said.

I don't think the parents were ever interested in them.

Some of them are worth real money, Nate said. The whole collection, who knows.

Then I'll pay them, George said. He didn't say it would make him feel better to have this connection to her, across him to Nate, like a bridge. Something like family has.

When the cat had eaten enough for the moment and walked away Nate washed the water dish and food dish and George dried them, packed them in a grocery bag with all the cat food she'd kept in the cabinet over the stove.

Get a bag and help me with the litter box, he said to Nate. Nate held the bag, George emptied the litter. Packed up the massive litter supply—it was like farm seed, in a big sack—ran water in the tub over the litter box, dried and packed that too in a blue IKEA bag. Nate had found the cat's travel box and was sitting beside it on the couch with the cat in his lap, purring and crinkling its eyes.

That cat has never been this friendly, George said. To anyone. Except her.

I wonder if he knows, Nate said.

The cat went quietly into its box. George was expecting a fight: the lack of it, again, moved him. They waited for the elevator to go down: George with all the bags and Nate with the cat.

That was sad, Nate said.

George just looked at him, then looked away.

You're going to have to say something soon, Nate said. You can't just keep looking at me with that expression on your face.

What expression on my face? George said.

Dead. It's a dead expression. Casting call for the zombie movie—that expression.

Okay, George said. He was looking down. Then up at his son, then down again.

Yes, it's sad, he said. It's beyond sad. I'm afraid if I talk about it too much, or at all, I'll come apart and you'll have to hold me up and hail a cab and pour me in it. Really, you don't need that.

There, that was better, Nate said. You won't come apart. You never come apart.

That's what you think, George said.

They stepped into the elevator. The door closed, they started down.

Anyway, George said. Thank you.

You're welcome, Nate said. So now we have a cat.

You'd never know it, he's not making a sound.

I think he knows, Nate said.

They got a cab.

Anyway, yes, now we have a cat, George said. I'm going to have to get shots.

He tipped the cat box a little and looked in it. Tears started to drop down onto his shirtfront, his lap.

Hi, cat, he said. Jesus fucking Christ.

27

Grief was like carrying a stone, it bent you; it bent you double, pressing down on your shoulders, and it filled you inside, a grief-stone within you, something you'd swallowed or something hardening in your gut, a pain of petrification. He could never have imagined it: he'd had plenty to grieve over, his father, his mother, his marriage perhaps, but he'd never allowed himself to grieve, he went on instead, numb and more numb. Here, it overwhelmed him, there was no putting it off. Not after watching the fire from the jagged matte black hole, not after the smoke and dust and paper peppered the air, not after standing on the street corner ready to fold himself up and die as the building she was in folded itself up and died.

Fall passed to winter passed to early spring. All of it mild—God's little favor. Arthur was getting an award from the Press Photography Association, he'd invited George. For photographs taken on September 11, 2001, and in the days thereafter . . . Arthur Townes. Awards that May. Arthur had asked for Louis to introduce him, an odd choice and not a member of the society of professional photographers but a celebrity now and politically burnishing so they said yes and they got Louis.

George bought a table and filled it with various eager souls from Brown, including a couple of photography enthusiasts; and Nate. Nate was a high school sophomore who owned his own tux. This made George strangely proud. He wondered if Arthur actually owned a tux, or had to buy one for the event. Or god forbid rent one.

Louis said, I met Arthur when I was writing and editing for the Columbia *Daily Spectator*—there was some sparse applause here and Louis looked up with surprise and a genial smirk—we're in the house, I see, he said. Anyway. Arthur's work *always* startled me. He had a funny habit back then, he'd hand you a pile of seven or eight work prints and he would *never* put the best ones first. Never. It was a test. He wanted to know if you knew what you were doing with a picture. Like are you a part of this sacred enterprise or just some godless interloper? I went out a few times back in those days with my camera and I said, oh I'm going to take pictures like Arthur's pictures! It'll be *swell!!* Of course they looked like shit. Pardon my language. I have no idea what makes a photographer like Arthur such a good photographer. I couldn't figure it out then, and now, well, I'm more self-absorbed and not as smart as I was then, so forget it. But I think photography, like writing, requires just a huge amount of practice and a huge amount of failure. To withstand all that failure! It's biblical, really, but of course I'm obsessed with the Bible as you know so don't listen to me. But you look at Arthur—

Louis waved his arm toward Arthur down the dais. Look at him!

People laughed, Arthur laughed.

That's an artist, people.

Louis looked back at him.

Like all artists, he said, you're a mess. But you're beautiful.

He turned back to the audience. Because that's what it takes. Which is everything. Every single thing you have has to go into the pit. That's all I can tell you. Arthur is an artist and I don't think he has spent many moments on this earth not being an artist. You can see the stone-hard determination in him the first second you meet him. And the lunacy. I did. And now you can! Ladies and gentleman, without further nonsense or palaver, I give you Arthur Augustine Rutherford Townes.

They applauded. Some stood, not all. Arthur was not, in the end, that popular. He was a pain in the ass and he hadn't always done the right things to have a good career. Failed marriages, strange projects and obsessions, a kind of physical failure of a man, like a weary shopkeeper from a century back. But they applauded. They liked Louis, after all.

Arthur waited at the podium. Clearly uncomfortable, physically too aware of his body, until he settled down. He hand-checked his jacket front, shirt, bow tie. George could see the hand move, that he wanted to check his fly too but thought it best not to. The applause settled.

He said thank you. Then he said: Photographs are not memory, John Berger said. Read Berger, everyone should read Berger, uh huh. Doesn't matter what book, they're all good. Anyway, Berger said that photographs have in contemporary times begun to replace memory. He was responding to Sontag, who was getting at something similar in a much more complicated way, which of course, right, it being Sontag. Photographs replaced memory. But I think they *started* as *part* of memory, an assistance to memory—memory wants time to stop but can't make it stop, it's a constant struggle and we always get things wrong, remember wrong—but then we had pictures. So now I think he's right. We all of us have a few frozen images in our minds about that day, about September 11, and they signify. Someone says 9/11, and if you didn't lose anyone that day, what stands in your mind in response is one of these images. Some of those images I made and I'm grateful for that, grateful I was alive and could be there. Yes. And my Nikon kept working in all that dust, thank you, Nikon.

Some scattered applause in the house.

Pronounced *Nee-kohn* in Japanese by the way. I sent the camera and two lenses off to them for repair and cleaning after, and at my request they took all the dust that came out of these things and put it in a double baggie and sent it back with the camera.

He reached into his pocket and held up the small bag, about a cigarette's width along the bottom of the bag, pale gray dust and particles of darker shades.

Here, he said. For the reliquary. It's safer there than with the EPA, I'll venture you that, because the EPA is burying that stuff as fast as it can and claiming all's well.

A bit more applause. He smiled at them, rubbed his nose.

Anyway, the thing is, right, no plain image can evoke all of what it felt like, all of what *happened* there. The sound of falling bodies . . . you know. The enormous roar. Enormous. Roar. It felt bigger than the air when the towers came down. I kept imagining after the South Tower fell the sounds of thousands of people screaming: it was as if I could hear it. And after that it never let up, uh huh, never let up! A kind of tinnitus of horror. Uh huh. Yes. This is what the mind does in such places: no photograph can do that for you. Or to you. Film or video can't do it. Only the mind, only the human imagination, stirred by the facts. I kept working, kept looking and shooting not because I had some heroic impulse to photograph, I mean, right? What did it matter at that point, right? But because if I didn't keep working I'd go insane. Uh huh. Insane, yes. I mean, think of all that death. Think of it. Of course in certain less fortunate places they have to deal with that scale of death not once in a lifetime, as we hope is true for us—they have to think of it every day or every week. I can't imagine what that does to you. That our country is often the cause, or even just the supplier, of such death should make us weep. Uh huh, yes, right. Weep.

He paused there. Took a moment to collect himself. There was no applause for this.

Anyway, he said. Then the second tower came down. I had to move north, uptown, right? Yes, uh huh, away from it, we all did, yes. Running up the road. Yes. The air was poisonous and thick, right, I mean we still don't know, right? And I'm sure, right, the bureaucrats will never allow us to know, sure, of course, what was in the air then. And in the months after. But my god the police and firefighters and EMS people, these incredible women and men, they kept going south. Kept going into it. I didn't see one hanging back, not one, and I was looking, I *wanted* to see that. I took a lot of pictures of them. They ended up looking like World War I soldiers in the fogs and mists of the French woods. Right? Like *Dulce et decorum est*, right? Of course what could they do? But they went. They didn't know yet, so they went. Listen, these people are not saints. I'm a black man, I can testify with *total* confidence, these people are not saints. Not even close. But they went. And whoever could come, came. And whoever could help, helped. For days, for weeks, toxins and soot, whoever could help helped. That's my city.

Here the applause started.

The ironworkers, he said. Huge men. They came in and

the soles of their boots were melting, every day. I mean you've read this, you know. And they stopped and took their helmets off for every body, for every part of a body. Hundreds of guys. Stopped. Waiting. Heads bare. With fire beneath their feet.

More applause.

I have pictures, I can tell you, I have pictures. Standing still until they carried the body out. So that's my city. And no matter what, I will always love it. Always.

Here they stood up. Applauding.

He gestured them to quiet. He wasn't finished. He thanked them. He thanked them again. Then he asked them for five minutes' silence.

Five minutes, he said, when everyone was down and quiet again. Not one short minute but five full ones. Okay, right, it's going to be very uncomfortable. I'm just warning you. I'll stand here and keep time. Little Casio but it works. Yes. Five minutes in a public place like this is an immense amount of time, absolutely, yes, but this, this was immense, right? That's actually all I'm trying to say, it was really frigging immense, excuse my language, and anyone who was down there when two of the tallest buildings in the world came down in jet fuel flames will tell you it's impossible to describe how immense it was. No they cannot. So we need to be immense back. Right? I'm not asking anyone to pray who doesn't pray, I mean that's silly, right? But close your eyes—let your minds wander. I don't care where, or to what—you know, nice shoes or feet—

Some people laughed at this, who knew his work. He smiled out at them.

Yeah, he said. Or whatever.

More laughs.

Okay. We're all going to close our eyes. Five minutes. Just let go of time and expectations. Starting . . . now.

He had warned the waitstaff ahead of time. All the table staff stood against the back wall. There were the hundred clinks of crockery being put down, of forks, knives on plates. Then silence. It went on forever. It was painful. People were writhing, some of them, or so it felt to George, who kept his head down at first, then lifted it and looked around. Arthur's head was down too, but George saw the watch on the podium. His head down he still kept a slitted eye on the room and on the time, he peeked from beneath his brow. George got him, at this moment, Louis was right, he was an artist, and he wanted to make these people *feel* something, to take them beyond where they'd willingly go without him, and he was controlling the moment and the place with a Casio watch. Tonight, five minutes was his art. Down to two minutes. Coughing of course. Coughing every few seconds, then none, then it would start again. A number of the men had begun checking their expensive watches before the three-minute mark and more of them after, as they approached four. George saw them. He also saw bodies, body after body after body, plummeting like heavy sacks or whirly babies through the air, and he imagined the sound, he hadn't been close enough but he imagined it, the sound of bodies hitting the hard ground: just like Jeffrey Goldstein all those years back. A hard thump with a bit of squish like a mark of punctuation, a comma or an apostrophe. The sound would be hideous. Awful. Every time he saw this in his mind's eye and heard it in his imagination, he felt something break. Four and a half minutes. He wanted to shout out to the squirming room that it was almost over. Then finally it was.

That was very hard, Arthur finally said. Thank you.

People were looking up. Hard to read their faces. Some, a few, with tears. Dabbing with their napkins.

Our souls are immense too, he said. That's why. More immense than we know. I mean, yes, I bet. It's what my father would have said. Yes. So three hundred souls here, offering that silence, difficult, yes, but it might do some good. You never know. Thanks again.

He waved oddly, like Nixon, George instantly thought, and went back to his seat. Again they rose, and they all rose. It embarrassed Arthur; he looked as if he wished that they hadn't and that he was anywhere else but there, being applauded. So he rose too and clapped back at them. When he sat again, they all sat too. So that was okay.

≡

How like Pearl Harbor it was, had been, as signifier, as unifier, yet how unlike. George's father's generation; Arthur's too. George knew that Arthur's Methodist father had been chaplain on an aircraft carrier in the Pacific. George's father had been sent to England and there he stayed, a clerk, filing the paperwork after D-Day. Pearl Harbor. *December seventh . . . a date . . . which will live . . . in infamy*. It changed everything. But it had become clear to George at some point in his youth, listening to them all, that for those who were not maimed or killed or psychologically destroyed; or who did not have a loved one maimed or killed or psychologically destroyed—for many, in other words—it changed things for the better. These were the best days of their lives, during the war and in the years just after. It not only effectively ended the Depression and brought back jobs, it blasted their world with meaning and that meaning would last most of the rest of their lives. As they aged, they missed it. That's why they reacted so badly to the rebellions later, of their children. Couldn't those children see what American Life was all about? It was about the just rewards for putting on a uniform and saving the fucking world. A naïve notion, but they all believed it as deeply as they believed in their own hands and feet. That the Soviets might have saved a little more of the world than the U.S. had, that dropping two nuclear weapons to make sure the war ended before the Soviets could march into Manchuria, that didn't save much of the world; and commencing a forty-five-year war of nerves and guns and lost lives, largely the lives of people darker of skin than Europeans and white Americans, for some ephemeral geopolitical idea about *influence* and *markets*, might not have saved anything at all, might have destroyed quite a bit in fact, but *that* they didn't think about. It was a glorious thing, that war, if you didn't die in it, if you didn't get your leg shot off, or have your soul destroyed. It gave them a vision of themselves that sustained them.

This, though. This. This attack and the infinite spreading endless war against ghosts that was sure to follow, this drained meaning right out of the world. It exposed the rot and cobwebs and vacant spaces they'd all been walking above, on a latticework of broken planks, for two decades, gingerly moving about while never mentioning that the floor beneath them was disappearing, then was gone. It made *Sex in the City* look like the product of a mental disorder, when before it had only seemed the product of a moral disorder. A week after the attack Susan Sontag had written in the *New Yorker* that the widespread reaction, indeed the required creed—that *the terrorists* were *cowards* and that we were blameless—was purely delusional, ahistorical, ignorant; the statement was brief and almost innocuous in its plain logic and to George's lasting amazement every well-meaning liberal from Maine to DC and NY to LA then condemned her. Not that it mattered, except to her (seeing the butter on her bread drying up, she recanted); what a woman, some half-European called Sontag, wrote in the *New Yorker* didn't much penetrate the red states and the red states, red signifying blood and meat and flushed pre-heart-attack Caucasian faces, were in charge now. And the country would fight and fight and fight for years to come—anybody sensible, it seemed to George, could already see it. What the fuck were we going to do, had anyone ever been able to do, in Afghanistan? Against the mountain tribes? Or in Iraq and Iran? Everyone would get rich off the guns. Truckloads of cash—billions—vaporizing in-country. And the military contractors. Fighting on, because somehow if the U.S. were able to kill enough of the people who hated it then everyone else would revert to loving it, and the country could magically return to the conditions that obtained when the world did not despise and ridicule it. Redemption through bombing and assassination.

And now it was our turn to taste the smoke and the rubble.

28

It was not that beauty had been drained from the earth: that was false; George could see it for false in front of his eyes. That entire autumn, in fact, had been the most stunning of his lifetime, a kind of balm to the wounded. The situation felt much more as if something had been drained directly from *him*. Personally. Not merely from his spirit but from his body. From his own relationship with himself as a body, a corporeal being. Some hope in the future of his body as an instrument of force and pleasure and meaning in the world. As an active agent. Pointless. It all felt pointless. And it *hurt*. Grief hurts physically, a kind of low-grade ache that flared at odd times like a volcano flame. Each day he proceeded quietly, feeling tired, doing what he did without conviction. Some measure-taking of the vividness of experience was gone. He had been drained. So beauty no longer meant, fully, beauty. Beauty meant beauty minus something. Beauty meant .71322 beauty and the rest was charcoal gray. Some diminishment of efficacy and effect. He walked through his days as if he weighed more. But he was working out almost daily: weights, floor, three or four miles on the treadmill. He remained his thick white self but he was a hard thick white self. This was not depression such as he had known off and on in his twenties. This was a rock inside him. Wind blew paper in the street. He saw it and later he could close his eyes and see it again, see it before sleep: the grit and old leaves churning and the paper flying above it, an unholy white bird. Brown & Co. stores every few blocks but often he'd be out and wanting coffee and not be near enough to one, he'd have to take a cab unless he had time for a ten-minute walk out of his way. *How could this be, when it had not been so before? Are we closing stores? Am I wandering into exotic neighborhoods?* No. And a rage would rise up then: rage, not mere anger. He wanted to put his fist through the glass corner windows of the Middle Eastern bakery/sandwich place on 23rd and Park Avenue South. Where he could not buy a coffee. Buying a coffee from the other places was no longer an option. He could, quite literally, be photographed doing so and the company would lose two percent of its market capitalization in a week. He met a woman at the gym. She could read him as rich. He knew this. More paper blew in the streets. How she tried to please him. Finally he told her: 9/11. Goodbye.

≡

GEORGE'S ASSISTANT, KATRINE: she had gotten the green slacks—key lime—and found herself matching flip-flops. She was wearing the dress flip-flops today. Little glass beads on them.

We're wearing flip-flops to the office now? George said.

You're not, Katrine said. Just me. And they're not flip-flops.

I'm glad, George said.

These are one-hundred-and-eighty-dollar sandals, you should know.

I'm tempted to say we're paying you too much but I know we're not.

No, you're not, she said. But occasionally one buys oneself something.

One does, George said.

Spring 2004, the cat, the Fat One, was sick and at the vet. Anna's cat, two and a half years after. El Gordo. George's heart rate was accelerated, he was feeling beside himself, he was surprised the degree—desperately, enormously—to which he did not want this cat to die. He was on the verge of a full-fledged anxiety attack. Perhaps this *was* a full-fledged anxiety attack: the thought made him more anxious. But the cat. Poor thing had a lump in his throat. They were going to operate to remove it. George had called three times already for reports; they kept telling him the vet would call after the operation. At three thirty or so he couldn't take it anymore and left the office and took a cab to the vet's. The vet was in another operation and would be out soon. He paced. They asked him to sit (he was agitating the other pets in the waiting room, it was thought); he said, I'll wait outside, please come get me. Cars went by, it was 79th Street just off West End Avenue, a big crosstown street with entrances to the West Side Highway, which in none of its parts was officially called the West Side Highway. Here it was the Henry Hudson Parkway. South of 59th, it was West Street. North of Van Cortlandt Park, the Saw Mill River Parkway. This was an exit and entrance point. Four lanes of traffic. Suburban SUVs. Cabs. Immigrants in Corollas. He tried to slow his heart rate: breathe. Breathe. How could this cat do this to him? He could see it all again, the rubble, the smoke, the white lights. The flyers posted everywhere with pictures and short biographies of the missing. He'd never put one up for her, he'd known it was useless but now he regretted that, it seemed callous, lazy, selfish, like not providing a headstone. She had been officially declared dead in a legislative gesture in late 2003, no remains ever identified. So no grave. He was thinking of buying one; getting her a stone. He would. He would. Let this cat be okay and I'll buy you a fucking stone okay? Like the diamond you never got.

The cat was, in fact, okay. No cancer, it appeared, and so the labs proved days later. Soon he was eating again with gusto, putting back on weight he'd lost, showing his usual contempt, peppered with moments of affection, usually first thing in the morning when he wanted fresh water and new food. So George bought Anna a headstone and a plot, up above Tarrytown in Sleepy Hollow, she'd be buried where Ichabod Crane had last been seen, until she'd spotted him that night in John Jay Hall almost thirty years ago. He told her parents, then took them to the site—what ritual? Who knew what ritual; the cemetery had a chaplain for a fee, they used her.

≡

THOUGH HE'D SWORN that he'd avoid the neighborhood he couldn't really, not while Nate had friends down there. Battery Park City. A little town of ten thousand souls, all in the top ten percent of United States earners and most far better, constructed in the 1980s across busy West Street from the Trade Center site. Battery Park City was not of itself interesting but a strange sight now that other place was, across the road, the former WTC, twenty-foot-high cyclone fencing tarped on the inside, and lights of white fire glowing above it night and day. People with apartments nearby were known to buy blackout curtains for the nights. Two years and not much visible progress had been made. George had come down to pick the boy up and prior to making himself known he stood watching his son play basketball with his friends; there was a park along the river and he watched from a kind of parapet separating the upper portion of the park from the lower, where the basketball court lay. Beyond that, westward, some trees and the Hudson River. He had a car service driver waiting on the roadway, a flight of stone steps above where he stood. He was content to let the driver wait and watch the game. There was Nate, with his luxurious hair, at the center of the scene. Tied back into a stubby ponytail, like a samurai's. Sweaty gray tee hanging off his chest. George looked out toward the water, the trees affording him just fragments of a Hudson view, and reenvisioned that night in 1976—he tried to place himself in memory on the dirt, the landfill, beneath all this construction . . . with that gorgeous young woman; he felt it in the gut, again. How he'd envisioned growing old with her, traveling . . . She hadn't wanted to give up her apartment, her sanctuary, so they had decided to buy a house in the country and furnish it together. His little ice chest, durable plastic, likely still somewhere below them: the Igloo. The Igloo™. That was the difference between then and now, or one of them: in those days one felt no need to call a thing by its corporate name. It was the mid-'80s or later before he even knew they were called Igloo™. Hell, Brown & Co. had introduced more corporate marketing jargon into the lexicon than most and the company still trained the assistants to correct those not using the proper text. *Soy half-caff latte* baby, tall, grande or venti. Back then, for the ice chest, he'd used *ice chest.* Now there would be no other way to refer to it except by its corporate name. George watched Nate with the ball. Nate was only five feet eight and broad of chest and back, his mother's son, her family's brand of peasant genes in him. George had been late in his growth, Nate might grow an inch or two still; George knew the matter pained him. He was a good ball handler. Back to the basket, a man on his shoulder a good three inches on him. He cut to his left, his shoulder in the defender's chest, and angled for the baseline. Watch the hook! one of the other defenders yelled from the far side of the lane but too late, Nate went up, his entire width separating the taller boy from the ball, his right leg lifted high, and he lofted a classic hook shot. That's right, George thought—you can only *watch* the hook. Nate could have been Bob Cousy in 1958, thicker and heavier but formally flawless with this ancient shot. He didn't wait to see it swish but turned as soon as he landed and trotted back to a defensive position beyond midcourt. One of his teammates went by with hand out at waist level—they briefly touched fingers; a gesture suggesting another gesture.

What was this, when you saw your son do something so practiced, fluid, known: when you saw his personality in his work, as it were. The retrograde quality of the shot—very Nate. He had asked George lately about waistcoats, fobs, and spats. What was this feeling? Commonly called pride, but the word did not suffice. Like a sentimental television commercial with beautiful smiling third-world children and a time-lapse film of a flower blooming while cloud formations whizzed by overhead, except the child was his child and the flower was . . . what? His own self, his identity, his life, his love for his son, his existence on the planet, unfolding like the long uncertain legs of a newborn calf just rising—what was this feeling of completion, of fulfillment, you underwent when watching your child succeed, thrive, exist on terms utterly his own, out in the world, against the world or with the world, what was it? Undercut by grief, still surrounded by the ache of terrible loss. This was why the mayfly died after mating, after the dropping of the silted eggs. Completion. Human children had no pupae in which to lie and grow beneath the stones. One had to stick around for a good long while to protect them. Parents became accustomed to this role and weren't programmed to understand that at a certain point, a very early point, it was over. But then one day you knew. All the future years were uncertain but you had no more say over them than you would for whether the trains ran on time. All the years, what to make of them?

Yes. There was a question. What to make of them. Here is where he had the full taste of his solitude.

≡

GEORGE HAD BECOME fascinated with the Golden Ratio. He asked Nate endless and, Nate repeatedly pointed out, profoundly unmathematical and pointless questions about it.

Okay, you have a line, AC call it. On that full line a point, called B, is situated such that the full line, AC, over the partial AB line is the same ratio as the AB line over the shorter BC line.

Right, Nate said. There are many other ways to express this. Like with rectangles. Or as one plus the square root of five, divided by two.

Yeah, that's a complete mystery to me. Anyway, that ratio in both cases is represented by *phi*, or roughly one point six one.

No, Nate said. One point six one eight zero three three nine eight. I mean you have to keep at least the eight. One point six one eight.

So you know the Fibonacci sequence?

Yeah, Nate said. One plus one is two, two plus one is three, three plus two is five, five plus three is eight, next thirteen, twenty-one, thirty-four, fifty-five, yeah. Each number plus the one before it yields the next number.

So this is insane, George said.

I know what you're going to say, Nate said.

We didn't do math at this level in high school.

That's not what you were *going* to say, Nate said. What you're going to say is once you get up to fifty-five and eighty-nine and one forty-four, the larger number divided by the number before it basically equals one point six one eight.

How can this be? George said.

It is, Nate said.

Yeah, right, that's how God answers—I am who am.

No, but it's a mathematical fact, that's all.

No no no, George said. It touches infinity. The Fibonacci sequence goes on to infinity and the principles go on—around and around and around—like the tigers in *Little Black Sambo*.

Yes, Nate said, all keeping the same proportion *ad infinitum*—

Nate pronounced the phrase in school Latin—*ahd eenfeeneetoom*—providing George a sense of pride and annoyance, a paradoxical mix he'd found common in parenthood.

What's *Little Black Sambo*? Nate said.

Never mind, George said. Forget I mentioned it. A boomer slip of the tongue.

Of course Nate googled it.

I can't believe you were told this story, he said.

That's only the beginning of the injuries, George said.

Nate was down in DC with Marina, for a long weekend. She called George.

How are you, she said. More like a declarative than an interrogatory.

I'm fine, he said.

No you're not, she said. Nate says you're a ghost.

Thank him for me when you see him, George said.

How do you know he's not here now?

I can feel it through the wires, the lack of a certain vibration. The Nate effect. Where is he?

At a friend's.

He has friends down there?

He does now, she said. A girl. Daughter of some people we went out to dinner with last night. I brought son, they brought daughter. The twain met.

What time will the twain get to the wailwoad station? George said.

Funny, said Marina. Meanwhile, forget Nate. What are *you* going to do?

What is there *to* do? George said.

I don't know, she said. I'm sorry to be so useless. Do you want to get together?

By this she meant go to a hotel and enjoy their bodies for a while.

No, George said. Thank you. I want to find a way . . .

What, she said.

To come to terms. To accept. To stop hurting. To go on. To love well. The rest . . . I don't know. The rest is up to God.

You believe in God? Marina said. That's new.

I believe in . . . creation? The workings of the universe? Mathematics? Fate? The constant *phi*? Something. Call it God.

Um, okay, Marina said.

Call It God: A Memoir, he said.

Call It Cod: The Life of a Massachusetts Fisherman, she said.

Call It Odd: The History of ESP, he said.

Call It Bod: The Art of Looking Hot in Tight Clothes, she said.

Call It Sod: The Laying Down of Patches of Grassy Earth.

They could do this all day.

Enough, she said.

I'll stop if you will.

Deal, she said. Although we still had mod, nod, pod, plod, wad, clod.

That's not stopping, he said. I was working on Christopher Dodd but I'm holding back. I expect the same.

Oh no, you have to tell me the Christopher Dodd, she said.

Call Me Dodd: The Man from Willimantic.

Willimantic?

Willimantic, Connecticut, is the home of Senator Christopher Dodd, yes. About forty miles north of Old Saybrook. Up Route 32 there.

George gestured with his hand to the unseeing phone, despite the absurdity of doing so, a dismissive gesture upward. *Up 32 there.* Likely she could see this in her mind's eye: hear the gesture in the tone of his voice.

≡

ON BREAK FROM his junior year at Berkeley, Nate for Christmas gave George *The Last Waltz*. The new DVD. Or, George discovered, the reissue of what had been the new DVD a couple of years before. It was enhanced. It had more songs. There were the special features. There were the weird studio pieces at beginning and end.

Let's just get to the concert part, George said. They watched together.

Interviews, etc. Nate manipulated the DVD remote. All George could think of was a collection of warm summer nights in 1978—a more merciful summer than the one before—and of seeing the movie on one of them with a pale, highly cultured girl, a classical singer in training, a Canadian, from Toronto, easily bruised—literally—by his light stubble which burned across her white skin, by his mustached lip which chapped hers so thoroughly that she looked as if she'd gotten drunk and smeared her lipstick across her mouth. He hadn't known for certain if he should kiss her, some fear or doubt he felt, he didn't know her signals, which was just waiting, talking, laughing, past one, past two. No physical movement toward him, no gestures, hints. Except they'd held hands in the film—why hadn't he known she wanted him, she asked him later. What did he think she was sitting there for at that hour? Finally they kissed—it must have been two in the morning by then, in his apartment. She wore a dress and heels, and stockings in the heat; the movie had opened at the Ziegfeld, where all the big movies opened, and the place had just installed its first Dolby sound system, which rattled their bones. The Ziegfeld was on 54th near Sixth Avenue; soon after the film started, once the actual concert portion started, he was so happy he reached for her hand and then paused as he was almost to it; she sensed it there; the millimeter-by-millimeter coming together of two young hands at a New York City movie theater in 1978. It stirred him now, to think about it. Such tentativeness. The erotic power of it at that granular level. The communication between them, without speaking or even—especially—looking. They inched toward each other, and touched, and fingers found fingers; they never looked at each other or acknowledged what was happening, the fingers' slow movements each like a miniature caress. Then she moved, or he moved, one of them coughed perhaps, smokers as they were, and it ended, and after that he didn't touch her, there beside him, and wondered later why he hadn't. She told him she wondered too. After the film they walked east to the newly opened Citicorp building, which had a nice restaurant that had impressed her. They both ordered scotch—Johnnie Walker maybe? She had hers neat, adding a touch of water on her own, he had his on the rocks and she chastised him for the ice, which she thought was criminal. So did he, now. Lex and Third Avenue above 42nd Street was still a kind of no-man's-land in which stood this shining new aluminum-clad tower and various side buildings; other than that, this stretch was hookers and sandwich and hot dog places with sales windows open onto the street, no interior but the kitchen, and steam table bars and, directly across Third Avenue, an old strip bar with a couple of men standing around outside looking mobbed-up and unwelcoming. It was a barren neighborhood with a silver tower standing in its midst, utterly medieval; outside its walls lingered various highwaymen, heretics and harlots. The banking complex included, anomalously, a church built partially underground and partially exposed by a glass pyramid on the corner. He hailed a cab on Third and took her away from there, to the living room of the apartment on 110th Street that he'd sublet for the summer. His roommate was away. They played records and she'd waited and waited and finally kissed him—while he stood at the record player she rose from the chair she'd sat in and put her arms around his neck. It was two in the morning, where else was she going to go? She had the most amazing and elaborate underwear. Stockings with garter and bloomers over panties and a lace brassiere with four hooks. He would forever, thinking of this, attribute it to her being Canadian, which made no sense. Her breasts were white globes. Nipples of the palest pink.

Nate said, Here?

George said, What?

This good?

Yeah. They were doing Up on Cripple Creek.

I had this idea, George said, hard to believe—in the fall of '76 I was going to hitch to San Francisco to see this concert. Leave school a week early for the Thanksgiving break.

Thanksgiving? Nate said. Didn't you have to go to some dinner somewhere?

I had no relations, George said. Now I have you and your mother, so you shouldn't be surprised. I always regretted I didn't do it. I didn't have the nerve. It was cold, you know.

Now there's one thing in the whole wide world I sure do love to see . . . Levon Helm was singing.

They *are* really tight, Nate said. He was watching the screen with care. From Nate this was a high compliment.

Being tight was what they did.

There's like twenty instruments going on here, Nate said. The keyboards are amazing.

Richard Manuel. He'd soon be dead.

The mandolin.

Danko. He'd die soon enough too.

Out of nine lives, I've spent seven—how in the world—do you get to heaven?

George had seen the film too, with another girl, Ninah, pronounced Nigh-nah—a tall blond girl with long hair. Ninah also from Canada; a friend of the first Canadian girl. Who was conveniently back in Toronto at that point.

The thrill of the girls. Even more thrilling—this was the sad part of life, wasn't it—in memory than they had been in the anxieties of the moment. The Toronto girl kissing him. Gorgeous full lips. Ninah's long legs out of her jeans, her panties down them, he pulled them across her feet, she opened like a gate allowing him in. He felt he should, almost could, remember the taste of these women. Ninah had a large clitoris that responded to his tongue without the usual mysteries or doubts. The pale brown and rust of her pubic hair. One could remember some of them—or was the memory just making it up as you went along, asking for certain information and the memory providing the full picture, falsely, like an Italian when you inquired for directions. Yet so vivid. When the Toronto girl came, he was behind her and had his hand on her stomach and he felt a wall of muscles rippling. She was a singer, a serious one, a classical singer. All those muscles were the work of her singing. His left hand on her breast and his right hand on her belly, pulling her against him: he could remember this, now, watching Mac Rebennack—Dr. John. Such a night.

And then so many years later, Nate gave him the DVD for Christmas.

And he watched it, and tears began running down his face, and tears kept coming.

Oh my god, are you *crying*? said Nate. Again?

What again? George said. I'm sorry. Or, no, not really. I'm not sorry. But excuse me anyway.

The tears took their time, gathered, and rolled out of his eyes, one, then another; not sobbing: just tears, like drops from the eaves as the ice melts on the first warm day, drip drip drip. Sniffle.

Why, Nate says. What could possibly make you cry about this?

Well, part of why, you already know.

Okay, said Nate. Sorry.

But no, George said. Look at their faces. Look.

Nate looked. What? he said.

Look how free they are, George said. They don't even *know* how free they are. It keeps occurring to me that no one, possibly—

He cut the sentence off.

What? said Nate. No one possibly what?

George waited a moment. I wonder if these people had any clue what they were watching the *end* of. It's possible no one in my lifetime will ever be that free again.

Buzzkill, Dad.

It's not the legacy I expected to pass on, George said. A distant memory of freedom.

You know you're kind of full of shit, right? Nate said.

Only kind of?

Only kind of. I mean, I can see what you're saying, I think. They're not doing any of that posing everyone does now, you know, performing or whatever.

Except Neil Diamond, George said.

Who?

He hasn't come on yet. You'll see.

But you're full of shit because they're white and privileged. Nineteen seventy-six in San Francisco, great, but if you were a black man in Oakland you wouldn't be so free. Weren't they still exterminating the Black Panthers at that point?

I think they were finished exterminating the Black Panthers by then, George said. But I'm impressed you even know about this.

American history? Nate said. Hello? Documentary films on the Internet?

Like you went looking for info on the Black Panthers? George said.

Yeah, I did. I got interested.

We'll have to look up the dates. Wait. You hear that voice? The backup? That's Joni Mitchell. Look, there she is. Neil Young's from Canada and she's from Canada and it's a song about Canada. The film, while she was offstage singing backup to Young, showed her silhouette behind the musicians where the audience presumably couldn't see her. Then she came onstage and did a beautiful version of Coyote.

Anyway, I think they were finished exterminating the Panthers by then, he said, while Neil Young was still singing.

Well, even more so, Nate said. I mean there's a kind of freedom in fighting to be free, and even that was already over by then.

He was watching the screen. Muddy Waters looked kind of free, he said. I'll admit that.

Oh, I don't know, George said. Some people perform it. But all their faces. You simply cannot see that look on the faces of American humans today. White, yellow, pink, brown. Nowhere that I've been anyway. Not onstage or in the street or in the bedroom. It's over. And until seeing this I hadn't understood it was gone or how gone it was. We killed it. And what you're saying about Oakland, I'm not sure it was any favor to the people who were less than free to destroy the freedom of the people who momentarily were. It's not a they-lose-I-win kind of proposition. It's an everybody-loses proposition.

Merry Christmas, man, Nate said. He clapped George on the shoulder, stood and went to the kitchen. He came back with a yogurt. There's never anything to eat, he said.

That's not true, George called back. Lourdes packs the fridge full of stuff to eat.

That's like meals, Nate said. There's never anything to just eat.

We're going to have a like-meal. Just not for a little while. What is there.

Some kind of peppers with meat inside.

Is it five yet? The new evening guy should be here. What's his name.

Andy. His name is Andy.

In a casserole dish? George said.

Yeah. There also appears to be a chicken. I think it's a chicken. It's small.

Just talk to Lourdes, George said. Tell her what you want to have. She'll get it.

You're dreaming, Nate said. You think I haven't talked to her? She's all like—he does the Spanish without trying to imitate the voice—*okay mi amor, oh yes mijo*, sure, and then she goes to Citarella and buys like swordfish steaks at forty dollars a pound. I'm like, how about a bag of chips.

Watch the movie, George said. Look. It's Joni Mitchell. Singing about Sam Shepard. You'll be brushing out a brood mare's tail while the sun is ascending, boy. C'mon. Sit down.

≡

AFTER GEORGE STARTED seeing Clarissa, Marina, who'd taken him to lunch, said from behind her menu, How did you let this happen? Burke's daughter? I mean I understand you're in grief and all, but still. That's insane.

I don't know. What can I say. The day I saw her again after lo, these many years, who knows how the stars were aligned. It sparked.

Fuck the stars, Marina said. Fuck the spark. We're talking about you.

Well, she was a bit late and when she got there she just glanced at the menu and ordered, no fuss, George said. And she wore a lovely frock. I succumbed.

She's twenty-eight, Marina said.

Thirty-two, George said. She's thirty-two.

Thirty, Jesus Christ. Remember thirty? I don't.

Thirty-*two*, George said.

Marina lowered her menu, which she'd been studying and not merely glancing at, and gave him her full evil eye. Malocchio.

Yeah, she said. Keep insisting on that two years like it makes all the difference. You're fifty-two. Twenty years older. Does she know Dylan? Has she read *Heart of Darkness*? Ever heard of Hazel Motes? Travis Bickle? Can she end the sentence *Forget it, Jake*? Does she know whence comes, historically, the phrase *Peace with honor*? Does she know where on the planet Malcom X was shot? Does she know what day World War Two began in Europe? Can she name at least five of the dozen or so democratically elected regimes we've taken it upon ourselves to topple since the end of that war? There were three in 1964–65 alone, maybe she could get one. Can she state in one brief sentence why we were attacked on 9/11? By a bunch of Saudis, no less? And *they hate our freedom* doesn't count. Frocks, schmocks, you can't trust the young.

George said, She is lovely and she is kind and we like each other a good deal.

Notice you don't say *love*, Marina said. Okay, people who can order that way at a restaurant—and granted, it *is* socially graceful to the max—don't actually care about food. Which is good, but alien.

When, said George, did you turn into a man? You know, psycho-politically.

Oh, honey, I never wasn't. You just took all these years to notice.

All those magnificent blow jobs blinded me, George said.

I should hope so, Marina said. Although many men are good at those too, one hears.

George said nothing to this.

When George had first arranged to have dinner with Clarissa, the first evening, Burke had known he was going out with someone, though not with whom.

Make sure it's not a dismal woman, Burke said. So you can enjoy the meal.

I don't date dismal women.

We all date dismal women. Sometimes we need dismal women. Just not now, for you. Not for dinner.

They wanted each other. They wanted each other's company. How peculiar and how he, who was having very few physical feelings these days and no romantic ones whatsoever, would not have predicted it, not even slightly. She wanted to heal him. Very kind of her. It took him weeks to be able to perform with her sexually. He assumed this would be true for him with anyone new. He'd been shattered and he had not since he was in his twenties felt so endangered by intimacy.

They talked much of her father. That was part of why she was there but George would never say such a thing to her. Let her figure it out for herself.

I am *so* not above taking his money, Clarissa said. Money is not moral. It doesn't bring with it any moral value. There is no morality in earning it and there is no morality in inheriting it and there is in many cases very little morality in stealing it. It's like saying to me, this air you're breathing, did you pay for this air or are you just freeloading on the earth's atmosphere?

It didn't take long to be found out.

Are you fucking my daughter? Burke said.

The language made George physically rear and wince. No, he lied. We're friends. She's a lovely young woman.

They—George and Clarissa—returned over and over to the question: Why did they both love the man? His narcissism. His beauty. His seemingly infinite energies, which became a kind of gravitational pull, him being a planet one revolved around, from which one took all measures of light and time.

Clarissa said, you know how the most beautiful visions of Earth are images taken from the moon? Like that. This large, gorgeous, inexplicable thing. All the Earth's horror and pain are completely absent in these images. That's how it is when I'm looking at him: not *dealing* with him, mind you, not remembering my history with him, not experiencing my *emotions* toward him. Just looking at him, taking him in, watching him *be* him. He's like the dumb Earth.

He shouldn't be allowed to be that big, George said.

Oh yeah? Clarissa said. He's not that big to you?

No way, George said. No way.

Right, Clarissa said. Say it twice, maybe that will convince me.

When she was a kid and Burke was broke and fucked up on one thing or another, he had hit her. Two or three or four times, she said. And paused.

Maybe more, but I only remember a few times. With those enormous hands of his, she said. I am haunted by those hands.

At the sight of the large, two-ringed hand: she would cry—a child, she had only been a little child, George couldn't stand to think of it—of course she'd cried—her mother who said nothing to the violence of the father, who did nothing to keep the—but why talk about it anymore.

You can't let this get inside *your* relationship with him, Clarissa said. Don't judge him. He needed to change and he did change and he loves me now like crazy and he affirms me and supports me in whatever I want to do. I respect him and I love him. So don't let this cloud your thinking.

I won't, George said. He was lethally young. And to be a parent is to fail every day in some way or another. You look all right to me.

Overall, she said.

She did, though, have a bit of a thing for hands. She held George's hand against her when he was using it, a standby when he was working out his other problems. The way she touched the hand was like some kind of extra level of communication. And women's hands she loved too. For all the trouble women encountered with the male gaze, with men objectifying them, the true connoisseurs of female beauty were women themselves. It was they who most ardently appreciated physical beauty—not the enticement and rapture of flesh that men saw and dreamed of, but actual beauty of bone and shape and posture and gesture. They saw in it a moral achievement, even a touch of the divine.

Clarissa said, I go mad sometimes, seeing a woman's hands, beautiful hands. A woman who moves gracefully, dresses well, I want to *be* her. It's an erotic feeling but it's also beyond erotic, or at least it's not satisfied in the erotic. Certain gestures. I die.

You already are one of those women, George said.

Oh no, Clarissa said. I'm not. I'm an imitation. It's just that men are easy to fool.

≡

EVENTUALLY SHE LEFT him to go to Italy. In part she wanted to get away from her father and his influence but soon the world would not be large enough for that—there were more than twenty Brown & Co. outlets in Italy. None in Malaysia yet, George told her. But he was at peace with it; he was grateful to her in fact. She was generous and kind and that worked on him on both the spiritual and physical levels. He commenced actual long-term healing with her. But she was, as the clock ticked, a person who wanted to raise children, have a nice home, and be liked. There was something almost comforting for him in accepting the normative bourgeois flavor of this realization; here was a person who wanted a pleasant life. People her age, he was coming to believe, took comfort living inside the boundaries. Took comfort thinking there were still boundaries one *could* live inside.

29

They were near a decade through the twenty-first century. Nate finished college in 2009 (he'd taken a year off). On that occasion, after George gave him his gift (a turntable and receiver and twenty requisite vinyl albums not already in Anna's collection, searched out in trips to Kim's and Colony and a couple of small used record shops downtown), Nate presented George with a letter he had written, a special life-moments note, with actual pen and paper: perhaps the last ink-and-paper letter he would ever produce. George read it in front of him. In it he said he loved George, was grateful to George, but his generation was despicable, and the one after no better. He wrote that the financial system had collapsed the way the habitat was going to collapse—*because you fucking Boomers and Gen Xers just drained it all dry*. It was all pure greed as far as he could see. He went on: *You people are showing no signs of being committed to changing anything at all, nothing whatsoever.* His generation, he said, was totally fucked.

George finished the note, looked up. This is very well written, he said.

That's not the point, Nate said.

Well, George said. Yes. It's bad. And apparently all you kids are gonna live at home until you're thirty-nine, like old-school Irishmen. Then you marry the spinster schoolteacher. She doubles as the village's only postal clerk. A sad wee girl.

Oh fuck you, Nate said.

You're coming into the world now, soon it's yours, George said. Make it yours, take it, and change it. You're going to have to break down the power structures governing things, and that's formidable. You'd better start now. You got everyone born since 1980 and you got the kids coming up behind you. Figure it out. You're right: I failed. I looked at it all when Reagan was president and I said, I don't have a chance. Politically speaking, in the face of industrial-strength narrative production, individual agency and desire don't have a chance. There was no longer any way to be heard. That was a mistake of course. But I basically gave up. So did everyone else. We went for the money.

≡

AND ON. OBAMA was making beautiful speeches. They really were terrific. As he neared reelection in 2012, you knew that the more gorgeous the speech, the less likely there would be a policy to support it. George was past fifty-five now, heading downhill toward sixty. He knew what it was to be a henchman. The associate guy. The Nick Carraway, there to see and report, never to drive. Ed Norton, Barney Fife, Barney Rubble. Uncle Charlie, Mr. Fucking French. An essentially comic role in which the assistant's unlikely personality is forced to fit in—garrulously at times, okay—with the schemes of the main character. Such was his relationship with Burke, after all these years. Always had been. What was he there for? From the beginning it had been the money but it had been a certain kind of money, money made from thinking shit up.

And now here he was at his desk in a rare enough visit to the office: and the little circle on his laptop in a smog-sky screen just twirled around and around and around with everything he tried to do, he couldn't shut it off, he couldn't reboot it. His rage built over a couple of minutes—not long, perhaps even one minute only—and then came surging up in him like vomit, total red rage, and he stood and picked up the laptop and smashed it and smashed it and smashed it until the screen portion he was holding was severed from the body, which bounced away, and then he commenced trying to break the screen in half with a terrible cracking of bones until, unable to snap it in two, he threw it across the room where it hit the bookshelf and knocked down some goddamned tchotchke that broke on the floor. He wanted to smash some more shit but Katrine dashed in and was looking at him. So he straightened himself, looked at her. The alarm on her face.

Call IT, he said. I need a new laptop.

It happened that day. He decided enough. He was going to resign. Really resign, not half resign. Pull away. Thirty years, nearly thirty years, was enough.

It happened after one of the meetings.

Stirred by his growing realization that there is a difference between serving a real need, based in the habits and desires of a community, a society, a culture, and instead constantly creating needs, deploying vestigial nostalgic notions of community and culture, George said: Wanting things leads to misery.

Katrine, beside him, shifted, looked at him. Yes, he knew he was becoming ever less helpful.

People wanting things is how we live, Burke said.

But we have to promote an idea of not wanting things while selling people things. It's the final lie. Spare. Zen. Wooden walls, tatami floors, empty rooms, what little you own in jars and bowls behind the cabinet doors. And one-hundred-and-sixty-dollar-a-pound white tea. With proper service.

A manufactured lifestyle of peace, Burke said. One you can almost afford.

Right.

I'd call it consciousness of the moment, Katrine said. Presence. This is really what people are going to want next. The ability to be and know you are in a place, in a moment of time. Awareness. The final, single drop of espresso falling slow-motion into the demitasse.

She was already building an image campaign.

These manipulations of reality are starting to make me sick, George said. I think they're giving me cancer.

They're not manipulations of reality, Katrine said. They are the discovery of some vein of common desire.

Burke said, Right, and the assurance that we *know*—that we share that desire.

I mean, Katrine said, we know you're not going to get peace from a caffe macchiato. But we know that you want, you need, to create a little space around yourself. You want to hearken back to something simpler, something easier, than all this. All this bullshit. We'll need new cups. Little square white china cups in square saucers, perhaps.

George watched the marketing and advertising directors writing it all down. A few of them wrote on their iPads, with little nibs that looked like colonial-era floor nails.

After the meeting, George took Katrine by the elbow and guided her into Burke's office.

Burke walked to his desk, turned to face them.

George said, Here she is. She can replace me. You don't need me anymore.

Essentially that's true, Burke said. We have some details to work out, though, don't we?

I can leave, Katrine said. She seemed eager to do so.

No, stay, George said.

Details, Burke said again.

The lawyers can do the details, George said. I want to go to Mexico for a while.

You and Mexico, Burke said. You and Mexico, it's like watching a fat man trying to seduce a cheerleader.

Lawyers, George said, and left Burke and Katrine together to talk. Burke, once she'd been elevated, would want to sleep with her. George had to remember to warn her.

≡

He did go to Mexico. He almost bought a house on the Pacific coast: with its boathouse it would have been a place to keep a lovely wooden sloop he'd discovered for sale in Boca del Cielo. He came back to New York, and managed, in a kind of isolated desperation, to start up again, by Skype, with Clarissa. After a month of long conversations he flew to Geneva, where she'd moved to work with an NGO doing refugee relief in sub-Saharan Africa. He had written to declare his love and need. He would help her have a child, he knew she wanted one, even at his advanced age, fifty-six going on fifty-seven in the fall—he didn't care. She was seeing some guy. She was into this guy. She was into him, to be specific, as an erotic obsession. She saw no future there, she admitted. George and she skyped. They skyped and skyped—all hours. Perhaps taking the long view, she had allowed him to visit her. Now she was asleep.

George tried to sleep but couldn't. He rose and sat at her dining table in the darkened apartment—it was a kind of European loft, all one space formed by two rectangles in an L position. Moonrise had come from France, to the southeast, emerging from behind the left haunch of the mountain; it's always a struggle to be born. But it had managed to slide out and over the course of the past hour he had found it by turns symbolic, historical, divine, mundane. It shone for a time over the city, and then passed, almost the color of flame, into invisibility behind a black cloud. It was just past three a.m.

In her apartment, a simple, elegant place in a middle-class district not far from the airport, rather surprising, she could have afforded anything, a house in the old city if she'd wanted it, he was sitting at her table, by the wide window, with its view of the low mountains, watching this passing cosmic drama. The larger of the two mountains, Mont Salève, was to the right. *I read, much of the night, and go south in winter.* He loved Europe, loved it firmly but almost always from a distance: he had never been free in his life—he'd lived his life in chains. And now, here, he had woken to the intolerable. Behind him, she breathed audibly, snored just a little, delicate, like a baby's snore; occasionally she moved in her sleep. He heard her move, and half hoped she hadn't woken from his having risen, and half hoped she had, and would rise too, and join him, so that he could sting himself again in the beauty of her company.

He watched the sky: the moon underwent a second slow birth, from behind its heavy cloud: it was now whiter, more still: less maudlin: cold. His eye registered these changing attributes and delivered them, already catalogued, to his brain.

The dreams: he had been dreaming with a kind of manic fervor. He dreamed that her newest lover had denounced him in the pages of the *New York Times Magazine*, which was absurd and almost wonderful—the man was barely literate, and it was George himself who sometimes appeared in magazines. He knew this *in* the dreams, this symbolic reversal. He had dreamed she was his (George's) wife, that she was holding a party, and was upset about the hors d'oeuvres. He tried to give the dreams code words while he was dreaming, phrases to remember so he'd be able to put the dreams back together, but now he remembered only a few of them: hot oil: she was in charge of the deep fryer in a restaurant and she was frighteningly angry that every time she put anything in the basket and lowered it, the grease spat up and stained her clothes. He was working in some other part of the kitchen, he could see her and wanted to tell her to stand farther back, to immerse the food a bit more slowly, to find an apron . . . But he was too busy and not allowed to leave his post so could tell her nothing at all: just let her burn and rage.

The rock? Was there a rock? Bare feet gripping wet rock? Something—but he couldn't remember.

He would have to work very hard now not to fall under the train again, depression; his companion of many disparate months over the past few years; to survive in the face of pain, to accept it, to feel it, and to go on, feel it again the next day, go on. Etc. So far, he felt a lot of pain, but no depression, no perfect paralyzing isolation, no rich gray blanket of melancholy. Indeed, he was vitally energetic; he was profoundly pissed off, pissed off over a lifetime of enforced failure; his dick was hard for the first time in two days; he was eager for game two, for which he would change his strategy, take a different approach.

The bright moon had disappeared again, leaving a glowing nimbus behind the clouds; the sky was a velvet black curtain, impenetrable.

Words words words: another black curtain. He stood behind it, waiting.

Eventually he tried to sleep again, and almost did, but then began to shiver. He settled, grew drowsy, but then she moved; he looked at her; he was electrified. Her limb, her shoulder, her hair. In the silver light. Soon he was hard again, and it felt to him as if every nerve in his body would jump out of his skin. He thought about waking her and shoving his cock into her; this was broadly speaking the M.O. of the character she was enamored of at the moment, but for that reason and for others in his history, and in hers, and in theirs together, he knew he would not do that. Could not. More rage at this. And he could not stay in bed with her; another minute or two and he'd start screaming. His situation was comic, was idiotic; last night when they were talking he had an easy time making his little position into a dirty sitcom sequence—he had needed very much to relax and laugh at himself and at her, but the hours between three a.m. and the waking life of sunlit morning are notoriously the least funny of the day; these are the hours for dying.

She was in Geneva for the year. When he'd flown in, the previous Wednesday afternoon, she had insisted on meeting him at the airport, but she was twenty minutes late—she looked tired, no makeup, a little unhappy. That day, a Wednesday, and the next, Thursday, were very bad. Confrontations—he was pushing her, he was arriving here in the middle of her life and insisting on some right or privilege that he did not have or deserve to have. Friday was nice in the a.m., foul after lunch. Nap, work. He apologized. They walked through the center of town and had a dinner in the old city, which initiated a loveliness that carried through the rest of the weekend. They rented a Peugeot at the airport and drove to Ticino, stayed in Lugano for the night and saw Bellinzona and Locarno before driving back in the afternoon on Sunday. He was aware of traveling paths Anna had talked about, had loved, from so many years before. The mountains were as she had described them—astonishing.

He would leave on Monday morning. He and Clarissa had sex, briefly, incompletely, in the Lugano hotel, the Splendide Royal, after drinks at the bar overlooking the lake; from the hotel they walked out for dinner, stopping at a place they liked the looks of, on a plaza between the shopping district and the lake. The dinner was superb. It was late April, and the resort was only mildly populated. A long walk back to the hotel: his leg hurt, as it did intermittently since he'd torn the knee ligament two years prior, running; when it did, as now, he limped and because of this she was, he could tell, mildly irritated with him. The next day they ate breakfast in the big dining room, analyzing the other guests—a few of them were frightening, seemed actually insane, two large men, severe, both Americans, which he thought odd as Americans on holiday usually looked like dumb cows in shorts and striped shirts. Then they drove to Bellinzona. She received her second speeding ticket of the trip (a hundred Swiss francs each) en route, though they wouldn't know this until later when it was mailed to her—everything was automated and efficient, this being Switzerland after all. Lunch in Bellinzona was perfect, with a wholly unexpected perfection; perfect in that way when something was lovely and you knew it in the moment and experienced it in the moment and knew too that you would never lose it. And then you didn't lose it. Fettuccine alla carciofi. A light fresh tomato sauce with artichoke hearts. Wine. A neighborhood place just off the small piazza they'd parked in; families eating midday dinner on a Sunday. He had seen in a brochure that included a few pictures that there was a church nearby, with frescoes—Santa Maria delle Grazie—nothing spectacular or famous but it looked more interesting than the endless castles of the place, the buildings in which these Europeans had all held up between bouts of slaughtering one another with arrows and spiked clubs: deadliest race on the planet: when the Europeans do it, they do it full scale, all out. And so it was, the church, more interesting than the castles—especially in the rearmost chapel on the church's north side, one of a half dozen chapels running up the two sides of the apse, for there had been a fire a few years before and in this particular chapel the fire hoses had washed away all the paints of the frescoes—a tragedy, one would think—leaving the plaster bare and haunted with faded remnants of the original charcoal cartoons on white plaster, ghostly figures reaching toward him, or turning to look at him, or gazing upward, some scene now erased, barely tangible, eyes outlined but empty and white as in some living death, all of it like a memory of communal sadness and joy. And yet these shadows of art, these ghosts, were the most compelling and beautiful art in the building. He prayed here—joking with her that they should fuck behind one of the altars, the place was abandoned now that it was afternoon and the last Mass had been said—he prayed silently to himself for her, for him, for them. She wanted a child. He prayed for that. They drove back to Geneva that afternoon; they got lost looking for the highway and ended up on a one-lane road crossing the Alps—one lane, literally, so that at every curve, and there were many curves required to get up and down these mountains, you had to stop and crawl forward to make sure no one was coming down, unseen, to plow into you. She drove and endured the stresses of this—he looked out the window, across at ridges and down into chasms rich in water and leaf and stone, wet and dappled and at play in ten zones of light. The place vibrated with the divine. They reached Montreux at nightfall and stopped for dinner—another fine meal—and she drank a third of a liter of wine and staggered laughing and holding him back to the car. He drove them into Geneva, grinding gears, riding the clutch, awake and alert to the bright lights and tricky reflections of the night and universe. And then he did not sleep.

Monday morning: the airport. The look on her face as she walked away: she hugged him quickly, not hard, with a yielding sense of affection; she was glad though, to have him go. Her face, her eyes especially, presented a complex mixture of sadness, regret, and, most of all, have-tos. He smiled at her after she kissed him. He was jovial: Have a good time kid, he said. Meaning with her other man. She slipped under the ribbon barricade and walked toward the exit. Perhaps she turned to wave at him, but if so he didn't see it—he was determined to look away from her. He didn't begin to face his emotions, the digging pain in the gut, until after he boarded the plane, stowed his bags, sat, and considered the possibility of her getting pregnant, that very night, by this intermittently employed construction worker she was fucking.

The flight was interminable. The data on the screen told him it was already after four o'clock in Geneva and they were just passing Newfoundland. He could see her, moving through her day without him.

Two months later Clarissa returned to New York. She was,

indeed, pregnant. Just as he'd predicted: that very night. She'd known too, by next morning, and had dumped the guy by the end of the week; then, she said, she'd had to endure the fifty SMS messages per day. For almost a month. Night rings of the buzzer. She did not call the police though she threatened to do so, because she didn't believe he was altogether *legal*. Eventually it stopped and then she left the country. He would never know.

George wanted her to live with him. He would be father to the baby.

I don't think so, she said.

He took *think* hopefully.

Burke said to him, at lunch, two weeks later: I'm going to be a grandfather.

George looked at him. Really?

I hope so. It's early yet.

How far along?

Only twelve weeks. I suspect you knew this already.

I know nothing, George said. I see nothing.

Right, Burke said. Like Sergeant Schultz.

≡

To Burke, who asked him one day about his financial *position*, he said, Well, I have considerable stake, sharewise, in this outfit called Brown et Co.

Yes, we know that, Burke said.

My big financial score was that I put a hundred grand in Apple in late 2002, another hundred in early 2003. It was shortly after Nate got his first iPod. I knew when I saw the kids with that thing that Apple would own that market. I didn't even realize the phones.

What was it? Burke said. I'm gonna cry when you tell me.

Eleven dollars a share. By early 2003 it was a little more.

Jesus. How many times has it split?

Fourteen essentially, George said. Two to one in '05 I think. Seven to one a few months ago.

So you made like ten million?

More like thirteen.

Right, like nine thousand shares became a hundred and twenty-five thousand shares going at a hundred ten bucks a pop. Fuck. What have you got in Brown, like three hundred thousand shares?

Closer to four, George said. But I've been selling them off a little.

Yeah, I noticed. That's very inspiring.

I'm converting a little to cash and munis. Coming apocalypse.

So you're worth like fifty million?

Plus cash and real estate and a few good paintings, yeah. So maybe fifty-five.

That feels like enough?

It's enough for three small countries, Steve.

You called me Steve.

Yeah, warm feelings now that we're talking about net worth. And I don't work for you anymore.

Anyway that wouldn't be enough for me. I got big plans.

I know. You're worth three hundred times that. We're different that way.

Yeah, Burke said. I'm three hundred times *better* than you.

What George would not tell Burke, at least not yet, was that he was selling out gradually in order to give his money away. He was in the midst of making a trust of ten million for Nate and after that he was willing to die with just enough in the bank for a funeral. It turned out, however (something he learned after twelve thousand dollars in lawyer meetings), it was quite difficult to give your money away. You couldn't just *give* it. You had to have a foundation. A foundation had to have a mission. It had to have a board. Its gifts had to comport with the mission. Its gifts in any one year should, for fiscal responsibility's sake, only be equal to the earnings minus the operating costs—leaving the investment intact. *The tax consequences the tax consequences the tax consequences the tax consequences*, they sang. It was the show-stopper tune from a big Broadway musical: the tax consequences. His secret weapon was that he didn't give a shit about the tax consequences. In theory he didn't pay enough taxes as it was and if he'd had a better government he'd accept that as a fact in practice as well. The lawyers looked at him with peculiar expressions, except the one, a woman who was originally a labor specialist Brown had used in establishing employee practices, whom George had admired, and who now did the law of charitable institutions.

Well, we can all kiss our fees goodbye, right out the window, she said. But what you want to do is find existing organizations to give the money to, not set up some cumbersome operation yourself. Of course my firm would be glad to help.

This last she delivered with a smile and all four of the other attorneys hooted at her.

I can't believe you're actually hooting in my meeting, George said.

The woman lawyer said, Oh, it's okay. It proves I'm one of the boys now.

George looked at her and wondered. Where was her left hand? Ah, the ring.

When the coffee and fruit and pastries were brought in, a

break in the proceedings, he said to her, in a low voice, Would it be rude to ask someone who's wearing a wedding ring whether they mean it?

She jerked back a bit, looked at him. A slow smile.

Then, she said, we must further ask, wouldn't it be equally rude to *ask* if it were rude to ask? I think so.

Well then, he said. I withdraw the question and propose never to have spoken the words.

But funny, she said. I'm separated. The golden ring's days are numbered I'm afraid. I'm also amused that you propose never to have spoken words you'd just spoken. You should have been a lawyer. Or a president.

George felt himself visibly lift, brighten. Enough that she laughed.

Well, he said. My mother always said I should be a lawyer. I started working with this guy on his coffee truck in Brooklyn instead.

And the rest is history, she said.

Yes, it's history. Entrepreneurialism and cutthroat marketing. The American legend. Killing all the bad guys with no help from anyone legitimately representing the law. It's great. Like Natty Bumppo. Bruce Willis. Clint Eastwood. Et cetera. I'd like to call you but I should consult my counsel.

Your counsel says go right ahead, she said. What have you got to lose? Except half your marital assets?

I'm not married, he said.

Her name was Rachel: they went out a few times. They made it about four weeks, then she called to tell him she was ending it.

You're a good man, she said, a decent man. But you're not

actually present. I've seen this before. I'm going to leave it for someone else to try to cure.

≡

THOUGH HE'D OFFICIALLY separated from the company, in retirement, he acceded to Burke's request that he troubleshoot problems at the larger stores—he'd agreed to do New York metro area only for a year, then train others what to do out of town. He wanted no travel. Stores that had been profitable and now weren't, stores with one kind of difficulty or another, mismanaged, without leadership, not performing. One store had given birth to five lawsuits for mistreatment over three years and not even under the same managers: the place just bred hard feelings. He spent maybe four weeks at most in any one place, didn't work for a month or two after, until Burke's assistant Alice called him and said, Hold for Mr. Burke! She was always so excited, she was part of the new sincerity, everybody talked and messaged in exclamation points all the time. And Mr. Burke! He was a famous man after all, now. He might even run for president. Not yet. Probably 2020.

Burke came on the line.

While you were gone, he said. Where were you? One of your trips skiing or sailing in the tropics?

I wish I could ski in the tropics but I went to see Nate in North Carolina, George said.

Nate was teaching politics and literature at UNC. The politics *of* literature, with an emphasis on postcolonial literature, was his distinct specialty. Appointment in two departments. Twice the departmental bullshit! he'd said.

He'd spent his first sabbatical in Nigeria. Now just back.

Yeah, whatever, Burke said. While you were gone, there was a *New York Post* story. People are going to our bathrooms to die. That's the kind of country this is now. You know what we spend on prisons in this country? Do you have any idea?

Fifty billion? George said.

Eighty. Eighty fucking billion. I swear to god I'm going to quit this, run for president, lose, then go to Tuscany. I swear. In any case there's a store uptown: Hamilton Heights. A fucking mess.

George went in only after the manager was released. He wouldn't do the firing: he didn't have the stomach for it. All the ones fired before his arrival, he had made Burke promise, got three months' pay and six months' health insurance, with the offer of a return to barista level at another store if they wanted. Generally they didn't want.

On the way uptown George was chatting with his Russian cabdriver. Not that many lifer drivers anymore. Guy had come over in the '80s when Brezhnev had let out a few thousand Jews and a sprinkling of low-level dissidents.

The driver said, When I came here, twenty-five years ago, this was a free country. He looked at George in the mirror. It's not a free country anymore, he said.

Freedom scribbled in the subway. A line Anna had liked. He'd have to remember from where. He kept waiting to see it now. You kept expecting to see the samizdat, the slogans and graffiti signifying a pulsing subcutaneous revolution in the works. Instead what you saw now were sixteen new luxury condominium towers in every neighborhood of Manhattan and the nearer, more fashionable districts of Brooklyn and Queens; eighty or ninety stories if possible. Who was paying off the zoning boards was what he wanted to know. Surely these people could be reported on by the papers. He couldn't remember the last time he'd seen a zoning board story. The whole fucking skyline had changed. Coming up the New Jersey Turnpike from North Carolina or DC, visiting Nate or Marina, for a time he had seen the painful absence of two astonishing towers. Now there was some putzy little Flash Gordon thing there and the whole rest of the skyline, all the finger-thin towers, like a bunch of kids behind some short hedges flipping him the bird. And what possibility was there for revolution when most of the people who went to college graduated already married to their debt; and when those who didn't go to college got shot by the cops for a missing taillight or selling loosies on the street? Answer: none. When those two stupid kids bombed the Boston Marathon, what proved more memorable as their violence was the instantaneous military occupation of the city. Any major city apparently could be put under curfew and held under martial law within hours of some outbreak, any outbreak.

George said to the cabbie, I'm glad someone's noticing.

Nobody's noticing, the driver said. Nobody's doing nothing. I know what it looks like. I know how, how, how it *taste* in the mouth. How it taste. Like this. Putrid.

≡

The ineluctable modality of the visible. Today's *visible* comprised a liter can of olive oil, now empty, and a paring knife, with which George was attempting to pry from the lid of the can its plastic nozzle, so as to wash the can and recycle it, and recycle the plastic nozzle, too, but separately from the aluminum can—even though the knowledge had been brought home to him at least two years prior that all their plastic shit, the bags and bags of it they—Lourdes mostly, of course—dumped into the basement blue bins wasn't in fact being recycled anymore but crushed like cars and put up in bales in various zones of poverty around the world, a reality that was up front in his mind, that was doing battle against the fantasy inherent to tossing another plastic item in the bag. But honestly what was he supposed to do about it? This fantasy was still legally required. And nowadays too, he couldn't look at most basic objects to be disposed without thinking how precious they would become, after the upcoming eco-apocalypse and breakdown of postindustrial hypercapitalist civilization. The modalities, in other words, were becoming considerably more fluid. This Tunisian olive oil can—perfect to the hand, compact, light, holding a liter of precious liquid, would be like gold to the frightened and bereft, those who survived, squatting in the woods, drawing water from diminishing streams.

≡

Six months later, George, invited to the opening of Arthur Towne's new show, *Natur/Nurtur*, brought the phonetically-appropriate Nate, who was visiting for the weekend. Clarissa and her son, named Andrew, his grandfather's middle name, would join them for dinner later. Perhaps Burke too. Marta was *in the country* apparently. What country was that? George always wondered. He and Nate stood outside the gallery after. Nate asked, regarding some new construction on 25th Street, I suppose that's being built for rich people?

Everything built here is for rich people, George said. The answer came automatically but then it struck him: what an extraordinary thing to happen to a society. Every single construction, for rich people only. Bankers. Russian thieves. Rich Chinese from the world of Communist capitalism.

And there are no revival houses anymore, George said, apropos of not much—rich people somehow. There used to be—

Don't tell me, I already know them all, Nate said.

Then he grabbed George by the shoulders. Dad, he said.

Yes? George said.

I'm only going to tell you this once, Nate said.

Yes? George said.

The revival houses are all in your phone now.

Oh fuck that, George said. But, so okay, yeah. Good point. But the city is pathetic and self-deluded now. Have you seen the new world trade center?

Just in passing, Nate said. Like on the Jersey Turnpike. Blink and you miss it.

It's a piddling little thing, George said. More than a decade in the making. And everyone is pretending it's a glorious patriotic victory. Twelve years to put up *that*? George hated the sight of it on the skyline. It was like seeing a man in the locker room with a freakishly small penis. One shuddered.

That was us, he realized. His country had become the man in the locker room with a freakishly small penis. And a mean expression on his face, to compensate. Probably a cop, that man. Forever turned down for promotion.

At George's level of wealth there was no way he was not part of the problem but he felt at least he'd gotten rich and bought a rich person's apartment; he hadn't turned a teacher's apartment, a librarian's apartment, a photographer's apartment, a whole neighborhood once middle class, into an investment banker's enclave, a whole borough of investment bankers. He hadn't forced or participated in the destruction of city blocks so that the developers could make him a tower to live in. He understood that he was likely fooling himself. When it came time to gather up the rich and take them out in white Ford Econoline beat-to-shit vans like the one he'd driven those—what, almost forty years ago, shit—gather them up like cordwood and take them out to Citifield and shoot them all, they weren't going to spare him because he lived in a nice old building on Riverside Drive. The one he'd kept, no matter how much his Brown and Apple stock was worth.

≡

He took off Monday and Tuesday. Nate flew back to North Carolina on Monday afternoon. George had taken over managing a shop on Fifth and 18th Street; something sweet about it if he could save it: that store was among their first. The Tuesday afternoon after Nate flew out he went in just to check on things; he saw a man, an old man with a walker, and looked twice. He was indeed very old now, this man, but George had him inside a second, from recognition of face to placement of identity—the identity came with recognition of the eyeglasses, the traditional tortoiseshell you never saw anymore. Mr. Goldstein. He sat with a vestigial bony elegance at one of the tables, a walker folded beside him and a vigorous-looking caretaker, large and self-confident, sitting across. Goldstein was reading the *Times*, he had it folded and was leaning over it with a glass. She was doing something on her phone.

George walked to the table, stood over it a moment and then said, Mr. Goldstein? Goldstein looked up at him.

You will likely not remember me, sir—

A little louder, son, Goldstein says. He pointed to his hearing aid.

You probably don't remember me, George said again. I was at Columbia when your son was there. I worked for the newspaper.

Goldstein stared at him wet-eyed through large glasses.

I remember you, he said. You came to the apartment.

Yes, sir, I did.

I don't remember your name, Goldstein said.

George, George Langland.

There was a third seat. George took it.

Langland, the old man said. *Pilgrim's Progress.*

Yes, sir, same name.

Did you ever read it?

No, George said. I tried. It was impenetrable.

Even when you penetrate it I'm not sure it's worth the time, Goldstein said. There was a pause. Like certain women, I guess, Goldstein said, and when he laughed he showed long yellow teeth. This made George laugh too.

Listen to you two, the nurse said. There's a lady here. So act like gentlemen.

This is Julia, Goldstein said. She rebukes me several times an hour.

Hardly, Julia said. Only when you need it.

Goldstein said to George, I read about you in the Columbia magazine. You're a high-up with these people. He nodded up and down to indicate the space.

Yes, George said. I'm kind of retired now though. Half-retired. He looked down at the front page of Goldstein's *Times.* The Russians were arming the Taliban. Oh good.

What are you going to do with yourself? You're young.

I'm thinking of taking up sailing again. Boats and water, it's where I started out.

Goldstein blinked at him. Finally he said, Well, the city has changed. Profoundly. Since then.

Yes, George said. It has.

Money, Goldstein said.

I know, George said.

You're not innocent of it, Goldstein said. All this.

He gestured over his head, toward the counter.

You do your part to hold the system aloft.

I know, George said. It didn't seem that way when we started, but now it is, and yes, I do.

So did I, Goldstein said.

Goldstein was the type of man you could sit with in silence, and this George did for a while. And then George said, This is an intrusive question, but I have to ask, have you found any peace? I used to see the ads in the classifieds every year, seeking information, and feel so sorry.

Found peace? No. Not peace. The old man stared down at the table for a second, two, long enough for George to formulate an apology, then he looked back up with his watery old eyes. *Our gaze is submarine . . .*

It was torture, Goldstein said. Torture, not knowing what happened. And you never get over being tortured, I suppose. Look at Primo Levi.

Another bit of silence, George let it rest. He didn't apologize. An apology seemed unnecessary. Goldstein touched his hand: the almost powdery softness of old people's skin.

Here it is, Goldstein said. I've thought of it this way before. Imagine you lose your legs. So much of what you do for the rest of your life is constricted, or painful. Or humiliating. You feel ashamed. But over the years despite all that you still hear a good piece of music or read something fine or successfully make love to your wife—without legs that really must be something but never mind—

George laughed at this. Julia said, Listen to you now still going on.

So at these times you feel what other people feel, you know. Satisfaction. Pleasure. Happiness. Even joy. You can see the largeness and beauty of life. You have snatches of happiness. And does anyone have more than that? Visionaries maybe. Ecstatics . . . Otherwise no, they have the same little passing lovely moments of happiness as this, but they have it or don't have it or strive for it or forget it—*with legs.* But you have no legs. Every day you wake, having dreamt of your legs, and you find again you have none. Every morning that flash of hope, every morning that smash of truth.

He made a small gesture, as if to say, that's it.

George nodded at him.

Can I get you anything? George said.

Goldstein looked at him, amused, as if George had offered him a little something, a piece of fruit maybe, to compensate for a lifetime of pain.

A little more tea would be fine, he said.

George turned to Julia. Oh yes, she said. We'll have a piece of that chocolate cake if you're offering now. That big one they have there in the case.

George spoke to the head barista, returned to the table.

I told her to bring two forks, he said to Julia.

We don't need any two forks, Julia said. Unless you're having some. Look at him now, does he look like he eats cake? He hardly eats, just pecks like a chicken.

Goldstein said, I still talk to him, you know. And I feel as if I hear him.

Really? George said.

Not as if he says, *Hi, Pop*. I talk sometimes, I wander around muttering, imagining him as he might be now or as he was then, it depends, different times. And then sometimes I feel something. A goodness in the air. Like love. Like a fine, thin joy, a scent. He's joyful. I'm a mess but he's joyful. Being dead is like finding the right religion, apparently.

The old man talked very slowly, considering his words as he had considered them so carefully when he'd been interviewed in his apartment forty years ago. With long pauses, as he paused here.

After a time, he said: The cliché is, like all clichés, true. The years *do* fly by. But they are *years* after all and eventually one has had enough of them. One dies.

Not yet, George said. Just not yet.

Right. Exactly. That's what we all say.

Another pause.

Goldstein said, You've reminded me of Bergman's *The Seventh Seal*, remember when Max Von Sydow, the knight, says to the death figure, wait, hold on—and Death replies, that's what everyone says.

They looked at each other. George considered death, as he understood it. As he understood it, now, it meant to be pulverized under a flaming heap of rubble, or to die as his mother had, round-eyed in fear and mute with tubes.

The old man patted George's hand.

Well, son, carry on, in the meantime. That's another quote. What Vladimir says to Estragon, right? You remember?

George had to think. Vladimir, Estragon.

Beckett? he said.

Yes, Goldstein said. *Waiting for Godot*. I saw it when it opened with Bert Lahr. I was young. Nineteen fifty-six? I can't remember. Then years later when it was revived at the Vivian Beaumont and some other time, too, awful, with Madonna and Robin Williams. *She* at least was humble. He was out of control.

What did Vladimir say to Estragon? George said.

Oh, near the end, just a few lines before, Estragon says, *I can't go on*, and Vladimir says, *That's what you think*.

Ah, George said.

That was my guidepost, that line of that play. I used to say it to my wife.

Oh great, George said. She must have loved that.

The poor woman, no wonder she hated me, he said. Then he laughed and showed his long mottled old-man teeth. His cackling laugh again made George laugh.

That's right, you laugh, Julia said. You two just laugh. You don't know what women know. Men are like mules. You need the mule, yes, for the work, for the field, but when that mule's not doing what you need him for, then all he does is eat and kick and go to the bathroom all over the barn. He's stupid too.

She said this with both irony and conviction and a proper dash of rancor.

I love her, Goldstein said. I'm Lear and you know who she is.

George rose from the table.

Julia, said George, offering her his hand, which she took. You are wise. Please, take good care—of him *and* you.

He turned to the old man and bowed. It's good to see you. More than good.

It was good to see you too, Goldstein said. I have to go home now and handle the memories.

Ah, said George. I'm sorry.

No, Goldstein said. It's what I do. You'll see. Getting old is all about remembering.

You forget everything *I* tell you, Julia said.

He looked at Julia, pointed at the plate. I think I will have a bite of that cake.

Hallelujah, Julia said. It's a miracle.

≡

Early in 2016, an ad started appearing on the subway and various bus stops, heavily concentrated in north Brooklyn and eastward out to Bushwick and Ridgewood, the young people zones: it was around only briefly before the MTA corrected its mistake and rooted it out. The Authority took them all down but not before the thing had gone viral, pictures on 300,000 mobile phones, Instagram, Facebook, Twitter. Thirteen million likes. Futura type, in all caps:

ADVICE TO THE YOUNG:

EARN ENOUGH MONEY . . .
TO BUY A LITTLE PROPERTY . . .
FAR OFF THE USUAL GRID . . .
WITH A SOLAR GENERATOR . . .
GOOD WATER FROM THE NORTH . . .
HAVE A FEW CHICKENS . . .
GROW SOME GREENS . . .
POTATOES AND BEANS . . .
BRING A FRIEND (IF YOU CAN) . . .

BECAUSE THINGS ARE NOT ON THE MEND.

—RVD

This was the first of what became an unpredictable sequence of publicly placed, non-NPR-friendly admonitions of this kind. No one knew who RVD was. Or what. It was as if Banksy had gone on an apocalyptic life-advice-printing binge. This first message looked perfectly reasonable to George. The only thing he puzzled over was the placement of ellipses at the end of every line. Gave it a haiku flavor—*Frog jumps . . . eternity!* kind of thing. Perfectly good message though. For the young. For him, too late. Here's what it meant to be closing in on sixty: he just wished them all good luck.

≡

AND THAT WAS it. Good luck. George tried to take pleasure in his life. He at least took amusement—people could never stop being how they were. God had a sense of humor, this one thing was certain, if there was a God. In George's life, if not in his house any longer, there were people whom he loved and who loved him: he had Nate, who would be married soon, to a smart and, most important, kind young woman; he had Marina, in Washington, sending exasperated texts and more philosophical emails, loyal and still loving most of the time and sharply entertaining always; he had Clarissa and her boy, Andrew, whom he took places and did things with like a grandfather, which people often mistook him for; he had Burke, and Burke was Burke; he occasionally had Louis, like once or twice a year but enough, and occasionally, too, Arthur and a few other old friends. He believed there would be another woman in his life, so one should be keeping one's head above water. That hope and the demands of sailing kept him going to the gym. He had books and films and travel—he had Mexico, which he had come to love—and he had memories. He found himself, like the old man Goldstein, talking to Anna in his head, and sometimes he detected an answer.

He did not know how it would all turn out, all of it; or when the turn, all the turns leading to the final turn, would happen. Here it was, this might have been life's secret, left in plain sight—the crux of every story and every dream, summed up in a common, impenetrable phrase: no one ever knew how things would turn out. Except to say there would always be sorrow, like stones in a sack; and there would always be loss, from the birth of self-consciousness forward, a constant set of cuts and burns and dissipations. Sometimes the loss was slow and invisible like time itself, until you looked and there was no more water in the jar; at other times the loss came shocking and large and loud, and left broken glass, ragged holes, smoldering steel, blood and bodies in the rubble . . . All this destruction not merely from the working of bullets and bombs but from the larger powers of time and human will. He felt now as if he spent a portion of each day in the recognition of dying. Not in a bad way, just in a knowing way; this is what life's later phases contained, this solid knowledge. Despite his fears and weaknesses, he knew he endured it; just endured it, gave it minimum space to move, as everyone endured it, most human beings, almost all—endured it and distracted from it, with love and desire and hope. To die, whether by one's own hand or fate's, was to relinquish those things. And so we continue to endure it, all of it, all the suffering and loss and the passages of despair, the dying itself—endure it and endure it and endure it—until that moment of severing mercy, when all the enduring is done.

Acknowledgments

My deep thanks to Patricia Towers and Vanessa Haughton, two superb editors who gave me careful readings of earlier drafts of this novel and invaluable advice, as well as to my beautiful friend Joshua Furst for his smart reading, encouragement and moral support. N read it *twice*, which shows she must be fond of me. Yvette Grant at Simon & Schuster was a life saver and a spirit saver (as well as a true *literature professional*). Finally, grateful acknowledgment must be made here to *Agni*, where part of this novel in different form first appeared, and to Jennifer Alise Drew of that journal, whose sensitive, intelligent, rigorous editorial assistance has many times, over many years, added to the possible beauty of my work and whose friendship has added to the certain beauty of my life.